KU-780-890

"When I'm casting about for an ant..... .. .. sugary female sleuths... Kate Shugak, the Aleut private investigator in Dana Stabenow's Alaskan mysteries, invariably comes to mind." *New York Times*

"Fast and furious adventure." *Kirkus*

"Stabenow is blessed with a rich prose style and a fine eye for detail. An outstanding series." *Washington Post*

"Excellent... No one writes more vividly about the hardships and rewards of living in the unforgiving Alaskan wilderness and the hardy but frequently flawed characters who choose to call it home. This is a richly rewarding regional series that continues to grow in power as it grows in length." *Publishers Weekly*

"A dynamite combination of atmosphere, action, and character." *Booklist*

"Full of historical mystery, stolen icons, burglaries, beatings, and general mayhem... The plot bursts with colour and characters... If you have in mind a long trip anywhere, including Alaska, this is the book to put in your backpack." *Washington Times*

THE KATE SHUGAK SERIES

DANA STABENOW

MIDNIGHT COME AGAIN

HEAD
of
ZEUS

First published in the UK in 2013 by Head of Zeus, Ltd.

9 7 5 3 1 2 4 6 8

A CIP catalogue record for this book is available from
the British Library.

ISBN (BPB) 9781908800718
ISBN (E) 9781781850206

Printed and bound by CPI Group (UK) Ltd,
Croydon, CR0 4YY

Head of Zeus, Ltd
Clerkenwell House
45-47 Clerkenwell Green
London EC1R 0HT

www.headofzeus.com

For Jeannie DeLavern Stabenow—
thanks for loving Dad

PROLOGUE

ST. PETERSBURG, MARCH 25

THE ELEGANT COLUMNS AND fabulous spires of the old city seemed to float in the pale gold light of the soft spring dawn, adrift on a sea of morning mist.

And why not, thought Kiril Davidovitch, bouncing in his seat as the armored truck lurched through yet another pothole. With Lake Ladoga to the northeast and the Gulf of Finland to the southwest and the Neva River and its many tributaries between, the buildings designed with such grace and style by Peter the Great's imported French and Italian architects almost three centuries before were in perfect position to set sail at the first high tide.

He propounded this thought to the truck's driver. The burly man with the bushy eyebrows deepened his scowl, shifted down to take the bridge over the Kanal Griboyrdova and growled, "Good. Ship the whole goddamn place across the Atlantic and let the Americans buy it. They'll buy anything, even," he sneered, "St. Petersburg."

Fyodor still resented the return to Leningrad's original name. It was an insult, to the state, to Communism and to Lenin himself, that poor mummified bastard. He'd roll over in his glass casket if he knew.

After seven months of riding next to him, Kiril was aware

of Fyodor Chirikov's deep resentment over the fall of Communism in Mother Russia. That fall had, in Fyodor's view, led directly to the loss of his subsidized apartment in the Nevsky Prospekt, which in turn compelled him to take his present job with Security Services, Inc., one of the new companies springing up like weeds all across the new nation, half of which were fronts for what Bobbie Batista had taken to calling the Russian Mafia.

Kiril loved Bobbie Batista. He loved CNN, and the ten-second clips of pictures showing him life in the West. One day he hoped to travel there, and perhaps convey his respects to Ms. Batista in person.

Just past the Gostiny Dvor Department Store Fyodor swerved the truck around a shabby orange barricade with "Detour!" marked in large, hand-painted letters. Kiril didn't flinch. Nobody obeyed street signs in the city. They had a nasty habit of having been set there by thieves who had the intention of separating you from your vehicle and putting it up for sale in pieces in the city marketplace a kilometer away.

Fyodor spoke Kiril's thoughts out loud. "Lousy thieves. Stalin would have known how to deal with them."

Kiril was more tolerant. What could you expect? The only people who had any knowledge of a free market were the crooks who had been running the ubiquitous and extremely profitable black market since before Lenin was elected. It was natural that the crooks would step in to fill the gaps in supply and demand, in production and distribution.

He, Kiril, was content to wear a stiff blue uniform and ride shotgun, like John Wayne in *Stagecoach*, to earn enough to buy black bread and sausages and the occasional bottle of vodka. It was also enough to pay for his own bedroom in a shared flat, to which more often than not he could entice a girl

2

to share his bed. His bed was his most prized possession; a four-poster relic of a more gracious (Fyodor would say degenerate) age, with a marvelously carved headboard and box springs, and a mattress and linens he had cheerfully beggared himself to buy.

Which reminded him of the little cashier in the black sedan in front of them. She was pretty, with smooth skin, velvety brown eyes and little breasts like apples pushing up the front of her suit jacket. It had been cold outside the bank that morning as they stood waiting for the branch manager to unlock the door. The little cashier had had no coat on, and the rough wool fabric over her breasts had peaked where her nipples had hardened. He would have liked to have slipped a hand beneath that jacket to see if those breasts were as firm as they looked. She had caught his appreciative glance and her smooth skin had flushed a delicate pink, the color of the dawn sky above, but she hadn't looked angry and she hadn't looked away.

The neat blond head was framed now in the rear window of the sedan, and he imagined that she could feel the weight of his gaze, enough so that he wasn't surprised when she turned to flash him a shy smile. The truck's windshield was masked with plate steel, leaving only a narrow horizontal slit through which to see and be seen, but Kiril knew she smiled at him. The branch manager next to her must have thought so, too, and must not have liked it, because he snapped something that had her obediently facing forward again. Strands of blond hair cupped her collar in a neat, shining line. Kiril imagined running his fingers through that hair, imagined the little cashier rubbing her head against his palm like a cat, purring like a cat, too. She would purr, he was sure of it. He couldn't wait to find out if he was right. That night, perhaps.

Fyodor observed all this with a sour expression. "The Romeo of the Rentacops strikes again."

Kiril grinned and gave a modest shrug. "What can I say? The ladies, they love me."

Fyodor grunted. The heavy truck bounced again as they ran over another, deeper pothole.

"Whoa there, pardner," Kiril said in his best Duke impression, and grabbed hold of the armrest to keep from rolling into Fyodor's lap. "Watch it. Don't want to upset all those rubles riding around in back."

Fyodor grunted again, disdainfully this time. He didn't approve of money, or currency transfers, or banks either, for that matter. Property, all property, should be held in common, by all citizens. Profit, especially profit earned by lending money at extortionate rates to those who knew no better, was an abomination.

Still, it wouldn't do to lose their escort entirely. The truck slowed almost to a halt. "Can you see the soldiers?"

Kiril bent down to peer into the rearview mirror. He laughed. "Yes. One fell off the outside of the troop truck. They've stopped to wait for him to catch up."

Fyodor swore and double-clutched into second. The gears crashed together and the armored truck began to jerk forward.

Kiril braced both hands against the dash and tried to keep his spine from snapping off at the neck. "What are you doing," he said, dutiful but not really alarmed. It was only Fyodor, rebelling against the new world order on schedule. "You know the rules, we wait for the soldiers."

"Fuck their mothers," Fyodor said, and broke another rule by opening the door to spit contemptuously. The door crashed shut again and they roared over the Nevsky Prospekt bridge, only to be brought to an abrupt halt on the other side when

4

Fyodor cursed and slammed on the brakes.

Kiril's hat fell over his eyes and the knuckles of one hand hurt where it had slipped and hit the dash. He swore a few times himself and shoved his hat back on his head.

The square was teeming with soldiers, commanded by a tall, broad-shouldered captain in a pristine uniform with knife-sharp creases down the legs of his pants and red tabs on his epaulets. He strode toward them, an expression of sharp annoyance in his hard blue eyes. His cheekbones were high and flat in a narrow face and his mouth was a wide pair of thin lips pressed together in an uncompromising line. Kiril, who had served thirteen hellish months in Chechnya before the pullout, recognized at a glance the look of a professional officer, one who got the job done and never bothered before the fact to count the cost in soldiers' lives. No matter what the situation was, no matter what Fyodor said, they were going to wind up in the wrong, Kiril thought glumly, and cast an anxious look at the sedan in front of them. The little blond cashier had twisted around in her seat and was watching the officer approach the truck. He hoped that wasn't admiration he saw in her eyes.

The army officer arrived at Fyodor's door and thumped it with an imperious fist. Without much hope Kiril said, "Don't open it, Fyodor, you know it's against the rules." Fyodor ignored him and opened it anyway, and Kiril gave up and sat back with a sigh.

"Captain Kakhovka," the officer said. "Fifth Battalion, assigned to assist the St. Petersburg militia in keeping the peace."

And not liking the situation, Kiril thought. The captain would rather be in Chechnya, slaughtering civilian rebels and having his own troops slaughtered in turn.

"What's the problem, captain?" Fyodor said.

The captain, still tight-lipped, said, "There were reports of violence in front of the General Staff Building this morning, a workers' demonstration gone bad."

Fyodor's lip curled. "Another one?"

The captain gave a curt nod, his field cap squared just so on his brow. "We've had information that some had weapons. You should have stopped at the barricade."

Fyodor spread his hands. "What barricade, Captain? There was no barricade." He looked at Kiril for conformation.

Kiril opened his big brown eyes as far as they would go. "No, no barricade."

Captain Kakhovka looked skeptical. Kiril didn't blame him. "You'll have to go around. We've rerouted the traffic down Plekhanova."

Indeed, the black sedan was already turning. The little blonde was still twisted around in her seat, wide curious eyes on the truck.

Fyodor muttered a curse and slammed the door to put the truck in gear again and jerk forward in pursuit of the sedan. In the rearview mirror Kiril noticed the captain waving the truck filled with soldiers to a halt, and that the soldier who had fallen off the truck into the pothole almost fell off again. He laughed.

"What?" Fyodor said grumpily, and, when Kiril relayed the news, grumbled, "We'll have to go all the way down to Gorokhovaya, maybe even Antonenko."

Plekhanova was a narrow street lined with tall, thin buildings blocking out the morning sun. Its surface was even rougher than Nevsky, and the noise the steel plates of the truck made as they rumbled down it precluded any conversation. Fortunately there was hardly any traffic, Kiril thought, because between the narrowness of the street, the width of the truck and Fyodor's sunny disposition, oncoming vehicles would have been at severe risk of winding up in someone's parlor.

They came upon an intersection with another, smaller street with no street sign and were there halted by yet another soldier. "What now?" Fyodor grumbled.

The soldier was carrying an automatic rifle over one shoulder. He waved at them, indicating an even tinier street to their right. The black sedan obediently turned down it.

"What the hell?" Fyodor said. "This isn't the way to Gorokhovaya." The soldier looked stern and waved again, and Fyodor swore and jammed the truck into gear. "Goddamn military. Fuck all their mothers. We are never going to get our lunch."

This street was if possible even narrower than the previous one, the houses smaller and leaning up against one another like they could use the support. They weren't fifty feet down it when the taillights of the black sedan flashed six feet off their front bumper. This time Kiril had himself braced against the dash before Fyodor stamped on the brake.

Another soldier was standing in front of the sedan. He, too, was armed with an automatic rifle. An older-model Kalishnikov, Kiril had just enough time to see, before, in a single, practiced motion the soldier had the muzzle trained on the black sedan.

"What the hell?" Fyodor said, startled out of his sulk.

Time seemed to slow down, enough for Kiril to notice the total lack of expression on the soldier's face as the rifle went off with a stuttering clatter, shattering the glass of the sedan's windshield. The branch manager's shoulders jerked once and went still. Half of the little clerk's blond head separated from the other half and flew back to smear against the rear window. The perfect little body seemed to relax back against her seat, as if she had decided to take a nap.

"No!" Kiril yelled and opened his door.

"Don't! Keep the door closed!" Fyodor shouted.

"No!" Kiril yelled again, already half out of his seat when he heard the quiet burping of automatic-rifle fire and felt a bullet slam into his right side. He bounced off the door, spun around and fell clumsily to the street, face down, his cheek pressed against the damp, patched tarmac, his outflung hands grasping at the cobblestones, the light layer of frost dissolving at his touch.

From a great distance he heard what sounded like a lot of firecrackers going off all at once. They weren't firecrackers, though; he knew that sound all too well. All he could think of was the smear of red against the rear windshield of the black sedan, all that was left of the little cashier's head. "No," he whispered, and tried to pull himself up. His arms and legs would not obey. The right side of his chest was warm, the warm area growing larger the longer he lay there.

A foot clad in highly polished army boots stepped over him. "What the hell?" he heard Fyodor say again, just before the shot that killed him.

"Set the charge," a familiar voice snapped. It was the officer with the blue eyes, Kiril thought. He remembered the coldness in those eyes, and with the small remnant of reason left to him concentrated on not being obvious about breathing.

A few minutes later there was a loud *Crump!* The truck rocked forward, the right rear wheel almost rolling over his arm. The two rear doors fell into the street with loud clangs that reverberated painfully inside Kiril's head.

"All right, bring up the truck."

There was the sound of an engine approaching. Tires rolled into Kiril's view. Feet clad in bright red Reebok sneakers thudded to the pavement next to the driver's door. Kiril heard more doors slam and more footsteps. Someone gave an excited laugh.

"The soldiers?" the first voice said.

"No problem," a second voice said cheerfully.

"All right. Come on, get it out, all of it. Let's get going before the real militia show up."

There was another laugh. "Aren't they getting their share?"

"This time it's all ours."

"America, land of the free, home of the brave, here we come!"

"Come on, move it!"

There was a flurry of furious activity between the back of the armored truck and the new vehicle. It lasted about ten minutes. For every minute Kiril lived a year. His side was beginning to hurt, but he knew enough to make no sound. He had not survived Chechnyan rebels to die at home, on a street in St. Petersburg not a mile from his apartment. He thought about the carving on the head of his bed. He thought about the little blond clerk lying beneath it, smiling and holding out her arms, before half her face slid off. A scream fought its way up his throat. He held on to it, repressing the fine trembling that had begun in his legs.

"All right," the first voice said. "That's all of it. Move out."

"What about you?" the cheerful voice said.

"I'll be right there." There was a sound of a round being jacked into the chamber of an automatic pistol. "No witnesses this time."

WASHINGTON, D.C., JUNE 12

"HALEY!"

"Yes, sir?"

"Where the hell are Carroll and Casanare?"

Special Agent Dennis Haley looked wildly around the cramped bullpen of the Russian Mafia task force, as if his extreme need would cause the two agents to crawl out from beneath one of the dozen desks jammed into the room. Instinctively he said, because even at his grade level deniability was all, "Uh, I don't know, sir."

"Well, find them, goddamn it!"

Golden slammed back into his office. Special Agent Haley's computer monitor rocked slightly on its stand from the aftershock.

Special Agent Haley was small and thin and red-haired and harried. He was also easily cowed, and in spite of the mountain of paperwork piled on his desk he didn't hesitate to go in search of the errant agents. He found them two floors down, assisting in the sorting of evidence from the bombing of an airliner which had gone into the Atlantic off the coast of South Carolina.

Carroll looked up and saw Haley in the doorway. "We're saved," she told Casanare. There were only so many ways a witness could describe a plane blowing up, all of them resulting in the death and dismemberment of everyone on board. When you've read one eyewitness report, you've read them all, whether they were knee-deep in the ocean off Myrtle Beach, revering or reviling the memory of John Brown at Fort Sumter, or visiting your mother-in-law under duress at Tybee Island.

"Who says there's no god?" Casanare replied. If he had to look at one more report of a severed limb floating to shore, he was afraid he might vomit. You just don't vomit at headquarters. In the field, yes, neatly and discreetly behind a bush, and at a crime scene no one blamed you, but not at headquarters.

Maxine Carroll was a tall blonde with deep blue, almost violet eyes. Alberto Casanare was an inch shorter than Carroll, fifty pounds heavier, all of it muscle, and as dark as she was fair.

They were key members on the task force investigating the Russian Mafia presence in the United States, recently covering themselves with glory following the successful cracking of a multinational organization controlling but not limited to credit card fraud, money laundering, illegal alien smuggling, white slavery, weapons trafficking and tax evasion, and the indictment (if not the trial and imprisonment, Haley thought regretfully), of one Pyotr Razikin, AKA Peter the Great, the alleged leader of the organization.

"What's up?" Carroll said in the hallway.

Haley, preoccupied with watching her walk, didn't hear her at first. Casanare, grinning, nudged him in the side before Carroll turned around and caught him. He colored and stuttered, "Uh, the boss wants to talk to you."

"What about?"

"I don't know," Haley said.

Carroll halted to examine him through narrowed eyes. "Like hell. You're worse than a Soviet mole in the CIA. You always know what's going on."

11

Haley's red face darkened to purple and he very nearly wriggled with pleasure. "Really. He just said to find you, he didn't say why."

"But your best guess would be—?" Casanare said.

Haley only shook his head and marched determinedly to the elevator. Casanare raised an eyebrow at Carroll, who shrugged and followed.

The lack of windows in Samuel Golden's office was disguised by the blizzard of memos, department communiques, ten-most-wanted lists, crime reports and handdrawn, crudely lettered cartoons scatological and profane dealing mostly with Senate oversight committees tacked to the walls. Golden himself was an intense, wiry man of fifty-two years, smart, tenacious and a Bureau man down to his toes. His family was Jewish, originally from Minsk, and he was fluent in Russian. He'd been a twenty-year veteran when tapped to head up the Russian Mafia task force. At first the task force had been him and one administrative aide. After the Berlin Wall fell and the Soviet Republic broke up, the power and global reach of the Russian Mafia expanded exponentially, and eventually he was allocated his pick of the personnel roster. His first choice had been Alberto Casanare. On Al's recommendation, his second was Maxine Carroll. As they settled into their seats, he ran a mental review of their jackets, which were very nearly as colorful as his own.

Maxine Carroll's great-grandfather had been born Anatoli Chernofski, which became Carroll on his way through Ellis Island in 1899. He had traveled by train across the country to Dawson City, where he met a dance-hall girl named Norma Swensen. They married and moved to Seattle, where Anatoli used Norma's savings to establish himself in the timber industry, gradually diversifying into paper products, soon landing a lucrative and apparently infinite contract with the Department of the Interior and thereby ensuring the security and comfort of his family well into the next century. In the fullness of time, Anatoli and Norma had children and grandchildren and great-grandchildren, of which Carroll was the third. At her great-grandfather's insistence, his children had grown up speaking both Russian and English, a tradition passed down through the generations. When Carroll graduated from the University of Washington in 1989 with a degree in economics, she was recruited by the FBI. She was thirty-four years old, single, with no children. Golden looked at her beneath drooping lids. If he could have said the same, and if he weren't her superior officer, she wouldn't have been for long.

Carroll's family was one generation up on Alberto Casanare's, whose grandfather had waded across the Rio Grande in Texas, picked lettuce until he had enough money to send for his wife, and who, by the time the Immigration and Naturalization Service got around to asking, had sired nine children, all born safely north of the Rio Grande and the eldest of which was an attorney specializing in civil rights. Al, the sixth of the grandchildren, had grown up speaking Spanish and English, which facilitated his talent for linguistics. He majored in foreign languages at the University of Texas, specializing in Russian and Japanese and, like Carroll, was recruited by the FBI on graduation. He'd spent four years in El Paso, that black hole of the FBI, intercepting drug shipments, before his fluent Russian got him seconded to Golden's task force. He was four years older than Carroll, happily married and the father of three, all of whom called Carroll Auntie Maxie, which she said made her sound like a Southern spinster, but that was all she said, so Golden figured she didn't mind that much.

They'd been partners for five years, and speculation was rife in the Bureau over the possibility of an ongoing affair. Golden knew better. Casanare was married to one of the smartest, prettiest women Golden knew, not excluding Carroll, and Carroll had all the moral flexibility of Carrie Nation. No, they were partners, and friends, no more. He approved. There was nothing worse than sex to fuck up a relationship, not to mention the job site.

Carroll moved restively in her seat, and Golden tried not to admire her legs, displayed to advantage beneath a slim skirt and a jacket that made everything else nip in and stick out the way it was supposed to. The woman was a first-class clotheshorse. "You wanted to see us, sir?"

Golden got his overactive imagination back under control. "Yes." He chucked a file across the desk and she caught it neatly. Casanare rose to read over her shoulder. "Couple of reports out of Russia. First one's a bank robbery. The ruble equivalent of $10 million. First National Bank of Commerce and Trade, St. Petersburg, March 25. They were transferring the rubles from the branches to the main bank."

"Seems like a hell of a lot of money for a provincial bank," Casanare observed.

"A hell of a lot," Golden agreed. "But then they do a hell of a lot of foreign trade. Finland, the Baltic states, like that."

"Over or under?"

"The table?" Carroll nodded, and Golden shrugged. "That's up to the Russian cops. Anyway, it's about eleven-thirty; there are three vehicles: a four-door sedan with a driver, the bank manager and a clerk, an armored truck with a driver and a guard, and a troop truck with twenty soldiers on board bringing up the rear." He paused.

"Let me guess," Carroll said. "A detour sign."

14

Golden nodded. "Except they didn't take the detour."

"Figures," Casanare said.

"Yeah, but it didn't help them, the crooks knew they wouldn't, and a couple streets on they were met by an army captain with a detachment who directed them down a dead-end street, ambushed them with automatic rifles, blew the doors off the truck with a handful of homemade C-4 and got away with all the marbles."

"Job inside or outside?"

"Outside."

Carroll made a face. "Everyone dead?"

"All but one," Golden said coolly, ignoring Casanare's wince. "Which won't surprise you."

"Why not?" Carroll demanded.

Golden jerked his head at the file in her hands. "Check out the description of the police captain."

She skimmed through the pages and came to a halt, her eyes running rapidly down the page. She went very still. "Ivanov."

"Ivanov?" Casanare said, sitting up.

"Ivanov," Golden said, nodding.

"Back in business," Casanare said.

"He was never out," Carroll said.

Ivanov, the only name by which he was known, had been the missing person in the Peter the Great case. There was no clear file photo of him, only a description of a tall, broad-shouldered blond with blue eyes, Slavic cheekbones and a thin-lipped smile that one terrified informant had described as "a fucking throat-cutter, and happy in his work. I mean, Jesus Christ, if Ivanov smiles at you, you know you're dead." Ivanov had sat at Peter the Great's right hand, had been his enforcer, had been, literally on one memorable occasion, Pyotr's hatchet man.

Carroll's gaze was narrowed and fierce. "You said there were two reports."

Golden tossed her a second file. "This one's a theft. A military base near the Ukrainian border was hit. We have reason to believe Ivanov was involved."

"What reason?"

"A description of one of two men in a white van that drove into the base late the night of the robbery. Tall, broad-shouldered—"

"—blue eyes—" Carroll said.

"—Slavic cheekbones—" Casanare said.

"—and a smile you could cut yourself on," Golden said, nodding.

"Two men?"

"Two. The other man didn't seem to make much of an impression on our witness, other than being shorter, heavier, older and with less hair. Of course, he was covered with Russian prison tattoos."

"Mafia."

"Looks like."

"And who is our witness?"

"Was. He died after he gave a statement."

"How'd he die?"

"He was shot. At point-blank range."

Casanare said grimly, "That sonofabitch doesn't like to leave any loose ends lying around, does he?"

Golden shook his head. "Wasn't Ivanov."

"Bullshit."

"Our witness was one of two guards on the gate that night, both of whom had been alerted by the base commander to expect company, with full descriptions of both so they could be passed through. The guards followed, as per instructions. Ivanov went into the general's office and stayed there, coming out only once, the guard thought while the general was on the phone."

"What general?"

"The base commander. Armin Glukhov. Four stars, much-decorated veteran of Czechoslovakia, Afghanistan, Chechnya, and on loan for a dozen little insurrections around Africa and South America."

Carroll's brows twitched together. Casanare said, "What did they steal?"

"Ten kilograms of plutonium."

Silence. "Plutonium?" Carroll said.

"Plutonium," Golden confirmed.

Another silence. "They make bombs with plutonium," Casanare observed.

"Yes."

"Nuclear bombs."

"Yes."

"With, like, fallout and radioactive poisoning and nuclear winter and all the other modern conveniences."

"Yes."

Another silence. "And you're telling us Ivanov stole ten kilograms of it? What's that in pounds?"

"Twenty-two," Carroll said.

Of course she would know, Golden thought, she knew everything, or thought she did. "And you only need about a pound to make a bomb with a one-mile blast radius, according to the mad scientists in the lab. Even a marginally competent design would fit into a suitcase, they say. Imagine a dozen suitcases placed strategically in bus-station lockers around Israel. Or India." He paused. "Or the United States."

17

"Jesus Christ," Casanare said, shaken out of his sangfroid. "I know things are bad over there, but—"

"But nothing," Golden said. "The Russian Mafia and the government pretty much run the country now, and business is along for the ride. People are making millions selling off government property, a dozen tanks here, a battery of ground-to-air missiles there. Everyone's involved; government, business, and they're both in bed with the gangs. Yeltsin's own minister of defense was caught hiring a hit man from a local gang to take out some undersecretary who didn't hand over the minister's share on a deal. Hell, Al, they are averaging a little under a hundred contract killings a month in Russia right now. There are five, almost six thousand separate criminal gangs in Russia, at last count. It's worse than Columbia, Venezuela and Bolivia combined. At least the drug cartels aren't electing presidents and appointing judges and misappropriating government funds. Yet."

"I hadn't heard that about the defense minister," Carroll said, affronted, as though the defense minister should have apprised her in advance before taking out a contract for a hit.

"You know how they do business over there nowadays? Say a ministry needs a million dollars to fix a road. They apply to the Russian parliament for the funds, the lawmakers—hah!—approve them, and then the ministry takes three percent off the top and hands it back to the lawmakers. Who then bank it in Switzerland or the Bahamas or Macao, or launder it through the Bank of New York." Golden wasn't telling them anything they didn't already know, but they also knew that it was useless to try to derail him. "Christ, I miss the good old days when all we had to worry about was a KBG mole bugging the men's washroom at Langley."

"Why didn't Ivanov just buy the plutonium from the

government? If everything's for sale, why not that, too?" Carroll said with a frown.

Golden grunted. "He doesn't believe in bribes."

After a moment they all realized how funny that sounded, and the three of them burst into a roar of laughter that jolted Dennis Haley at his desk in the office outside.

"So how did it go down?" Casanare said, sobering.

"Report says the driver handled the actual trade, while Ivanov and Glukhov waited it out in Glukhov's office."

They considered this. "Glukhov nervous, wanting insurance," Carroll said. "He keeps Ivanov with him while the transaction goes through."

The stakes had just gone through the roof, but both agents were maintaining, although Carroll's fair skin was a little flushed and Casanare tugged at his tie. "Yeah," Golden said, "that's my take on it, too. The whole thing's pretty slick. There's a forklift warmed up and waiting, one of the workers rides one of the forks into the plant, I guess pointing the way. They weren't inside more than twenty minutes. So, maybe an hour all told later, Ivanov comes out, walks past the two guards to the outer office door. They turn to escort him out, and the general shoots both men in the back, bang, bang, a walk in the park."

Carroll examined him with a shrewd eye. "They were in on it with Glukhov, weren't they, the two grunts."

It wasn't a question. "Yes. But—"

"But what?" A crook was a crook, in Carroll's book. She had no sympathy or regrets to waste on a crook.

For the most part, Golden agreed with her. Still—"One of the guards had been with Glukhov since Czechoslovakia, the other since Afghanistan."

"Cold," Casanare said with distaste. "When he decided to

go, he decided to go all the way."

"Price of entry into the brotherhood," Carroll said, curling her lip. "Ivanov would require it."

Golden smiled inwardly, anticipating their reaction to his next news. "He's been seen. Two days ago."

Carroll's voice was tense with excitement. "Ivanov?"

"No," Golden said, still smiling. "Glukhov."

Her enthusiasm waned noticeably. "Oh. Where?"

"Anchorage, Alaska."

"Alaska?" Casanare said blankly. "You mean like the Arctic?"

"Yes, Al, the Arctic, with dog teams and Eskimos and blubber," Carroll said, but then she was from Seattle, which was practically a suburb of the Last Frontier. "Where in Anchorage?"

"Outside the midtown post office," Golden said, enjoying himself. "To be precise, he was spotted standing on the curb, talking Ukrainian into a cellular phone."

"Who spotted him?"

"Remember Alex Kornbluth?" He waited.

Carroll's frown cleared. "That's right, Kornbluth, he's from Fairbanks. He transferred up when they opened the new office in Anchorage. They needed someone who spoke Russian because the border's opening up between Alaska and Siberia. Alaska Airlines is flying between Anchorage and Magadan and Providenya nowadays, and they've got Russian trawlers docking at Dutch Harbor and other ports during the fishing season."

"Lot of trade, lot of immigration," Golden agreed. "Anyway, Kornbluth was coming out from checking his mail and there was General Armin Glukhov, chattering away on the cellular. He said Glukhov was letting his hair grow and he

20

was wearing a suit that would have cost Kornbluth a year's pay, but Kornbluth recognized him right away from that file we've got on all those generals Yeltsin keeps firing."

"What did Kornbluth do?"

"He climbed in his car and pretended to read his mail. Pretty soon, Glukhov climbs into his car, a brand-new Cadillac El Dorado, I might add, and drives over to a bank about twenty blocks north, Kornbluth says, although I find it hard to believe they have ten blocks in Anchorage, Alaska, let alone twenty. He meets another guy, Kornbluth didn't recognize him, big city business type with a Michael Douglas duck's ass, they have some conversation, in English. Kornbluth got close enough to hear something about shipments, and then they split up."

"What happened then?"

Golden sighed. "The battery on Kornbluth's cell phone was dead, and he had to go find a pay phone to call in. When he got back, they were gone."

It happened. "So Ivanov's recruited Glukhov," Carroll said in a dreamy voice. "In effect, Ivanov has become Pyotr, and Glukhov has become Ivanov. Right down to the hatchet, or in this case, the gun."

There was a brief silence. Casanare broke it. "Ivanov wouldn't turn him loose this soon without a keeper."

"No," Golden said, still smiling.

"So he'll be there, too," Carroll said, sitting up straight in her chair. "Up to his neck in whatever Glukhov is fronting."

"Yes," Golden said. He held up an admonitory finger. "One thing. We don't talk about the plutonium. It's zirconium we are officially looking for. That's what our people in Anchorage will be told, too."

"What's zirconium?"

"Hell if I know. I'm told it's used in nuclear reactors to make plutonium, so we've got a legitimate reason for looking for it. That's good enough for me." He grinned. "It's only worth about five hundred a short ton."

"At five hundred a short ton, who's going to believe anyone could smuggle enough to make a profit?" Casanare said skeptically.

"Who's going to know? What any of us knows about the stuff could be written on the head of a pin. Us and ninety-nine percent of the rest of the world, especially in this country, in which educational institutions are barely managing to graduate students who can read, let alone tell one element from another. Nobody knows what zirconium is. Plutonium, on the other hand, is a hot button. Everybody knows what plutonium is, or does. So we don't talk about it. No need to start a general panic."

"Do we get a tap?"

"When we find a phone to listen to," Golden said dryly, "you'll get a tap."

Without knowing it, Carroll and Casanare were on their feet. "This time," Carroll said, "we nail the bastard," and she met Casanare's high five with a stinging slap that echoed around the room.

Golden sat back in his chair, linked his hands across his belly and gave a contented sigh. He loved the sound of agents on a mission in the morning.

CHAPTER 1

NINILTNA, JUNE 25

"Lots of spirits all over, this year,"
They whisper.

—*A Quick Brush of Wings*

THEY WOULD ARGUE LATER about when it all began, perhaps with the death in July, or maybe the meeting in Washington, D.C., the month before, or even with the fall of the Berlin Wall in 1989, but as far as First Sergeant Jim Chopin was concerned it began that day in late June when he flew his Bell Jet Ranger from the regional post in Tok to the Bush village of Niniltna on the Kanuyaq River, and drove the twenty-five miles of rough gravel road through a green and fecund Park to Kate Shugak's homestead.

"She's not there," Bobby had said when the trooper asked for the loan of Bobby's pickup.

His wife, Dinah, a worried look on her face and baby Katya on her hip, added, "We haven't seen her since before Thanksgiving, Jim. She's just vanished."

"Can I borrow the truck or not?" Jim said.

"Goddamn it," Bobby roared, "I said she ain't there!" He rolled his chair forward so that he could glare straight up into the trooper's face. "We drove out three weeks ago. The Ford's parked in front of the garage, the snow machine's parked in the garage, and the cabin's empty except for some canned food and a lot of dust. She ain't there, and she ain't been there."

"Where is she, Jim?" Dinah said. "Have you heard something? Is that why you want to go out there? Billy's really worried. He hasn't seen her since the funeral."

"She was at the funeral?" Jim said, startled. "I didn't see her."

"I didn't either," Bobby said, making it sound like an accusation.

"She was standing in the back," Dinah said. "I only caught a glimpse of her. She left right after, before everybody started telling Jack stories."

"Goddamn it!" This time the tops of the trees seemed to sway in response to Bobby's roar. His black face was made blacker with rage, made all the more furious by a dark fear no less tangible for remaining unspoken. "I will kill her when we catch up with her, I swear I will kill the bitch!"

Katya, used to Daddy's decibel level, was so upset she burped, loudly. Dinah, looking at the trooper, said, "Why are you looking for her, Jim? Is it something to do with the case?"

He shook his head. "No. The suits are fighting for extradition to Germany, but it doesn't look like it's going to fly. Their own country doesn't seem much interested in getting them back. Big surprise."

He pulled the gimmee cap from his head and ran a hand through a thick pelt of hair. He'd recently abandoned the more formal Mountie-type hat for the baseball-style hat with the trooper insignia above the bill. The Mountie hat, especially the way Chopper Jim wore it, was a first-class babe magnet, which had been its chief attraction to him when he opted for it at the beginning of his service. He had suffered a great deal of joshing at the switch over the last six months. All he would say in response was that wearing the smaller hat made it easier to get in and out of aircraft. The uniform, his size and a look in his eye that dared comment kept people from remarking that in fourteen years of wear his Mountie hat hadn't kept him from flying before, at least to his face.

They were standing on the porch that ran the width of Bobby's A-frame. From there the ground gradually sloped down to Squaw Candy Creek, the southern border of the one hundred and sixty acres Bobby had home-steaded in the mid-seventies, when he had come back from Vietnam minus both legs from the knee down and decided to abandon his home state of Tennessee for the last frontier of the Alaskan Bush. On the eastern horizon, the blue-white spurs of the Quilak Mountains scored the sky, Angak or Big Bump the biggest spur of all.

Half an acre of cleared land sprouted leaf lettuce and broccoli and arugula and radishes and cauliflower and carrots and sugar snap peas. Tomato plants had grown to the roof of the greenhouse, so that it looked like a jungle in a box. A garage stood open, revealing a small tractor parked inside, the snow-clearing blade it donned in winter leaning up against one wall. A new green pickup was parked next to it, and the outline of a snow machine could be seen beyond them. The shop was between garage and house, and it too stood open, displaying a U-shaped bench just the right height for someone in a wheelchair. A circular saw, a sander and a router had been built into the bench; from pegboards on the walls hung every imaginable tool, each handle worn smooth from years of use.

Not for the first time, Jim wondered where Bobby Clark had acquired the money to finance his homestead. Not for the first time, he decided to let it go. "So can I borrow your truck or what?" he said.

Bobby let loose with a string of imaginative curses that Jim had to admire for their almost Elizabethan flavor, graphic detail and physical impossibility. He waited, maintaining his placid facade with some effort.

Looking for a fight and not getting one, Bobby growled out one last ripe and frustrated oath and wheeled into the A-frame, reemerging almost immediately with the keys to the truck clutched in one fist. He hurled them at Jim. "Take the goddamn thing!"

Jim took a quick step back and stretched up a hand, and the keys smacked into his palm like he was catching a fly ball. He caught his balance just before he fell off the edge of the porch and said, "Thanks, Bobby. I'd thought I'd drive out to the Roadhouse after, talk to Bernie. That okay?"

"I don't care if you drive it into the goddamn river!"

"I do," Dinah said, "we're almost out of diapers."

"Again? Jesus god, that kid produces more shit than a herd of moose!"

Katya gave Daddy a blinding smile and launched herself from her mother's arms into her father's. Dinah gasped and Jim clutched, but Bobby caught the one-man Flying Clark Troupe solidly in both hands and arranged her on his lap, scolding all the while. "Christ, kid, you trying to give your old man a heart attack? Don't try that trick again without a parachute."

She reached up and punched him in the nose. Bobby, his worry for Kate in temporary abeyance, was still laughing when Jim climbed into the truck and drove off.

Dinah's last words, delivered in a low voice beneath the ring of her husband's laughter, echoed in his ears. "Find her,

26

Jim. Do whatever you have to do, but find her and bring her home."

The rough gravel road was all that remained of the roadbed of the Kanuyaq River and Northwestern Railroad that had once run from Niniltna to Cordova, hauling copper from the Kanuyaq Copper Mine four miles north of Niniltna. It had been a dry summer so the road was in pretty good shape; Jim was bounced off the roof of Bobby's truck only three times, which had to be some kind of record. He swerved once to avoid a moose cow and two calves, and again to miss a two-year-old grizzly who was looking a little peaked, as if his momma had just kicked him out and he had yet to learn how to forage for himself. He'd learn or die, Jim thought, and stepped on the gas.

At mile twenty-three he pulled into Mandy and Chick's, the hunting lodge turned sled dog ranch and, since Abel Int-Hout had died, the nearest neighbor to the Shugak homestead. "I haven't seen her since before Christmas," Mandy said. "I went over to invite her for Christmas dinner. She wasn't there."

"Did it look like she'd been there recently?"

The musher spread her hands, worried down to the elegant bones of her Boston Brahmin face. "You know what a neatnik she is. It's hard to tell sometimes if anybody's ever lived there."

Chick put his hands on his roomie's shoulders and squeezed. His eyes met Jim's. He gave a tiny jerk of his head.

"Yeah, I know what you mean," Jim said, and drained his mug. "Thanks for the coffee, Mandy." He got to his feet and donned his cap. "I better get a move on."

"Jim?"

He paused at the door, looking back over his shoulder.

Unconsciously repeating Dinah's admonition, Mandy said, "Find her."

"I will," he said, although they were talking Kate Shugak here. If Kate Shugak wanted to be lost nobody was ever going to find her, and they both knew it.

Still, Mandy added, "And Jim? When you do, kick her butt for me, good and hard."

He touched the brim of his hat and gave his first real smile of the day. "My pleasure."

The sound of the door closing behind him was lost in the howling that ensued when he stepped outside. There were tens and maybe hundreds of dogs chained to tree stumps across a couple of acres of yard, all of them yapping in a cacophony that would have drowned out even Bobby Clark. He threaded a careful path through the pack and walked back up the trail to where the truck was parked in the pulloff. He opened the door and sat sideways on the seat, arms folded across his chest, watching a squirrel stuff her face with spruce cone seeds, the individual petals of the cone raining down in a tiny shower of debris, her cheeks pouched out like an overstuffed purse. She was an efficient if messy eater.

There was a rustle in the branch above, and they both looked up to see a magpie fold his black-and-white wings, the branch bouncing lightly beneath his weight. The squirrel dropped the cone and scampered up the branch to the trunk, up the trunk to a higher branch and leaped to the next tree. The magpie gave a grating squawk, and swaggered down to take the squirrel's place. It was loaded with pinecones bursting with seed, the reason the squirrel had chosen it.

"Greedy guts," Jim said.

The magpie paid him no mind. He was an even messier eater than the squirrel.

A few minutes later Chick came trotting up. "Let's talk quick," he said. "She thinks I'm in the outhouse."

"You know something?"

"Just that I saw Kate after Mandy did," Chick said. His face was round as a melon and as brown as a walnut, with dark hair flopping into his narrow brown eyes.

Kate had hair like that, a thick, shining fall as black as an October night in the Arctic before the first snow. "When did you see her?"

"The second of January. You know Kate lets us run teams across her property?" Jim nodded. "So I was on a training run and I dropped in. What with everything that happened last year, we've been keeping a closer eye on her than usual. You know." Jim nodded again. "Well, she was there."

"Was she packing to go somewhere?"

"I don't think so." Chick paused.

"What? Tell me, Chick."

"She didn't invite me in," Chick said. He didn't like saying it, didn't like acknowledging the fact that Kate Shugak was in such bad shape she couldn't even keep to the rule of Bush hospitality, especially in January.

Jim took his hat off and studied the trooper insignia with care. "Chick, were you sober by the time she moved back from Anchorage? After she killed that baby raper and quit the D.A.'s office?"

Chick frowned, unoffended by the reference to his chronic alcoholism. What was, was. "Yeah."

"You remember what she was like then?"

Chick did, and he didn't like it. The frown deepened. "Yeah."

"Was she better or worse than that this January?"

Chick thought. "Worse," he said finally. Their eyes met. "A

29

lot worse. That's why I didn't tell Mandy I'd stopped by." His shoulders gave an uneasy shrug, as if trying to wriggle out from under something, and failing. "You know how it is when Kate walks into a room, Jim. Snap, crackle, pop, sometimes you've got to duck, the sparks are so big and so fast. She's alive, you know?"

"And she's not, now?"

The shoulders hunched, against the blow of Chick's own words. "No snap, no crackle, no pop, no sparks at all. She's pulled the plug, Jim." He rubbed his hands down his thighs, as if the friction might warm them, and shoved them into his jeans. "She's not even angry, you know? Kate's always pissed off about something. Not now." He paused, thinking over his words. "She doesn't care enough to be angry."

They stood in silence for a moment. Jim moved first, pulling his hat back on and squaring it away. "Thanks, Chick."

"Jim."

He paused, door open, and looked over his shoulder. "Yeah?"

Chick Nayokpuk, more popularly know by his worldclass dog-team driver sobriquet, the Billiken Bullet, was a rotund little man with a rotund little personality to match, but today his round smiling face had hardened into something approaching severity. "We gonna get 'em?"

"We already got 'em, Chick. They aren't going anywhere."

"Trial still on for September?"

"September 23."

"Good," Chick said. "First time I been sorry we don't have the death penalty."

"You're not the first person to have said that."

Chick nodded, face still set in severe lines. "Good to know."

He met Jim's eyes. "Too bad you can't just turn 'em loose in the Park."

Jim smiled, this time a thinning of his lips with no humor to it. "Really too bad." He raised his hand in a semi-salute. "Take care, Chick."

"Find her, Jim," Chick replied. "Find her, okay?"

Jim nodded and drove off, Chick staring after him in the rearview mirror until hidden by the curve of the road.

CHAPTER 2

Gone
the voices, singing.

—The Light on the Tent Wall

A COUPLE OF BIRDS were serenading each other in the trees when Jim came down the path, but he didn't know anything about birds and so could not identify them. There was a rustle of undergrowth here and there as some small mammal heard him and moved unhurriedly out of range. There were salmon still up the creeks and hunting season was two months off; there was no need to rush. Summertime in Alaska and the living was easy. The trail ended in a clearing a hundred feet across, and Jim paused on the edge of it, trying like hell to look at the scene through the eyes of a trooper.

Instead, all he saw was history, the history of a woman whose life could stand as metaphor for the last thirty-five years of the history of the place in which she lived. She had been born Native and raised white, giving her a foot in both worlds. It had cursed her with perspective. Perspective was a quality essential in seeing things clearly for what they were, but not so good when it came time to take sides, to commit to family or, as in this case, tribal loyalty. As her grandmother would have been the first to tell her, and probably had on occasions too numerous to mention. Kate would never tell.

Whatever problems Kate had had with Ekaterina would go with both of them to their graves.

Jim Chopin was a state trooper, by virtue of his profession trained and dedicated to the gathering and evaluation of information. He knew a good deal more about Kate Shugak than most people, far more than she would have been comfortable with had she known.

Her father had been an Aleut fisher, and a veteran of Castner's Cutthroats, a specially trained commando unit that had fought in the Aleutians during World War II. After the war there had been few villages left standing to go back to, and like many other Aleuts, including his mother, Ekaterina Shugak, he had moved north to the Park, although it wasn't a Park then, just a big chunk of land, owned by the federal government, that at that time wasn't being watched too closely. So people moved in, Aleuts, miners, trappers, hunters, fishers, even a few misguided folks who gave farming a try and almost invariably failed; they all staked out sections, built cabins, and refused to move when Alaska became a state in 1959. The fight over who owned what land was on. A lot of lawyers later, the homesteads were grandfathered in, and in 1980 the Park was created around them.

Stephan Shugak ignored the fuss, married Zoya Dementieff, and in 1961, when they'd given up on ever having children, their daughter, Ekaterina Ivana, was born. Ekaterina for Stephan's mother, Ivana for Zoya's. Billy Mike still told the tale of how Ivana had lost the toss to be the first name. Jim figured Ekaterina snuck in a double-headed coin. That old broad hadn't been one to leave much to chance.

Stephan supported the three of them by fishing salmon in summer and trapping beaver in the winter, and if he and his wife had managed to stay off the sauce it would have been a good life. They hadn't. First Stephan was gone, then Zoya, and little Kate had been shipped off to Niniltna to live with her grandmother.

She had stuck it out for a week. The morning of the eighth day she got up early, tucked half a loaf of homemade bread down the front of her snowsuit, shouldered the little .22 rifle her father had given her and walked the twenty-five miles home. This had been the first week in December, with the highs below freezing and the lows below zero.

She made it all the way to the homestead and had a fire going in the wood stove before anyone in Niniltna knew she was gone. Abel had told that tale, of how he'd seen the smoke from the chimney and snowshoed over to see who was trespassing on the Shugaks' cabin. Kate had welcomed him inside and made him a cup of Lipton tea, sweetened with honey just the way he liked it, and a slice of buttered bread. She didn't invite him to stay the night. "Here's your hat, what's your hurry," was how Abel described it. He'd snowshoed back to his own homestead and waited for Kate's grandmother to arrive, which she did, the next morning at first light on a snowmobile, bundled in beaver and spitting mad.

Ekaterina brought Kate back to Niniltna and locked the girl in the spare bedroom. Kate climbed up on the dresser, kicked out the window and got a mile down the road before Ekaterina caught up with her the second time.

Kate didn't fight her grandmother. She waited. Old Sam Dementieff had visited Ekaterina's house during that time, and described it as an armed camp—"She don't know where it was coming from, but Ekaterina knew it was coming, and she was ready to repel boarders." Old Sam would pause, giving his punch line its due dramatic weight. "Kate was readier."

When she brought her back the second time, Ekaterina

tried reasoning with Kate. She was only a little girl, barely in kindergarten, how could she take care of herself all alone way out there on the homestead? And what about school, she had to go to school, it was the law. And what about her old grandmother, all alone in her big house by the river in Niniltna?

This last should have carried weight. Kate was always susceptible to guilt, and Ekaterina could lay it on with a shovel. But at the time it was delivered, to the accompaniment of sad brown eyes squeezing out a single, forlorn tear, Ekaterina's house was filled to the rafters with fourteen cousins making their traditional after-school stop for fry bread and cocoa, one uncle there on tribal business and three aunties making a quilt. Kate looked at them, looked at her grandmother and curled her lip. Auntie Vi told that story— "Ayah, that girl, she one inch high then, and she look twice as big as her emaa."

The next day Emaa walked up to the school to escort Kate home. Kate never did come out.

Kate always knew where the back door was.

Until that day, Ekaterina Moonin Shugak, village elder and tribal leader, had never been confronted with a will as strong as her own. To her credit, she did recognize it, finally, and cast about for an acceptable solution, one that would save everyone's face and provide for Kate's safety. Abel Int-Hout was a widower with four sons who had the homestead next to the Shugaks'. He knew Kate, and Kate knew him, and if not quite with Ekaterina's blessing then at least with her grudging consent Kate had moved in. There she stayed until she turned eighteen, commuting to school on first Abel's and then her own snowmobile, paid for out of summer jobs Abel got her. Bowing to matriarchal pressure, for a change, she went off to the University of Alaska in Fairbanks, where she completed a degree in social sciences with a major in justice. A year's additional training Outside and she went to work as an investigator for the Anchorage District Attorney's office, pissing off her grandmother all over again, who had thought Kate would be coming home after graduation and putting her degree to work for her family and her tribe.

It might have happened, Jim thought now. Yes, it might have. If Kate's boss in Anchorage had not been Jack Morgan. Shortly thereafter he was her lover.

She'd specialized in sex crimes, in particular sex crimes against children. It had taken her five years to burn out, five years and being attacked by a perpetrator caught in the act. He didn't survive. She did. Sort of. Bernie told that tale— "That scar, man, that scar just scared the hell out of me the first time I saw it, right across her throat, all red and ropey and swollen. Kate could barely talk. You gotta wonder what the other guy looked like."

She had come back to the homestead five years before, followed a year and a half later by Jack with a job offer. Find a ranger lost in the Park. Find the investigator sent in after him, also lost. She did, and from then on worked cases for the D.A.'s office on a contract basis.

Until last fall, Jim thought. Last fall, everything changed. He pulled off his cap and let the breeze ruffle his hair as he walked to the middle of the clearing.

Her father's homestead wasn't much different today than it had been when he and Zoya were alive. A one-room cabin, a shop, a garage, a greenhouse, an outhouse, a cache, a woodpile. The buildings, old but in good repair, grouped themselves in a neat half circle, their backs to a narrow creek that ran swiftly between high, rocky banks. The current of the creek had carved out enough of a backwater in the bank next to the cabin to form a small pool suitable for swimming when it warmed up. Not that Jim had ever been invited for skinny-dipping.

He thought of the four-bedroom, split-level home in San Jose in which he'd been raised, and the kindly but clueless couple who were his parents. James and Marie Chopin, in their mid-sixties now, both retired, he from his mail route, she from nursing. They traveled, taking yearly trips to cruise first the Volga and then the Nile, and where was it this year, the Panama Canal? He'd tried to get them on a cruise to Alaska, but they weren't quite ready for that. He didn't think they were ever going to be ready for that, and had long ago resigned himself to taking his yearly vacations in California. Family was family, and he was all they had.

They wouldn't have been ready for this homestead, either, he thought. His mother believed absolutely in the curative properties of hot water and disinfectant, his father in ESPN. Marie couldn't have baked her own bread if her life depended on it, and James routinely traded in the family sedan every three years, carefully timing it to just before the warranty ran out. Jim thought of his father's expression if he'd had to drive any new car down the old railroad bed that served as road access into the Park, and grinned involuntarily.

The red Ford pickup was parked in front of the garage. He walked over and looked in. The keys were in the ignition. He left them there.

He opened the garage door, and as Bobby had said, found the Arctic Cat pulled up to the far wall. No tools appeared to be missing from the shop. The greenhouse was empty except for a fireweed that had pushed its way through a seam in the corrugated plastic walls, purple blooms halfway up the stem.

Through the glass panes he could see raspberry canes hanging heavy with bloom and beginnings of berries. The square plot of garden had not been spaded this spring, and was covered in chickweed and horsetail, the occasional bright yellow head of a dandelion peeping through.

He went around to the back of the cabin and knocked against each of the six fuel oil barrels in turn. They were all near empty. So she'd been here through the winter, and had not yet reordered. But she wouldn't really need to until fall, when the last tanker truck rumbled down the road.

The door of the cabin was unlocked, ready to offer aid and comfort to whatever lost soul might stumble through. He wasn't lost, he wasn't freezing, and he had no warrant. He opened the door and went in.

The bright rays of the eight o'clock sun filtered through the trees and the windowpanes to make gently moving patterns on the walls. It was neat enough to make your teeth ache, but Bobby had been right about the dust. Jim ran a finger across the counter and looked at the resulting smear. She hadn't been here in weeks, probably months.

The room was twenty-five feet square, with a counter, a sink with an old-fashioned water pump handle, two stoves, one oil for cooking, one wood for heat, an L-shaped built-in couch made of plywood and two-by-fours, foam cushions newly upholstered in blue denim neatly patched together from old jeans, and shelves on every available inch of wall space filled with books. There weren't any noticeable holes on the shelves; she hadn't taken any reading material with her.

A ladder in the center of the room led to the loft. He climbed up, the first time he had ever done so, and saw a bed with a down comforter, a Blazo box dresser with four shelves and not so much as a sock on the floor. The shelves seemed pretty bare to his eyes, but then Kate never had been much of a clotheshorse. Jeans with a T-shirt in summer, a sweatshirt in winter, tennis shoes year round. Still, the emptiness of the shelves could be an indication that she had packed a bag when she left. His heart lifted at the thought.

He put a hand on the mattress and pressed down. Well-padded but firm.

A sound came from outside the cabin and he snatched his hand back as if it had been burned.

He climbed back down and looked out the door. A moose was grazing on a mountain ash that would never be more than five feet high. Jim stepped back into the cabin to see the guitar hanging next to the door. He'd never heard her play it, but he'd heard tell that she used to sing sea chanteys before her throat was cut and her voice had been reduced to a raspy husk of sound.

He couldn't imagine the combative, unsentimental Kate Shugak he knew softened by song.

There was a box of photographs on the kitchen table. He leafed through them with the feeling that he'd seen them somewhere before. It took a minute before he remembered where: all over her grandmother's kitchen walls. Kate must have taken them as her legacy after Ekaterina died; she'd certainly given everything else away, including the house.

He pulled out a chair and sat down to leaf through them. They were a record of family and Park history, baby pictures, grade-school and high-school graduation pictures, wedding pictures, anniversary pictures, potlatch pictures. A few looked as if they had been cut from posters on post office walls, and given the size of Kate's extended family, probably were. He thought he recognized Kate in a beaming little girl with laughing hazel eyes, a mass of black tangled hair and chubby knees. He'd never seen her beam like that. It unnerved him, somehow, that she could have been a child like any other. Silly. He'd been a child like that, everyone had. Why would Kate be set apart, dissimilar, sprung full-grown from the brow of Zeus? He gave himself a mental shake and concentrated on the pictures.

There was another of her high-school graduation, thinner in the face and much more serious. She stared the lens straight in the eye, looking as if she were trying to project fearlessness and succeeding only in showing a bravado that failed to hide the apprehension beneath. Again, nothing so different from any other teenager who had wondered what the hell he or she was supposed to do now. He remembered his own panic at the realization that the days of the parental safety net were numbered, that in ascending the stage to receive his diploma he was also taking steps to assume sole responsibility for his actions, of cooking his own meals, washing his own clothes, making his own bed, paying his own rent. He was lucky, he'd always wanted to be a cop, which put him one up on many classmates who were still dithering between majoring in philosophy and electrical engineering. Knowing what he wanted to do was no guarantee of a job in that field, however, and he knew it.

By the time he had his college degree, he was much more confident of his ability to fend for himself. So was Kate. Her college graduation picture had attitude in spades; chin up, shoulders back, eyes confident, even arrogant. The picture of a woman who had found a calling, who was on her way up the ladder, and who knew it.

The last picture he found was of Kate and Jack Morgan. It was at Bobby and Dinah's wedding the previous August, where Kate had acted as best man and maid of honor and, he recalled with a shudder, at the last minute, midwife. When it was all over and she was making motions toward stepping in as the cleanup crew, too, Jack had picked her up, tossed her over his shoulder, grabbed up a sleeping bag and disappeared into the woods, from which they had not emerged until morning. The picture was taken from the side, with their faces turned toward the camera. Kate's long black braid was falling over her face, from behind which she was pretending to be angry. Jack was laughing and about to give her an admonitory slap on the behind.

Jim stared at the picture for a long time before coming back to himself with a start. His watch said it was eight-thirty. Time to head for the Roadhouse. Maybe Bernie would know something. He dropped the picture in the box and walked to the open door.

It was a beautiful evening, warm and serene and still but for the sound of water rushing down the creek in back of the cabin. It soothed nerves rubbed raw by the rush and bustle of modern civilization, gave senses chafed by the noise of life in the city at least the illusion of calm. The Alaskan Bush, the Last Frontier, the last retreat for the weary of spirit and the troubled in mind.

It was, however, only an illusion, and no one would know that better than Kate Shugak, especially after the previous September, when all the rules changed, and peace and tranquility were overrun by malice, mayhem and brutal murder, and nothing would ever be the same again.

He walked back to the box and picked up the picture of Kate and Jack. Tucking it into a breast pocket, he stepped outside and closed the door behind him.

The same birds called all the way from Kate's cabin to Bobby's truck.

The Roadhouse was a big barn of a room with a bar down one side, tables scattered around a dance floor, a jukebox in one corner and a twenty-five inch television suspended from the exposed beams of another.

Tonight the television was black. "No games," Bernie said, pouring Jim a Coke.

"Nobody to watch them, either," Jim said, nodding at the nearly empty bar.

Bernie nodded. "Everybody's out fishing."

"Old Sam tendering this summer?" Bernie nodded again. Jim sipped his Coke. "Kate go with him?"

He must not have sounded as casual as he might have wished, because Bernie gave him a sharp look. A refugee from the sixties, Bernie, tall, skinny and pony-tailed, had not smoked enough dope then to make him stupid now. "No. Dandy Mike went out with him this summer." He produced a rag and began polishing the bar with great vigor.

There was a black-and-white cartoon by Wiley blown up big and tacked to the wall behind the bar. "Bert's Bid For a Utopian Society," read the caption. The drawing showed an irascible-looking old fart hunched over a cane, sitting next to a sign which read, EVERYBODY SHUT UP AND DO THINGS MY WAY! "Bert's" had been altered to read "Bernie's."

The cartoon was right next to the sign which read, FREE THROWS WIN BALL GAMES. Bernie coached the high-school basketball teams, men's and women's, and the shop class had made the sign a class project the first time they took the Class C state championship. It was two feet square, made of three-quarter inch plywood, the lettering burned neatly into the wood, with a glossy varnished finish. The occasion of the sign's presentation was the only time Jim could remember Bernie allowing anybody underage in the Roadhouse, as the sign had been escorted by all forty-two members of Niniltna High School.

Jim raised his glass in a silent toast. Bernie, like Bobby, had burrowed so deep into the Park that both men had become part of the fabric of it, as solid as the Quilak Mountains, as essential as the salmon in the Kanuyaq. Unlike himself, the deus ex machina who flew in for a day and flew out the next, no responsibilities except for those delineated by statute, and god forbid no emotional ties beyond a lusty romp between the thighs of a series of willing Park wenches. It was a life he had crafted for himself with care, it suited him exactly, he had never wanted any other.

Unsettled by the trend of his thoughts, Jim said abruptly, "Have you seen her, Bernie?"

"Who?" Bernie said, frowning down at a stubborn spot on the bar.

"My great-aunt Fanny. Kate Shugak, asshole. You seen her lately?"

Bernie scrubbed harder at the spot. "Nope."

"When was the last time you did see her?"

Bernie stopped scrubbing and stared at the ceiling for inspiration. "Gosh, I don't know. When was that?"

"Bernie." Something in Jim's voice made the bartender meet his eyes, albeit reluctantly. "It's important. When was the last time you saw her?"

Bernie looked around. The nearest people were a couple of tourists necking at a table near the door. If he read the signs right, they'd be asking to rent one of the cabins out back in the next five minutes. They were dressed in a yuppie version of safari chic; jackets by Banana Republic, jeans by Eddie Bauer, boots by L. L. Bean. Bernie mentally raised his room rates twenty percent for the night.

Two old men were shooting pool and arguing over every shot, and that was it for this last Saturday in June, typical for the beginning of fishing season, a time of year the trooper in Jim loved because people were making money on the water instead of spending it in bars. Far fewer calls to domestic disputes during the summertime, and domestic disputes were the calls dreaded most by any law enforcement official. Jim had often wondered if it would be possible to keep men and women separated year round, with time off for good behavior, and conjugal visits, of course. It would make his job so much easier.

Either that or prohibit the manufacture, sale and consumption of alcohol entirely, which hadn't worked real well the last time the country had tried it. And wasn't working real well, come to think of it, in those Alaskan Bush communities that had chosen to go damp or dry during the last ten years. Mostly because they wouldn't stay damp or dry, in spite of an eighty percent drop in alcohol-related crimes such as drunk driving, robbery, sexual assault and murder when they did. He remembered the last bootlegger to inhabit the Park, and his removal, vividly. The Kate Shugak Extraction Method was quick, he'd give it that. As well as effective. And longlasting. There hadn't been a bootlegger within a hundred miles of Niniltna since.

"She was in here in March," Bernie said, and Jim snapped to attention. "I don't know when she came, I don't know when she left. We were busy as hell that night—breakup, you know how it gets around then—so by the time I got over to her table she wasn't there anymore. Weird."

"What's weird?"

Bernie shrugged, brow creased. "She always sits at the bar. This time she was at that table." He pointed at the small circular table tucked into the corner farthest from the bar. He frowned, and began scrubbing the bar again. "First time she's ever been in here that she hasn't even bothered to say hello."

Take a number, Jim thought. "She meet anybody?"

"Not that I saw."

"Who was in that night?"

"Oh, hell." Bernie abandoned the rag. "Everybody. Old Sam, Demetri Totemoff—he's moving around pretty good, now—the Grosdidier brothers drinking down their weekly case of Michelob. Vi and Joy were having their quilting bee, knocking back the Irish coffees like Brazil was running out of beans the next day. The belly dancers were in the back room, the Presbyterian congregation had the big table. Mac Devlin was hustling for mining leases, like usual, making one Oly last all night. Ben and Cindy Bingley."

Jim raised an eyebrow. "Cindy come unarmed?"

Bernie smiled. "They're behaving themselves nowadays. Couple of beers, couple of dances and they're outta here. Whatever Kate said to them last spring must have took."

"Who else?"

"Dandy Mike and Dan O'Brian." Bernie grinned. "Both of them chasing Cheryl Jeppsen, I might add."

Jim stared. "Cheryl Jeppsen? Cheryl Jeppsen of the Kanuyaq River Little Chapel? Cheryl Jeppsen the I-been-saved-now-how-about-you? Cheryl Jeppsen, the self-appointed moral arbiter of all things godly in the Park? Dan and Dandy are chasing that Cheryl Jeppsen?"

Bernie chuckled. "Cheryl's fallen off the born-again wagon. She walked out on her husband and got a job changing sheets

45

at Vi's bed and breakfast. In her off time, she's catching up on what she'd been missing, and from all I hear tell, she'd been missing it a lot."

"I'll just bet she had," Jim said. A reminiscent smile crossed his face. "I remember her before she ate the apple."

"So do I," Bernie said, and looked around hastily to see if Enid had come in without him noticing. His wife had an unnerving habit of sneaking up behind him when he was in the middle of conversations just like this one, and hearing all the wrong parts out of context, too.

"So? Who else?"

"God, Jim, I don't know, everybody. The Moonins, the Bartletts, the Kvasnikofs. George Perry. Billy Mike. Everybody."

Great, Jim thought. Too many people to talk to tonight, even if he could track them down in the middle of fishing season. Well, it had been a forlorn hope at best. He rose. "Thanks, Bernie. I better be going while I've still got light to fly."

"Why are you looking for her? There isn't something going wrong with the trial, is there? Nobody trying to beg off on a technicality?" Bernie's words were light. His tone wasn't.

Jim shook his head. "Nope. They're up for murder times six, attempted murder times four, assault and accessory to attempted rape. If they were found guilty on only one charge, they'd still be going down."

"Christ." The bar rag swiped slowly down the gleaming surface of the bar, and back up again. "I didn't know about the attempted rape." The rag stilled, and Bernie looked up, all levity gone. "What the hell happened out there, Jim?"

"What have you heard?"

"Only what Old Sam and Demetri have said, which isn't much, because they're both witnesses and can't talk about it,

46

or that's what they say. Myself, I think they'd just rather not, which tells me a whole lot right there." He paused, hopeful, but Jim said nothing, and he sighed and continued. "The word is that George organized one of his back-to-the-basics big-game hunts for a bunch of rich Euro cowboys, and Kate, Demetri, Old Sam and Jack signed on to guide for him. Next thing we know, Old Sam's home with his leg broke and his arm shot up, Demetri's in the hospital with a perforated lung, and Kate's back on her homestead with the 'No Visitors' sign up in neon letters twenty feet high. And then people started bringing newspapers into the bar, and we heard about Jack. And the rest of them."

"Yeah."

"So what the hell happened?"

"What they said. What you read." Jim drained his glass and dropped a couple of ones on the bar. "Gotta go."

"Jim?"

"I'll find her, Bernie. You know how she is, she won't make it easy, but I'm a trained law enforcement professional." Jim pulled his cap on with unnecessary force and screwed it down over his ears. "I'll find her."

"Good," Bernie said.

Jim wasn't sure if Bernie believed him.

He wasn't sure he believed himself.

Bobby dropped him off at the airstrip just as George Perry was on his last approach of the night into Niniltna. Jim climbed back out of the Jet Ranger and waited for the Super Cub to taxi up to the hangar.

The pilot saw him as soon as he stepped down from the plane. "Hey, Jim."

"Hey, George."

"What brings you into the Park on such a fine night?" George tried to smile, but the events of the preceding fall had taken their toll on him, too, and it was a poor effort. Both men couldn't help but remember the scene that had met their horrified gazes on the airstrip at George's hunting lodge south of Denali National Park. There had been too many bodies, seven in all, one of which Kate had to be separated from forcibly before they could load it into the plane.

The dead had outnumbered the living by one. Jim didn't like to think about it even now, with ten months between him and that terrible day.

By his expression, neither did George. Jim got right to the point. "Have you seen Kate lately?"

George, in the act of opening the Cub's cowling, paused. "No."

"When was the last time you did see her?"

George turned to face Jim, a spark of anger lighting his eyes. "They aren't going to let them go, are they? You didn't forget to read them their rights or something stupid like that, did you?"

"We aren't letting them go," Jim said wearily, "and no, I didn't forget to read them their rights. I'm looking for Kate, is all. When was the last time you saw her?"

George stared at him long enough to decide Jim was telling the truth. He turned back to the cowling. "I don't know. It's been a while."

"Try to remember. It's important, or I wouldn't ask."

George's shoulders slumped. "Look, she's been through enough, all right? Leave her alone."

Old Sam had said almost those same exact words when

they had landed at the strip ten months before. *Leave her be.*

"I need to know where she is, George."

"I don't know where she is," George said. His words had the ring of truth to them, but Jim had been a state trooper for more than fourteen years and he knew when someone was telling him the truth but not all of it. He waited.

With a muffled curse George slapped an open hand against the Cub's fuselage, causing the fabric to undulate in little waves. "I saw her in March, at Bernie's. She said she was leaving the Park for a while. She asked me for a lift to Anchorage. I took her that night."

"Where'd you drop her off?"

"Spernak, at Merrill. Last I saw, she was heading for a phone to call a cab."

"She say where she was going?"

"No."

"She say how long she'd be gone?"

"No."

"Okay." Jim paused. "When was this, do you remember? What day, I mean?"

"The fifteenth. The ides of March." A glimmer of a smile. "Why I remember."

There was something else, though. "What?" Jim said. "What else, George?"

George took a long, deep, steadying break. "Something wrong with her arm. Her right arm, above the elbow. She had it wrapped up, but there was blood seeping through. She wouldn't let me take a look."

"What did she say happened?"

"I knew she wouldn't tell me, so I didn't ask."

They stood without speaking, trying not to think back to

the last time they'd seen Kate Shugak hurt. "Okay," Jim said finally. "Thanks, George."

George watched the tall trooper walk to his helicopter and climb in. The rotors whined into motion.

"Bring her home, Jim," he muttered as the Ranger lifted off and headed high, fast and northeast for Tok.

"Just bring her home."

CHAPTER 3

He don't talk right, don't
Know when to sit down, get up.
He make too much talk talk.
                              —*Gisakk Come, He Go*

"WE'LL HAVE TO GO in without her," Gamble said.

"What do you mean we, white man?" Jim said. "I'm the one you're asking to go into a Bush village—"

"Over five thousand population," the FBI man protested. "That isn't exactly a village."

"—with no backup, not even the local cops—"

"Some of the local cops may be in on it. We won't know which ones. We can't risk it, not right away, not until we know more."

"—undercover—"

"The uniform does have a way of alerting certain people to the presence of a police officer, now, doesn't it?" The FBI agent gave Jim a benign smile and folded his hands over his belly, a comfortably plump little shelf at odds with the thin torso, the stick legs and the spindly arms. The toupee was such a mismatch that at first Jim had thought Gamble was wearing a beret.

Gamble wasn't much over forty-five, but he worked at projecting the benign air of an elder statesman. Jim decided that if Gamble patted him on the shoulder, he would bite

Gamble's hand off at the wrist. In the meantime, he continued enumerating his objections in a pleasant voice.

"—all because some informer who once helped you catch a Russian smuggling nesting dolls—big bust, that, by the way, really help the climb up the old promotional ladder—anyway, a Russian smuggling nesting dolls into the country tripped over his own feet in the Anchorage International Airport and says he saw some Russian bad guy getting on a plane for Bering?"

"And we don't know how long he'll be there," Gamble said, pouncing. "He won't leave until the money dries up, that's for sure, and that means he stays until the last dog is up the river. That gives us what, five, six weeks?"

"More like eight or ten, the run's later on the Yukon and the Kuskokwim. And you don't even know what this alleged bad guy is up to, by the way. If anything. For all you know, he might have gone straight."

This was the lamest of Jim's arguments against and they both knew it. The Fibbie was tactful enough not to point it out, but then he wanted something and it behooved him to be diplomatic.

They were sitting in Jim's office at the trooper post in Tok, a sleepy little town of twelve hundred hardy souls whose only reason for being was that it sat at the crossroads of the Glenn and AlaskaCanada Highways. It was the last stop out of Alaska, sitting sixty-odd miles from the Canadian border as the crow flies, longer by road. Jim had been stationed there for the last ten years, and he knew his posting better than the back of his own hand; every little town, village and homestead, every mayor and village elder and all the girls most likely to. He was on a first-name basis with every bootlegger, every dope dealer, dope grower and dope peddler. He knew who leaned toward fishing behind the markers or up a closed creek, or toward commercial fishing a subsistence site and selling the catch to an Outside buyer on the side. He knew who took bear in season and out, and who flouted the wanton waste law by harvesting only the gall bladder for sale to Asian smugglers.

The Park rangers were assured of backup when they called him in to arrest some guide who, after twenty years of holding a license, still couldn't manage to follow the game laws. Village elders knew he would fly in at the first call when trouble got too big in the villages for the village public safety officer to handle, and that he could and would shoulder the weight when the family and friends of the arrested gathered to boo and hiss, in a way their local police never could. The Pipeline operators knew he would be there when some welder got drunk and hijacked a Cat with intent to bulldoze an entire pump station, or took off in the pump station manager's Suburban on a trajectory for the Calgary Stampede.

He was on call, twenty-four hours a day, three hundred and sixty-five days a year, and they knew that, too. Fixed wing or rotor, whatever it took, First Sergeant Jim Chopin would have it in the air within fifteen minutes, partly because it was his sworn duty, partly because he was paid very well, partly because, deep down, he revered the oath he had taken the day he graduated from the trooper academy, and mostly because, hell, let's face it, he felt like Zorro every time he responded to a call. Zorro minus the mask.

It was a far cry from San Jose, where the air was too thick to breathe, the roads were too crowded to drive, and a cop's chance of being shot by a gangbanger was infinitely higher than was his chance of being stomped by a moose. Jim would take the moose any day.

The Park was his home, and now they wanted him to leave it, detached duty, temporarily assigned as liaison to the goddamn FBI, which, to Jim's jaundiced eye, was a less than stellar supplement to the law enforcement community, being as how they spent most of their time in Alaska arresting people cutting down the wrong trees in the Tsongas National Park and killing the wrong walruses off Round Island. Not to mention getting caught doing the lap dance with hookers on Fourth Avenue in Anchorage and shooting caribou out of season on the Glenn Highway.

He knew the Park, every rill and rivulet, every glacier and game trail, every village and town. But all he knew about Bering could be fit into one of Katya's shoes. He vaguely remembered a case where a bootlegger, Armenian by birth, got caught shipping one hundred and two cases of cheap whiskey into the still, last time he looked, damp town. When brought to court, the guy claimed it was provisions for his daughter's wedding. Upon investigation, it was revealed that the wedding was five months off. The jury, three members of which were related to the accused by way of a providential marriage into a local Yupik family, came back with an acquittal in less than ten minutes. The prosecuting attorney later allowed as how he should have petitioned for a change of venue. No shit, Jim had thought at the time.

Now he said, "If there are only five thousand people in the whole goddamn town, most of whom are each other's first cousins once removed, how is it I am not going to stick out like a sore thumb?"

"You'll be a seasonal worker," Gamble said. "There are a ton of them around this time of year."

"Something to do with fish, no doubt," Jim observed in a deceptively pleasant tone.

"It is salmon season," Gamble pointed out reasonably. "And one of the trawlers contracted to the Bering IFQ is Russian, so it's reasonable to expect that our boy is somewhere close by."

"What the hell do you think he's getting up to on a goddamn fish trawler? And if he's as hot as you say, why don't you just waltz in and arrest the bastard?"

Gamble's smile vanished. He leaned forward and tapped one finger on the desk, like a college professor making the point that would justify his whole seminar and screw you on the exam. "We want to know what he's up to, Jim. If even half of what his file reads is true, this Ivanov is a very, very bad boy. Drugs, prostitution, weapons smuggling, money laundering, industrial espionage, military weapons thefts, you name it, he's in it up to his eyebrows. Which is why we don't want just to catch him, we want to catch him in the act."

"In the act of what?"

"We don't know. That's what we want you to find out. He's too smart and too successful for whatever he's doing in Bering to be penny-ante. And there is a strong Russian presence in the Bering Sea lately. Lots of trawlers catching lots of fish, and delivering them, and who knows what else, who knows where, who knows to whom? Plenty of opportunity out there for those criminally inclined to take advantage of the slackening of tensions between East and West."

"You sound like my poly-sci instructor in college," Jim muttered. He changed tactics. "Why me? Why don't you send in some little Fibbie who speaks seven different Russian dialects, and who is probably hardwired in to D.C. through his belly button besides?"

"Because we don't have someone like that who knows the Alaskan Bush, too," Gamble said flatly, "or we would. You were assigned to Dillingham your first year of Bush rotation, you've lived around the Yupik, you aren't going to put your foot in it and offend some tribal law that will get you tarred and feathered and run out of town on a rail."

"And using a honeybucket won't throw my sensibilities into an uproar," Jim observed sardonically. "How long is this assignment?"

"Depends on how quick you are on the uptake," Gamble said, and smiled when Jim's eyes narrowed.

The voice on the speaker phone jumped in for the first time. "We've got you cleared for a month's TDY, Jim."

"Do you actually want me to do this, boss?" Jim demanded.

"It's up to you."

"Who'll look after the post while I'm gone?"

"Janine Shook."

"Well, at least she's had some Bush experience." Plus, she was close enough to retirement that she wouldn't get proprietary about his post. And though he hated to admit it, this special assignment wasn't a bad career move, especially if, however unlikely it sounded to him now, there turned out to be an actual case and he broke it.

Besides, he was getting damn sick and tired of sitting around wondering where the hell Kate Shugak was. If she'd wanted to be found, she would have been by now. In his memory she had never spent an entire summer out of the Park, except for the five years she'd worked in Anchorage, and even then she'd spent most weekends, every day of her vacation and, truth be told, sick leave on her homestead, or tendering with Old Sam.

Where the hell was she?

Gamble leaned forward. "Look, Jim, we lean on the troopers, I know that. We just don't have the manpower to reach out to all the Bush communities—"

"Oh, and we do," Jim said.

"—especially in a situation like this—"

"Yeah, I can see why you'd come to me. I put down half a dozen Russian gangsters dealing in small automatic arms before breakfast every morning. And I ramrod one of the slower districts, at that."

"They didn't steal a nuclear bomb, they stole something from which someone with the know-how could make a bomb."

"Nuclear bombs," Jim said pointedly.

"Yes. Providing they had all the other ingredients to go along with it. But there's more to the story, Jim."

There was an old Damon Runyon horse player who would listen to any tip on a race if a story went with it. What was his name? Jim couldn't remember, so he leaned back in his chair and put his feet up on his desk. "Talk."

Gamble raised his voice enough to be heard in the outer office. "Carroll! Casanare!"

The door to Jim's office opened so promptly that a suspicious person might think whoever was on the other side had been standing with their ears pressed against it. It swung wide, revealing a man and a woman, both with that chronic tendency toward blue-suited neatness displayed by all FBI agents. They must teach a class in neat at Quantico, Jim thought. Right after forensics and law.

Gamble waved them forward. "Special Agent Maxine Carroll. Special Agent Alberto Casanare. First Sergeant Jim Chopin of the Alaska State Troopers. Sit."

Carroll had a long, cool stare, and she used it to look Jim over as the silence stretched out.

"Tell him," Gamble said.

Casanare made a business out of dragging two chairs forward, and lounged back in his to examine the ceiling for cracks.

Jim met Carroll's stare head on. She was a looker, all right, a goddess even, tall, blond, blue-eyed, but his response to her challenge was more of a reflex than actual interest. He would have found the realization alarming if he'd allowed himself to think it over.

Gamble fidgeted some more, and finally gave. "Oh, come on, for crissake, he's not exactly a civilian. And we are asking him to go in undercover for us."

Carroll's eyes flickered, looking first at Gamble, then exchanging a long expressionless look with her partner. Casanare raised an eyebrow. Carroll sat down, and in a calm, even voice that ticked off hijacking, treason and murder the way someone else might call off items on a grocery list, led Jim down the trail that began in St. Petersburg and ended in Anchorage.

"Jesus god," Jim said, when she finished, and cursed himself immediately for betraying how impressed he was.

"Indeed," Gamble said.

Jim eyed him speculatively. "Can we spell promotion?" he said.

Nobody said anything.

"You said you couldn't show me a picture of this Ivanov, because you didn't have one," Jim said. "You said he was very careful about not being photographed."

"As careful as he is about never leaving witnesses behind," Gamble said, and smiled.

There was a brief silence. "You've got a witness," Jim said. "Somebody survived the hijacking. Or the robbery. Didn't they?"

Nobody said anything again.

"Yeah, well. Bering's a hell of a long way from Anchorage."

Gamble steepled his fingers and smiled over them. "FBI Anchorage contacted the Alaska State Troopers and put in a request to all communities with a Russian presence to be on the lookout for, et cetera. We got a bite. A trooper in Bering spotted someone whose description leads us to believe is another player, an Alexei Burianovich. Known associate of Ivanov. Probably was in on the hijacking."

"Uh-huh," Jim said again, managing to infuse the two syllables with considerable skepticism. "Plus you didn't mention we were taking on the goddamn Russian Army."

"I knew I forgot something," Gamble said.

"Save it. Why don't you just go in and pick them up? It's a small town, they'll be easy to find, and they can't be here legally."

Gamble's smile faded. "I told you, Jim. We need a line on that zirconium. If we swoop down and arrest the whole boiling lot of them, we'll never see it again."

"And we want Ivanov," Carroll said.

Casanare smiled. It wasn't a nice smile.

"What makes you think they haven't already moved it? They stole it, what, March twenty-eighth? That was three months ago. What makes you think it's still for sale? And why Alaska? For crissake, Gamble, how would they get it all the way across Russia and Siberia and the Bering Strait? There have got to be easier routes, not to mention closer customers. I can think of two or three in the Middle East without even opening up this week's issue of *Time*."

"To answer your first question, we've been monitoring our sources in the arms-manufacturing markets. There has been no word that it's out there. Yet."

Jim reflected. "That doesn't wash. What kind of self-respecting crook would steal that kind of thing if he didn't already have a buyer?"

"Maybe he did have a buyer, and maybe the warlord he was about to sell it to got knocked off his throne before he could take delivery." Gamble looked up from his steepled fingers with a too-bland expression. "To answer your second question, the FBI has come up with a projection that estimates a ten-year trend toward an increase in domestic terrorism. We're looking at weapons of mass destruction, Jim, biological, chemical, as well as nuclear. Hell, we don't even have to get fancy, all it takes is a couple of barrels of fertilizer and some fuel oil in a Ryder truck. The Oke bomb was just the first shot in a long war."

Casanare examined his fingernails. Carroll looked bored.

"As for why Alaska?" Gamble said. "Because, along with Montana and Idaho, Alaska is a breeding ground for radicalism, and the numbers are only increasing. Have you taken a close look at the Juneau legislature lately? Some of those people are slightly to the right of Adolf Hitler, and there's more of them moving up here all the time. They can't get far enough away from the federal government to suit them."

"What a laugh," Jim said, "considering about ninety percent of the state of Alaska is owned by the federal government."

"Yes, well, no one said these people are all that bright. Just homicidal."

Jim remembered a couple of summers ago, when Kate Shugak had run headlong into one of the radicals Gamble was referring to, a right-wing Christian pastor who had assumed the offices of judge and jury, and anointed his parishioners as executioners. Pastor Seabolt and his gang made Gamble's story at least plausible, if not entirely convincing.

He looked over at Carroll and Casanare. "What are Boris and Natasha here going to be up to while I'm in Bering, probably getting my ass shot off by renegade remnants of the Red Army?"

Carroll flushed and opened her mouth. Gamble's glance silenced her, but her eyes promised retribution.

"They'll be stationed in Anchorage," Gamble said. He didn't see Carroll and Casanare exchange glances, but Jim did. "Reaching out to informers," Gamble went on. "Gathering information. Amassing evidence. Building a case."

Carroll stifled a yawn, Casanare a grin.

With sudden gravity, Gamble said, "This isn't a case we can afford to let slip, Jim. And we need your help to make it."

The silence stretched out. It was after ten, and the miles he'd flown and driven that day were starting to catch up to him. He rose to his feet and stretched. Through the window he could see a bunch of kids shooting hoops across the street. A truck went around the makeshift court very slowly, and speeded up once it was past. If he listened hard enough, he could almost hear the music from the Tap down the road. His mouth felt dry. He could use a beer. Or three.

"I'll go. For a month," he said, turning and raising an admonitory finger, "and only a month. If I don't find something in thirty days, there isn't anything to be found, and I'm just wasting my time and the state's money." He put his hands in his pockets and regarded them placidly. "Take it or leave it."

He waited for his boss to tell Jim that Jim would stay however long his boss told him to, but the squawk box remained silent. With the price per barrel of oil more in the toilet than out of it these days, and the attendant legislative funding cutbacks, Colonel Gordon's willingness to cooperate with a brother law enforcement organization went only so far.

"Great," Gamble said, breaking into a smile. "We'll take it."

Yeah, right, Jim thought, great.

Bering.

Jesus.

CHAPTER 4

BERING, JULY 1

We live long time,
We live on salmon, bear.
We care for land.
Gissak come, he go.

—*Gissak Come, He Go*

FROM NORTON SOUND TO Kuskokwim Bay, the western coastline of Alaska bulged southwest, pushing out like the belly of a pregnant woman very near her time. The drainage basin for the two-thousand-mile-long Yukon River and the eight-hundred-mile-long Kuskokwim River and all their tributaries, the Delta stretched two hundred and fifty miles from Norton Sound to Kuskokwim Bay, and two hundred miles inland from sea's edge to the Kuskokwim Mountains. The river channels doubled back upon themselves to form lakes and flow through others until from the air the area resembled nothing so much as a basket of silver snakes, skins shining in the sun. Jim Chopin, looking out the window of an Alaska Airlines 737, in fact found it hard to tell where the water left off and the land began. Most of both looked below sea level as it was.

He'd been boning up on the area during the seventy-minute flight from Anchorage, courtesy of the Alaska Geographic

Society. Gamble had made him spend a week in Anchorage for something he called orientation, which consisted of looking at a bunch of mug shots and Russian Mafia organizational charts, which did not seem very organized and which seemed to chart mostly demises of said Mafia members.

He'd had to sign up at Job Service, too, one of the more humiliating experiences in his life. It didn't matter that he wasn't really out of work and that the fix was in for him for a particular job; the people behind the counter greeted all applicants with the same weary, disillusioned expression that said they'd heard it before, save the sob story for someone who cared, thanks. The people in line were tense and anxious and eager to please, some of them looked hungry, and Jim was pretty sure he saw among them a man from Wolf Lake he'd put away for child abuse ten years before, a woman who'd bankrupted her Chitina employer by writing checks to herself from his bank account in her capacity as his bookkeeper, and a kid from Tok, barely twenty, who had shot his sister while fooling around with a loaded shotgun nine years before. The district attorney had declined to prosecute, calling the incident a tragic accident. Tragic for the dead sister, certainly, Jim had thought at the time. He distinctly remembered wanting to take the kid and his father, who had left the loaded shotgun lying around in the first place, out back to beat the crap out of both of them.

The kid was the only one who recognized Jim. His eyes widened and seemed to fill with tears. Jim couldn't get out of the building fast enough.

But one afternoon he managed to get loose and visit Alaska Geographic's office on International Airport Road to thumb through the racks of quarterly publications, which featured titles from *The Aleutians* to *Yakutat* with stops at every other

Alaskan location north, south and in between. A fair, pleasant woman named Kathy, plump in all the right places and whose eyes twinkled when he told her where he was going, directed him to the Society publication called *The Kuskokwim*.

It was an engaging twinkle. Although she was wearing a wedding ring, out of habit Jim tried to strike up a flirtation, but it was soon obvious to both of them that his heart wasn't in it. He bought his book and left, worrying about the low level of his libido all the way to the hotel. What was worse, he had slept perfectly soundly that night, all alone in his queen-size bed.

The jet flew into a bank of clouds, obscuring his view, and he looked back at the book.

Bering, the largest settlement in western Alaska, was on the Kuskokwim River, maybe—he measured with thumb and forefinger and compared it to the legend on the map—forty miles upriver, on the undercurve of the pregnant belly. It had been founded by Moravian missionaries in 1886, who had wanted to call it Bethlehem. Natives protested and began a movement to call it Manilaaq, after a legendary shaman. Eventually a compromise was reached and the town was named for Vitus Bering, a Dane on the payroll of the Imperial Russian Navy who was credited with the discovery of Alaska in 1728, and who died there in 1741. His memory was dim enough in everyone's mind for the partisan fervor to die down and for the missionaries to get on with moving the Yupik out of their sod houses and into the church. They were amazingly successful at both.

Twenty years later, the Gold Rush brought measles and influenza to Alaska, from which the Natives had no immunity, and from which neither the missionaries nor the missionaries' god could protect them. Half the adults and all the babies in the Delta were dead from one disease or the other within a year. Bering was one of the few towns that survived.

Tracing the curve of the belly, he saw that traditional names had prevailed elsewhere. Tununak, Umkumiut, Chefornak, Kipnuk, Kwigillingok, Tuntutuliak, Napakiak, Nunapitsinchak and others he would bet had more letters in their names than people in their villages. The Alaska Geographic Society didn't provide translations, but most of the names were probably variations on the Yupik word for "mosquito." Or "salmon." One species was as ubiquitous in the Alaskan Bush as the other, with the mosquitoes, taking up less space per unit, possibly having a slight edge.

Although the birds were giving both a run for their money. A lot of the Delta was the Yukon Delta National Wildlife Refuge, created in 1980, at the same time the Park was created around Kate Shugak's father's homestead, and just how had Kate managed to creep back into his consciousness? Annoyed, he read on.

The Yukon Delta National Wildlife Refuge was comprised of nineteen million acres and change, supporting the lifestyles of a hundred million shore and water birds, among them Canadian, brant, Emperor and white-fronted geese, tundra swans and duck species from mallard to green spectacled eider.

It was also, of course, the spawning ground for one hell of a lot of the aforesaid salmon. Kings, reds, silvers, humpies and dogs, so plentiful that this species alone went a long way toward explaining the presence of the largest and healthiest population of aboriginal Americans, the Yupik. Easier to catch salmon than to hunt whales or chase caribou, Jim thought, and probably a lot less dangerous.

There were also rainbow trout, Dolly Varden, sheefish,

whitefish, arctic char, tomcod, and northern pike, the most rabid sports fisherman's dream date, although Jim had never seen the attraction. Pike were bony and virtually tasteless. If you couldn't eat it, why go to all the trouble of catching it?

The teeming bird and fish populations explained the teeming small mammal population, in particular aquatic mammals such as mink, otter, muskrat, and beaver. Aquatic mammals with nice pelts, Jim observed, and wondered what the trapping was like in the area. There were also red and arctic foxes, hares and voles.

Large mammals, the moose, the black bear and the grizzly generally turned up their noses at the Delta. Didn't like getting their feet wet, maybe.

Kate Shugak, a large mammal herself, didn't like getting her feet wet, either.

Goddamn it. He shook his head angrily and didn't return the flight attendant's smile when she walked down the aisle.

Below Bering, there were hardly any trees. There were stands of willow and the omnipresent alder, and occasionally a lone spruce, but that was it. The rest was virtually a sea of brush and grass.

The plane shuddered as the gear came down, and the flight attendant's voice came over the intercom. "Ladies and gentlemen, we are on our final descent into Bering. Please check to make sure that your seat back is in its original upright position and that your tray table has been stowed and locked. Please return all handcarried items to the space beneath the seat in front of you or in the overhead racks. Thank you."

She hung up the microphone and smiled again at Jim. She was attractive, a brunette in her mid-thirties with flirtatious eyes, and she had been very attentive to the big, good-looking man wearing a Sonics cap and sitting in the window seat of the exit row. She had managed to let fall the information that she flew out of Anchorage. Normally, he would have had her phone number before she had moved the drinks cart to the next row of seats.

Their shadow passed over the town, curved like a three-quarter moon around the upper bend of the river, houses and roads hopscotching over and around lakes and streams and ponds and trickles, connected by gravel roads on raised beds and a few boardwalks. Most of the dry land looked like a poorly drained swamp. Most of the swamp looked like an overgrown river. Too thin to plow, too thick to drink. The water table had to be right below the surface. Jim wondered what the sewer system was like. He shuddered to think.

Gamble had told him he was going in as ground crew for an independent airfreight business which operated out of the Bering airport. "You're a pilot, you'll fit right in," the Fibbie had said with an airy wave of his hand, and right then and there Jim should have known enough to run for his life. When he located the ramshackle building at the other end of the airstrip that housed Baird Air, he wished he had.

The hangar slanted to one side like a sailor on shore leave for the first time in months. The office, a smaller version with windows, leaned against the first building as if it was a drinking buddy the first had picked up on the town. Both had corrugated tin roofs adorned with generously sized rust spots, and the orange-and-white logo over both doors had faded almost to invisibility. A large lake nibbled at the back edge of the property, on which there seemed to be a float plane landing or taking off every five minutes. Baird Air was directly below the approach. A seedy operation in a seedy location. Wonderful.

Like most pilots, Jim was uneasy when anyone's hand but his was on the stick. He tried not to flinch each time a plane roared overhead. Adding to his unease were seven propellers of various sizes mounted on the exterior wall of the hangar, all with textbook groundloop curls to their tips. He counted to be sure. Seven times someone had dinged a plane. He hoped it wasn't the same someone. He hoped if it was that that someone wasn't still flying, in particular any of the planes taking off out back.

Inside the office everything, chairs, desk, file cabinet, coffee pot and radio; everything was patched with duct tape. Some of it was held together with duct tape, like the cushion around the back of the visitor's chair. A Budweiser clock ticked loudly on the wall, next to a map of the Yukon-Kuskokwim River Delta framed nattily in silver duct tape. There were a lot of lines drawn on it in grease pencil from Bering to outlying villages. A bundle of rolled-up maps had been tossed carelessly behind the desk, all of whose corners had been reinforced with duct tape.

He turned and tripped over the coffee table sitting between the couch and the desk. It was cheap veneer with three of the four corners chipped down to the pressed wood. The fourth corner was caked with mud, as if someone propped his feet there early and often. There was a corresponding hollow in the seat of the black Naugahyde couch, which appeared to be held together with, someone's original idea, electrician's tape. At least the colors matched.

On the desk was a notepad, blank, and one Bic pen with the top chewed off. A desk calendar had been ripped all the way down to April twenty-seventh. A copy of *Aviation Week* lay folded back to an article on a float-plane accident in Southeast, the last words of the pilot reported as, "Oh, s***." An overflowing ashtray made from a one-pound coffee can and what looked like river silt sat on a pile of paperwork. On top of the pile was a check for—he blinked, and looked again. He moved the ashtray to be sure. Twelve thousand dollars. Dated June fifteenth. Two weeks before.

"Who the hell are you?"

Jim looked up to see a man in the doorway, scowling at him from behind a squat stogie which glowed red and emitted regular puffs of smoke like a miniature steam engine. He was short and fat, with thin white hair that had arranged itself in a kind of tonsure effect. Pendulous pink cheeks quivered when he talked, and enormous saddlebag hips moved independently of the rest of him when he walked. His bib overalls were gray, stained beyond all hope of washing clean and cut off to just above a pair of pink, pudgy knees. Shiny black rubber boots came up to mid-calf. He appeared to be wearing nothing else. "Well?" He reached inside his overalls to scratch at something, or maybe to go for a gun.

Unhurriedly, Jim set the coffee can down. "I'm Jim Churchill. Your new hire. Job Service said you were expecting me."

The man looked Jim over, grunted, shifted the stogie from his left cheek to his right and a wad of chewing tobacco from his right cheek to his left. He spat out a stream which landed three inches from Jim's right toe. Jim noticed the generally brown character of the rest of the office floor, and deduced that this man didn't hold with spitoons.

"Well, you're big enough to handle the freight, I guess. You know how to run a radio?"

"I—"

"Cause you don't, you can just hightail your butt on outta here. I've had it up to my eyebrows with the yoyos them dopes in Anchorage send me; most of you couldn't find your ass with two hands and a flashlight. Not to mention which you're

70

all lazy." He glared. "Not to mention which every last one of you's fresh outta jail."

Jim met the man's fulminating gaze head-on without flinching, and spoke to the only inference that mattered. "I'm not lazy," he said firmly. "I'm just very well organized."

There was a brief pause. A slow smile spread across the man's face. "Jacob Baird," he said. "You can call me Baird." He pulled his hand from beneath his overalls and stuck it out.

With real heroism, Jim took it.

"I'm your boss."

"I got that much."

"I own this here operation."

"I got that, too."

"You'll be working twelve on, twelve off, noon to midnight, 'cepting the days you work more, no exceptions."

"I was told."

"Time and a half is all I go, no double time for the holidays."

"Understood."

"It gets to be the Fourth of July and you're whining either cause you have to work or cause you're not getting paid enough, I'll kick your ass into the Kusko."

"I'll bend over and kiss it good-bye," Jim said amiably. He liked Baird.

"All right then. What's today?" Baird picked up the desk calendar. "Well, shit." He slammed it down again.

"July first," Jim said.

"Jesus, is it July already?" Baird looked around for the time.

Jim looked at his watch. "It's two o'clock."

"You're on then, until midnight, when your relief shows up." He looked over Jim's shoulder. "Well, hey, what the hell are you doing here?"

"I brought the grocery list," a voice began from the doorway, and then cut off abruptly.

Jim spun around like he'd been shot.

A joyous bark rang off the tottering steel ribs of the hangar and four sets of toenails skittered across the cement floor. One hundred and forty pounds of half wolf, half husky hit him square in the chest and knocked him solidly on his back on the floor stained brown with tobacco and spit.

"Oof!" He didn't have time to say anything else, as his face was being comprehensively licked by a very long, very sandpapery, very enthusiastic tongue.

He sat up with a jerk, toppling Mutt to the floor.

A small woman stood in the doorway, framed by the afternoon sun streaming in around her. Her face was in shadow, but he would have recognized the outline of that figure in his sleep, as he had recognized the low rasp of her voice. "Kate?"

The familiar husky rasp of her voice was welcome, if its words were not. "What the hell are you doing here, Chopin?"

He stared at her, his mouth literally hanging open, unable to believe his eyes.

Baird's voice seemed to come from a long way away. "You know this joker, Kathy?"

There was a long silence, while Kate and Jim stared at each other. For a moment he thought she would deny all knowledge of him. "Yeah," she said finally. "I know him."

After that first startled exclamation, she had, it appeared, nothing further to say to him. She met his eyes with no hesitation. She displayed no curiosity. She wasn't happy to see him, not a big surprise, as he couldn't remember a time when she had been. She wasn't upset, either, as he might expect, considering the circumstances surrounding their last meeting.

72

No, she stood, hands hanging loosely at her side, one grasping a slip of paper, probably the aforesaid grocery list. She seemed, of all things, patient. Waiting. What for, he wondered.

He heard Chick's words echo against the inside of his skull. *No snap, no crackle, no pop, no sparks at all. She's pulled the plug.*

"Mutt," she said, without force. "Here. Mutt."

Mutt swiped Jim with a final, lavish caress and trotted over to take up her usual position at Kate's right side. She had a new scar on her flank, and another on her face, but both had healed cleanly, showing pink and firm beneath new fur. Her iron gray coat was thick and shone with health, and her yellow eyes were bright and alert. She moved easily, with all of her old strength and grace, a far cry from the wounded, and Jim had thought dying, creature of the previous fall.

The summer sun had turned Kate's pale brown skin a dark gold. Her narrow hazel eyes were clear and sane. She looked thinner, in the hollows beneath her high, flat cheekbones, in the way her clavicle pressed against her T-shirt, in the way her jeans hung from a belt pulled in two extra notches. It emphasized the upward tilt of her eyes, making her look more Native than white, and more Tatar than Native.

The tan made the scar on her throat stand out in bold relief, five inches of rough, roped tissue. It never shrank in size the way most scars did, it was always right there, right out front, above the neck of a T-shirt or in the open collar of one of her ubiquitous plaid Pendleton shirts. He had always suspected that she used it like a dare. Yeah, somebody tried to cut my throat, what of it? Think you can finish the job? Come on ahead.

Few men Jim knew, at least those who were not practicing lunatics, would have taken up that gauntlet. Kate had always projected the demeanor of someone who was willing to do whatever it took to win. It didn't matter that she topped out at five feet, or that she weighed a hundred and twenty pounds; all the old jokes aside, size didn't matter. Determination did. Kate had taken out one man Jim knew of with a pack of wolves, another with a boathook. Whatever was ready to hand was what she used, if she deemed its use necessary.

Not a religious man, he was reminded suddenly of that old Biblical verse, something about if thine eye offend thee, pluck it out, if thine hand offend thee, cut it off.

Or Kate Shugak would do it for you.

Her hair was short and neatly cropped, fitting her head like a smooth, ebony cap. He remembered the braid that used to hang down in back almost to her waist, hacked to the scalp by the time he and George had arrived at the lodge last September. He wondered again why she'd cut it.

The new style made him uneasy. It turned her into a different woman. He knew how to act around the old Kate, he knew which buttons to push and when. They had a history he could rely on, cases worked together—again he was reminded of the right-wing cult in Chistona—not to mention years of persistent flirtation on his part and blunt rebuff on hers.

He had no history with this new Kate. This new Kate might have a different set of all-new rules to go with her different appearance.

He got to his feet, brushing the debris of the floor from the seat of his jeans. Dog and woman stood without moving, staring at him, one with adoration, the other with apprehension.

The sight made Jim want to shout hallelujah.

It also made him want to knock the both of them on their collective ass. He opened his mouth to say so, and remembered just in time that they had an audience. He closed it again with an audible snap that made Mutt's eyes widen and Kate's eyes narrow.

"Way-yull, hay-yull." Baird strolled over to stand next to Jim. "If I'd known you come with an endorsement from Kathy Sovalik, ground crew extraordinaire, I'd've sent in a request for you personal." He paused. "Churchill," he added, with extra emphasis. Kate's use of Jim's real name had not gone unnoticed.

They said nothing. Kate's face had closed down. Jim couldn't hide his anger but he could restrain his wrath, for now. Mutt stood with her head pressed to Kate's hip, gazing worshipfully at Jim, gray plume of a tail waving back and forth in a graceful arc.

"At least somebody's glad to see you," Baird observed. "Okay, Kathy, since you're still up, run the new guy through the routine. What's going out and when is on the board." He jerked his head toward the hangar. "The bunkhouse is out back." He jerked his head in the opposite direction. "Kathy'll show you that, too." He grinned, displaying teeth with shreds of tobacco caught between them. "Separate bunks. Sorry, buddy."

Jim was watching Kate. She did not respond with so much as the flicker of an eyebrow to the salacious intent of Baird's remark.

"You got a choice for lunch," Baird said, "cheese on your burger or not."

"Cheese," Kate said, not breaking eye contact.

"Not," Jim said, maintaining his stare.

Baird chuckled low in his throat, a deep, surprisingly attractive sound, and left the room. Jim waited until he heard a car door opening, the creak of oppressed springs, an engine start.

When it had moved out of earshot, he said, "Kathy?" in a dangerously soft voice. "Kathy Sovalik?"

She answered in kind, although her voice displayed only the most passing interest in his answer. "Churchill? Jim Churchill?"

"Where the hell have you been?"

"What business is that of yours?" There was no antagonism in her answer, and even less interest. It was something to say, already laid down in the text.

"Do you know how many people are looking for you?"

"Unless you're here to serve me my subpoena?"

"Or maybe you just don't give a damn that anybody who ever cared about you is scared shitless because they haven't heard from you in months!"

"I told you I'd be in town in time for the trial."

The very indifference of her tone maddened him beyond all bearing. He had her shoulders in angry hands in one quick step. He shook her hard, snapping her head back.

Mutt's tail stopped wagging.

"Goddamn it, Shugak! Nobody's seen you for four fucking months! You couldn't have called? You couldn't have dropped somebody a postcard? Bobby and Dinah are worried sick, Bernie and George don't know what the hell is going on except that it's bad, and Billy Mike and Auntie Vi and the rest of your family think you're dead!"

He let her go with a shove, and she staggered back a step.

"Wuff?" Mutt said, the only time in living memory anyone had ever heard her sound uncertain.

"You shut up," Jim told her, and turned a furious gaze back on Kate. "Why am I bothering? You obviously don't give a shit." He swept off his cap with one trembling hand, smoothed his hair with the other and resettled the cap squarely on his head.

He couldn't remember ever being this angry. He never got angry, he never permitted it, not ever, not in the face of the grossest possible provocation. When a drunk pipeliner stuck a .357 in Jim's face at Bernie's Roadhouse, Jim did not even pull his weapon. Just last year, again at Bernie's, when a couple of feuding homesteaders had shot his hat from his head, he had remained calm. When he got passed over for promotion, when he got dumped by a woman, when he was assaulted by a suspect, when a case went sour at trial or an especially undeserving perp got off with a light sentence, Jim let it roll off his back. He had decided long ago that being angry took far too much energy best spent elsewhere.

Now he wasn't just angry, he was enraged.

He marched through the door, forcing Kate and Mutt both to give way before him, and strode into the hangar to glare from side to side, barely taking in the boxes, pallets and totes of freight stacked everywhere, the large, walkin cooler in one corner filled with wet lockboxes, the approaching roar of a taxiing aircraft.

He turned to look at her, very much under control, at least for the moment. "I are a ground crew and I cain't even spell one," he observed in an even tone he congratulated himself on. "You going to give me the rundown on this job, or what?"

CHAPTER 5

Yes, I said.
I know what they have done.

—*The Last Wolf*

JIM DISTINCTLY REMEMBERED "FORKLIFT operator" printed in the job title slot of the form he had filled out in Anchorage, and he did operate the battered old propane-powered forklift from time to time. When he could be spared from loading and unloading the Piper Super Cub, the Cessna 206 on floats, believe it or not the DC-3 and, holiest of holies, the C-130 Hercules when they roared up, he was set to weighing freight, packing totes and pallets, making out waybills and load manifests, loading freight that had come in into the backs of pickup trucks, unloading freight to go out from the backs of other pickup trucks, answering the phone and the radio, entering times and locations for freight to be picked up and delivered on a grubby chart on the wall of the hangar, taking telephone reservations, and trying to satisfy Yupik callers who spoke little English and had no patience with those unfortunates who spoke even less Yupik.

He looked for Kate to handle the last of those calls, but she had long since disappeared, back to the bunkhouse, he presumed. Fine. Good. Let her keep her distance. Let her get on the next plane out of here. Let her get off in Anchorage, or better yet, Seattle, or best of all, Etadunna, Australia. Good for her to move her sweet little ass as fast and as far out of range of the toe of his boot as she could get it.

The metal banding he was currently winding round a loaded pallet twisted and snapped like a splinter of wood. He took a deep breath, removed the mangled end from the bander, and started over.

During a rare lull in the day's activities he did point out to Baird the check on the office desk and mentioned the date on it, keeping his voice offhand. His new boss grunted and spat, picked up the pile and rifled through it impatiently. He handed Jim half a dozen pieces of paper, which proved to be checks totaling over thirty-six thousand dollars, some of which had been cut in March. Baird saw Jim's expression and said defensively, "Well, hell, starting with herring I just don't have time to catch up on every little thing there is to do around here. Write me up a deposit slip and I'll take 'em down to the bank. I'd have Sovalik do it but she's even worse at bookkeeping than I am."

Since any mention of Kate under whatever alias instantly raised Jim's blood pressure twenty points, he ignored Baird's comment and dutifully made out the deposit slip, totaling it twice because he didn't believe the sum the first time. Baird stuffed slip and checks into the bib pocket of his filthy overalls and promptly forgot about them.

He would not think of Kate, not yet. He banished her completely and ruthlessly from his mind until he had time to deal with the fact of her presence—here, in Bering, at Baird Air for crissake, his employer for the duration of his TDY or until he uncovered the nefarious plot allegedly being brewed by the Russian Mafia on Bering's front doorstep. The way he felt right now, this minute, he'd have it cleaned up and the perps in custody within twenty-four hours, no matter how unlikely he considered the possibility that Gamble's assessment of the situation even approached accuracy. Russian Mafia in Bering. Christ.

He could feel the rage coming back in a great wave and he knew it had little to do with Russians or the FBI. He choked it back, not for the first time that day, and not for the last.

Fortunately, the job kept him busy, frantically so. Business at Baird Air was conducted at full speed and top decibel. Baird was everywhere, yelling, cursing, pushing Jim out of the way, shoving him in closer, head beneath the cowling of the Cub, fueling up on the wing of the DC-3, disappearing into the open maw of the Herc, backing up the forklift at full throttle, the warning beep ringing off the metal interior of the hangar and threatening its already perilous list.

In direct contrast to the aforementioned seedy appearance of the rest of the operation, the planes looked and sounded as if they were in excellent condition, well maintained and, if the affectionate slap he saw Baird give the flank of the Herc was any indication, well loved. The pilot in him approved.

He was awed by the Herc, an aircraft surrounded by myth. Viewed from one angle, it looked like a flying wing, from another like a pregnant whale. The Lockheed C-130 Hercules aircraft had been in production since 1956 in various incarnations. Originally designed as an assault troop transport, over the years they had been adapted for search and rescue, fire fighting and midair refueling. Hercs were the planes the National Weather Service flew into the middles of hurricanes to gauge the strength and direction of the storms, from the hurricanes' very eyes.

A Herc was also one helluva freight hauler. Jim paused in his work to watch the rear of the Herc open up like a clamshell, the bottom half forming a ramp so Baird could drive forklift after forklift loaded with frozen salmon into the bowels of the plane. Baird was very careful with the forklift then; it never came within sneezing distance of the fuselage on either side.

Baird's care extended to his tools, as Jim discovered when he went in search of a screwdriver. The tool crib was in the northwest corner of the hangar, the tools clean and oiled and very well organized in the multiple drawers of tall red metal tool cabinets, three of them. Every drawer had the names of the tools inside written on the front. There were also several parts lockers; they too were labeled and organized within an inch of their lives.

The roar of a jet on takeoff drew him to the door, and he looked out to see a 737 with no markings but black tail numbers too far away to read lift off from the end of the runway. No windows, had to be a freight plane, and one of the shorter, stubbier ones, too, probably a 200. Another plane was already taxiing for takeoff. He'd never seen so much air traffic in and out of one airport before in his life, not even at Merrill Field in Anchorage on a CAVU summer day. Or maybe it was just the variety of aircraft. On that first day he saw a Lockheed Electra, an old Connie, two other DC-3s, four Beavers, three on floats, seven twin Otters, although they all wore the same logo and in ten hours he could have seen the same one more than once, a couple of Navaho Apaches, two more 737s, one all-freight 727 and three all-passenger Fairchild Metroliners.

That didn't even count the small planes, the Cubs and the Cessnas and the Lakes and the Stinsons and some models he didn't recognize and wasn't sure should be in the air they were so old. Once he thought he saw an open-cockpit biplane, although he was squinting into the sun at the time.

The pilots were on the ground long enough to drop one

load and pick up another, and the engines never stopped running. Baird Air employed four pilots in all. The Cub pilot was a dour, angular man in his fifties who wore a cowboy hat that made him six inches taller than his already six feet. He introduced himself as Shep Whitfield, but Baird called him Tex. The Herc pilot, one Larry Maciarello, was five feet two, weighed at least two hundred pounds, looked like Pooh Bear and left a trail of M&M wrappers in his wake. The DC-3 pilot never stopped moving long enough for Jim to get a good look at him, much less catch his name, but the license posted in the office showed it to be Calvin Kemper. He only saw Ralph Whitmore, the Cessna pilot, from the back as he was trotting down to the dock to take off again. No one took a second look at Jim; Baird's shouted introductions were usually productive of nothing more than a hand cupped behind an ear, a puzzled look, a dismissive shrug, and a shouted "Later!"

The noise was loud and continuous, the already almost unendurable roar of planes on constant takeoff and landing reinforced by the music blaring out of tape decks and radios, by the screaming of thousands of birds, by backup signals beeping and heavy equipment loading and unloading freight and ferrying it from pickup to flatbed to hangar to yard to plane. The smell of fuel exhaust was constantly in his nostrils, the whine of engines constantly in his ears, and both seemed prepared to go on around the clock.

At eleven that night he was in the hangar strapping more boxes to yet another pallet when his stomach growled loudly enough to be heard in Anchorage, or at least loudly enough to be heard over the noise outside. Baird, glaring at a freight manifest that wouldn't total, eyes narrowed against the smoke curling up from his stogie, looked up, startled. "Jesus! Dinner! I completely forgot!"

He climbed into the bright orange Chevy pickup with the flaking orange-and-white company logo on the side and was gone. By the time Jim finished strapping the pallet he was back, driving the pickup right into the hangar, bringing lasagna and green beans and salad in Styrofoam containers, one quart of Cherry Garcia, another of lemon sorbet ("That's mine," Baird growled) and a body bag in the back of the truck.

Jim, busy wolfing down the lasagna, which was amazingly good, thick, meaty, hot and loaded with cheese, didn't notice the body bag at first. It was only when he finished and went to stuff the container into an overflowing garbage can that he glanced casually into the truck bed. It halted him in his tracks. "What the hell—"

He wheeled around. "Baird, is that what I think it is?" he demanded, pointing.

His voice was stern enough to raise Baird's eyebrows. "It's a body, what of it?"

"Whose body? And how the hell did it get to be in the back of your pickup?"

Baird grunted, shifted his stogie from the right corner of his mouth to the left, his chaw from his left cheek to his right and spat. The tobacco stains on the floor of the hangar were overpowered by years of spilled oil, but not by much. "Not that it's any of your business, bub, but the Herc's going on to Anchorage this morning at two A.M., and the last Alaska Airlines jet left at nine. We're taking the body in for them."

"For who?"

"For who? For the goddamn state, who else. Everybody who dies accidentally in Alaska has to get autopsied, and we don't got us a corpse doctor here in beautiful downtown Bering." He spat again.

"Why isn't there a uniform with it?"

Up went the eyebrows again. "A uniform? You mean like maybe a cop?"

"No shit like maybe a cop," Jim said, feeling his neck go red. He'd been looking for an excuse to lose his temper all day, and here was a dandy one, cut, dried and delivered to his doorstep. "There is such a thing as chain of evidence, you can't just—" He shut up, suddenly conscious of Baird's increasingly suspicious stare and well aware of already having said far too much.

"Chain of evidence," Baird said, still staring. "What are you, some kind of defrocked lawyer?"

Jim was spared the necessity of answering by the arrival of a white Ford Suburban bearing the shield of the Alaska State Troopers. With more haste than grace he retreated into the rear of the hangar and busied himself with the arrangement of boxes in a tote, which required him to be head-down in the tote the whole time the trooper was there. He was supposed to make contact, but not here, and not now.

Baird's voice growled something, a female voice answered, crisp and confident and self-assured. The door to the Suburban slammed and the engine started. He stood up in time to see it drive away.

Baird was looking at him. "You want to tell me what all that was about, boy?" he said, mildly enough.

Jim tried for a rueful grin. "Nope."

It didn't work. Baird's eyes narrowed to tiny creases, lost between those pendulous cheeks. "Not running from the law, are you?" He paused, and added, "Churchill?"

Jim shook his head. "No, sir, I am not," he said definitely.

Baird stared a moment longer, then shrugged. Jim had proved himself a hard worker. Besides which, he could add. In

Bush Alaska in the summertime, that was more than enough to set the price of an employee far above rubies. The only real requirement was a pulse, and was frequently the only requirement a prospective employer could hope for. Over the years Baird had had his share of deadbeats on staff. He'd managed to acquire himself a live one here, and he wanted to keep him, and if that meant looking the other way when the law was around, he was okay with that. "Good to know," he said, dismissing the subject, and put a period to it by pretending to examine the paperwork on the transport of the body left behind by the trooper.

Jim came up behind him and read over his shoulder. Yeah, the standard form for shipping a body to the lab. Baird's greasy thumb was over the first part of the name of the deceased; it was the second half that held him transfixed. He took a deep breath, and with studied indifference said, "Who is this guy, anyway? What happened to him? What did he die from?"

Baird finished writing out the waybill and scribbled his signature at the bottom. "Fell off a boat tied up to the dock down on the river. One of them processor boats, so the deck was pretty high up. Trooper said his head looked like a squashed tomato. Yuk."

He separated the copies of the waybill and thumbed the clip on the clipboard. Before the copy of the waybill covered it, Jim saw the name typed on the form in full.

He removed the clipboard from Baird's hands.

"What the—"

"I just want to look," Jim said, and again there was that unconscious authority in his voice that comes only from years on the job. It silenced Baird. He watched Jim read through the form once again.

No witnesses were listed, but then they wouldn't be, this wasn't an incident report. All it said was that the body of one Alex Burinin, having died an accidental death, was being released into the custody of the medical examiner for confirmation of cause of death, signed off by Trooper M. Zarr.

He unzipped the bag, ignoring Baird's protest, and looked at the face. All dead faces looked like something out of Madame Tussaud's, waxen and lifeless, soul and spirit on their way to somewhere else, but Jim recognized the features from the mug shot in the file Gamble had shown him, in spite of the fact that the top of the skull had been flattened to his eyebrows, forming such a beveled crown that comparisons to Frankenstein were irresistible. Someone had very kindly mopped up the blood, revealing a nose like the beak of a vulture, eyes set deeply into dark-skinned sockets, a chin so weak Jim was surprised he hadn't grown a beard to hide it; a chin, again according to Gamble's files, Alexei Burianovich had made a career out of disproving.

He zipped up the bag and turned to Baird, ready with an innocuous explanation of his interest, when he saw Kate standing in the open hangar. She looked tense, and tired, as if she hadn't had much sleep. Too bad.

Mutt stood next to her, shoulder to knee. They were a pair, a duet, a unit entire unto themselves.

He realized he was staring, and made a business out of fussing over the body bag's zipper.

Baird noticed, and looked around. "Hey, Sovalik." He looked at his watch, surprised. "God damn, is it midnight already?" He shook his head and offered a grin. "Time flies when you're having fun, don't it? Churchill?"

Again with the slightest hesitation before the name, Jim

noticed. Damn it all anyway, he wasn't a day on the job and his cover was already compromised. It was all Kate's fault, he thought, and the rage came back as if it had never been away.

"Well," Baird said cheerfully, taking no notice of either the red creeping slowly into Jim's face or Kate's silence, "I'm going to go catch me some Z's. You hand over to Kathy, she'll show you the bunkhouse. You're due back on duty at noon. Don't be late or I'll fire your ass."

This was a threat so hollow the words rang off the insides of themselves, but no one said so. Jim helped him move the body to a pallet, and Baird climbed into the pickup and was off without further ado.

Kate stood where she was, silent, still enveloped with that eerie patience. She could wait for him to talk first, she could wait for doomsday to arrive. No hurry.

Yes. An entirely different Kate Shugak.

He didn't like it. He didn't like her much, either, at the moment.

"The Cub's at the tiedown outside," he said curtly. "The Cessna's overnighting at Russian Mission; they're scheduled to take off for Kaliganek after daylight, then back here. The DC-3 is in Dillingham, and the Here's inbound from Aniak and scheduled to make a fish run to Anchorage for Northwest Packers at two A.M." He nodded at the truck. "Got a full load, including the body."

"The what?" She peered down at the body bag as if she had never seen one before.

He handed her the clipboard. "I'm assuming you know the drill."

"Yes, I—What the hell are you so pissed off about?" she demanded, her voice rising, and for the first time there was a hint of the old Kate Shugak in it. "I don't owe you any explanations. I don't owe anybody any explanations, but I especially don't owe one to you."

He stared intently over her head at a section of hangar wall with nothing of interest on it but a calendar featuring Miss Socket Wrench in a provocative pose with a three-sixteenth box end. "Where's the bunkhouse?"

A brief silence. "This way."

They detoured through the office to pick up his duffel bag. He tripped over the coffee table again; she avoided it with the habit of long practice and led him around the side of the hangar to yet another ramshackle building that was little more than a plywood and two-by-four shack with two bunks, a table and a stove. So far as utilities went, there was electricity, and that was all there was. "Is there a shower?"

She jerked her head. "There's a community shower up at the terminal. Say you work for Baird and they won't charge you." She gestured at the shelves on the wall above the table. "There's fixings for sandwiches, the hot plate for coffee or soup. There's a water faucet the other side of the hangar. You know where the outhouse is?" He nodded. "Okay, that's everything, I guess. You—"

"Fine. Thanks. Good night." He more or less shoved her outside and shut the door in her face.

An hour later he'd showered, shaved and eaten a peanut butter and grape jelly sandwich. He brewed a cup of coffee and stretched out on the left top bunk to drink it. He finished the coffee, read ten pages of the latest John Grisham thriller without retaining a word, and turned off the light.

Half an hour later he turned it back on. He was too physically exhausted to relax—he hadn't done this much manual labor since the physical training at the trooper academy—and it didn't help that the Herc was taxiing up to the hangar, its low-throated, wallowing roar rattling the tin on the roof. His bunk was too short, too, and it was too light out. The sun wouldn't be up until five-thirty, but it never got very dark at this time of year, and there were no curtains on the bunkhouse's windows, although they were dirty enough to block out most of the light.

It didn't help either that the woman he had last seen ten months before, bruised and bleeding and cradling the body of her dead lover in her arms, was working a hundred feet from where he lay at this very moment, evidently whole and sane and very much all right in spite of the fears of family and friends. Why this should irritate him more than he was already he didn't know, but it did and he embraced it with enthusiasm.

Until he discovered to his fury that he had an erection. Son of a bitch.

"Where were you when I needed you?" he demanded, looking at his lap. "Where were you when Carroll was in my office? Where were you on the plane in? Where were you at goddamn Alaska Geographic?"

The hell with this. He bounced to the floor and yanked his clothes on and slammed outside with no very clear idea of where he was going. Kate was loading a pallet with the body bag strapped to it into the Herc. Mutt was asleep with her nose under her tail on a rug in front of the office, and Jim took advantage of the noise of the Herc's engines to slip by unnoticed.

A rutted gravel road led around the lake that served as a seaplane base, unsignposted and, if the grass growing in the ruts and the occasional mudhole that had been reclaimed by the surrounding swamp were any indication, underused. It looked neglected and abandoned. It suited his mood exactly, and he set off, seeing how far his legs could stretch. After a hard day's labor, it felt good to move without bending, stooping, lifting heavy objects, or needing to dodge out of the way of Baird's unpredictably driven forklift.

The sky was that pale mauve that characterized Arctic summer nights at the more southerly latitudes, where the sun actually went down for a few hours. The horizon stretched on forever, unsettling to a man used to mountains taking up more than their share of sky. He passed a small clump of alders, a lone diamond willow. The rest of the landscape was covered in tall grass, where it wasn't a lake or a marsh, or a stream draining one into the other, or both into the Kuskokwim.

What was that illness when you were afraid to go outside your own home? He remembered reading a story once about a woman who hadn't left her house in twenty-one years. They'd given it a name, interviewed doctors, sounded Greek—agoraphobic, that was it. Why agoraphobic? The Agora was an area of shops in Athens dating back to classical times. He'd traveled in Europe the summer after he'd graduated from college, a gift from his parents, relieved that their son had made it through school without their having to pick up child support as an additional expense. He remembered the women of Greece fondly. One minute you were looking at a statue carved two thousand years before, the next you saw the model for it strolling down the street with that marvelous Hellenic arrogance that says, "We were building the Parthenon when you were chipping out arrowheads and don't you forget it." Greek women brought that arrogance to bed with them, where it said, "Okay, show me what you got, I dare you." Jim dared every chance that came his way.

Yes, there was something special about the women of Greece, something extra, a bonus. Of course, there were more than a few Alaskan women you could say that about, too. He immediately thought of the five-foot package of dynamite back at the airport, and tripped over a rock thrown up by the gravel fill of the roadbed. He caught himself and swore. A goose, species unidentified but about the size of a Stearson, exploded out of a hummock of grass two feet to his right, honking angrily. When Jim got his heart restarted, he moved on.

Slowly but steadily, he left the hum and bustle of the municipal airport behind, and so it was with annoyance that he heard the buzz of something airborne nearby. He saw the plane soon after he heard it; small, single-engine, a Cub, he thought, although the engine sounded thin and tinny. It was red with white letters, and as he watched, it climbed, stalled, dipped a wing, dropped into a brief spin, leveled out and gained speed to climb again.

Jim disapproved. There wasn't enough light at night for acrobatics, not even in Bering in July. There was a pilot who was just sitting up and begging for a crash.

The Cub banked right and dipped below the tops of another cluster of alder trees nestled into a bend in the road. Jim quickened his step, rounded the trees and saw that he'd been right, the plane was on a short final to the gravel road that looked more like a controlled crash than a landing. It bounced twice, hard, before giving an almost perceptible shrug and settling down on the ground, rolling out to a stop, not five feet from his toes.

He looked down at the plane. It was a Cub, all right, but the wingspan was only three feet wingtip to wingtip.

"I'll be damned," he said. It was a model aircraft with a working engine, ailerons, rudder, rolling tires that were miniature tundra tires if he was not mistaken, the whole nine yards. If it were life-sized and it was September, he could have climbed in and headed out in search of caribou. He crouched down to examine it more closely, astonished by the accuracy of the detail.

Hasty feet thudded up the road, and he looked up to see a girl approaching at a trot, a control box clutched in one fist. Eyes wide, out of breath, she skidded to a halt on the loose gravel ten feet away.

They stared at each other. "Hello," Jim said finally.

She said nothing.

Jim nodded at the Cub. "Nice plane."

Silence.

Jim squatted on his haunches, elbows on his knees, hands dangling, and did his best to look harmless. "You build it?" He dusted off his best smile.

She moved forward a step, pulled closer either because of his charm of manner or because she was afraid he might steal her airplane.

"My name's Jim," he said, and held out a hand. "I'm a pilot, too."

Later, when he got to know her better, he would realize that it was the "too," the implied equality, that had brought her the rest of the way. She stopped on the other side of the Cub and squatted down in an imitation of his stance.

"What's your name?" he asked, letting his hand drop.

She gave his question the same careful consideration he would learn she gave all questions put to her. "Stephanie," she said at last. "Stephanie Chevak." Her voice was a mere whisper of sound he had to strain to hear.

"Jim," he repeated. "Jim Cho—Churchill." He held out his hand again, and after a moment she took it, obviously unaccustomed to the gesture but equally obviously determined to meet him courtesy for courtesy. Her hand was tiny in comparison to his, and felt a little sweaty against his palm. Her fingernails were clipped short and grimy, her fingertips callused. She worked with those hands.

She was Yupik, round-faced with narrow brown eyes tilted toward her temples and a ponytail of long black hair. Her skin was a smooth, dark gold in color, her cheekbones high and flat. Her chin was pointed and very firm, and Jim had a suspicion it would grow more so with age. Kate had a chin like that. Shut up, shut up, shut up.

She wore a kuspuk made of blue flowered corduroy trimmed with white rickrack, over a pair of faded blue jeans with nothing left to the knees and a pair of hightop Reeboks with heels that lit up every time she put her feet down. They glowed now, a neon pink that would have looked more appropriate on a cafe sign in Anchorage flashing "Eats! Eats! Eats!"

She put her hands on the leading edge of the model's wings and with great care turned the red model airplane belly up. There was a square of black plastic cut into the belly. Stephanie ran her hands down the fuselage and pressed a corner of the plastic. It popped open to reveal a lens.

"A camera!" Jim said, surprised.

She looked at him, her expression unsmiling but not unfriendly.

"You taking pictures from up there?" He jerked a thumb up.

She hesitated, then nodded once.

"Well, hey," Jim said. "That's kind of neat. I suppose you take the tape home and show them on the television afterward?"

She said something in her small voice.

"I'm sorry, what?" Jim said.

"Transmitter," she said again.

"Oh," he said. "You've got a transmitter in there?" He gestured at the body of the model airplane.

She nodded.

A smile spread across Jim's face. "What do you do, broadcast?"

She nodded.

"Where to?" he said. She didn't answer, and he thought he saw a hint of a challenge in her glance. "Of course," he said. "You're a ham, aren't you?"

There was the barest allusion to a smile at the corner of her mouth.

"A ham radio operator," he said. "I know a ham. Name's Bobby. Operates a transmitter out of Niniltna. You ever talk to him?"

"Clark the Park Spark?" Still in the tiny voice, but her first indication of real interest.

"That's him." Something in the quality of her expression changed. It was the first time in Jim's life that his consequence had been increased simply by knowing Bobby Clark. "Anyway, I remember him telling me that there are cable channel frequencies reserved for hams."

"Fifty-seven to sixty," she said promptly.

"Yeah, Bobby called it the ham band. So you broadcast pictures from your plane on the ham band to, where? Your home television?"

She nodded.

"How far is the signal good for?" he said, trying to entice her into more than a nonsyllabic reply.

"Five miles."

"No kidding?"

"So long as you have a direct line of sight."

He looked around. "It's a little dark to be taking pictures, isn't it?"

She nodded.

"Special film?" he said.

A pause, another nod.

"Who's watching?" She looked confused. "At home," he said, "right now. Who's watching television?"

Her face closed up. He had trespassed, who knew how. He went for a change of subject. "You build the plane?"

A pause, a slight nod.

"Nice job," he said, and meant it.

"Thank you." Her voice was a little stronger this time.

"You have help?"

She shook her head.

"You do it all yourself?"

A pause. "Yes."

"Wow." He looked at her with an admiration that was not at all feigned.

An expression flashed across her face and Jim tried to identify it. It wasn't, as he might expect, pride. Embarrassment? Why embarrassment for a job so well done? She'd done all the work, she should take all the credit and then some. "Well, you did a terrific job. This looks just like the one I fly. Different colors, is all. Plus maybe a little bigger."

She almost smiled that time.

"It was a kit?"

She nodded.

"You send away for it?"

She nodded.

"How long did it take you to build?"

She considered. "Five months."

"You're kidding. From the time you got the kit, only five months?"

She nodded again.

"Wow." Jim's whistle was low and admiring and honest. "That's pretty impressive. You build the engine, too?"

She shook her head. "Not this time."

This time his smile was natural and without guile. "Next time?"

This time she did smile back and it was a revelation, lighting the little face with humor and intelligence.

"How old are you?"

"Ten."

"You going to be a pilot when you grow up?"

"Yes." It was a simple statement of fact. "And an engineer."

"What kind?"

"Aerospace."

"You want to build rockets?"

"I want to fly them," she said.

"Oh," Jim said. "You a *Star Trek* fan?"

Her smile came back, wider this time, matched by a twinkle in the brown eyes. "*Star Wars*."

"Aha," Jim said. " 'Ancient weapons—"

"—and a hokey religion—" she chimed in irresistibly.

"—are no match for a good blaster at your side, kid,' " they both intoned.

She giggled. It was an enchanting sound. In the next instant she was serious again, her voice back to its whisper. "They never should have taken Darth Vader's mask off."

"In *Jedi*?" he said.

"Yeah."

"What should they have done instead?"

She thought about that, very grave. "They should have let

us see his face in Luke's," she said at last.

Jim was trying to decipher this cryptic utterance and form a reply that wouldn't get him laughed out of town, when Stephanie's face changed. Jim watched her realize that she was talking to a stranger on a lonely road late at night, a male stranger, and a gussuk male stranger, at that. She stood up.

Jim did, too. She was right; she shouldn't be talking to strangers. Still, he said, "You want some help getting your Cub home?"

She shook her head, ponytail whipping vigorously back and forth.

"Yeah, well, I guess you got it out here all right." He stood looking down at girl and model plane. "Why are you out here so late at night, Stephanie?"

Her change of expression was swift and immediate. All she did was shrug, but Jim felt the definite slam of a door in his face. "I'd like to see you try out her wings in daylight sometime. If that's okay?"

Another shrug, a good way to return a noncommittal answer to a specific question. She tucked the plane beneath an arm and set off down the road in the opposite direction from the airport.

"Good-bye," he called after her. "Nice meeting you."

She hesitated, and looked over her shoulder. Their eyes met straight on for the first time, and he thought he saw her smile, but he could have been wrong. She started walking again, a sturdy, determined little figure, neon pink lights flashing from her heels.

It was a lonely stretch of road, and he worried about her for a moment. But she lived here and he didn't, and she obviously knew where she was going. Still, he wondered what her parents were thinking, to let her out at this hour.

He wondered if her parents knew she was out at all.

He shook his head and retraced his steps back to the airport.

"Hey, you need a ride to town?"

The question came from a guy in a pickup, the bed loaded with gear, parked in front of the main terminal building.

"Yeah, sure, thanks," Jim said, and climbed in.

"Where you headed?"

"Ah, the docks," Jim said with sudden inspiration.

"Great, me, too," the driver said, and put the truck in gear. "Mike Mason."

"Jim Churchill."

"You looking for work, Jim?"

Jim shook his head, hooked a thumb over his shoulder at the receding airport. "Got a job. Baird Air."

"Oh, yeah?" Mason laughed. He was a wiry, sandy-haired man with a thin face and an eager expression, as if he was excited about what was around the corner, as if life had not yet kicked him in the teeth too many times to dim that excitement. He wore a shiny new gold band on his left hand that he kept touching, tapping against the wheel, rubbing between his fingers, as if to reassure himself that it was really and truly there.

"Yeah," Jim said, "I just started today."

"What's he pay?"

Jim realized he didn't have a clue, but he had his pride. "Top dollar."

"He ought to," Mason said frankly. "He works his help like dogs, is what I hear."

"Woof," Jim said.

Mason laughed. "I'm a fisherman myself."

"I figured, from the gear. Salmon?"

Mason nodded. "I just tore up a set on a deadhead last week." It didn't seem to bother him much, in spite of the dollar value of the gear involved, which ran into the thousands. Maybe the wedding band accounted for his unquenchable optimism.

Just wait, Jim thought. He himself couldn't get along with women he wasn't married to. He skittered away from that thought and said, "Who do you deliver to?"

"Whoever pays the best," Mason replied.

"Who's been paying the best lately?"

"Lately, it's a tossup," Mason said, braking for a pair of Canada geese and nine fuzzy offspring grumbling sleepily along in their wake. They made it safely across the road, and the truck rolled forward. "The Japanese are usually the highest bidders, but there's buyers coming from all over now. Korea, Taiwan, Russia, you name it."

Russia. Suddenly Jim remembered why he was in Bering. Not to mention the body bag currently en route to Anchorage and the medical examiner. "Russia?" he said casually, trying to sound like a rube. "You mean like actual Russians from actual Russia?"

"Yeah, although they're awful picky about what they'll take. Guess the communist manifesto has given way to crass commercialism. About time, too. Better they should spend their money on fish than on bombs."

"Ahuh," Jim said. "I personally have never felt the need to glow in the dark."

Mason gave him a suspicious glance, as if he doubted Jim's patriotism, but you get that a lot in the Alaskan Bush and Jim felt safe in ignoring it.

Jim thought for a moment. Mason was a fisherman,

Burinin aka Burianovich had purportedly fallen from a boat on the docks. It had to be common knowledge by now, and natural curiosity should serve as a reason for asking. "Speaking of Russians, we had to load the body of one on a plane for Anchorage this evening. You hear anything about that?"

"Oh hell, yeah, I practically saw it happen."

Jim went on alert, but he said casually, "No shit?"

"Oh yeah, man, it was a mess. I was just finishing up delivery to Peter Pan when there was this big hooraw about three boats down. We all went to look." He shuddered. "Man, he was a mess. Blood everywhere."

Jim reflected on how odd it was that Baird and Mason, two men who wrested their living from sea and air, could be so squeamish about a little blood. To be fair, he'd seen more than his share.

"What happened?"

"He fell. Pitched headfirst right off the side of the boat and landed on his head next to the gangway."

"What did he fall from?"

Mason shrugged. "Nobody really said. There were Russians all over the place yelling in Russian, and then the trooper showed up and tried to calm everybody down. Easy on the eyes, the new trooper, you seen her yet?"

Not from head-down inside a tote, Jim thought. "No."

"Not that I'd be interested," Mason added hastily, fingering his wedding band.

"Doesn't hurt to look," Jim said soothingly.

"Right, right, looking's no sin." Mason didn't seem convinced. "Anyway, this one Russian, hairy little bastard, looks like Mr. Spock, you know, with the ears, he yells at the rest of the Russians to shut up, or at least they did so I guess that's what he said. The trooper asked him if anybody saw what happened, and he said no, and they all went along with him."

Jim caught the inference. "But you don't think so?"

"Well…" Mason's voice trailed off. "There were about thirty of them, is all. Seems like somebody would have seen something."

"Anybody from shore see anything?"

Mason shook his head. "One guy, beach ganger, said he heard the sound of the fall and went to look. That was about it."

"What do they think happened?"

Mason shifted down to cross a narrow, railless wooden bridge over one of many streams. "The trooper got out a tape measure, and did some climbing around on the boat. Said from where he landed he must have fallen from the starboardside ladder to the catwalk outside the wheelhouse."

Again there was doubt. "But?"

Mason shrugged again, irritably. "Hell, how should I know? Trooper's paid to look into that sort of thing, she said how it was, that's how it was."

Jim maintained a not unhopeful silence.

"Hell," Mason said again. "It's just that the bulkhead of the *Kosygin* is well inside the gunnel, four feet or more. If he fell from the catwalk he'd hit the deck, maybe the gunnel."

"But not the dock?"

Mason shook his head. "Maybe in high seas, with the boat rolling back and forth. But not tied up in Bering."

"Could he have fallen from the gunnel?"

"Could have. He even could have tripped and fallen down the gangway, except he was to one side of it instead of at the foot."

"What makes the trooper so sure he fell from the catwalk?"

"She found something caught on the catwalk railing, a piece of clothing or something. She put it in a Ziploc and took it away. Might have been a piece of his shirt, something like that."

"Oh."

"Anyway. Seen lots of nutty stuff happen at sea, never mind shore."

"I guess."

Of course, Jim thought, if the body had been found on the deck of the boat, the boat would have been subject to search. As things stood, the scene of the accident had been removed to the dock, public property as opposed to private. Domestic territory as opposed to foreign. Convenient for the owners of the boat however you looked at it.

The road meandered around lakes and more lakes, and houses grew gradually closer together as they reached the center of town. Jim had heard that Venice, another city built on lakes, was slowly sinking into the Adriatic; he wondered where Bering would be in another decade or so. Of course, by then they would have fished out the salmon the same way they had the king crab and the halibut and it wouldn't matter, except to the Yupik.

Mason let Jim out with a wave good-bye and drove away. Jim looked at his watch. It was three o'clock, and although the dawn was more than two hours away the sky was perceptibly lighter, having faded from mauve to a pastel shade of lavender. No stars, he thought, standing still and staring up. They disappeared from the night sky from May to August, displaced by the midnight sun.

He remembered stars in California, lying on his back in an artichoke field, next to Sally Ann Schaefer, the artichoke field's owner's daughter. She'd been two years older than he was, a senior to his sophomore, and in those few sweet hours he'd learned about artichokes, and about other things as well.

He imagined telling Kate Shugak that story. He imagined the sneer that would follow, the snide comment, something about how every one of his memories seemed to be tied to a roll in the hay, or in this case, artichokes. Why shouldn't she; it wasn't as if he hadn't lived that life, cultivated that image, and had a great time while he was at it. He'd never intentionally hurt anyone, he'd made sure his partners were on the same page before they turned it with him, together. He had no regrets, and some great memories.

He realized his teeth were grinding together, and made a deliberate effort to relax his jaw muscles.

The town itself was quiet. A hum of activity came from the direction of the river. A lane led between two two-story buildings, one a warehouse with a Sealand sign on the side. From the other he heard the drone and clank of machinery. He walked down the lane to emerge onto a wooden dock as wide as a two-lane road, where he was nearly run over by a forklift.

"Get outta the way, dipshit!" the driver yelled.

Not anything Baird hadn't been yelling at him all day. He dodged back a step and the forklift roared by.

The dock seemed to go on forever in both directions, curving with the northern, convex edge of the shoreline. The water was deep brown and moved slowly, almost sluggishly, bearing boats, skiffs, tankers, uprooted trees, deadheads, a loose oar, a half-submerged cardboard box, a plastic Sprite bottle, a waterlogged dory, a tangled section of meshed gear, maybe part of Mike Mason's; all of it ever and inexorably down, down, down to the bay and the ocean beyond. It looked like something out of Mark Twain, and Jim caught himself looking for a raft with a boy and a man on board, heading down the river before one of them was sold there.

Floodlights fixed to the walls of buildings and the rigging of boats lit up the scene. Processors taller than the canneries on shore were moored to the sea wall bow to stern to bow, and occasionally side by next. The fishing boats were most of them open skiffs with only the most rudimentary of cabins, if they had cabins at all, and were rafted together three and five at a time. The area was a hive of activity, forklifts beeping, hydraulic lifts whining, lines snapping and tackle clattering, black rubber fuel hoses slithering up and down, beach crews yelling and cursing as they loaded and unloaded fish and supplies.

Fishers never sleep. Not between May and August. Unlike the stars.

Some of the fishing boats were tied up to some of the processors and were delivering their catch direct. Other boats were tied up to spaces between the processors and were delivering to onshore buyers. Here, a buyer sorted the best-looking reds to be frozen in the round and shipped air freight to points Outside and international. There, a tote of more scarred fish was dumped onto a conveyor belt that disappeared into a cannery, destined for one-pound talls and half-pound flats beneath generic labels on Safeway shelves.

Jim dodged people and fish and made his way up the docks, passing the *Kyoto Kozushima* out of Edo, Japan, the *Chongju* out of Seoul, South Korea, the *Northern Harvester* out of Anacortes, Washington, the *Arctic Princess* out of Freeport, Oregon, until he came to the *Kosygin*, out of Vladivostok, Russia.

Alone among the processors, the *Kosygin* appeared deserted. The bridge was dark. The boom was still. The deck was bare, of fish, deckhands and beach gang. There was no one at the head of the gangway that stretched down to the dock. There wasn't anyone at the foot of the gangway, either. The hull was rusted right down to its trim line, which was riding three feet above the water. It wasn't exactly overloaded.

He found an overturned fiberglass tote in a corner that left his line of sight unhindered in both directions and settled in to watch. A half hour passed. The light increased, the beach gangs finished unloading half a dozen gillnetters, and knocked off for a break. Jim ambled over and got in line for coffee and enormous sugar doughnuts.

"Great morning," a voice next to him said.

He turned to see a short, slight man, about fifty. His hair was hidden under a Greek fisherman's cap and he wore stained brown Carhartt overalls. His chin was stubbled with three-day-old beard and he looked at Jim out of deepset dark eyes, face creased into a slight smile. "You're new."

Nothing to do but agree to that, so Jim said, "Yeah."

"Thought so. I'm the foreman, so I would know."

"Oh hell," Jim said.

The smile widened into a grin, deepening the crow's feet at the corners of his eyes. "Gene Brady."

"Jim Churchill." Jim stuck what was left of the doughnut in his mouth, wiped the sugar from his palm on the seat of his jeans and accepted Brady's hand. "Sorry about this," he mumbled around the doughnut.

"No biggee." Brady examined him with a critical eye. "You don't look like a bum."

"I'm not, I'm gainfully employed."

"Where?"

Jim made a vague gesture with his coffee cup and swallowed the rest of the doughnut in one indigestible lump. "Baird Air."

The grin became a laugh.

"What's so funny?"

"You working for Baird. Anybody working for Baird."

Jim relaxed. "Yeah, well." He shrugged and did his best to look rueful.

"Step into my office." Brady indicated the edge of the dock.

Since Jim had a bellyful of Brady's doughnut and he was working his way through a cup of Brady's coffee, he accepted the invitation.

"How'd you wind up in Bering?" Brady said.

Jim gave a fleeting thought to Gamble. "Job Service."

"Ah." He caught Jim's sideways glance and grinned again. "No offense. Some of my best friends were sent out from Job Service."

"Yeah, right," Jim said.

"You sticking?"

Jim shrugged again. "Long as there's work, I guess. I don't plan to make Bering my home."

"You could do worse." Brady drained his cup, and pointed at Jim's. "Want a refill?"

"Sure." He watched Brady take the cups to the coffee urn set up on a folding table against the wall of the cannery, wondering at Brady's interest.

The coffee was hot and strong, the second cup as good as the first. "Good," he said.

"Yeah," Brady said with satisfaction. "They used to give us Folger's until I put my foot down. Now it's Kaladi Brothers all the way or I walk."

"What do you do?"

"I'm the head of the beach gang. Also known as the bitch gang." He listened with a contented smile as a chorus of disapproval rose from the employees sprawled around them on the dock, primarily young, male and Anglo. Brady eyed Jim over the rim of his cup. "They're a good bunch. The problem is, working the hours they do and considering the overtime, they make too much money too fast, boom, they've got both semesters paid for, tuition, room and board, and off they go to visit their mamas before they have to go back to school." Another chorus rose, this one half-hearted. Brady drained his cup. "If you're working for Baird, you might maybe know how to run a forklift."

"I might."

Disappointed at this lack of encouragement, Brady said, "Yeah, well, you get tired of Baird running your ass off, you let me know." This time the grin seemed to have grown fangs. "I'll put you to work."

"I bet you would," Jim said. "You just unload the little boats?"

"I work for Half Seas Under, we unload who delivers to us. Sometimes big, sometimes little."

"You ever have to take on one of those?" Jim hooked a thumb over his shoulder at the processors lining the dock up and down river.

"Sometimes."

"The foreign vessels, too?"

"If the price is right."

"I've never seen so many foreign-registered ships in an Alaskan port before."

"Yeah, well, then you haven't been on the coast much. We get 'em all, Koreans, Japanese, Taiwanese, Polish…"

"Polish?"

"Yeah, believe it not, they've got a pretty big foreign fleet. Back before the fall of the Wall, Polish sailors liked to jump ship in Alaskan ports. I was working down on the Chain one time that happened."

"They get to stay?"

"For a while they got to stay in the hospital, recovering from exposure. This was February."

Jim winced. "Brrr."

"I'll say."

Jim nodded at the *Kosygin*. "And I see you've got Russian fishers, too."

Brady's voice flattened. "Not hardly."

"They don't deliver to Half Seas Under?"

"They're not hardly fishermen," Brady clarified. "They don't deliver to anyone most of the time."

Jim was about to ask him about Burinin aka Burianovich's death when an engine sounded right behind them, and both men looked around to see a thirty-two-foot drifter sidling up to the dock, wallowing beneath the weight of a catch that was spilling over both gunnels. The man at the wheel looked tired but content, and the two boys standing on the deck hip-deep in red salmon looked cheerfully exhausted. The drifter was moored in a smooth, three-step process that indicated long practice. The beach gang looked on with critical and not unadmiring silence. It was always a pleasure to watch work done well, especially when you weren't required to do it yourself.

"Okay, people," Brady said, rising to his feet. "Let's get back to work."

"Thanks for the coffee and the doughnut," Jim said.

Brady waved a hand. "Anytime. Keep my offer in mind. I could use someone who isn't just out of diapers to back me up with this bunch."

There was another chorus of boos and whistles, and Jim stepped back to watch the team go into action. It was as efficient as the boat's crew had been, no hesitation, no wasted motion. Two shinnied down the ladder to help the deckhands fill the brailer, one operated the hoist, another maneuvered a forklift loaded with an empty tote, two others steadied the brailer so it stayed directly over the tote before pulling the line that opened the bottom and caused the fish to cascade down in a slippery silver stream. Gene Brady was everywhere Jim looked, on the drifter pitching fish, on the dock looking over the hoist operator's shoulder, walking behind the forklift with an eagle eye on the edge of the dock, next to the men maneuvering the brailer. It was a smooth operation, Jim decided, if a bit slimy. His respect for Brady increased.

He woke up to realize that the hoist operator looked familiar, and why. Thickset, Hispanic, his hands were very nimble on the controls. Jim wondered if they taught heavy-equipment operating at Quantico, too. Probably. Somewhere between forensics and neat, would be his guess.

Someone lurched into him. "Sorry," a voice muttered.

"No problem," he said, and moved out of the way of another member of the beach gang, who had exchanged the blue suit she'd been wearing the last time he'd seen her for a dark red plaid shirt, yellow rainpants and steeltoed black rubber boots.

He knew now why Gamble had kept him in Anchorage for six days, and felt a slow burn that, for a change, had nothing to do with Kate Shugak.

Empty, the drifter pulled away and another swung in to take its place. The glow of the sun was evident on the northeastern horizon, and he glanced at his watch to find that it was almost four o'clock. He hadn't had any sleep, and he had to be at work at noon.

He thought about finding a telephone and calling George Perry on his cellular phone to pass the word that Kate Shugak was found and that she was all right. He spotted a pay phone, started toward it, and hesitated.

George would want to know where she was. George would also be beating the Bush telegraph like a bongo drum the minute he hung up on Jim, beginning at Bernie's. Auntie Vi would hear, and Auntie Joy and Auntie Belasha and all the other aunties, not to mention Billy Mike and Mandy and Chick and Bobby and Dinah and who knew who else. Jim wouldn't put it past the whole boiling lot of them to commandeer themselves a plane and fly into Bering to see with their own eyes that their straying lamb was found. He wouldn't have a hope in hell of maintaining his cover if that happened.

And she could have called them if she'd wanted to, if she'd cared enough to, the inconsiderate little—

He headed down the dock.

As he passed the *Kosygin*, he noticed again how deserted it seemed. His footsteps slowed, then stopped.

Well, what the hell. It was a Russian ship, he'd been seconded to Bering to ferret out a bunch of Russians of dubious moral and ethical character, one of whom was now dead in what could, without too much of a stretch, be called suspicious circumstances, and there wasn't anyone around to tell him not to.

He looked around. The Half Seas Under crew had disappeared into the cannery, and everyone else was too far away to see, or were minding their own business.

He walked up the gangway and went on board.

CHAPTER 6

*...there is no time
in the summer of midnight sun.*

—*Crazy Dogholkoda*

KATE FINISHED LOADING THE Herc and watched it taxi out to the runway and take off with its distinctive grumbling roar, shouldering the world into the sky. A flatbed thundered past, on its way to the Alaska Airlines terminal. Traffic in and out of the airport had slowed, but probably wouldn't entirely stop until sometime in late September, if not October, certainly not until the last salmon had made it up the river.

And then Baird would put the seats back in the planes and begin ferrying Outside fishermen to Anchorage for their flights home, local residents to Anchorage for winter supply runs, and Natives to Anchorage for the AFN convention. In January he'd take the seats out again and start hauling dog teams to Anchorage and Fairbanks and Whitehorse. After the last musher made it under the burlwood arch in Nome, he'd hose down the insides of his fleet and the cycle would begin all over again.

After four months, the last two filled with fourteen-to eighteen-hour days, it was all pretty much routine. When Baird had suggested splitting her job into two twelve-hour shifts and hiring a second person for the ground crew, her first instinct had been to protest. She wanted the work, she needed the work, she had to have the work to occupy her every waking moment, to keep her so busy she wouldn't have to remember, to exhaust her enough so that she could sleep without dreams infiltrating her subconscious.

She couldn't think of the past winter on the homestead without a shudder, without the lurking fear that the anguish of those months all alone in the middle of that enormous, echoingly empty Park would return and take her right back down to the bottom. She wasn't sure she could pull herself out again. She wasn't sure she would want to.

Here she was too busy to be lonely, the only people she knew were her boss and his pilots, and the only things even remotely recognizable were the makes of the various planes flying in and out. There wasn't a relative within five hundred miles, or a mountain close enough to see, or one single fishing boat tied up at the docks named after the daughter of someone with whom she'd graduated from Niniltna High.

There was nothing here to remind her of her life, of the people in it, of the people she'd lost. She could breathe here, with care, but she could breathe. If she went home, she'd start to suffocate again, and there was still enough of an instinct for survival to get out while she still could. If she had stayed...

Against her will the memory of that day in March surfaced, when the trees and the mountains and the very sky itself seemed to close in on her, when after it was over, all she had was the wound on her arm to remind her of what had almost happened, of what would happen if she didn't get out. She'd driven to Niniltna that evening and flown George to Anchorage that night. She'd been waiting when Job Service opened its doors the next morning, invented a name, made up a social security number, inverted the numbers on her driver's license, lied about losing her identification, and had been on a plane to Bering that afternoon. The good old state Job Service. If you wanted away from your life and you could walk without scraping your knuckles on the floor, Job Service would take you there.

From the instant she had stepped foot on the Bering tarmac she'd been working flat out; nonstop, hard, back-breaking, strenuous work, work that left her spent and depleted, work that left her too tired to think, too tired to move, too tired to feel, too tired to remember anything beyond the arrival time of the next load and the maximum tonnage and load limits of the plane it was shipping out on. She worked, she ate, she slept briefly for a few hours snatched from the work, and then she got up and did it all over again. There were plenty of birds for Mutt to hunt in every direction, a hot shower not too far away, and if the toilet was an outhouse, at least she didn't have to haul a honeybucket. Baird, thank god, had it pumped on a weekly basis by the local service.

So far as Baird knew she had no friends or relatives, no life to infringe on her devotion to the task at hand. In four months she had never taken a day off. She rarely left the airport, sending him to the Eagle store with a grocery list when needed, which always included whatever new bestsellers were on the checkout stand, nothing to stimulate her imagination or challenge her intellect, just words on a page to occupy the front of her brain while everything behind lay dormant and detached. She hadn't dared to bring any poetry with her. She hadn't listened to music in eleven months.

The old gods were silent as well. Agudar, Calm Water's Daughter, The Woman Who Keeps The Tides, they no longer spoke to Kate. She didn't miss them, she told herself. She didn't even miss Emaa anymore.

Kate was in neutral. The motor was running, but it wasn't

going anywhere. It was just so much as she was capable of, and no more.

There was a tentative knock at the door and she looked up. A short, pudgy man with a tentative expression on his elfin face stood in the doorway, eyebrows raised. "Is a bad time, yes?"

She smiled, glad to be diverted from her increasingly morbid thoughts. There was one other person she knew in Bering besides Baird and the pilots. "Is a bad time, no. Come on in, Yuri. What are you doing up at this hour of the night?"

He came in and sat down across the desk from her. "I have the problem with sleeping," he said. "I can't. So I get up and wander around the little town. Everybody is having this same problem, I think, because everybody else is up, too."

"No. It's just summertime in Alaska." And she was struck again by how normal everything was, how ordinarily everyone went about their business, the fishermen setting their nets and pulling in fish, the postal workers distributing mail in the post office, the waitresses bringing coffee to their customers, the gas station dispensing gas, the grocery store selling groceries.

Suddenly she wanted to rip the door off its hinges and scream, "How can anything be normal, how can anything be ordinary, don't you people get it, Jack is *dead*!"

"Ekaterina?" Yuri peered at her worriedly through a shock of thick, untidy black hair, ragged around the edges as if hacked off with a knife. Like hers.

"Ekaterina?" he said again, and this time his worried voice brought her back. Her breath was coming rapidly, her heart thudding painfully in her throat, her hands had clenched into fists.

"Something is wrong, yes? A bad time this is." He half rose from his chair. "I go."

"You stay." She summoned up another smile from somewhere, aware that her supply was running low, and with a deliberate effort calmed her breathing and relaxed her hands. Her heartbeat obediently steadied, and slowed to a more normal rate. "Did you want to ship something? Or did you just drop in to say hello?"

He brightened. Fumbling through his pockets, he produced a grimy deck of cards. He looked at her hopefully.

Her smile was more genuine this time. "Snerts?" She rummaged through the desk and came up with her own deck. "Remember, I told you, it's more fun with three or more people."

"I don't care," he said, clearing a space. "You teach me to beat you."

"In your dreams," she said without force.

He stayed for two hours, during which they played six games and drank Diet Coke she fetched from the cooler in the hangar.

"Diet?" He made a face.

"You're awfully picky, for someone who didn't used to be able to drink any pop at all."

His face fell into tragic lines, and Kate was about to apologize when she noticed the twinkle in his eyes. "Just for that, I'm blowing by you with thirteen cards left on the pile."

"Hah! Just try, you—you American! I leave you in dust!"

It wasn't the first time he'd made a late-night visit. He was a native of Russia, and worked off one of the processors that put into port a couple of times a week. She'd met him one morning when he came in with a box to ship to Anchorage. He'd explained that the crew of his boat loaded up at home on nesting dolls and saints' icons with gilt haloes and surplus Red Army watches for resale in Fourth Avenue shops in

Anchorage, in order to get around the currency laws, so they'd have a little cash to spend in America. She had found him to be no threat, even amusing, and he had dropped by the next time his boat was in, the first time she'd taught him Snerts. Thereafter it was part of both their routines; when his boat was in, Yuri showing up at the hangar in the early hours of the morning when he knew Kate would be alone and probably not very busy.

He'd made a mild pass at her the third time they'd been alone together. She had refused as kindly as she knew how, using up as much nice as she had energy for because she was glad of his company when three o'clock rolled around and she started thinking about September. The early morning hours were the worst. She'd acquired her new scar at three A.M.

Yuri had taken his refusal with good humor; mostly, she suspected, because he was looking for an easy way into the country and was prepared to put the moves on any likely American female who might be susceptible to a proposal of marriage. That night she had risen to the top of his list. Now she had been eliminated, and they could be friends.

Over the weeks he had told her about himself in little snippets dropped here and there, about his boyhood, about the filthy, freezing, losing war in Afghanistan. He had been invalided out of the Army, no great loss to the Army as he'd been a lousy soldier, and no great loss to him as the Russian Army was no longer able to meet its payroll. He had been unable to find work, and one day had come home to the apartment his family shared with two others to find that his wife was gone, along with their two daughters.

"What did you do?"

He shrugged and put a five of spades on a four of spades a second and a half before she did. The back of his hand was thick with the same black hair that grew from his head with such exuberance. "What I had to. I move out because I have no money for rent, but I find a friend who will let me sleep on his floor and use his bathroom for a few rubles. I speak the English well, no?"

"Yes."

"My mother insists. Very smart, my mother, she say America will win Cold War and we will all have to speak English. So. I hire as interpreter to American who wishes to sell Coke in Russia." He regarded his Diet Coke with a proprietary air, drained the can and set it down with a satisfied smacking of his lips. "Before that I drive truck for a while. Before that I buy and sell on black market, a little."

"Did you ever see your wife or your daughters again?"

"No. I am stuck." He held up his deck as evidence.

She ran through hers once more, and then, on the count of three, they shifted one card from the top of their decks to the bottoms and began dealing in threes again. "I'm sorry."

"Me, I am sorry, too. But then I get this job, on this big boat—" he flung out his arms "—and I come to America, and I meet you!" He grinned. "Even if you won't marry me."

"Find yourself another way to get into the country, buddy," she said.

He looked wounded, but not mortally.

She managed to throw the fifth game.

"Hah!" he said, triumphant. "I get better at this Snerts!"

"Hah," she said in turn, "I get revenge next week."

His happy grin faded. "I don't know, Ekaterina. Next week we may not come to Bering."

"Oh." She was silent for a moment, searching for dismay, and found none. Her smile this time was obviously forced. "Then it was very nice meeting you, Yuri."

"And for me to meet you, Ekaterina." He took her hand and bowed over it, a gesture that would have looked ridiculous on anyone but a European with two thousand years of civilization at his back.

Yuri hadn't been gone for five minutes before everything she had been feeling before he showed up came crashing back in on her.

Jim Chopin, of all people. Chopper Jim, First Sergeant of the Alaska State Troopers, also known with some truth as the Father of the Park. He just had to show up and destroy what fragile peace of mind she had managed to achieve after four months' effort. He even had the gall to be angry, not just angry but furious, almost violent in his rage. It had roused a brief spurt of answering anger in herself, which had died almost immediately, much to her relief. She didn't want to feel like that.

She didn't want to feel.

She thought, without much interest, that she'd never seen Chopper Jim angry before. Certainly he'd never been angry with her. Irritated, amused, intrigued, challenged, impressed by and yes, aroused, but never angry.

He was here under an assumed name. That could only mean one thing, that he was working undercover. Was there something hinky going on at Baird Air? Slowly, reluctantly, engaging gears rusty with disuse, she thought back over the past four months, of the loads of airfreight going in and coming out, of the shippers and the receivers.

It had seemed like a fairly routine operation. The season had started with supplies, groceries, parts and gear coming in, and had progressed to fish going out. There were some special shipments, personal belongings for families moving to or from, a load of liquor for an upriver village that had just voted itself dry to wet for the third time, an unending stream of airplane engines going back and forth to Anchorage for annual inspections. There were the regular shipments of supplies to support those government bureaucracies maintaining a presence in this southwest Alaskan hub; the state courts, the Departments of Corrections, of Public Safety, of Fish and Game. Now and then one of the staties hitched a ride on a pile of freight, not strictly kosher but what the FAA didn't know wouldn't hurt Baird Air.

She looked at her left wrist, which sported a large stainless-steel watch with Russian letters on the face, a gift from Yuri that he'd broken out of the first shipment she had expedited for him. Baird had one just like it, only larger. So did each of the four pilots. Jim would probably be offered one if he were on duty the next time Yuri brought in a consignment. Baird Air treated all its customers as if their goods were on fire and the nearest fire hose was at the other end of a plane ride, but the gifts made Yuri feel that his goods would be handled with extra care. "What the hell," Baird said, admiring his watch, "it ticks."

No, Kate couldn't pinpoint anything out of the ordinary in the day-to-day operations of the air taxi. Baird made money hand over fist, but then a lot went out, too, in maintenance, lease payments on the hangar, mortgage payments on the plane, insurance liability and replacement. He shared, too; Kate was pulling in almost five thousand a month and the pilots more than that.

She didn't want to think about any of this. She didn't want to wonder why Jim was here, she didn't want to speculate over what might or might not constitute a case for him, she didn't want to look at Baird Air's customers as anything but letters and numbers entered neatly on a manifest form. Baird ran an airfreight service out of a Yukon-Kuskokwim hub, paid her to help him do so, provided her with a bunk and meals and didn't hassle her about Mutt. She didn't need to know any more than that.

She wanted Jim to go away.

She decided to tell him so.

But when she went to the bunkhouse for lunch at six A.M., he was gone. From the evidence, he'd showered, changed, napped for a while, and then left. He'd eaten, washing it down with his own coffee.

She hadn't had anything but Hill's Brothers in so long. The bag smelled good. The label identified it as Tsunami Blend, from Captain's Roast in Homer, Alaska. It was ground for cone filter, and Jim had been so obliging as to bring all the fixings with him. She filled the tea kettle from the five-gallon white plastic jerry can beneath the table, and the hot plate brought it to a boil quickly. She put the cone on a mug, a filter into the cone and spooned coffee into the filter with a generous hand. She inhaled the steam rising from the surface. Heaven had to smell like that. Seasoned with a touch of evaporated milk, it tasted ambrosial.

She carried the mug back to the hangar, sat down at the desk and began completing cargo manifests. Mutt woke up and padded in. "Hey, girl," Kate said, one hand dropping automatically to scratch behind the big ears.

Mutt leaned up against her, long enough for the warmth of her body to penetrate through Kate's jeans. She'd been doing that a lot lately. Ever since that morning. One hand rubbed absently at the flesh of her right arm. The scar was now only a lump of rough tissue, barely discernable as individual tooth marks.

Her hand dropped. She drained her mug and went back to work.

Mutt went looking for an early morning snack and came back with a tight belly, a satisfied expression on her face and goose down hanging from her chin. The sun shone horizontal rays through the office window, the clear, pale gold of early morning.

Baird showed up at eight with a tray of breakfast burritos, the Cessna landed right after the Here, the phone started to ring and the day began in earnest.

At eight-thirty the pilot of the Herc perched a considerable hip on one corner of the desk and bit into his burrito. "God, but the old man can cook. I swear I'd marry him if he ever took a bath."

"Can't you keep the grease off your paperwork, Larry? You know some of this stuff goes to the FAA."

"Fuck the FAA," the pilot said amiably. "You're about to go off duty, aren't you?"

She didn't look up. Completing government forms was an art in and of itself; instructions incomprehensible to anyone who spoke English as a first language, tiny spaces totally inadequate to hold the information required. "Not until noon," she said, as she always did.

"Did I ever happen to mention that I've got an apartment in town?"

"At last count? About one hundred and eleven times." Kate signed Baird's name and picked up the manifest. Fish, fish and more fish, in from Kwingillingok. Plus a baby carriage. A baby carriage? Oh, right, Mrs. Christianson was sending her daughter's baby carriage to her daughter, who was due any day now. Baird frequently carried things of a personal nature at minimal or no charge. Said it made people who wanted to ship stuff by air think of him first when the time came. Personally, Kate thought he was just a big softy who fell for every sob story laid on him, and she liked him the better for it.

Larry leaned across the desk and touched the scar on her neck. "Well, then, have I ever told you how sexy that scar is?"

"Nope."

He dropped his voice. "It is. Very sexy."

Nothing.

Larry was nothing if not an optimist. "So, I've got a bottle of Jameson's up to the pad, and I was thinking you might like to come on up and help me put some of it away."

"I don't drink."

The pilot stuffed the rest of the burrito into his mouth and leered around it at Kate. "Well then, maybe give me a back rub. I've got a bad back, and I'm a little sore from holding that damn Herc up in the air all night."

Kate sat back and looked at him, really for the first time since they had been introduced. He was as wide as he was short, with thick brown curls, velvety brown eyes and what he was sure was an invincible way with women, a delusion common to many men of the air.

"Listen to me carefully, Larry," she said. "I would rather spend the rest of my life at a monster truck rally."

He grinned. It was, in fact, a rather charming, slightly lopsided grin that wrinkled the corners of his eyes into engaging creases and displayed an alarming number of very white teeth. "Well then, why don't we just adjourn to your bunk and fuck?"

It didn't catch her on the raw the way it had the first ten times he'd said it, but neither did she feel any desire to deal with him as gently as she had Yuri. "Tell me something, Larry."

It was a variation on her usual response and he had to hide his surprise. "Anything." Anything that will get you into the sack with me, was what he wasn't saying but what they both knew he meant. Alaskan summers were long of day and long of duration, and wearing on a transient worker with all the normal hormones. It made for brief, passionate and highly unlikely couplings that went south with the birds.

Kate leaned forward and said earnestly, as if she really needed to know, "You know why men don't suck their own cocks?"

His jaw dropped.

"Because they *can't*."

She leaned back and watched without interest as his face flushed a dark and unbecoming red. He backed up a step, caught his heel on the coffee table and went sprawling on the couch.

Kate knew a momentary flash of gratitude to that crusty old RPetCo communications operator from whom she had first heard that joke, back when she worked that dope case on the Slope, back when she'd been spending every other week in Anchorage with—she stopped that line of thought with an efficiency all the more ruthless after ten months' practice.

The pilot's mouth opened but whatever he was about to say was interrupted by a bray of laughter. They turned to see Baird standing in the doorway, clad in his usual uniform of bib overalls and black rubber boots.

"Give it up, Maciarello," he said to the pilot, still laughing. "You're outclassed, outmanned and outgunned. She ain't interested. I oughtta know." He gave Kate a friendly leer that somehow was not nearly as smarmy or as offensive as Larry's.

She handed him the clipboard. "North Star has another shipment of smoke fish going out this afternoon, and Frank

Malone just lost the engine on his Cub. He wants to know if you can overnight it into Merrill instead of International. He's got a mechanic standing by there."

Baird grunted, skimming through the pages attached to the clipboard. "This ain't a goddamn on-the-ground freight service, it's a in-the-air freight service. We'll land where we got a load to deliver." The crotchets of his reply were immediately nullified when he added, "See if North Star minds picking up their fish at Merrill." Kate nodded. "Anything else?"

"American Seafoods has a new lidder in Anchorage waiting for a plane, while they've got fish rotting in the hold here and they're having to turn away more because they can't get room on a commercial flight today. Alaska Airlines has no cargo space available for something of this size until Thursday. American Seafoods wants to know if the Herc's available."

Baird grinned. Unlike Larry's, his was downright nasty. "I heart Alaska Airlines. Tell Carl his lidder's got a ride if he's got the price."

"Okay." Kate picked up the phone and made the call.

Baird waited. "That it?"

"Yeah."

He reached his hand inside his bib and scratched. "Hell, you might as well knock off then. Take an extra hour. Get that big bastard out of bed and on the job by noon, though."

Larry Maciarello had been loitering in carefully disinterested fashion near the door. His head whipped around. "You got a guy here?"

Kate said coolly, "We all do. New ground crew, name of Jim Churchill. He'll be working noons to midnights." She nodded at Baird. "See you at midnight."

He winked broadly, and gave the pilot a meaningful nudge that nearly knocked him over. "Sweet dreams."

But Jim's bunk was still empty. There was no sign that he'd been there since he had left it originally. She looked at her watch. Almost eleven o'clock.

This was Chopper Jim they were talking about, the man who rumor said had had more women than Warren Beatty. By repute, Jim Chopin was constitutionally incapable of going without nookie for longer than twenty-four hours; he'd probably hit the bars this morning and gone home with the first reasonably attractive woman who would allow herself to be seduced by those come-hither blue eyes.

Only there weren't any bars in Bering. Bering was a damp town; you could have booze in your house for personal consumption, but you couldn't sell it in quantity, and you certainly couldn't sell it in a bar or buy it in a liquor store.

Where else would Jim go to pick up women? Kate knew herself to be momentarily at a loss. Considering she'd known him for, what, ten, twelve years now? she knew very little about the man. Did he read? What kind of music did he like? She knew him, trusted him, even secretly admired him, professionally. Personally was a whole different ball game.

He'd kissed her once, a couple of years back, when he'd dropped out of the sky into her front yard in his Bell Jet Ranger to warn her about a mass murderer on the loose in the Park. He'd made his interest obvious to her, to everyone, in fact. Even to Jack. Especially Jack, last summer on Alaganik Bay.

Next to her Mutt gave a soft whine. She had to blink to see the big yellow eyes fixed on her face. "It's okay, girl," she said, and had to clear her throat. She fought back the tears, fought back the pain, fought back the memories, and concentrated on what she did know about First Sergeant Jim Chopin, other than the known facts that he was a first-class law enforcement officer and a notorious lecher. The second fact could explain why he hadn't called in his location, but the first negated the second. Undercover, even under the covers, he would have called in. Kate didn't stop to wonder why she knew that.

She had relieved Jim at work. The last she'd seen of him was when he'd pushed her out the door at midnight. She took a longer, more careful look at the bunkhouse.

Jim's duffel was open. She hesitated only a moment before tossing it. His badge and gun, with two spare clips of ammunition, were wrapped in a Banana Wind T-shirt at the bottom.

The T-shirt was the oddest thing about her find. Badge and gun, he'd never leave those behind, whether he was doing a job without benefit of uniform or not. The T-shirt, though. Banana Wind? Jimmy Buffett? Who'd have thought Chopper Jim could get that mellow?

With a faint shock she realized that yesterday was the first time she'd ever seen Jim Chopin out of uniform. He'd been wearing jeans and a long-sleeved blue checked shirt.

It unnerved her. He wasn't Chopper Jim without the official blessing of the blue-and-gold of his service. He wore the uniform the way a beauty queen wore a tiara, as if he were strutting down a runway, all eyes upon him and some Las Vegas crooner in the background about to burst into song. If he wasn't Chopper Jim, how was she supposed to act around him?

She rewrapped badge and gun in the T-shirt and stuffed it back in the duffel. There were dirty clothes in a Carr's plastic garbage bag, so he had showered and changed. The loaf was the lighter by several slices, coffee grounds were spilled on the table. She checked the square plastic tub she'd been using to wash dishes; a saucer, a knife, a mug. He'd had a sandwich, some coffee, so he hadn't gone anywhere to eat.

Or had he? Of course, that was one answer. There were five restaurants in Bering; Jim probably wandered into one and charmed the pants off the first waitress he saw.

Still, he hadn't called in.

She went up to the terminal and showered. She stopped in the office on the way back to the bunkhouse on the pretext of adding to her grocery list. Jim wasn't there. Baird was. He greeted her with a scowl that told her he was well aware that the clock was ticking down. "Where the hell is he?"

"He's still not here?" She stepped through the doorway into the hangar.

Baird followed her. "No, he ain't here, and he's late. Goddamn Job Service." His hand dipped beneath his bib and he scratched, adding in an absent-minded tone, "Fucking state."

It just wasn't her problem. Kate went out the door.

Halfway around the hangar she turned, went back to the office and picked up the phone.

"Who're you calling?"

"The cops."

Baird blinked. "Why, you think he got picked up or something?"

"Hi," she said into the phone. "I'm calling for Baird Air out at the airport. We've got an employee missing, name of Jim Churchill. Caucasian, late thirties, six-two, a hundred seventy-five pounds, dark blond hair, blue eyes, no obvious identifying moles or scars. Ring any bells?"

Baird's eyes narrowed. "You sound like some kind of cop yourself, Sovalik. What the hell's going on here?"

"You watch too much television," she told him. "They've got me on hold." He was about to say something else when she held up a hand. "What?" Her brow creased. "What? When?

Where?" She listened. "Where is he now? Okay, thanks. We'll get right over there."

"Right over where?" Baird said, mystified.

"The hospital." Kate's lips were set in an unsmiling line. "Somebody shot our new employee last night."

The hospital was a prefabricated structure, built in sections in Seattle and shipped north on a freighter to be assembled on the shore of the Kuskokwim River like a gigantic Lego toy. Jim was lying flat on his back in one of the rooms, skin very pale against the white pillow. The nurse, a young Yupik woman with a glint in her eye that said she didn't get patients often and liked to keep the ones she did, whispered, "He's asleep, but he was awake for a few minutes an hour ago. That's a good sign."

"What happened?"

The nurse, identified as Sadie Guy on the nametag pinned to her uniform, was striving to maintain a professional detachment but she couldn't quite hide her excitement. "He was shot," she said impressively.

"They told me that much on the phone," Kate said. "Where, and how bad is it?"

"Oh, well, it's not that bad." Nurse Guy tried not to sound too regretful. "It only creased his scalp, just over his left temple. He's got a new part in his hair." She compressed her lips and shook her head, looking stern. "A fraction of an inch lower, and—well. He'll have a terrible headache for a while, but it doesn't look like there will be permanent damage."

Kate realized that she wouldn't have known who to call if there had been.

Nurse Guy looked at Kate, obviously trying to place her.

"Are you a relative?" Her eyes dropped to the scar on Kate's throat and her eyes widened.

"No." Kate didn't elaborate.

The single word, spoken in her low, rough voice, triggered Jim into consciousness. His eyes opened and focused on Kate's face. "Hey."

"Hey yourself," she said.

Jim's bed tilted dangerously floorward when Mutt placed her forepaws on the side to peer down at him anxiously.

"I really don't think—" the nurse began.

"Hey, gorgeous." Jim's voice was low and caressing, and Nurse Guy shut up.

"Mutt. Down," Kate said, and Mutt dropped back to all fours. Kate scowled at Jim. "You can't wander around goddamn Bering, Alaska, for godsakes, without getting yourself shot? Lucky your head is so hard."

He gave her a drowsy smile. "I like the hair. Did I say? Makes you look sorta like Demi Moore. *Dasvidanya*." His eyes closed again.

"Jim?"

A rustle and a whisper from behind the door made her turn. Three people stood there besides the nurse. One of them wore the uniform of the Alaska State Troopers.

"Who are you?" Kate said.

"Who are you?" the trooper said.

They stared at each other in silence, as reflexes Kate didn't know she still possessed kicked in. "I'm Kathy Sovalik," she replied, lying without compunction before a sworn officer of the court. "I work with him," with a backward jerk of her head. "We're both ground crew with Baird Air. He didn't show up for work at noon, so we called the cops. They said he was here." She paused expectantly. When no reciprocal information was forthcoming, she said, with emphasis, "And you would be...?"

The trooper, a short, wiry woman in her forties, said woodenly, "I'm Trooper Mary Zarr. These people found him dumped in the backyard of a house on the river. The ambulance brought him to the hospital. The hospital called me." Her gaze lingered at the scar on Kate's throat. Unlike the nurse, she wasn't shocked; rather, she seemed to be intent on solving the puzzle Kate's scar had posed for her.

Kate looked, first at the tall, fair woman, then at the short, dark man, both dressed for work on the slime line in yellow bib rainpants, heavy shirts and black rubber boots. "When did you find him?"

The two exchanged a glance, and the shifting of gears was so smooth she almost missed it. The man stepped forward, a broad, admiring smile on his face, his hand outstretched. "Kathy—Sovalik, did you say? Al Gonzalez." His hand enveloped hers in a warm, firm, rather insistent grasp. "Me and my partner here, Maxine Casey, we work the beach gang down at the dock. We knocked off around eight this morning, didn't we, Max?"

"Around eight," she agreed, eyes never leaving Kate's face.

"Yeah, and we were heading back up to the bunkhouse when we stumbled across your friend here."

"Where exactly did you stumble across him?" Kate demanded. Mutt's ears went up, and then back. She stepped to Kate's side without crowding either one of them, ready for action.

Gonzalez looked at Mutt, looked at Kate, and rolled his shoulders as if to work out the kinks, maybe get ready for a little action himself. His Hispanic accent became more pronounced. It would have worked better if it didn't sound as if it had been used before, and to more effect. "Gosh, I don't know, Kathy, we only got in a week ago and we been working nonstop ever since, you know? We don't really know our way around. It was one of those houses between the dock and the bunkhouse, s'all I know."

Kate looked from him to Casey. Casey's blue eyes were cool and steady. "Between the dock and the bunkhouse," she confirmed. "Around a corner and up a street. We were passing a yard, heard a groan, and looked in and saw him lying there. He was just covered in blood." She affected a shudder which did not go well with the appraising expression in her eyes.

"Scalp wounds bleed like faucets," Nurse Guy agreed sympathetically.

"Lucky for him you found him when you did," Kate observed.

Jim roused. "Damn straight, lucky for me. *Spasibo*," he said strongly. He smiled at Kate. "You can ride to my rescue next time," he said, and slid back into sleep.

Nurse Guy bustled forward. "Now, wasn't that nice? We'd better let him sleep it off. Come back tomorrow morning, and we'll see how he's going on."

Kate and Mutt found themselves hustled out of the room. The trooper and the two beach gangers did not immediately follow.

If they were beach gangers. Oh, they had the requisite amount of fish scales per square inch, the proper smell of brine. But Gonzales was clean-shaven, Casey's nails were manicured, and both had haircuts that looked fresh out of a salon. That kind of tidy usually came government issue.

Mutt nudged her knee. Kate heard voices on the other side of the door and moved down the hall. The door to a rest room came up on her right and she shooed Mutt inside just as she heard the door to Jim's room open.

She shot the bolt on the door and leaned against it, listening for the footsteps to pass down the hall on the other side. Mutt looked at her quizzically.

"Who the hell was that woman?" Casey's voice said.

"I don't know," Gonzalez replied.

"You buy her story that they're working together at Baird?"

"Easy enough to check out."

"That scar—" Zarr's voice said thoughtfully.

"Goddamn it, Al, I want a wire on that damn boat."

"They don't have a phone, Max."

"We've seen at least four of them talking on cells. How about a directional receiver?"

An invisible shrug. "The hull's made of plate steel. I doubt anything's going to come through that. And what are we going to do with it, mount it on top of a forklift and park it next to their gangway?"

"I'm going to call Gamble anyway—"

The footsteps and the voices faded. Kate relaxed.

Gamble. That would be Fred Gamble, special agent assigned to the Anchorage office of the Federal Bureau of Investigation. Kate had burgled the office of a prominent Anchorage attorney in company with Fred Gamble two years before. He wasn't a very good burglar. If Jim was working with Fred Gamble, it was no wonder he was flat on his back in a hospital bed.

She caught sight of her reflection in the mirror on the wall. She was not yet comfortable with her shorn head. She missed the weight of the braid on her back.

But she could also remember rough hands using it to pull her around the yard of the hunting lodge, like a dog on a leash.

She braced her hands on the sink and stared at herself.

Who was Demi Moore?

She stood like that for a long time.

CHAPTER 7

keep an open countenance
stand lance-straight

                            —*To a Young Warrior Woman*

BAIRD'S REACTION WAS SIMILAR to hers and completely predictable: "Jesus gawd, he's not even in Bering twenty-four goddamn hours and he gets himself shot in the head? How the hell did that happen?"

"Probably the husband got home early," Kate said.

"I say we ship his butt back to Anchorage and let goddamn Job Service inflict this pain in the ass on some other poor, defenseless business!"

"Works for me," Kate said. "I never wanted you to hire a second roustabout anyway."

Baird eyed her with suspicion. "You sound awful goddamn chipper, Sovalik."

She raised her eyebrows.

"For someone who's going back to a twenty-four hour on, none off shift," he explained, still suspicious.

She gave him a sweet smile that put Mutt's ears straight up. "You must be talking about someone else. I'm not on until midnight." She held a hand up against the resultant sputtering. "Hey, this was all your idea, taking on more help. I just pulled a full shift, and I haven't had any sleep. You cover things for a while. It's not like you haven't done it before. I'm going to go catch some Z's."

Instead, she went into town.

• • •

She walked down the gravel road, dodging taxis—there were almost as many taxis in Bering as there were in Dutch Harbor—and trucks and trying not to choke on the dust they raised. She passed a housing subdivision so painfully new the houses on their lots of naked dirt hurt her eyes to look at them. A little further down the road and on the opposite side was a supermarket, a trailer court and what looked like some kind of state housing, half a dozen small buildings of a similar size with the same brown paint and white trim and, like all buildings in Bering, up on stilts to keep them out of flood's way.

Then there was the hospital, with Jim tucked safely inside, and the state jail, followed in rapid succession by the Delta Branch of the University of Alaska, the local radio and television station and a building housing the local police, the state police and the library. Kate didn't quite understand the juxtaposition of tenants, but then construction materials for projects in Bering had to be freighted in by barge or plane; the first method was expensive enough; the second, as she now knew from firsthand experience, prohibitively so.

Roads began to appear, mostly from the left, as the river was on her right, with private homes interspersed with public businesses. There was a bowling alley next to a cabin that looked as if it had been built by the first Moravian missionary, all decaying logs and mud-and-moss chinking. Fireweed grew from the roof and was beginning to bloom. As Kate passed, a woman came to the door and poured a pan of slops to one side of the front steps, where another clump of fireweed was thriving. An outhouse, in better repair than the main house, stood in back. Tall grass obscured the foundation, and bid fair to cover the first-floor windows as well.

The pattern continued as Kate moved into the heart of downtown, small houses mixed in with large buildings sheltering half a dozen businesses each. One large, two-story building housed the post office, two restaurants and the AC supermarket, a second the armory, the elementary school, Swensen's Variety Store and the Catholic church, a third the Moravian Church, Moravian Bookstore, Moravian Seminary and Moravian Museum, and a fourth the Klondike Cafe, the local newspaper, a branch of Alaska First Bank of Bering and the Mormon church.

A surprising number of the homes were two-story. None of them had yards. All the buildings were on pilings with steps up to the front doors or porches.

There were outhouses everywhere. There was no community sewer in Bering, although there had been some talk of an above-ground flowline system connected to a sewage treatment plant. The sooner the better, as the current nonsystem had the city of Bering acting as a leach field for the city of Bering. Enough to turn the entire state Department of Health a pale, algaeic green, the same color as some of the many shallow lakes that interrupted the city lots and streets in every direction.

It was so typical of the state government's reactive style of administration. Take a bunch of people who had been migratory hunter-gatherers for thousands of years and tell them they had to settle down in villages. They comply, and then the government won't give them schools so their kids have to be sent away from home to receive a high-school diploma. Molly Hootch and eleven hundred other village kids had sued to correct that situation. So now the villages had schools but no sewers, and the legislature wouldn't fund them, either, and probably never would until forced to by a lawsuit.

In the meantime, a cloverleaf was being built at the corner of Minnesota and International in Anchorage, a city of less than three hundred thousand people, at a cost of eighteen-point-two million dollars. Ninety-five percent of that was in federal funds, true, but those funds could have been allocated to something more beneficial to the Alaskan population than another road in Anchorage.

It soothed Kate to focus on the folly of the Alaska state government in their dealings with Bush communities, rather than dwell on the fact that this was the first time she'd been into Bering since she had managed to strongarm Baird into buying her tampons so she didn't have to go in herself. It was the first and only time she'd seen him blush.

She was, well, not comfortable, exactly, at the airport, doing her job at Baird Air. Content wasn't the right word, either. Safe didn't work because she didn't feel safe anywhere anymore. Call it uninvolved, for lack of a better word.

Uninvolved was good. Uninvolved, nonpartisan, uncommitted. The world rolled on but she wasn't part of it. She was one layer removed, insulated from the joys and sorrows and laughter of daily life by her very indifference to it. She wasn't hurting anyone, she kept herself to herself, she was the cat waving his wild tail and walking by his wild lone.

Nobody's seen you for four months! You couldn't have called? You couldn't have dropped somebody a postcard?

The words had been reverberating in her head since Jim

shouted them at her the night before, and for the first time in nearly a year she felt something.

Guilt.

There was almost as much activity in town as there was at the airport; people loading trucks with boxes and bags and case lots of groceries, two marine chandlers doing a roaring business in propellers and engine oil and mending twine, the post office preparing pallets of wet-lock boxes filled with Kuskokwim River reds. Villagers from up and down river, identified by the strong smell of hard smoked king salmon, jostled for space with fish buyers from Seattle decked out in cargo pants and olive green T-shirts from Banana Republic. Fishers in hip boots covered with fish scales formed groups to discuss and embellish their most recent catch. Japanese workers fresh off the processor staggered out of Eagle and AC with bags and bags of beef cut into rib eyes, New York strips, T-bones, filet mignons, tenderloin, pot roasts, rolled roasts, rib roasts. From another door came Koreans loaded with boxes of Camel cigarettes, unfiltered.

The restaurants were full, with lines to get in. The post office was jammed with locals and transients sending red salmon packed in dry ice to friends and family Outside. The fish were up the creeks and people were making money fast and spreading it faster. Busy, bustling, it would have been brawling if there had been any bars; the *ka-ching* of the cash register played a joyous harmony to the melody of commerce in this Kuskokwim River hub.

The source of all this activity was one continuous dock that ran between downtown and the river. The surface was made of two-by-twelve wood planks stained dark with the drippings of engine oil and fish gurry, and edged with twelve-by-twelves which served as mounting blocks for hoists and seats for tourists and a safety lip for the forklift backing up a little too close to the edge. The dock rumbled like thunder as trucks, tractors, forklifts and jitneys passed down the alleys created between canneries and warehouses and shippers and processors, and dust clouds from the gravel roads hung like ephemeral visitors from another world until they were exorcised by the next truck carrying a crew to work or an engine to a boat or a load of fresh frozen fish to the airport.

Kate, Mutt padding at her side, walked the dock slowly, taking it all in, if she but knew it retracing Jim's footsteps of that morning almost exactly. She saw the man and woman from Jim's room unloading a tender full of reds. The fish were averaging about nine pounds, she thought, and Gonzalez and Casey were hustling with the best of them. They both seemed to know their way around a dock. They both had at least ten years on every other member of their crew, too.

Gonzalez saw her and smiled. Casey saw her and frowned. She didn't stop.

One of the processors was pulling away, a boat registered in Seoul, Korea, and when it had cleared the dock and stood out to the middle of the channel, she saw the *Kosygin*, one hundred and twenty-five feet of rusting steel and deserted deck.

Dasvidanya, Jim had said, and then, *spasibo*. Kate didn't know much Russian but she knew enough to say goodbye and thank you, mostly due to Yuri, that sweet Russian man who had given her something to look forward to on those nights that stretched out too long.

She looked down at the stainless-steel watch on her left wrist. A shout came from the head of the gangway, and she looked up to see Yuri himself beaming and waving at her. "Ekaterina! Come up, come up!"

She looked around and thought she saw Casey glaring against the rays of the sun. "Hey, Yuri," she said, and let Mutt precede her up the gangway.

He greeted her with an enthusiastic hug and three kisses on alternating cheeks. Still beaming, he dropped a hand to Mutt's head and scratched vigorously. Mutt, taking her cue from Kate, stood still for it, a resigned expression on her face. She'd met Yuri before, so his advances were marginally acceptable but, like Kate, she never cared much for strangers pawing her.

Yuri stood back, hands on Kate's shoulders, and continued to beam. "Ekaterina! Finally you visit me, instead of me visiting you! I have not seen you down on the dock before this day! What do you do here?"

She shrugged, unobtrusively relieving herself of the weight of his hands. "Thought it was time I took a look around. All work and no play..." She smiled.

He laughed uproariously. "Makes our Kate a dull girl, yes? I remember this American saying! Well, come, come, I will show you our ship, yes?"

"Sure, I'd like to see it." She followed him inside, almost tripping over the raised lip of the hatch. It felt like a long time since she'd been on a boat. But then it felt like a long time since she'd been anywhere but Bering, and done anything except clean, service and load airplanes.

It was dark and cool inside, a relief from the glare of the afternoon sun, and quiet in contrast to the hustle and bustle of the dock. "Not much going on today."

It was in fact very quiet for a working processor, but Yuri shrugged, spreading his hands wide. "We deliver our fish, we deposit our check, we take on supplies, we leave soon. Today, we rest. Come!"

He led the way to the galley, a long room that ran nearly the width of the beam of the ship. It smelled of the deep fat fryer and it was shrouded in a haze of cigarette smoke. Mutt sneezed.

A group of men were gathered around a table that ran the width of the room, which was set with half a dozen bottles of vodka, two brown sausages hacked into uneven slices and several round brown loaves of bread. Yuri stepped to one side as Kate followed him in, bellowing something in Russian and revealing his prize with a flourish of hands. There was a rumble of feet to equal the thunder of the dock boards outside, and Kate was surrounded by a group of young men with admiring eyes. Everybody was talking at once, until Mutt barked, a single, warning sound.

There was a momentary silence, until one of the young men, plump and dark, made a respectful remark. Everybody laughed and Kate was swept forward into a place of honor. Room was made for Mutt at her side, and Yuri put together a plate of bread and salt. He made a little speech and offered the plate with a bow. Kate got back to her feet and accepted it with a return bow, which went down very well.

Kate didn't think any of them were over thirty, and they were all dressed in Western clothes that looked just off the rack at the Gap. Everyone's hair looked as if it had been cut beneath the same bowl Yuri's had been, and to a man they chain-smoked Marlboros. "We are Marlboro men, no?" one of them said, flourishing his cigarette in Kate's face.

"You are Marlboro men, no," she said, trying not to cough. She never could abide the smell of cigarette smoke.

Jack, learning this, had quit the week they met.

Yuri began introductions. There were Sergeis One and Two, Danya, Karol, Fadey, Gregori and Yakov and some others whose names Kate didn't manage to catch. They were very glad to see her and determined to make her feel at home, probably partly because she was the first woman they'd seen to talk to since they had left their's. They nudged each other over her scar, but nobody asked any leading questions, or Yuri didn't translate them.

One man, older than the rest, asked Yuri a question, and looked at Kate with more interest at the response. His eyes were deepset beneath thick brows, his nose was large and fleshy, his mouth a rosebud pout. "You work Baird?" he said. "You—" He said another word, and when she didn't understand, made large, swooping gestures with his hands.

"Oh, am I a pilot," Kate said, and shook her head. "Sorry. No. I am not a pilot."

The man lost interest immediately, retreating to a corner of the room to brood over a bottle.

"Sorry, Ekaterina," Yuri said in her ear, "Ziven thinks everyone who is not pilot is not here." He looked anxious. "You are not offended? You understand?"

Kate thought of some of the pilots she had known, and how there was barely room in the cockpit for them and their egos, and smiled. She ought to introduce Ziven to Larry Maciarello. There was a couple made in heaven. "I understand," she said.

The bread was a little dry, but she rubbed it in the salt and took a bite as they watched anxiously. She smiled. "Good," she said thickly, "thank you." A shout went up and several hands hit her shoulder approvingly. A thick tumbler of vodka was shoved beneath her nose and it required a great deal of tact to refuse it. Disappointed, a Diet Coke appeared in its place, Yuri beaming that he could serve her in kind. She looked up to see Yakov on his feet proposing a toast. He raised his glass to her and tossed it off. Everyone else followed suit, and looked at her expectantly.

"Welcome to Alaska," she said and tossed off her Coke. Mutt sneezed again. There was tremendous applause, and a boombox began to blast the Beatles' *White Album*. Back in the USSR, indeed.

They wanted to know everything about her. How old was she? Was she married? Did she have children? Had she been born in Alaska? Had she lived there all her life? What did she do? Did she have a fiancé? Where in Alaska? Had she been to Disneyland? The Grand Canyon? Tombstone, Arizona? The Rock and Roll Museum in Cleveland? New York? Hollywood? Did she have a boyfriend? Was Mutt a sled dog? Did Kate mush the Iditarod? Did she have any sisters? Had she ever seen Michael Jordan play basketball? Well then, had she ever seen Wayne Gretsky play hockey? Was it true that all black Americans were seven feet tall? Did she have any cousins? Any nieces? Did she know any girls in town who might like to go out with a nice Russian boy?

"Nice Russian boys?" Kate said, peering around. "Where?"

There was another shout of laughter when Yuri translated this and more vodka disappeared. Kate was a little apprehensive but nobody wandered outside to fall overboard or picked a fight with anyone else or made a pass that couldn't be resisted. When Yuri decided to take Kate on a tour of the ship, it was unanimous; the entire crew fell in behind to form an honor guard.

The *Kosygin* was as rusty on the inside as it was on the outside. It wasn't very clean, either, the crew evidently content to allow the next batch of fish to wash away the evidence of the previous batch. The gear looked similar to what could be found on an American processor, only older and some of it in serious need of service. There were storage areas closed off by waterproof hatches, but none of the doors were locked and

Yuri was more than happy to demonstrate the sealing mechanisms for a wide-eyed, admiring Kate. She didn't see anything behind the doors while they were open. The crew quarters were the standard two-man staterooms with the obligatory pinups and piles of dirty clothes. There was a laundry and a kitchen that looked a lot like the ones on board the *Avilda*, a crabber she'd shipped on some years before.

Kate was disappointed. This was a Russian ship, after all. It seemed odd that Russians would wash their clothes in a machine made by GE.

They went back to the galley and began another round of toasts, pledging eternal friendship between Russia and America and undying devotion to Kate. Danya, red-faced and hoarse, embarked on a story that looked hilarious and which Yuri refused to translate. Kate laughed dutifully when everyone else did, which appeared to give them a good opinion of her, although she thought privately that merely by being there and being female she had fulfilled her role in their lives.

She waited for a break in the conversation to offer Yuri her condolences.

His brow wrinkled. "What are these condolences?"

She assumed an apologetic expression. "I'm sorry, I probably shouldn't have brought it up. I saw the body when I came on duty last night." His face changed, and she added, "Alex? Burinin. He was off this boat, wasn't he?"

The sound of his name brought all other conversation to a halt. In the strained silence that followed, she realized how feverish had been the determination to have a good time. These weren't men in the mood for partying, these were men intent on burying recent events in a shroud of alcoholic forgetfulness. "I'm sorry," she repeated insincerely, looking from face to face and finding the same wooden expression repeated there. "I just assumed—he was one of yours, wasn't he? The name was Russian, so…"

Through stiff lips, Yuri said, "It was accident."

"Well, of course," Kate said soothingly. "What happened?"

"He falls," Yuri said.

"Yes," Sergei One said. "He fall."

"And break his head," Sergei Two said.

"Where did he fall from?" Kate said.

"From the catwalk," Danya said.

"From the bow," Fadey said at the same time.

"Over the side, and he hits his head on the dock," Yakov said firmly. "He never was much of a seaman."

"He hated the sea," Karol said, nodding his head vigorously. "Not like us."

"Have some more sausage," Yuri said to Kate, although this time his smile did not reach his eyes.

After that, the mood changed from welcoming to wary. Kate was beginning to think it was time to make her good-byes when the door to the galley opened.

Gradually laughter died all over the room. Yuri looked over his shoulder and leaped to his feet. "Sir!"

Everyone else followed, including Kate. She turned and beheld three men. The first was older, shorter and heavier, with a clean-shaven jaw, neat dark hair and shoulders held with military precision. She'd met soldiers before, and this man was one or had been one very recently. The second man was younger, taller and slimmer, and the third fell somewhere in between.

All three of them were looking at Kate.

Yuri, stammering a little, said, "Kathy, this is our captain. Captain Malenkov, this is Ekaterina Sovalik. She works for Mr. Jacob Baird at Baird Air, who ships our trinkets to

Anchorage for us. Ekaterina, this is Captain Malenkov." He added, lamely, "We didn't expect you back so early."

"I can see that," the third, intermediate man said in faultless English. "It is very nice to meet you, Miss Sovalik, but it is perhaps time for you to return to shore, yes?"

"Yes," Kate said baldly. There was a threat behind the words that underlined just how alone she was on this rust bucket. Mutt, on her feet, eyes narrow and ears up, felt it, too, and Kate needed to get her ashore before she decided to take on the entire crew.

She turned to Yuri and shook a hand that was suddenly clammy to the touch, gave a general wave to the rest of the crew, and started for the door. The captain stepped back and so did the military man, but the younger man did not. She looked up to excuse herself and the words died on her lips.

He was the most beautiful man she had ever seen in her life. Blond hair shining like a golden helmet, eyes the color of a dawn sea, a face like an archangel. He was tall and lithe, just wide enough across the shoulders, just narrow enough at the hip, with legs that went on forever. He wore a dark red flannel shirt tucked into a pair of black jeans, and a pair of loafers that gleamed with polish.

Her jaw must have dropped, and it must have been a reaction he was used to, because the lines at the corners of his eyes crinkled. He took one of the hands lying limply at her side, raised it to his lips and met her eyes over the top of it. "How do you do, Ekaterina Sovalik," he murmured, and his voice was deep and low and very intimate—they could have been the only two people in the room. "It is very nice to meet you."

She swallowed and stammered for what was probably the first time in her life. "Th—thank you, Mr.—?"

"Nikolai Kamyanka. But please, call me Nick."

"Uh—er—of course," she said. "Nick. I'm Kate—Kathy, I mean," thereby nearly blowing her cover, another first.

The smile deepened. He glanced down. "Your dog doesn't seem to like me."

Kate looked down to see Mutt eying Kate's hand, still clasped in Nick's, a low, steady growl issuing from her throat. "Mutt," Kate said. "Bad girl. Stop that."

Her voice sounded weak and unassertive even to her own ears. She looked up at Nick and was instantly snared again by that blue gaze. She knew an absurd concern about her hair; did it look all right? Had she dribbled Diet Coke down the front of her T-shirt?

Captain Malenkov cleared his throat in a meaningful way, and color rushed up into her face and the spell broke. She tugged her hand free, not without difficulty, and said, "Yes. Well. It was very nice meeting you all." She turned to see a sullen expression on Yuri's face. "Thank you for the party and the tour, Yuri, Fadey, all of you."

She turned and, prudently avoiding catching Nick's eyes again, stepped around both men and through the hatch, catching her toe on the raised lip for the second time and almost but not quite falling on her face. She didn't breathe again until she was safely down the gangway and back on the dock. She tried very hard not to look back as she walked away. She couldn't resist, though. She turned, and there he was outside the bridge on the catwalk, leaning on the railing, watching her walk away with that clear steady gaze.

She found the nearest corner and went around it, only to slump against the wall and take a deep breath and blow it out again. "Whew."

A forklift putted up and stopped. "What were you doing on board that processor?"

Kate looked up to see Casey scowling down at her. "None of your damn business," she said. "Come on, girl," she said to Mutt.

Mutt lifted her lip at Casey, and they left. Casey watched the two of them walk away until they were out of sight. They moved together with the unconscious assurance of a long-time relationship, the way she'd seen some human partners move on the job, secure in the knowledge that competent backup was instantly available should it be required. The fangs on that hound had to be two inches long. Casey decided she'd rather face down a perp high on angel dust holding a nine-millimeter Smith & Wesson than that hound when she was pissed off.

From behind her Gonzalez said, "What'd she say?"

"Nothing."

"Think she's in on it?"

Casey chose to answer this obliquely. "Chopin seems to know her."

"Yeah."

"According to Zarr, one of the crew off that boat goes up to see her at the hangar every time he's in port."

"Yeah."

"Could be a connection. Handy to have a friend working at an airfreight outfit. Especially when you've got something to ship. So far, Zarr says, it's been boxes of trinkets, toys, pictures, jewelry, like that. Tourist stuff."

"So far."

"Yeah. So far. Probably should keep an eye on her," Casey said, as if the idea was new to her. In fact Casey and Gonzalez intended to keep a very, very close eye indeed on the trooper's friend.

"Might be a good idea." Gonzalez got around to what they were both thinking. "Did you see the guy?"

"Which one?"

"Smartass. You think it's him?"

"Two bodies in forty-eight hours?" Casey smiled, a thin, cold smile. "Oh, yeah. I think it's him."

"Chopin's not dead."

"A mistake. A bad one. There will probably be another body shortly, in payment thereof, if he's running true to form, and why not. It's him, all right. He matches all the descriptions."

Gonzalez held up a cautionary hand, and wasn't surprised to see that it was shaking a little. "We'll need to be sure."

The smile vanished. "Yes. Better call Gamble."

Kamyanka watched the woman go around the corner, and heard someone come up to stand at his shoulder. "My apologies," Captain Malenkov said. "The men are idiots."

"Yes."

"They actually took her on a tour of the boat. Do you think she saw anything?"

"There is nothing for her to see." Kamyanka turned and smiled, although this smile was nothing like the one he had given Kate. "Besides, she will be able to remember only me when she thinks of her visit here today."

"How much longer must we wait?"

Glukhov came out from the bridge. "Until Monday, Captain. Our business will be done then."

"It's a long time to stay in port at this time of year," Malenkov said. "Especially when we have lost a crewman, which will cause the authorities to look at us more closely."

"Break something," Kamyanka said.

"What?"

"Break something. On the engine. Something that will take two days to fix."

Malenkov's brow cleared. "Yes. That will help." He looked at Kamyanka again. "No longer, though. I cannot risk the authorities looking too closely at the *Kosygin*."

"Two days," Kamyanka said. He looked at Glukhov. "We will be done then. One way or the other."

Glukhov smiled, and wiped surreptitiously at the sweat beading his temples.

The bank was as busy as anywhere else in Bering this afternoon of the second of July, and Kate gave up her place in line several times to get the teller she wanted. No one argued, as it was four-thirty and everyone wanted their check on deposit before closing time. Banks didn't used to be open on Saturdays at all, but if they had tried to close this one down there would have been a riot. There were five tellers and a sixth window, closed until the bank manager, a pudgy, genial man in his fifties, left his desk and opened it to accommodate the crowd of customers.

There were approving noises all up and down the line, which now doubled back on itself twice and pretty much filled up the lobby. "About time," someone said, and someone else said, "That Sullivan, always happy to take your money."

The manager heard both comments and looked up with a grin. "You bet I am, Dempsey. Hand it over." He removed the NEXT TELLER, PLEASE sign and opened for business.

Kate's teller became free and Kate moved up to the counter. "How may I—" She looked up. "Hey! Kate! Kate Shu—"

Before she could call Kate by name Kate held up a hand, forestalling her. Keeping her voice low, she said, "Hey, Alice."

"I didn't know you were in town!" The teller's voice dropped instinctively to match Kate's own.

"Here I am," Kate said, trying to smile. She seemed to have

150

lost all social skills, not that she'd ever had that many in the first place, so she said baldly, "I need to talk to you about something. Ask a favor, maybe."

"Oh? Sure, whatever, but—" Alice looked at the line. "Can you maybe wait until closing time?"

"Sure."

Alice brightened. "Good, great. Grab a seat over there in front of the manager's desk. We close in half an hour, but we have to take care of the people in line first."

"Not a problem." She began to turn away, paused. "Alice?"

"Yes?"

"Is there a pay phone around here somewhere?"

"Sure, there's one on the wall outside."

"Thanks."

"May I help the next customer, please?" Alice said, raising her voice.

Kate walked out the door and found the phone. It was unoccupied. She stared at it from a distance of ten feet, thinking.

Telephones wired into individual homes had still not made it into Niniltna, but the snake had slithered into the garden by way of the cell phone. Everybody had one now; George Perry, Bernie Koslowski, Auntie Vi, Billy Mike. His son, Dandy, had been first to sign up for a cell phone, and given his overactive social life it could be argued that he stood in more need of one than anyone else in the Park, but even Bobby and Dinah had one—Bobby, for god's sake, who was a ham radio operator and pirated his own radio station every night, who was more in touch with the outside world than any ten Park rats Kate knew.

"You gonna stare at that thing all day or you gonna make a call?"

151

Kate jumped and looked around to see a whiskery fisher with red-veined eyes standing next to her. "Oh. Sorry. I didn't know you were standing there."

"So you gonna make a call?"

"You go first," she said cravenly.

He shrugged and walked forward to insert a quarter and dial a number. "Hi honey, it's me. I'm on my way. You want anything from the store?"

If she called Auntie Vi, she might get tears. If she called Bernie, the whole bar would be in on it. If she called George, he would insist on knowing where she was, which meant so would everyone else.

If she called Bobby, it was entirely possible her eardrums would not survive the experience.

The fisher hung up and looked at her. "Tough one, huh?"

She nodded.

He smiled, and his broad, tired face was suddenly lit from behind with a disinterested kindness. "Just call and get it over with," he advised. "It's never as bad as you think it's going to be."

He walked away with a friendly wave.

She swallowed hard and fished a quarter from her pocket. Bobby picked up on the first ring. "Yeah?"

At the sound of his impatient voice barking out that single syllable, unaccustomed tears sprang to her eyes. She blinked them back.

"Who the hell is this?" Bobby said.

She tried to say hello, failed.

But he knew. "Kate?" His voice sharpened. "Kate, is that you?"

Kate heard Dinah's voice in the background. "Is it Kate? Bobby, is it Kate?"

"Shut up, woman, I'm trying to listen here! Kate, is that you? Goddamn you, answer me!"

"It's me," she whispered finally.

"It's about goddamn time!" he shouted so loudly that she winced and held the receiver away from her ear. "Where the hell are you? Are you all right? Say something, goddamn it!"

"I will if you'll shut up," she said, gaining voice.

"Where the hell have you been? We've all been scared shitless! You couldn't pick up the phone before this, you couldn't have set some minds at rest? Dinah's been worried sick! I swear I'll kill you when you get back, Shugak!"

"Now there's a great incentive for me to get on the next plane," she said wryly, and surprised herself.

"Yeah, whatever, just get your ass back so I can start. It's gonna be long, Shugak, and it's gonna be painful, and I plan on just purely enjoying the hell out of myself! Now when the hell are you coming home?"

"Not yet, Bobby," she said.

"When, goddamn it? Give me a time, a day! Tomorrow? Next week? Next month? It's your ass all over again if it's next year! When?"

"Sometime," she said, unable to say anything else. "I just called to let you know I'm all right. I am, Bobby. Honest. Tell Auntie Vi, okay?"

"Kate!"

"And George, and Old Sam, and Bernie. Tell them all I'm okay. I've got a job, a place to stay. Tell Auntie Vi I'm eating. I'm okay," she repeated, clinging to the belief that it was so.

"Kate, don't—"

"I've got to go."

"Don't hang up, goddamn you, Shugak, don't—"

She replaced the receiver and leaned her head against it for a moment, eyes closed. The anxiety and the concern in his voice nearly undid her. She was finding it hard to breathe, and almost regretted making the call. She heard again the distress underlying Bobby's bellow, and could not. Jim had been right, she should have called before now.

The thought of Jim lying in a hospital bed down the street steadied her, gave her back her sense of purpose and helped her regain her composure. She went back inside the bank, found a seat and read a six-month-old issue of *Money* magazine while the line grew shorter. *Money* told her to cut up all her credit cards. *Money* told her to start moving her stock portfolio from foreign to domestic holdings, warned against overinvesting in Internet stocks, and suggested some companies she might consider. *Money* told her to start a SEP, a self-employment retirement plan, something every self-employed person should have. Kate wondered if the two thousand and change left over from last year's fishing season was still in the Darigold one-pound butter can on the kitchen table of her cabin. Her Baird Air paychecks were accumulating in a stained manila envelope in a daypack under her bunk out at the airport. She probably should have brought them in and opened an account in Alice's bank. She was sure *Money* magazine would have said so.

Promptly at five the manager locked the door to forestall any new customers, and by ten minutes after five he was escorting the last customers outside. He spotted Kate just as he was locking the door again. "Oh, I didn't see you there." His eye ran over her appreciatively. "Mike Sullivan. I'm the manager."

"I know, I heard. I'm a friend of Alice's," Kate said, avoiding giving her own name.

"I'll be right there, I've just got to balance my till," Alice called.

"Not a problem," Sullivan said. He smiled at Kate. "Alice is our head teller. Very capable and reliable employee."

Kate nodded without replying, and after a moment Sullivan, disappointed at his inability to start up a conversation, went away.

She wasn't surprised to hear that Alice was a reliable employee. When they had attended the University of Alaska Fairbanks together, Alice had never been late for class, always had her homework done on time, always had her term papers finished by the due date, was always prepped and ready for every test. She should have been cordially hated by every classmate she had, but she wasn't. She was too nice for that.

She was a zaftig little brunette, even shorter than Kate, with a merry smile that nearly made her dark button eyes disappear in the round folds of her face, and a headlong manner of speech that made listeners want to breathe for her. She'd been trailed by a line of men that reached across campus from her first day there. She was merciless in dissecting their faults, and Kate remembered more than one night when the women of fourth-floor Lathrop dorm had gathered together to trash their latest boyfriends. Alice always had something to contribute, but it was always delivered with such rueful amusement and self-deprecation that even the men themselves, had they been present, could not have taken exception. Or not very much. Alice never hurt anyone's feelings if she could help it, not on purpose, not even in absentia.

There was a knock on the door and Kate looked around to see a man standing outside, nose pressed up against the glass and a hand shading his eyes.

"Chris!" Sullivan said, sounding pleased, and went to the door to let him in. "I heard you were coming to give the Fourth of July speech. Great to see you!"

"How are you, Mike?" Chris said, clasping Sullivan's hand and grinning. It was was a wide grin, practiced, polished and produced for effect. It looked familiar to Kate, but she couldn't place it or him. He wore a dark suit over a white shirt, and a bolo tie with a big ivory walrus nestled between the points of his collar.

Mike murmured something, and the other man laughed and slapped him on the back. "Nothing to worry about, everything's under control. We'll be meeting with them in the next day or so. As soon as I get the confirmation from Dillon."

"Good to know." The bank manager looked over his shoulder. "Alice, would you close up for me?"

She flashed her bright smile. "Sure, Mike, not a problem."

The two men went out. Kate waited as the rest of the tellers rectified their tills and departed and Alice went around checking the locks. "Let's take a minute," she said, plumping down in the chair across from Kate. "It's great to see you. How long has it been? What are you doing in town?"

One great thing about Alice—she never read the newspapers, and the local news on Bering's only television station was erratic at best. The story had been eclipsed by one of the spasms over presidential misbehavior growing ever more common to the national media, and had never been broadcast nationally, which meant Alice could not have seen it on CNN, either. She would therefore probably know nothing about the events of the previous fall. Current affairs were not Alice's forte.

Kate could feel herself relaxing, and they spent ten minutes playing catch-up and do-you-remember before she got around to answering Alice's last question. "I'm working out at the airport for Baird Air. Ground service."

Alice frowned. "I'm surprised I didn't hear before. You've been here for a while?"

"Since March."

Alice was hurt. "Why didn't you come see me before?"

Kate had known that question was coming since she had decided to contact Alice and she had no better answer for it now.

Into the silence, Alice said, "Didn't you know I was here?"

Kate thought of lying and discarded the idea. "Yeah, the one time I had to come into town for supplies, I saw you working in the bank."

"Why didn't you say hi? My folks would love to meet you. I told my mom all about Kate Shugak from Niniltna who almost flunked out first semester and then graduated with honors. She was impressed."

"Actually," Kate said, "I'm working under another name."

Alice puzzled. "You aren't here as Kate Shugak?"

"No."

Alice's eyes widened. "Oh wow, Kate! I heard a rumor you'd gone into business for yourself! Are you still being like a, what, a private eye? A detective?" She gave a little wriggle of pure pleasure. All was forgiven. "Are you, what do they call it? Undercover?" She sat forward on the edge of her seat, eyes wide and fixed on Kate's face, determined not to miss a word.

Kate cursed inwardly. "Well, I guess you could say—"

"Because I think that is soooo cool! Just like Sharon McCone!" Alice looked at her worshipfully. "What's going on? Who is the bad guy? Is it Jacob Baird? Although he's been around forever, it'd be kind of hard to imagine him being a bad guy, even if he ought to be arrested for the rates he charges. Even if he did bring Auntie Sylvia's dog down to the vet that time for free. Are you working with the police? The state? Oh wow, Washington? Do you—"

Kate held up a hand to stem the flow. "Slow it down, Alice." Alice lapsed into a hopeful silence. "I was wondering if you could help me with something."

Alice lit up. "You mean like with your investigation? You bet! Anything! What?"

"I need some information from the bank."

"My bank?"

"Yes."

Alice blinked. "Sure!" she said, a smile spreading across her face.

"Don't," Kate said. "Think about it first. I don't have a warrant, this is strictly a personal favor. It's private information. If you get caught, you could get fired. You could even be prosecuted."

Alice tossed her hair, a short, shiny bob parted on one side that cupped her chin in two curved black wings. "Hah. They couldn't run this place without me. What do you need?"

Kate hesitated, nerving herself.

For nearly a year Kate Shugak had been adrift in an unfamiliar world, with obscure landmarks and unknown beacons, her safe harbor a horizon away. The scar on her arm itched and she rubbed it. Mutt watched her through the glass door from her seat on the porch outside.

Bobby Clark threw a party every year for those Park rats who were Vietnam vets; she remembered hearing them talk about being "back in the world." "When I was back in the world," they'd say, as if the Nam was not and had never been part of the world, of the real world, of their real world which was defined by snow, not jungle rain, eating moose, not dog, and love with a woman you didn't have to pay to pretend to care.

Back in the world.

She wasn't sure she was ready to be back in the world, but Jim Chopin was laid out in a hospital bed, unable to do for himself, and the least she could do was make a stab at finding out why someone had put him there.

'The least she could do.'

Sounded better than 'back in the world.'

She took another breath and then did it, took that step over the line to move from passive observer to active participant.

She met Alice's eyes and said firmly, "I need to see the account records of every fish processor who's got one with your bank, for the past three or four months. Since the fishing season began, anyway."

She paused. "Especially the foreign ones," she added, and couldn't decide if the distant tumult resounding in her ears was the crowd roaring approval or herself, running scared.

CHAPTER 8

make her fearless like you
do not let her forget us

—Brother Wolverine

ALICE INVITED KATE HOME to dinner and Kate could not refuse
without giving offense, not that that had ever stopped her
before, but the phone call to Bobby had softened something
inside her. Weakened her defenses, maybe, but nevertheless
she followed Alice to the post office, where Alice checked
three different post office boxes—"Gramp's, Mom's and
mine"—and then to one of the grocery stores, where she
bought a head of leaf lettuce for $1.99, a bunch of radishes
for a dollar, and three bunches of green onions for $2.40,
almost exactly twice what they would cost in Anchorage,
about the same as they would cost in Niniltna. "What do you
drink?"

"I don't drink," Kate said.

"Not booze, you can't buy any here anyway," Alice said.
"Pop? Kool-Aid? Lemonade?"

"Lemonade sounds good," Kate admitted, suddenly feeling
dusty.

Alice paused with one hand on the cooler door. "Didn't
you used to drink Diet 7UP?"

"Yeah, got too sweet for me."

"How about Mutt?"

"She doesn't drink Diet 7UP anymore, either." Alice grinned, and Kate added, "She drinks water and there's already plenty of that around."

Alice giggled. It was an attractive giggle, joyous and dimpled. It hadn't changed much in thirteen-plus years, and suddenly Kate was very glad that Alice still lived in Bering. "Did you come home right after graduation?" she said outside the store as Mutt fell in between them.

Alice shook her head. "No, I moved to Anchorage, just like you. I used to read about you in the papers sometimes." She gave Kate a sideways glance. "It must have been a hard job."

The scar on Kate's throat itched. "Yeah."

"But I was always glad you were doing it. Somebody has to look out for the kids who have fallen through the cracks."

"Yes," Kate said.

"Anyway, I went to work for the state in the attorney-general's office—had to do something with that degree. I had a good time, but…"

"But?"

"It's a big town, Anchorage. Some people say it's Alaska's biggest Native village, you know, because there's more of us there than anywhere else."

"That's what they say."

"I missed Bering. I missed my family." She gave Kate another sideways look. "And then there was this guy…"

"I knew there had to be a guy in it somewhere."

Alice laughed. "Yes, you did, or you ought to have. His name was Paul. He was fresh out of school with a degree in marine biology, and he was so in love with me he couldn't see straight."

"Nothing wrong with that."

"No, except he was in love with the Bush more."

"Oh."

"Yeah. So I brought him home for Christmas in 1986. Mom liked him, and so did Gramps. The whole family did. He got a job with the state counting fish upriver, and we got married. I have a daughter," she added proudly.

"No kidding? How old?"

"Ten."

"What's her name?"

"Stephanie."

"Pretty name."

"Yeah, and she's really smart." Alice's proud smile dimmed a little. "I think she's going to want to go as soon as she can."

"Where? To school?"

"School, Outside, you name it. I don't think she's staying in Bering for much longer than it takes to graduate from high school."

"How about Paul?"

"Paul is long gone," Alice said with a wry twist to her mouth. "He did a study on the crash of marine life in the North Pacific, went totally tree-hugger on us and got a job with Greenpeace. Last I heard he was tying himself to a bridge in Seattle." A pause. "I was angry at first, but now I don't know. He's a believer, you know? Totally, passionately, completely. Must be where Stephanie gets it."

"Hey. Alice."

A man stepped into their path. He was short and dark, with intense black eyes and a sullen frown. He was weaving slightly on his feet, and Kate could smell the liquor on him from six feet away.

"Charlie," Alice said without enthusiasm.

"I wanna talk to you." Charlie spoke with the slurred diction and the peculiar emphasis of chronic drunks, I wanna

TALK to you, as if the forceful stress of one word above all others would draw attention and compel obedience. It achieved only the former.

"I told you, Charlie, it's over."

"I LOVE you, Alice. I can't live WITHOUT you." His sullen expression dissolved and he began to weep. "Why won't you TALK to me? I LOVE you. I know you love ME. Please TALK to me, please."

"I said I was sorry. Please, just leave me alone."

"Is it the booze? Because I can quit, anyTIME. Just come BACK to me."

"No, Charlie."

"Bitch." They stepped around him and walked past. "Bitch, bitch, GODdamn bitch. Think you're so great. Think you're BETTER than everybody else! Well you've got another THINK coming to you! I'LL show you!"

They walked on, Alice's head and color high, ignoring the curious or impatient glances cast their way.

"Bitch! I ought to—I ought to—you'll come back! You'll come back, and I won't BE here! THEN what'll you do!"

"Who was that?" Kate asked in a low voice.

"A mistake," Alice said briefly, and Kate said no more.

The Chevak family lived in one of the homes in the Tundra Subdivision northwest of town, by the side of a long gravel road that looked exactly like every other gravel road in Bering, laid down over reeds and brush and alder and avoiding the requisite number of ponds and lakes. "How do you find your way around this place?" Kate said when they reached the doorstep. "Mutt, stay."

"Oh, she can come in," Alice said cheerfully, and opened the door. "Mom? Gramps? Stephanie? I'm home, and I brought a friend!" She kicked off her shoes and Kate followed suit. "What do you mean, how do I find my way around?"

"There's nothing to tell where you are around here. It's just flat, no hills or mountains."

"There's always the river," Alice pointed out.

Kate was unconvinced. "I remember you used to talk about the river at school, it was almost like a person to you."

"It is. She is."

"She? The river's a she?"

"Oh you bet, about as contrary and cranky a she as you'd ever want to meet. Mom? Steph? Gramps?" She walked over to the wall and pointed. "We keep this one wall unpainted to remind us."

"To remind you of what?"

Alice pointed at a series of horizontal stains, one above the other. "High-water marks. This one is from 1979, this one is from 1983—" she pointed to a mark above her head"—and this one is from the Great Flood of 1994."

Kate remembered reading about the chronic flooding beneath which Bering labored five springs out of six. Baird had referred to it as flood season, without animosity, simply a fact of life in Bering. "It's why most everybody tries to have two floors," she remembered him saying now. "At least they can move their furniture upstairs while the downstairs dries out." He'd displayed marks similar to the ones Alice was pointing to now, left behind by various floods on the wall of the hangar, not without a certain perverse pride. You think you can survive in Alaska? Try spring in Bering.

"It's backed up ice that causes the flooding, right?"

Alice looked at her quizzically. "You're kidding. Aren't you? Doesn't the Kanuyaq ever flood? Isn't Niniltna ever under water?"

Kate thought of the tiny village on the banks of the eight-hundred-mile-long river that led to Prince William Sound and the Gulf of Alaska. "No," she said, too abruptly, and tried to cover it with a weak smile. "Not that I remember. We're farther south than you, maybe we don't freeze up as hard."

"Huh. Well, Bering does flood, big time, on average once every ten years. There are little ones in between, too. And yeah, it's ice that causes it. The river freezes over every winter, and come spring and breakup, the ice jams and the water backs up in back of it, and over the banks it comes. And the villages flood."

Kate looked at the line above Alice's head. "Must be awful."

Alice smiled. "It's kind of fun, actually. Everybody moves upstairs, and you have to use a rowboat to get to school and church and the grocery store. It is a mess cleaning up the mud afterward, though."

Kate looked at the marks again, two of which were over her head. "I'll bet."

There was the creak of footsteps from the floor above and an old man appeared on the stairs. "Hi, Gramps," Alice said, bustling forward. "Are you hungry? Where's Mom? She said she'd cook if I made the salad."

"She went to get a salmon from your uncle." He peered past his granddaughter. "And who is this?"

"This is a friend from school. Kate, this is my grandfather, Ray Chevak. Kate Shugak, this is my grandfather, Ray."

There was a sudden stillness about the old man. "Kate Shugak? Any relation to Ekaterina Shugak?"

"My grandmother, uncle," Kate said.

"Gatcha," the old man said softly. "Ekaterina's granddaughter."

Kate felt his eyes following her all evening. Over the broiled salmon, the boiled salmon eggs, over the salad and the sticky rice, she would look up and he would be watching her. He smiled in all the right places in the conversation and made all the right responses to remarks directed his way, but it was as if he were only half in the room; the most essential, the most vital part of him somewhere else, somewhere he'd rather be. Kate saw Alice glance at him in puzzled fashion from time to time, but she asked no questions to draw attention to his introspection.

Alice was the mirror image of her mother, Dorothy, who was as round and cheerful as her daughter. Alice's daughter, Stephanie, while bearing a close physical resemblance, couldn't be less like her mother or grandmother in personality. They were outgoing and verbal; she was shy and quiet. She wouldn't meet Kate's eyes directly, she didn't seem to look at anyone straight on. She set the table before dinner, she did the dishes and took out the garbage afterward, but she displayed no interest in Kate and very little in the conversation around the table. She ate her dinner with no real enjoyment, as if she was merely taking on fuel. She was waiting, Kate realized, waiting to be dismissed from the family circle so she could take up her own life again, and the more efficiently she completed her chores, the sooner she would be free to do so.

Mutt liked her, though, more than anyone else in the room, and Kate trusted Mutt's instincts as much as and sometimes more than she did her own. Stephanie's room was directly across from the bathroom, and when Kate needed help to figure out how to use the chemical toilet Stephanie came willingly enough to show her.

On impulse Kate followed her into the girl's room, and hit her head on a model of the space shuttle *Discovery* hanging from the ceiling. "Whoa," she said, and put up a hand to steady the model.

The room was a shrine to space transportation and exploration. There were posters of the Mir space station, of the Saturn V rocket launching Apollo Eleven, of all other shuttles including the *Challenger*. There were other models hanging from the ceiling, from a Wright Flyer to an F-16. A table made from an old door laid across two Blazo boxes was covered with nuts and screws and bolts and pieces of electronic equipment and tools and a lot of other parts and pieces Kate didn't recognize, some of them metal, some of them plastic.

There was also the terrific *Star Wars* poster of Anakin Skywalker standing in the sunlight of Tatooine, projecting the shadow of Darth Vader behind him. There were model ships of Naboo, the Imperial Senate, the Rebellion, and one lone starship *Enterprise*.

Kate didn't see any Barbie dolls. "So, my guess is you want to be Miss America and eventually go on to become the weather girl on the *Today Show*."

The joke fell flat. "Or a pilot," Kate said, looking up at the models from real and imagined worlds. "You build all these?"

Stephanie cast a swift look from beneath her lashes, apparently checking to see that the hallway was clear in case she had to make her getaway from this nosy and uninvited guest. "Yes."

"I'm impressed," Kate said, reaching up to touch the fuselage of some kind of jet. "I don't know anything about it, but these look well made. Very authentic. Like the real thing, only in miniature. You're very good."

Stephanie, sitting over an open book, said nothing.

"What are you reading?" Kate said, leaning over her.

The book was open to a diagram that looked like circuitry of some kind. With seeming reluctance, Stephanie held her place with one finger and showed Kate the cover.

"*Beginning Physics*," Kate said.

"You work with the big man."

"I'm sorry?"

"The big man. Jim. He's a pilot. You work with him at the airport."

At something of a loss, Kate said, "Yeah, I do. How did you know that?"

"I saw you."

"Oh." Kate looked up at the model airplanes. "Maybe you take your model planes out past the airport to fly them?"

"Maybe. Is he going to be all right?"

"Who, Jim? Why, yes, I think so. They say so, at the hospital. I didn't—how did you know he'd been hurt?"

Shrug.

There were only five thousand people in Bering. It was impossible to keep anything secret in a small town, always assuming you wanted to in the first place, and there was no reason to hide Jim's assault. Take it as read that Stephanie had met Jim, had heard of his injury through the Bush telegraph and was concerned. Kate wasted a brief moment wondering if there was any age limit on Jim's conquests—she already knew there was no limit on species—and said, "I went up to visit him this afternoon. He woke up and recognized me, and the nurse said that was a good thing."

"Huh," Stephanie said, and reopened her book.

Alice was pouring out after-dinner coffee in the kitchen. "That girl of yours is up there in her room studying beginning physics," Kate said. "It is July, isn't it? School has been out for two months, right?"

"It's what she likes doing."

"Frightening. What did you say she was, ten?"

Alice, trying unsuccessfully to hide her pride, said, "The

teachers say she could go all the way, college, graduate school, a Ph.D."

"What does she say?"

"She soaks it up." Alice looked around to make sure they were alone. They were, but Kate noticed she dropped her voice anyway. "I can't offer her too much encouragement, at least not where anyone can see, you know how it is with us."

"Yeah, I guess," Kate said. "Kind of. How do you mean, exactly?"

Alice put mugs on a tray. "You take milk? Good, so does everybody else." She poured a healthy dose of Carnation Evaporated Milk into the bottom of all the mugs. "It's a Yupik thing, I guess. She has to get good grades to get into college, but the way we do things won't help her."

"Meaning?" Kate found the spoons and a saucer and put them on the tray.

The coffeemaker burped its way to a finish and Alice poured out. "We don't act alone, independently of each other. We're a *tribe*. When we do something well, it doesn't reflect on us personally, it reflects on the tribe as a whole. We're not supposed to be singled out, to be set apart, to be praised for something we do on our own."

"To be individuals?"

"I guess," Alice said, pausing with the tray in her hands to consider. "Yeah."

"Tough on someone like Stephanie, who goes it alone, who excels in the sciences, who has ambition."

"She'll manage," Alice said. "To get what she wants, she'll have to."

But she would leave the village, Kate thought, and unlike her mother, she would very probably never come back. Alice was right about that.

They went out onto the porch, where they found Ray and Dorothy sitting on deck chairs. Dorothy was knitting a sweater. "What is that?" Kate asked. "Is that qiviut?"

Qiviut was the soft hair from the belly of the musk ox, a large, slow, stupid animal with sadly drooping horns and a very thick coat. They had once roamed the northern latitudes of Alaska by the thousands until hunters had killed them all. Reintroduced from Greenland in the 1930s by the University of Alaska, the various herds now numbered over three thousand. The qiviut, the softer hair that came from the belly, fell out naturally, was collected and spun into yarn and distributed among western Alaskan village women to be knit into hats, shawls, tunics and scarves, mostly for sale to tourists in Anchorage because nobody local could afford it.

Dorothy nodded, and waited patiently as Kate fingered the soft stuff and admired the intricate pattern that depended from the needles. Alice passed around coffee and Kate took a seat next to her at the top of the steps. Conversation centered around salmon, the legislature's total lack of ability in coming up with a subsistence plan, salmon, the move to the Chevaks' fish camp upriver to be undertaken in two weeks' time, salmon and the passage of the English-only initiative in the last election and the subsequent lawsuits popping up between Native-speaking villages and the state.

"Your grandmother would have had something to say about the English-only initiative," Ray said with a reminiscent smile.

"Yes, she would," Kate said. "She'd find a way around the bylaws to award Niniltna tribal money to the village of Tuntuliak to help with their suit against the state, and then she'd fly down to Tuntuliak and suggest that every federal and state employee who wanted to do business there hire a Yupik interpreter. And she'd probably tell them what to charge, and it wouldn't be cheap."

"Ay," he sighed, "I remember one time in Juneau this senator from Anchorage made some remark about villagers sucking on the public tit for so long they didn't know how to eat on their own. It was time to wean us, he said. Your grandmother was there."

Kate winced. "Is he still living?"

Ray laughed, his belly shaking. "Ekaterina didn't say anything. I don't think she ever said anything in public. Not to lose her temper, anyway, and she was as close to it that time as I've ever seen."

"What did she do?" Because, of course, Emaa had done something.

"We were talking about it that night in her room, a bunch of us, and she found out he was part-owner of a chain of gift stores in downtown Anchorage, along with some other tourism-related stuff, a bus line, I think, like that. So she got the president of the Alaska Federation of Natives to suggest moving the AFN convention from Anchorage the next year." Ray laughed again. "She didn't have to call him, he called her. The next morning a little before six, woke us both up. I figure it was about two minutes after the newspaper hit his doorstep. She invited him to the next meeting of the Rural Governance Commission."

"What happened?" Kate said, fascinated.

"He went. He didn't change his vote on anything important, as I recall, but he actually showed up and listened. Afterward, he said he had no idea there was such a split between rural and urban Alaska."

"How long had he been in the state?"

"Oh, he was born in Anchorage. He'd only been to the

Bush once, of course, to Barrow with his high-school wrestling team."

Alice collected the mugs and went upstairs to chase Stephanie away from her books and into bed. Dorothy packed up her knitting and said good night. Ray and Kate continued to sit on the porch and watch the sun travel around the sky in that horizontal fashion that seemed odd only to people who live south of the fifty-three. "You knew her well," Kate said. She was only just beginning to realize how well.

Ray cast her a glance that was half wary, half amused. "Very well."

"I didn't know."

He shrugged. "We didn't try to keep it a secret."

Implied was the suggestion that perhaps Kate hadn't cared enough to notice. She wasn't getting a lot of compliments on her attitude lately.

"She talked about you a lot," Ray said.

"She didn't talk about you at all."

He shrugged. "It was not her way, to talk of private things."

"I suppose not."

Kate was glad she was sitting down.

It had never occurred to her that Ekaterina might have taken a lover. She felt dizzy with the discovery.

Well, and why not? Emaa was a strong and powerful woman, and for some men strength and power were seductive qualities.

But she was old.

She looked at Ray, and Ray looked back at her, the twinkle in his eyes very pronounced.

Evidently not that old.

Kate got to her feet. "It was nice to meet you, uncle."

He held her hand. "It was good to talk of Ekaterina again.

172

When she died—" His voice failed him, and he seemed to look beyond himself, beyond them, seeing something he couldn't share.

"How long did you know her, uncle?"

He took his time coming back. "A long time," he said. "Yes, a very long time."

"Did you ever think of, well, making it permanent?"

Ray sighed. "I asked her. She couldn't leave Niniltna, and I can't live anywhere but Bering."

Kate was silent.

"I don't know what she would have said about this last election."

"I do," Kate said.

"English the official language, no subsistence bill, the state fighting tribal sovereignty. Seems like we're going backwards." He stood up. "That's not why I miss her, though." He looked at Kate. "That's not even the half of it. I miss her laugh most, I think. You couldn't help but laugh with her."

He paused, his eyes uncomfortably piercing. "This thing that happened to you in September."

Kate stiffened. Next to her, Mutt tensed and gave a soft whine. "What thing in September?"

"Don't get smart with me. I might have been your grandfather, if I'd met your grandmother first," he said sternly. "Unlike the rest of my family, I read the papers."

The fight went out of her. "All right, uncle."

"This thing in September," he repeated. "It has hurt you."

She said nothing.

"It could not be otherwise." He paused. "Just don't let it destroy you."

He went inside, and Alice came out. "You're leaving? Shoot, so soon?"

Alice walked her to the gate of the little picket fence surrounding the yard. "Who was the man who came into the bank this afternoon, Alice? That your boss let in after he locked the door?"

"Who? Oh, that was Senator Overmore. Senator Christopher Overmore, Bering's senator in the legislature."

"Oh," Kate said on a note of discovery. "That's why he looked so familiar."

"He's running for the U.S. Senate."

"Yeah, that's right. I forgot."

"Hard to with the nine million posters he's got plastered all over the state. You can't even watch *Frasier* reruns anymore without Chris Overmore butting in on Niles and Daphne." Alice sounded indignant.

"Maybe you should pay attention," Kate suggested.

Alice lifted one shoulder. "Who cares, anymore? Nobody believes anything politicians say. It's not like they're working for us, all they do after they get into office is run for reelection. Money, money, money, that's all it's about. I wouldn't vote for George W. Bush at gunpoint, just because he's made enough money to buy every American citizen's vote ten times over. It's obscene, Kate. And Chris Overmore's just as bad, got his hand out everywhere you turn. Why do you think he came to the bank and got all buddy-buddy with Mike?"

"Why, Alice," Kate said in mock surprise. "I didn't think you cared."

Her brief spurt of temper over, Alice laughed. "Remember, if you don't vote—"

"—you can't complain," Kate finished for her, and they both laughed at this echo of Kate's determination that Alice take an interest in politics when they were in college together.

"About the other thing," Alice said, suddenly serious. "What you asked me to do."

"Yeah," Kate said, uncomfortable. "I don't know, Alice, maybe you better forget it. You could get into real trouble—"

"I want to do it," Alice said. "And you wouldn't ask me to if you didn't have a good reason." She grinned. "My one chance to play Nancy Drew and you want to yank it? No way!" She hesitated. "And, Kate? Thanks for asking."

Kate walked back to the airport at a slow pace, thinking of Alice's unhesitating loyalty to a classmate she hadn't seen in thirteen years, but mostly of Ekaterina and Ray, marveling at his existence in her grandmother's life.

A lover. Emaa had had a lover. Kate shied away from the mental image that conjured up. Sex might not have offended Emaa's sense of dignity but it offended Kate's sense of Emaa's dignity. She didn't know whether to laugh or cry or rage. Emaa had had a lover, a lover serious enough to propose marriage, a lover in love enough to hang on when she refused.

A lover like Jack.

For the first time since his death, Kate thought about what it had meant to have Jack always there. She had been so sure of him, of his affection for her, of his faith in her, of her trust in him. It had never occurred to her that he would cheat on her. He wouldn't, she knew it right down to her bones. He would never endanger her health, he would never betray her trust. How many women could say that about the men they loved, and with such certainty?

The pain she had been suppressing for so long struck suddenly, straight at her gut like a knife, twisting hard and deep. It stopped her in her tracks, the breath going out of her body in a rush. She bent over, arms wrapped around her belly, and gasped for air which suddenly seemed in very short supply. Mutt pressed close, curving her body around to come into as much contact with Kate's as possible.

A truck went by, slowed as if to stop. She straightened up and waved to show that she was all right.

"Probably drunk," a disgusted voice said, and the truck kicked up gravel and dust as it accelerated away from her.

Another time she would have been angry at the assumption. Now, it was all she could do to put one foot in front of the other and move down the road. Mutt paced next to her, glancing up from time to time, never straying far from Kate's side.

It was nine-thirty by the time she arrived at the hangar. Baird looked frayed and irritated. "Did you have a nice day off?"

She looked at him blankly. "What? Oh. Yes. I suppose so."

"You ready to go to work now?"

"Let me grab a couple of hours first. I'm not due on until midnight anyway." She walked out without waiting for a reply, knowing he was fuming behind her and not caring much.

Jim was in the bunkhouse, stretched out on his bunk. He raised his head as she came in.

"What are you doing out of the hospital?" she said, stopping just inside the door.

"I hate hospitals. I checked myself out."

She pulled off her sweatshirt and sat down to take off her shoes. "I met a friend of yours tonight."

"Oh yeah?"

"A girlfriend."

"Who?"

"Name of Stephanie. Stephanie Chevak."

"Who? Steph—oh." A pause. "How did you meet her?"

"I know her mother, Alice. Ran into Alice in town, Alice took me home to dinner, where I met her family."

"Oh."

"Cute kid."

"Yeah."

"Didn't know you went after them that young."

"Knock it off, Shugak."

For the first time in their relationship she'd given him the needle and he didn't have a smart comeback. Kate let her second shoe drop. "What happened to you, Jim?"

He started to shake his head, winced and stopped. "I don't know. I can't remember. The doc said head trauma sometimes results in short-term memory loss."

"Permanent?"

"Don't know yet. All I remember is getting a ride into town. I don't even remember who from."

"Were you robbed?"

He nodded. "My wallet's gone."

"What was in it?"

"No ID, if that's what you mean." He was trying to sound indignant, and failing.

She knew that, she'd found his wallet with badge attached in the bottom of his duffel bag. "Money?"

"A hundred in twenties, maybe. A driver's license in the name of Jim Churchill. A VISA card, same. That's about all."

"You said something in Russian to me at the hospital."

"I did?"

"Yeah. *Dasvidanya*. And *spasibo*. Good-bye and thank you."

"That it?"

"That's it."

"I always did have a big vocabulary."

"What are you doing in Bering, Jim?"

There was a short silence. "I'm on the job, if that's what you mean."

"That's what I mean."

"Then you know I can't tell you about it."

"Yeah, well, study of empirical evidence accumulated to date indicates that that's not going to get you far."

Silence. A long sigh. He rolled to his back and stared at the ceiling.

"There's something going on with the Russians, isn't there? The ones on board the *Kosygin*."

He sat up, too suddenly, and stifled a groan. "Stay away from them, Kate."

"Why? Why should I? What's so dangerous about them?"

He touched the wound over his left eye gingerly. "Damn, this hurts."

"Those were Fibbies in your hospital room this morning, weren't they?"

His hand stilled. "How did you know?"

She snorted. "Who wouldn't? Why are they here?"

"We're working a case."

"To do with the Russians." He still wouldn't say yea or nay to that, but the quality of his silence told her her guess was right. "So what is it they're up to? Smuggling? Smuggling what? Dope? Guns?" She echoed his words of the week before. "And why through Bering, of all places? You'd think they could loose themselves a lot easier in Dutch, given the comparative volume of traffic through both ports."

"What do you care?" he said, lying down again and pulling the sleeping bag up to his chin. "I'm feeling all right now, by the way. In case you care."

"I don't."

"Didn't think so," he said, and closed his eyes. "I'll be okay to take my shift tomorrow."

"Sure you will," she said.

CHAPTER 9

knives flash
blood drips in dust

—Schizophrenia

SURPRISING HERSELF, KATE SLEPT two hours and got up at a quarter to twelve. She dressed quietly, in the dark, careful not to wake Jim, who was snoring loudly, and was on the job on time. Baird eyed her fulminatingly. "I suppose you're gonna want twelve hours off every damn day. I shoulda never hired no second roustabout. Now you're spoiled. I knew you were too good to last."

She ignored him. His big-soled black rubber boots were admirably suited for stamping off in.

Her shift was busy as usual, a load of lumber in from Anchorage on the Herc, a load of sports fishermen from England out on the Cessna, a grocery run into a homestead on the Tuluksak for the Cub, prepping the DC-3 for a charter for the board of the local Native corporation on a fact-finding mission to villages on both sides of the river from Anogok to Big Fritz, and over to lower Cook Inlet as well. This last entailed scrubbing down the inside of the fuselage to rid it of the fishy smell left by the last cargo trip to Anchorage, and reinstalling the seats, although she had to wait for Baird to come in the following morning because that was a two-person job. She was tired when noon rolled around.

Jim appeared at ten till. He'd removed the bandage wrapped around his head, replacing it with a piece of gauze taped above his ear, which gave him a rakish look half *Pirates of the Caribbean*, half refugee from Kosovo. Although a little pale, he declared himself fit for work. Kate showered up at the terminal, fixed a sandwich and some of Jim's coffee, and fell asleep before finishing either.

His head ached dully and continuously, but Jim was too busy to give it much thought. Cal Kemper strolled into the office an hour before the DC-3 was scheduled to take off, just in time to do a walk-around and meet the passengers with whom he'd be spending the better part of the next two weeks. "Little gal I found up to the laundromat just didn't want to turn loose of me," he said, grinning at Jim and Baird. "Can't say as I blame her."

"I thought you were married," Baird said crankily.

Kemper met the remark with an amazed stare. "What's that got to do with anything?"

"Well, you're late, anyway," Baird said. "Goddamn prima donna pilots."

Unflustered by this slur on his character, Cal strolled out again.

Ralph Whitmore, five feet tall when he wore high-heeled boots, which he probably did in and out of bed, brought the Cessna back from dumping off the English fishermen, and was not pleased when he was instructed to take a load of commercial fishermen to Toksook Bay. "Drunk or sober?" he demanded, and swore ripely at the answer. He swept off his Seahawks baseball cap to reveal a head as bald as an egg, rubbed fiercely at his scalp, and yanked the cap on again, all the better to glare at Jim and Baird impartially from beneath the brim. "If one of those sonsabitches barfs in the plane, I ain't cleaning it up!"

Baird jerked a thumb at Jim. "That's what we got him for."

Oh joy, Jim thought.

"All right, then," Whitmore said, and stamped out again.

"Thank you," Jim said.

"That's why you get the big bucks," Baird said, slapping him on the back hard enough to jar his tender head.

Jim stifled a groan, and remembered he still didn't know how big those big bucks were. His heart skipped a beat and he stood up straight. He might not know what he was getting paid, but he sure remembered the last time the topic came up, sitting in the pickup truck next to that fisherman on the drive into Bering. What was his name?

Suddenly it became very important to remember the fisherman's name. He backed up, tripped over the coffee table and sat down hard on the couch.

Mike Mason. That was the fisherman's name, Mike Mason. Newly married, if the shine on the wedding ring and the way he fiddled with it was anything to go by.

Jim felt a wave of relief sweep over him. It was all he could remember, but it was more than he could remember lying in that hospital bed. Maybe the docs were right. Maybe he'd remember everything in time. The sooner the better. It was unnerving to watch people walk in and out of the hangar and wonder if he'd already met them. If he'd met them thirty-six hours before. If one of them had been holding a gun when he had.

The Herc sat idle for all of four hours, before a local builder under threat of legal action rushed in and said he absolutely positively had to get a backhoe, a bulldozer and a dump truck to St. Mary's overnight. Baird smiled sweetly and allowed as how it could be done. The builder interpreted the smile correctly and reached for his checkbook.

At six o'clock a short man with very white skin who looked like a hairy leprechaun appeared on the apron. Baird handled his freight request personally, a wooden crate to be shipped to Anchorage the next day, to a gift shop on Fourth Avenue.

Jim got to the office as the bill of lading was signed and money was changing hands. "I'm going to grab some grub, okay?"

Baird grunted without looking up from counting out twenty-dollar bills, but the man twisted around in his chair. When he saw Jim, his white face went even whiter.

"Hi." Jim waited, curious at the expression on the leprechaun's face.

The man nodded once, stiffly, but said nothing.

"Okay if I take the truck up town?" Jim said to Baird. "I want to grab some dinner, and I don't want another sandwich."

"Go ahead."

"I'll be an hour."

"Don't be more."

Jim climbed into the orange truck and started it up with the nagging feeling that he was leaving something important undone, or behind. Why had the man in Baird's office looked so frightened?

He hated having no memory of what had happened to him. A cop with a lousy memory for faces was a cop who took early retirement, usually with disability pay. Since he'd woken up from his attack, it seemed that every face he saw had a reaction to his own that he should have understood, and couldn't.

He slammed the truck into drive and peeled out. It was noisy and only served to make him feel childish. Plus, he'd bet

Baird would have something to say about the ten feet of rubber he'd left behind on the tarmac.

He drove the three miles to town in a black mood and pulled up in front of the first restaurant he saw, the Klondike Cafe. There was one seat left at the counter. He ordered coffee and the meat loaf special, with extra gravy, and stolidly ate his way through everything. He wasn't really that hungry, but he knew he had to eat if he wanted to be well enough to chase bad guys.

He mopped up the plate with the last of his dinner roll and ordered a piece of cherry pie, a la mode. He got a check and a refill on the coffee at the same time. The waitress, a plump young woman with flirtatious black eyes, hovered until he looked up. "Any time you're ready," she said, smiling. She was tapping the check, but the check wasn't what was on her mind.

He drew breath for a graceful exit when the bell on the door jangled violently. Everyone looked around at the man standing there, who walked rapidly across to a table where a trooper was sitting. Jim hadn't even seen her come in, which showed how much he was slipping. Her nametag read M. Zarr. The same one who had signed off on the body in the hangar his first night on the job. She was listening intently to the man talking rapidly to her in a low voice. When he was done, she asked a question. He nodded.

The trooper looked around, ignoring all the stares, and found the waitress. "Sophie? I've got to go. Put this on my tab, will you?"

"No problem, Mary," Jim's waitress said.

The trooper pushed back her half-empty plate, reached for her hat and stood up. She was five-six, maybe a hundred and fifty pounds, and moved well, as if she worked out.

She was putting on her hat when she passed Jim. Her eyes widened and he thought she was going to say something. She didn't, though, and the bell jangled again when she followed the man outside. They were joined by another man, and stood talking for a few moments. The trooper and the first man went off, while the second man came into the cafe and sat down heavily next to Jim.

Sophie was right there with a mug and the pot, and he thanked her. She waited until after his first swallow before saying, "What's going on, Emil?"

He cradled the cup between his hands as if they were cold. "Alice Chevak is dead."

A ripple of comment ran around the little cafe, and then stilled, so that for a moment there was no sound at all except for the second pot of coffee filling on the coffee machine.

"How?" Sophie said finally. "Was it an accident?"

Emil looked down at the coffee cup in his hands as if he couldn't imagine how it got there, and shoved it away. "No. Somebody beat on her. Bad. Real bad. Looks like she died of it. Oscar found her body floating in Brown Slough."

Alice Chevak, Jim thought. Alice Chevak, where had he heard that name.

Oh, he thought. No.

Alice Chevak.

Stephanie's mother.

And Kate's friend.

He stood up, threw a twenty on the counter, avoided Sophie's inviting eye and left without waiting for change.

Outside, he stood blinking in the sunlight, wondering what to do next.

All Zarr knew was that he'd been shot, by whom he said he didn't know. If he could have shown his badge, it would

185

have been easy enough to drop in to exchange professional courtesies and hear all about the local homicide. If he went in without it, if she was even halfway competent Zarr would wonder at his curiosity, would ask how he'd known the victim, and then he'd have to tell her who Kate was. If Zarr didn't believe him, she could add him to the list marked "Suspects." He would have.

The Fibbies might have told her who he was. She might have been in the hospital room that morning, although along with everything else he couldn't remember her, and Kate hadn't mentioned it.

Even if she knew who he was, finding the brutal murderer of a local woman would take precedence over an operation with, so far as the trooper knew, no blood on it yet. He thought of Alexei Burianovich, alias Alex Burinin. No obvious deliberately spilled blood, anyway.

Reluctantly, he decided there was nothing he could do.

Other than tell Kate of her friend's death.

Kate came awake in a rush, heart pounding so loudly in her ears that she could hear nothing else. A great dark bulk was stooping over her, and instantly she was back in the clearing in front of the hunting lodge, her hands bound, Jack face down with a bullet in his back, Eberhard unbuckling her jeans.

She felt hands on her shoulders and struggled against them. "Mutt! To me! Mutt!"

There was a whine, a soft yip.

"Kate!"

She felt herself shaken once, hard. The drumming in her ears subsided. The stooping hulk reduced in size, became Jim

Chopin, sitting on the bed next to her, holding her shoulders in a firm grip. "Kate?"

"Jim?"

"You okay?"

She wrenched her shoulders out of his hands. "I'm fine. What the hell do you think you're doing?" She looked at her watch. "It's not midnight yet, what are you doing here?"

There was something about the quality of his silence that brought her to full alert. "What? What is it, Jim?"

A long sigh was her reply. "Kate," he said. "Oh hell. I don't know how to tell you this." A muffled curse. "I don't want to have to."

"What? Mutt? Is Mutt all right?" She looked down and was immeasurably relieved to see Mutt sitting there, worried yellow eyes fixed on Kate's face. She stretched out a hand. Mutt's rough silk head was a tactile reassurance to her skin, and her heart steadied. She looked back at Jim.

"Alice Chevak is dead," he said.

She blinked. "What?"

"Alice Chevak is dead," he repeated.

"Baloney," Kate said. She even gave a little laugh. "I just had dinner with Alice and her whole family last night. She's not dead. You've made some kind of mistake, she's—"

"Kate."

She looked up and met his eyes. "Jim, look, I know you think—"

"Alice Chevak is dead."

There was a long silence.

"I'm sorry I couldn't tell you sooner, but when I got back from dinner the Cessna was in and needed cleaning, and I just now—"

"How?" Kate said thinly.

"What?"

"How did it happen?"

"They found Alice's body floating in Brown Slough."

He stopped, and she said, "What else?"

"Kate—"

"What else?"

Reluctantly—if he didn't tell her she would find out on her own—he said, "They're saying she'd been hit. A lot. And hard."

Kate sat very still. She thought about Alice, plump and cheerful behind her nameplate at the bank. She thought of Alice, bustling about the kitchen of her home, helping her mother with dinner, making sure her grandfather got his coffee just how he liked it, harrying her daughter from her books into bed. She thought of Alice, offering the hospitality of her home to a classmate she hadn't seen for thirteen years.

She thought of Alice, thrilled at the thought of helping in a real live investigation. Alice, who had asked no questions, had only wanted to help out a friend.

"I am the angel of death," Kate said softly.

"What?"

"I get people killed."

"Kate, stop it."

"Abel."

"Kate—"

"Emaa."

"Kate, no—"

"Jack."

"Kate, don't—"

"And now Alice. I am the angel of death."

188

"Kate!" He shook her again, hard.

She fought him, shoving him away or trying to. He wouldn't let go. "Kate, you didn't beat up Alice, you didn't have anything to do with her death. Stop this, now, damn it, knock it off!"

She was quick and strong and slippery, and his head hurt abominably. Unable to subdue her any other way, he pushed her down on the bunk and lay on top of her. "Just settle down, damn it, Kate."

She tried once more to pull free, and couldn't.

She broke then. She broke quickly and she broke completely, sobs welling up from some bottomless subterranean pool, raw, painful sounds that hurt him who heard them as much as her who suffered them. She lay beneath him, helpless, out of control, as all the tears she hadn't wept over Jack's death overflowed in a deluge that threatened to drown them both.

"I couldn't even scream because they would have heard me," she said, gasping. "They would have heard me, and killed me, too. And I was careless." Her fist thumped his shoulder as hard as it could, which was pretty hard.

"Hush now," he said. He slid his hands under her and gathered her up, rocking her. "It's all right. It's all right, Kate."

"No, it isn't. It never will be again." She was barely aware of what she was saying. "I wasn't paying attention. Two people were dead, what was I thinking? I wasn't thinking. Jack was going to take early retirement and move to the homestead. He was happy. I was happy. I was scared, but I was happy. Two people were already dead and there were a couple of homicidal maniacs on the loose and I was too happy to be careful. How could I be so sloppy?" She hit him again. "How could I be so careless?" She hit him a third time, a fourth, a fifth. "How could I be so stupid!"

He caught her hands and pressed them against the mattress. "Hush now," he said, helpless to say anything else, determined only to comfort, only to soothe. "It's okay, I'm right here. I'm right here, and everything's going to be all right."

"I am the angel of death," she said in a kind of stunned mumble, tears halting at last, to leave her drained and exhausted. "I don't pay attention, and I get people killed. I got Alice killed."

He held her because there was nothing else he could do for her. "Shhh," he said, "there now, everything will be all right. It's okay, Kate, it's all right."

He held her, he rubbed her back with gentle hands, he rocked her, and he told her everything would be all right over and over again, and presently he saw that she had fallen asleep. He gathered her close, tucked her head beneath his chin, and whispered, "It's all right now. Everything will be all right now."

He closed his eyes against the insistent throbbing of his head, and followed her into oblivion.

When she resurfaced, minutes or hours later, she was still on the bed. Jim's hands had relaxed their grip, and he had shifted to lie next to her. He was big and warm and solid and alive. She turned her face into his throat. His pulse beat strongly beneath her lips. He smelled like man.

She raised her head and kissed him.

Still mostly asleep but automatically attuned to the female body next to his, his hands slid around her waist. He kissed her back. He was very good at it, and with an inarticulate murmur of pleasure she kissed him again, and again, soft, fugitive, luring kisses, nibbling at his lips, teasing him into kissing her back, retreating when he did so, responding when he pursued.

It had been so long, and he felt so good. She hooked one knee over his hip and urged him closer. She slid a stealthy hand down between his legs, pulled at his zipper, found the opening. He fit into her palm as if he'd been made for it.

His hands were busy, too, cupping her breasts, gently exploring the cleft between her legs, until—"What the hell? Kate?"

She didn't want to talk. She didn't want to think. All she wanted was to feel.

"Kate, wait a minute, I don't think—"

Hands slid from her breasts and she whimpered and dragged them back. She kissed him again, tightened her hand, rolled to her back. He made a sound deep in his throat and came over her, settling in between her legs. "Oh yes," she said, the merest thread of sound, and pulled at his jeans. Her panties were already gone. She felt him nudging at the entrance to her body, she felt how wet she was and how hard he was and how ready they both were, and she arched up langourously, opening to him, inviting him in.

Again, a shaken voice against her ear. "Kate, no, this isn't— we shouldn't—damn it, don't do that—"

"Please," she murmured, and crossed her ankles in the small of his back. He slid inside her as if he were coming home, a perfect fit, as arousing as it was comforting. "Jack," she whispered. "Oh Jack, I've missed you so much."

The big body froze over her, in her, and with a protesting murmur she arched up again, wanting, needing, so very ready, he couldn't stop now.

It seemed he couldn't. He began to thrust, deep, deeper, deepest, and she whispered her approval and dug her nails into his back and urged him on.

The man in bed with her swore in a rough voice, and fell over the edge with her.

She woke up thirty minutes before her shift started, just enough time for her to grab a quick, necessary shower and present herself at the hangar at one minute before midnight. Jim was unloading freight out of the back of the Cessna as Baird checked it off a manifest.

Baird saw her first. "About time," he said, rather unfairly since it was exactly midnight and she was exactly on time. But then she'd spoiled him over the last four months, coming in early, staying late, having no life but work.

"Here." He shoved the clipboard at her. "And don't even think about getting me up for anything less than an actual crash."

He stamped outside. The orange truck started up and was off with clash of gears.

"Kate," Jim said.

"Where does this shipment go?" she said, looking down at the clipboard.

"Kate, I—"

"I don't want to talk about it, Jim."

"Well, I do. I'm sorry, I—"

"You sure are."

A silence. "I beg your pardon?"

"You sure are sorry," she shouted. "You took advantage!"

"Excuse me. *I* took advantage?"

"Yes! You prick, you've been after me for years, and you knew you'd never get me in the sack any other way, so when

192

I was down about as low as I've ever been you took advantage!"

"Now just wait a minute here," he said. "Just wait one goddamn minute. I did not—"

"Like hell! I'd like to kill you, you bastard! How could you?"

"How could I!" he shouted in his turn. "How could I not? Whose hand was in whose pants? You were all over me when I woke up! I tried to stop and you wouldn't let me!"

"Liar!"

"You begged me!"

"I did not!"

"You know what?" he said, suddenly, dangerously calm. "All right, fine, I took advantage. I mean what the hell, there I was, there you were, we even had a bed. It was great. I loved every minute of it. Especially right there at the end, when you called me Jack."

He dropped the box he was holding, to what sounded like the total disintegration of whatever was inside. "It's midnight, my shift's over, I am out of here."

He stalked outside and was halfway to town before he realized that he'd even started walking in that direction. All he knew was he needed to get as far away as possible from the infuriating woman in the hangar. His legs ate up the ground at a furious rate, while he called Kate every name in the book and himself seventeen different kinds of a fool.

There were flashes in the distance that caught the corner of his eye, and he looked up to see fireworks. He remembered then that it was the morning of the Fourth of July.

Last year on the Fourth he'd been in Aleganik Bay, working a murder. And working it with Kate Shugak.

George had flown him out to Kate's aunties' fish camp, and they had caught Kate and Jack going at it on the shore of the creek. It was evident that they'd been playing grabass all the way to the airstrip, too; Kate had had her T-shirt half out of her jeans and Jack had had that look, the one men get when they are this close to getting some, eager, edgy, annoyed at the interruption and in a hurry to get back to it. He, Jim Chopin, had been irritated with Jack Morgan that evening. He, Jim Chopin, had wanted Jack Morgan on the other side of the earth.

He, Jim Chopin, had been jealous.

He stopped dead in the middle of the road. "What?" he demanded out loud of no one in particular. "Who said that?"

Nobody answered. He started walking again. "Jealous, my royal blue ass. She's just another woman, she held out longer than most, so what. I've had her now, time to move on."

He tried not to think about what would have happened if Bobby Clark had heard him say that. Or George Perry. Or Chick Noyukpuk. Or Bernie, or Old Sam, or Demetri.

Or Jack Morgan. He, Jim Chopin, would have been on his royal blue ass if Jack Morgan had been within a ten-foot radius during the last five minutes.

Try the last three hours.

Jim refused utterly to acknowledge any shame and moved on briskly.

On the outskirts of town a white Suburban pulled up next to him, and he looked up to see the insignia of his own service on the door. The trooper behind the wheel said, "Jim Chopin?"

"Sorry, wrong guy, I'm Jim Churchill," he said, wary.

She raised an eyebrow. "First Sergeant Jim Chopin?"

"I guess so," he said, yielding.

"We need to talk." She leaned over and opened the passenger door. "Get in."

"I take it somebody told you who I am."

"You take it right. How's your head?"

"Lousy."

"Remember anything yet?"

"No."

"I saw you in the cafe yesterday evening. You should have joined me."

"I didn't know we weren't playing Superman and Clark Kent anymore. How is your homicide investigation going?" He caught her look. "One of the guys you were talking to came into the cafe afterward and told us."

"Yeah. Well." The knowledge that she was talking to a fellow officer made her relax her guard. "We sent the body to Anchorage today for autopsy. That'll tell us whether she died of the beating or drowned. It looked like her neck was broken."

"Who was the last person to see her alive?"

"She was a teller, worked at the local bank. One of the other tellers said they were walking by and saw her inside yesterday at four in the afternoon."

"On a Sunday?"

"She told her mother she was behind and that she was going in to work some overtime."

And Kate had had dinner with her Saturday night.

"That's not unusual," Zarr said, misreading his silence. "It gets crazy around here in the summertime. Everybody gets in a lot of overtime."

Jim looked at his watch. "Including you."

She smiled. "Including me."

Carroll and Casanare were waiting for them at the trooper post. "Ah," Jim said, "Boris and Natasha, what a surprise to see you again. Especially since you're both in Anchorage, reaching out to informers, gathering information. Amassing evidence. Building a case."

195

Carroll didn't waste time. "What the hell were you doing on that boat?"

"What was I doing on what boat?"

"On the Russian boat, the *Kosygin*," Casanare said.

"I didn't know I was on it," Jim said. Carroll's face darkened and he held up a hand. "Wait a minute, okay? I'm not trying to weasel out of anything. Let me think, just for a minute."

His head was aching and he put up a hand to touch the gauze taped to his skull. The crust of the wound was hard beneath his fingertips. He'd have to soak it off in the shower. "Look, the doc told me I might experience some short-term memory loss. I expect she told you the same thing."

"Yes, she did," Casanare said with a warning glance at Carroll.

"So I don't know where the hell I was just before I was out."

"You remember who we are?"

"Yes," Jim said, feeling very tired all at once, "I remember who you are. I thought I made that clear."

"You remember what we're all doing here?"

"Yes." He held up his hand again. "Let me speed things up by telling you what I do remember. I remember hitching a ride into town after my shift was over with a fisherman named Mike Mason. I remember having coffee and doughnuts on the dock with the beach gang—"he looked up"—and I remember seeing you, Mr. Casanare, working the hoist, and you, Ms. Carroll, waltzing around in raingear like you had some fish to count. I also remember wondering why Gamble told me you'd be working background in Anchorage when you were so obviously all present and accounted for in Bering." He paused expectantly.

Carroll and Casanare exchanged another glance. The trooper straightened a piece of paper on top of her desk with great care and precision.

"Do you remember anything after that?" Casanare said. "After you saw us on the dock?"

"No," Jim said. "Have I mentioned how appreciative I am of the way you people share information? And you whimper when local law enforcement doesn't roll out the red carpet when you show up."

"What about the woman?"

"What woman?" he said, although he knew perfectly well what woman.

"The woman who visited you in the hospital. The woman working at Baird Air."

"Kathy Sovalik," Casanare added.

"That woman," Carroll said.

"What about her?"

"You know her."

Jim had his antenna up and in full working order. "Like you said," he said, shrugging, putting as much nonchalance into it as a nearly fatal head wound would permit. "I work with her. I didn't show up to relieve her. Baird probably sent her looking."

"She went on board the *Kosygin*."

"She did what!" His head gave a vicious throb. "Ah, shit. Do you have any aspirin?" he asked Zarr.

Without speaking, Zarr reached into a drawer and pulled out a year's supply of Bayer. There was a small refrigerator behind the desk, from which she produced a bottle of Evian. He accepted both gratefully and followed four aspirin with a long, continuous swallow that drained the bottle dry. "When did she go on board?" he said, looking around for a trash can. Zarr took the bottle.

"Saturday afternoon," Carroll said. "The day after you went on board. While you were in the hospital."

Jim closed his eyes and tried to think. "She said something tonight. Something about me speaking Russian to her in the hospital?"

"You said good-bye and thanks," Casanare said. "*Dasvidanya* and *spasibo*."

"That was it?"

"Yes."

"That would be enough to send her on board a Russian fish processor?" Carroll said, disbelief clear in her voice. "A Russian fish processor harboring international fugitives?"

"I don't know what the hell she would or wouldn't do," Jim said shortly. "Or why." He was trying to figure out if it would be better to say who Kate really was and thereby clear her of all suspicion, or to go along with her cover and try to bury her in the background.

"I ran her through the computer," Zarr said.

Oh shit, Jim thought.

"She came to work for Baird through Job Service. She gave them a phony social security number and a phony driver's license number."

"Okay," Jim said, his hand forced. He didn't know whether to be glad or sorry. "Her real name is Kate Shugak."

The trooper drew in a sharp breath. "Is she the one—"

"Yeah. Yeah, she's the one."

"She's the one Gamble wanted you to find," Casanare said.

"Yeah."

"Okay," Carroll said, folding her arms, "how convenient is it that she shows up right where and when we need her?"

Jim stood up, ignored his head, looked Carroll straight in the eye and said firmly, "I know her. She's a part-time independent investigator who worked five years for the Anchorage district attorney. I've worked cases with her. She has a reputation, a good one, that is very well deserved. She's not here working for anybody except herself."

"How do you know that? When was the last time you saw her?"

An image of the woman holding the dead man in her arms flashed through his mind, followed immediately by a picture of her lying beneath him, moving with him, coming with him. He pulled himself together. "I know her," he repeated.

"Maybe you don't," Zarr said. She met his eyes without flinching and said to Casanare and Carroll, "Shugak got into a situation last fall." She told them, keeping it brief. "You don't know how a thing like that affects someone," she said, as much to Jim as to the two agents. "Even someone you know real well."

"I know her," Jim said forcefully. "She is not mixed up in this."

"Yeah," Carroll said, clearly unconvinced.

"The Russians are shipping stuff out on Baird Air," Casanare said. "And I noticed she was wearing one of those Russian watches."

"So is Baird," Jim said. "So are all of Baird's pilots. It's grease, is all." He went on the attack. "Where did you find me?"

They exchanged a glance. "Like we said. Dumped in somebody's yard."

"Were you looking for me?"

"I saw you go on board the *Kosygin* that morning," Casanare said, and shook his head. "Man, I don't know what you were thinking."

"Me, either, considering the guy you told me to find is

dead." He nodded at Zarr. "You tell them?" She nodded. "Tell me this: How long has the *Kosygin* been in port?"

"Three days."

"And Burianovich came in on her?"

Zarr looked at the two federal agents, decided she could converse with a member of her own service if she so chose, and nodded.

To the agents Jim said, "I'm guessing the two guys you were talking about in Tok, the general and—"

"Yes," Casanare said.

"—they flew in about the same time?"

"Yes."

"And suddenly Burianovich, Russian Mafia highflyer, is dead, in an unexplained accident. Implying a change of command, not a, shall we say, amicable one."

Casanare and Carroll looked at him without expression.

"They can't stay tied up here forever," Jim said. "If that circum—seercon—whatever the hell you call that stuff is on board, they're going to have to offload it and ship it out."

"And Baird Air is the likeliest route," Carroll said, "since Zarr here says the crew has been using them since they first docked with a load of fish in June."

"What have they been shipping up to now?" Jim asked Zarr.

"Fish and trinkets, mostly. Fish because the *Kosygin* is affiliated with the local IFQ. It's a program," she explained in an aside to the agents, "designed to get Bering Sea fish delivered to villages so they can skim off some of the profit. The trinkets are mostly stuff for the gift shops on Fourth Avenue in Anchorage. Nesting dolls, amber jewelry, icons. Stuff like that."

"You check it all?"

"Customs has someone fly in from Anchorage on a random basis to check cargoes. I monitor the process when they do. Otherwise I don't get involved." Zarr added, "They have an import permit."

"Really?" Jim raised an eyebrow at Carroll and Casanare. "Boris and Natasha didn't tell me that. How convenient." He paused, thinking, and said slowly, "Now, I wonder who signed off on that permit? Do we know?"

He waited. No information appeared forthcoming. "I see that we do. What else is going on that you're not telling me?"

Nothing. "Okay, fine. You're thinking they've got the stuff on board, that they've been shipping junk up till now as practice. Why don't they move it?" He thought. "Because they're waiting for payment, of course. And it's such a hell of a big deal that the boss man showed up to handle the transaction in person. And Burianovich didn't like it, protested and was removed from office, so to speak. That about it?"

Casanare looked at Carroll and shrugged. "That's about it," he agreed.

"You've got a witness," Jim said. "What the hell are you waiting for? Get your warrant and go on board."

"We want them all," Carroll said softly, echoing Gamble's words the week before. "We want the sellers, and we want the goods, yes, but we want the buyers, too."

"Who are the buyers?"

"Well, that's the problem," Casanare said after a moment. "We mostly don't have a clue about who the buyers are. We've got some ideas, but until they show their hands…" He spread his own and shrugged.

"You're risking a lot to find out," Jim observed. "Why not just grab up your guy and sweat him? Offer him witness protection or something."

Carroll's laugh was short and unamused. "You don't know what you're talking about."

"You're right," Jim said, "I don't, and whose fault would that be?"

The agents left. "I can't believe I've had Kate Shugak in my own backyard for four months and not even known it," Zarr said.

"Yeah, well, she doesn't want to get noticed, she isn't."

Zarr stood up. "I'm knocking off for the night. Would you like a drink?"

She was an attractive woman, a nice smile, friendly eyes, made chunkier than she really was by her uniform. "I thought Bering was a dry town."

"Damp. I can have it in my home, I just can't buy it or sell it. At least that's what it is today. Who knows after the next election. So?"

Well, why the hell not? He deliberately forced himself to relax into a smile, and saw the usual and expected response on Zarr's face. "Sure," he said. "I'd love a drink."

Zarr smoothed back her hair, tucking a strand behind an ear. "Great." She paused at the door to look up at him, as she was about eight inches shorter than he was. "Play your cards right, I might even cook."

He grinned, the old, practiced grin full of lazy, seductive charm. "You play your cards right, I might even eat." He ran his eyes over her. "All of a sudden, I am hungry enough to eat a moose, whole."

She laughed, and he followed her out the door.

CHAPTER 10

Are these
Your Levi's or mine
Lying wrinkled on the floor?

— *Marked Man*

JIM CAME IN PRECISELY at noon, surly and uncommunicative. Kate managed to hand over ground operations without once meeting his eyes. She showered and changed, sat for a moment to gather strength, and headed for the Chevak house, Mutt padding next to her.

The first person she saw was Stephanie, the last person she wanted to see. She approached the porch with a step that slowed in spite of herself. "Stephanie."

The girl looked up from the model plane she was holding, a red Super Cub, beautifully made, correct in every detail. Her knuckles were white where they clutched the fuselage. Kate sat down next to her, Mutt on her other side. "I'm so sorry, Stephanie."

Silence. Mutt leaned up against the girl. Stephanie released her grip on the Cub to slip an arm around Mutt's neck. Mutt gave a soft whine and licked the girl's cheek. Stephanie buried her face in Mutt's ruff.

A woman came up the steps. "Hi, Stephanie."

"Hello, Mrs. Jenkins."

"I'm so sorry about your mother."

"Thank you."

"I brought you some banana bread, would you like a slice?"

"No, thank you." The little voice was thin but firm.

The woman hesitated, casting Kate a curious glance. "Oh. Well, I'll just go inside then, pay my respects to your grandmother and Ray."

"Okay."

Kate waited until the door closed behind her. "Your mom and I went to school together. I don't know if you heard us talking about that when I came to dinner the other night. At the University of Alaska. In Fairbanks."

Stephanie didn't move, didn't speak, kept her eyes trained on the airplane in her arms.

"She was the nicest person, one of the nicest people I've ever met. I—I was really scared in school, at first, and really lonely. Your mother helped me my first year, a lot. She helped me get my books at the bookstore, and showed me where all my classrooms were. She went to meals with me so I didn't have to walk into that big dining room all alone. Sometimes she would make me go with her to a movie. Whenever she had a party in her room, she always invited me, too."

The girl swallowed, and the guilt threatened to swamp Kate the way the tears had the night before. "She was one of the best people I've ever met. I'm really glad she was my friend."

Stephanie raised her head. "You came and she died."

Kate drew in a sharp breath.

Stephanie's brown eyes bored into hers. "You came and she died," she repeated.

They stared at each other in silence for a moment, until the accusation in the girl's expression gave way again to grief and she hid her face.

You came and she died. Kate would have liked to deny those words, but they were true. I am the angel of death, she had told Jim the night before, the words boiling up from the depths of rage and pain and despair, yes, but maybe it was true, maybe she was.

"There's a story I know," she began, hardly aware at first of what she was going to say.

There was no response but she knew Stephanie was listening. A couple approached. "Hello, Stephanie."

"Hi, Mrs. Mather. Hello, Mr. Mather."

"We're so sorry about your mother, honey."

"Thank you."

"I brought some banana bread, would you like some?"

"No, thank you."

"Okay. I'll put it in the oven to keep warm. You can come in and get a slice whenever you want."

"Okay. Thank you."

Kate waited until they had gone up the steps and inside, and then continued, because the words had come to her now. "It's about a little boy who lived in the mountains of Tibet."

She kept her voice calm and matter-of-fact as she recounted the story from the wonderful little children's picture book by Mordecai Gerstein that she had given Katya as a christening present, that she had given as a christening present to every child of her acquaintance, all about the little boy who loves to fly kites, who grows up to be a woodcutter, who marries and has children, who lives to be very old and then dies.

A voice then offers him a choice between going to heaven or living another life. As a woodcutter he had always wanted to see the rest of the world, so he choses to live another life. Pick a star, says the voice, and he does. Pick a planet around that star, says the voice, and he does. Pick a place on that

205

planet, says the voice, and he does. He remembers that he was a boy in his last life, so he decides to become a girl in his next.

A little girl who flies kites.

It was a book that had touched Kate deeply the first time she saw it; truth be told, she owned her own copy. She'd never been religious, hadn't been brought up to it by Abel or Emaa. When asked once what she believed in, she had replied with perfect honesty, "The earth." She did, she believed in its ability to nurture her, to sustain her, to challenge her; she believed in its ability to bury her in the end. She had never bought into the idea of heaven and hell, having witnessed too many, too successful attempts by people to create the latter in this life.

But she liked the idea of being offered a second chance. A do-over. And she especially liked the idea of being given a choice in that chance.

Next to her, Stephanie stirred. "You think my mom already picked?"

Kate took a long, careful breath. "I don't know, Stephanie. Maybe."

Her voice was muffled by Mutt's fur, a Mutt who was apparently willing to sit there as long as Stephanie needed to hang onto her. "She always wanted to go to Italy."

Kate thought about it. "I remember now. She had a poster of Michelangelo's *David* on the wall of her room at school."

"We just started studying Italian from tapes," Stephanie said, and began to recite from memory. "*Buon-giorno. Buona sera. Come sta molto bene. Per piacere. Dov'e il gabenetto?* Mom said the last one was really important," Stephanie added.

Kate nodded. She had no idea what it meant but she could guess.

"So maybe Mom's a baby in Italy now," Stephanie said, her head still burrowed into Mutt's ruff.

"Maybe."

"Or maybe she's in heaven like Pastor Dave says."

"Maybe."

Stephanie shifted a little, sat up. "Maybe I should keep learning Italian."

Kate felt the knot in her stomach loosening. "I think that's a very good idea."

"Someday I'll go to Italy. So I'll need to speak Italian."

"Yes."

They were silent. A man left, and two women came. "Hello, Stephanie."

"Hello, Ms. Sirilio, hi, Ms. Nicholson."

"We're so sorry about your mommy, Stephanie, so very sorry. You feel bad about anything, you know you can come to us, right?"

"I know. Thank you."

"We brought some banana bread, would you like a slice?"

Kate felt Stephanie's body tremble a little next to her, and resisted the impulse to put a protective arm around the girl.

"No, thank you."

"We'll keep it warm for you, honey."

"Okay."

The second woman had a thin, intelligent face beneath a short, permed frizz and sharp eyes. "You get that physics book I left for you at the library?"

"Yes, Ms. Nicholson, I did, and thank you."

"You have any questions, you come on over. Doesn't matter when."

"Okay. Thank you."

The two teachers went inside.

"Does everybody bring banana bread when somebody dies?" Stephanie asked.

"I guess so," Kate said.

"Weird."

It was the first childlike thing Stephanie had said since Kate had sat down, and she welcomed it with open arms. "Totally."

They sat in mutual contemplation of the oddities of humankind for a few moments.

Kate stirred first. "There's something I have to tell you, Stephanie."

The wariness was back in the child's voice. "What?"

"This kind of thing shouldn't need saying, but just in case you're too young to understand, I want to lay it out for you. You are your mother's daughter. I was your mother's friend. If you ever need anything, anything at all, at any time in your life, come to me. I'll help. Right now I work at Baird Air, out at the airport. Most of the time I live on a homestead outside Niniltna. This is my post office box number, and the cell phone number of a good friend. I'll tell him you might call." She tucked it into Stephanie's shirt pocket. "Anytime you need me, anytime you need anything, you write, or you call, or you just get on a plane and come. Okay?"

"Okay," the muffled voice said.

Kate reached out, hovered over the girl's hair, shoulder, settled for a light touch on one of the clenched hands. Her own hand was possessed of a fine trembling that, try as she would, she could not control.

Inside, a woman Kate didn't know was taking Saran Wrap from a loaf of bread that Kate would bet her last dime was banana and setting it on the table between two macaroni casseroles. The couch and chairs in the living room had been pushed back against the walls, the dining table chairs had been brought in to sit next to them, and there was a steady, low-voiced murmur coming from the kitchen.

Ray and Dorothy were sitting next to each other, wordless in their grief. Kate tried to say something and Ray grabbed her hand. "Sit next to me, Katya."

Kate sat. He kept her hand.

"Your grandmother called you Katya."

"Yes, uncle."

"She was so proud of you."

"Yes," Kate said. If he said so, it must be true. Emaa had not squandered speech on praise, unless she thought it would result in something of immediate benefit to the tribe.

"You knew Alice in school, didn't you?" He was wandering in his grief.

"That's where we met, uncle."

"She made many friends there. She tried living in Anchorage after she graduated, did you know that?"

"She told me."

"But she came home. She came home to Bering, to be close to her family, to raise her daughter. She was a good girl."

"She was a good friend to me, uncle."

He nodded. "She talked about you, too. She thought your job was exciting. I think she was kind of envious, sometimes."

The back of Kate's throat seemed to fill up. She was afraid she was going to be sick.

The door opened, and the bank manager walked in, followed by Chris Overmore, the man Kate had seen come into the bank the afternoon she had met Alice there. "Mr. Chevak," Sullivan said, coming forward with his hand out. "I am so sorry. Mrs. Chevak. What can I say? Alice was one of the best. We will miss her so much down at the bank."

Ray Chevak saw the other man over Sullivan's shoulder, and struggled to his feet. "Senator Overmore."

Kate stood up with Ray and Dorothy, and shook hands.

209

"Mike, Senator Overmore, this is Kate Shugak, a friend of Alice's from college."

The women setting food on the table seemed to pause with dishes in the air, voices seemed to still in the kitchen, Overmore and Sullivan froze in the act of extending their hands.

There was no way she could have stopped it. She hadn't told Ray or Dorothy that she was in Bering under another name, and Alice had introduced her to them employing her correct name. "Senator," she said, bringing the room to life again. The ladies setting the table vanished into the kitchen, the men seated around the room began to converse in low tones. "Mr. Sullivan. We met at your bank a few days ago."

"That's right," he said. "I must not have caught your name that day. How do you do, Ms.—Shugak?"

"Kate Shugak," she said. His hand was cool, his handshake brief.

"Ms. Shugak," Senator Overmore said, alive to the tension in the air and determined to take no notice of it. He gave her the practiced smile that had enough wattage to power a chain saw, but no real warmth. "A terrible tragedy, this."

"Yes," Kate echoed. "Terrible." The hair on the back of her neck lifted. Instinctively, she pegged both men as bent. In reality, she knew nothing against either of them.

Mike Sullivan, according to Alice, was the manager and one of the owners of Alaska First Bank of Bering, a regional bank with branches in those villages large enough to support them. She seemed to remember something about them opening a branch in Anchorage as well, always news in this age of megabank takeovers, which meant they must be making enough money to stave off corporate invaders.

Senator Overmore—well, he worked in Juneau. No more really need be said. He and Sullivan were natural buddies. He was married to a Yupik woman, as she recalled, which must explain how he, a white man, had been elected from the largely Yupik District S.

She wondered what tack to take. It was Sullivan's bank. Alice had extracted information from Sullivan's bank's files. If Alice proved to have been the victim of random violence, Kate need not come forward. If Alice had been killed as a result of pulling information Kate wanted from the bank's computer files, then Kate had a duty to come forward.

She looked up and saw Sullivan looking back, a considering expression in his eyes.

If he was bent, she could wind up like Alice.

There was a time not long since when that possibility would have been welcomed. Now she was up to indifferent.

Sullivan turned to Ray again, standing patiently in front of his chair. "Ray, this is just awful. I don't know what to say. They'll catch the bastard, you know that. Anything I can do, please, ask me."

Overmore was right behind him. "Terrible thing, Mr. Chevak. Awful that it should happen in a peaceful place like Bering. I know our law enforcement officials will do their best to apprehend this person or persons and put them in jail." He was a politician, so he couldn't resist the opportunity to work the room, and raised his voice, not to any vulgar pitch but loud enough to be heard above the serving of franks and beans. "The death penalty is too good for people like these. I've said so time and again, while I've been in office. I plan to make it my last work in the legislature to return the death penalty to practice in the state of Alaska, and I will continue that fight in Washington."

He shook Ray's hand again, he shook everyone in the room's hand, he admired Alice's high-school graduation and wedding pictures with Dorothy, he conferred with an elder on sovereignty, he listened respectfully as a member of the city council held forth on the need to lengthen and upgrade the airport, he sampled a plate loaded with fried salmon, macaroni and cheese, potato salad, fruit salad, carrot salad and banana bread, he praised the cooks adequately but not extravagantly, shook hands with Ray again, and left with a general and all-inclusive wave, Sullivan scurrying in his wake.

Ray said, "Have you ever noticed how all politicians sound alike after a while?"

"Right from the beginning, I always thought," Kate replied.

Both of them managed a smile.

At the back of the crowd Kamyanka and Glukhov watched the candidate mount the platform. A red-faced, beaming mayor introduced him with fulsome praise, the local Boy Scout troop paraded the colors as everyone stood to attention, a zither player accompanied *The Star-Spangled Banner* and *Alaska's Flag*, and the president of the Chamber of Commerce led the Pledge of Allegiance. The candidate took center stage and gave an impressive reading of the Declaration of Independence, punctuated by enthusiastic and rebellious outcries from the crowd.

He knew his audience, did Senator Christopher Overmore of District S. These were Bush dwellers, of whom many had settled in Bering because it was as far as they could get from the federal government, from government of any kind, and to which happy estate many others had been born and were glad to remain. Anything said against government interference in local affairs, state or federal, would be roundly welcomed, even if it was two-hundred-and-twenty-odd years old.

"He has called together legislative bodies at places unusual, uncomfortable, and distant from the depository of their Public Records, for the sole purpose of fatiguing them into compliance with his measures."

"You mean like Juneau?" somebody yelled.

Senator Overmore, a man who lived and worked six months of the year in Juneau, grinned and continued. "He has erected a multitude of New Offices, and sent hither swarms of Officers to harass our people, and eat out their substance."

"Sounds like the Park Service to me!"

"For depriving us in many cases, of the benefits of Trial by Jury…"

Somebody yelled something in Yupik that time, which was immediately applauded by everyone, white and Yupik alike whether they understood it or not.

The senator smoothly skipped over the section that referred to "merciless Indian Savages," and continued, "We have warned them from time to time of attempts by their legislature to extend an unwarrantable jurisdiction over us."

"Have we ever!"

"Yeah, like they ever listen!"

"Throw the bastards out!"

"Native sovereignty!"

"Rural subsistence!"

"Fly and shoot the same day!"

"And for the support of this Declaration, with a firm reliance on the protection of Divine Providence—"

"Praise the Lord!"

"—we mutually pledge to each other our Lives, our Fortunes and our sacred Honor."

The crowd erupted into applause as a chorus of catcalls

and rebel yells went up. Thomas Jefferson might have been two hundred years in his grave, but in the Alaskan Bush his words lived on.

Somebody shouted, "Is there a cold beer to be had in this goddamn town?"

"Fine words. That Jefferson really knew how to write."

"You think so?"

"Of course! Life, liberty, the pursuit of happiness. America, the land of the free and the home of the brave." Glukhov grinned. "And ice in the glass of water they bring you at restaurants, and the four-wheel drive."

"Give me a dictatorship every time," Kamyanka said. "The more repressive the better. Much more opportunity for profit." The applause had died down and people had begun to drift away in groups to other celebrations. "So that's our guy?"

Glukhov nodded, his eyes hidden behind Ray-Bans, his hair tucked beneath a Seattle Mariners baseball cap. He was wearing a brand-new black-and-yellow Nike windbreaker, and hightop Nike sneakers with artistically thick soles. They were leaning up against a storefront on the other side of the street.

"He's good with a crowd." It wasn't quite a question.

"He knows banks," Glukhov said. "He used to be a banker. And he's married to a banker's sister. They all have a vested interest in seeing the business go through."

"I hope you're right."

"Why wouldn't I be?"

Glukhov missed the annoyance that crossed his companion's face. "I've seen men like him before. They're fine until things begin to go wrong. Then they lose their heads and get people killed. The wrong people. He'll be fine, though. His type

214

always is. They wreak havoc with everyone else, but they always survive."

Glukhov was amused. "All this you can tell from seeing him once at a distance of ten meters?"

"Yes." Kamyanka turned to look at Glukhov's unrevealing face. "Yes, I can."

As they returned to the ship, Glukhov wondered if he shouldn't move up his retirement.

As they returned to the ship, Kamyanka wondered if he had made a mistake in allowing Glukhov to live.

CHAPTER 11

A naked tree leaned down, its
Chalkwhite skeleton jaunty
— *Hidden Creek at Northspur Junction*

KATE AND TROOPER MARY Zarr arrived at the hangar at precisely the same time, one minute before midnight. They nodded to each other, and since grunting and stacking sounds indicated that Jim was in the hangar, Kate went in the office, wondering at the odd look in Zarr's eye. Almost as if she were assessing Kate for damage.

In the office, she found a stack of checks underneath the ashtray with a note in a greasy scrawl that said, "Add these up." She extracted the checks, excavated the adding machine from the pile of paperwork it resided beneath and began to fill out a deposit slip.

With the best will in the world she could not avoid hearing the voices speaking just outside the door that led into the hangar.

"Why didn't you stay this morning?" Zarr said in a less than official voice. "I hate waking up alone."

Kate's pen stopped moving.

There was the sound of skin on cloth. "Especially after such an enjoyable night. I wanted to do something to show my appreciation." There was the sound of what could have been a soft kiss.

"I had to get back to work," Jim said.

"You're about ready to knock off now, aren't you? Want a lift?"

"Should you be here?"

Kate's pen fell from suddenly nerveless fingers, and it began to roll, unnoticed, toward the edge of the desk.

A note of annoyance crept into Zarr's voice. "Why not? No one knows who you are, so why should they suspect anything? Even if they did see us together?"

"I just meant, with your homicide investigation, if you shouldn't maybe be—"

"I'm a big girl, I can get my job done when it needs doing." A brief pause. "I can also sleep with whomever I want."

Jim said nothing.

"So you're one of the fuck-and-run guys after all."

"No, damn it. I didn't mean that, Mary, I—"

"Yeah, sure you didn't."

Quick firm steps, followed by the slam of a door, the hard start of a truck engine, the squeal of tires.

Jim's discouraged voice said, "Oh, goddamn it to hell, anyway."

Kate's pen fell off the desk and she made a mad grab for it, knocking over the ashtray in the process. It crashed to the floor, scattering sand, stogie stubs and ashes beneath the desk, under the coffee table and the couch and everywhere in between.

The hangar door was yanked open. Kate didn't want to look up, but she had to and, of course, there he was, standing in the doorway.

It was difficult to say who was more horrified. His skin turned a deep, dark red. Hers did, too. Mutt, until then having a peaceful snooze with her nose beneath her tail, was on her feet in response to the ashtray crash, looking wide-eyed and ready for action, even if she didn't know what kind.

The ticking of the Budweiser wall clock seemed to have slowed down, and also to have become very loud.

"Fuck," Jim said, with bitter and comprehensive emphasis.

The door slammed so hard that instead of catching it bounced back on its hinges and off the wall. Small pieces of already rotten Sheetrock crumbled and fell to the floor. Hasty feet were heard going the long way around the hangar toward the bunkhouse. If he'd gone the short way round, she could have seen him through the windows. And he would have been able to see her.

The Herc arrived, back from Anchorage, followed shortly by the Cub and the Cessna. All had to be serviced and ready for action with cargo stowed when the dawn came, five and a half hours hence. The DC-3 was in Dillingham with the Native association board of directors, being serviced by Cal Kemper. One plane less for her, and she was grateful.

Kate swept up the mess in the office, returned the ashtray to the desk, finished totaling the deposit slip, slid checks and slip into a manila envelope she marked DEPOSIT in large black letters with a Marksalot and ducttaped to the office door, and went back to work.

She was hanging up the phone when Jim came in at noon. "That was Yuri," she told Baird. "The *Kosygin*'s heading out tomorrow, and he wants to get another load off to Anchorage before then."

"Fish or trinkets?"

"Trinkets."

"How many boxes?"

"He said no more than six, same size as before, same weight as before."

Baird grunted. "Hey, big spender. Herc's taking a load of reds into Tenth and M Lockers later today. We'll put them in with that."

Jim felt his ears prick up. He wondered what else Yuri was shipping besides trinkets. Maybe the Fibbies' obsession with this zirconium stuff was about to pay off. And maybe then he could go home. The sooner the better. He couldn't wait to get out of Bering.

He wondered if Yuri was the Russian who had been visiting Kate late at night in the hangar. He wondered why. Not that he lent any credibility to the Fibbies' suspicions, or Zarr's speculations about Kate's state of mind. No, he knew Kate better than that.

But he wondered about Yuri. A young man, perhaps? Good-looking? Every Russian Jim had met had had terrible teeth. Not their fault, Russia had lousy health care. He wondered if Kate knew that Russian men were only interested in Alaskan women as a means of gaining entry into the United States. He wondered if perhaps someone should tell her.

Her voice brought him out of his speculations. "Oh, and Bill LaRue called from Koot."

"Oh yeah? And what did marvelous Mr. LaRue want, exactly?"

"Exactly, he wanted a ride into town."

"He offer to pay?"

"No, he seemed to think you'd be happy to put it on his tab."

"Four-flushing con artist swindling son of a bitch," Baird said without heat. "And you said?"

"I informed him that Mr. Baird had instructed me that until he, Mr. LaRue, paid his outstanding debt to Baird Air, which at the moment totals an amount approaching six thousand dollars and change, that he, Mr. LaRue, was unwelcome to fly the otherwise friendly Baird skies."

"Well put," Baird said, admiringly.

"Thank you. I also told him that his personal check was no longer good here. Cash, money order or cashier's check only." Kate almost smiled until she looked up and saw Jim. Her tone became very crisp. "Jessie Oscar called from Atmautluak; his wife is due to go into labor this week sometime and she needs a ride in to the hospital."

"Jeeze, how many is it now, six, seven? You'd think they'd have figured out how that works by now. Anything for the Cessna?"

"A few calls, nothing firm yet. Oh yeah, Shep says the Cub's tailwheel needed repacking. You'll have to sign off on it before he takes off for Atmautluak."

She looked between the middle two buttons on Jim's shirt and said, "I'm done. See you tonight."

Jim watched her very straight back march off with a vague, indefinite notion that he owed her an apology. He just couldn't figure out what for.

Mutt's head nudged his hand as she followed. The gesture offered him some comfort.

She showered, buttered two slices of bread, heated a can of cream of asparagus soup and forced herself to eat, managing to avoid even looking at Jim's side of the bunkhouse. Certainly she never strayed over the invisible line she had painted down the center of the floor.

A soft whine told her Mutt was back. She opened the door and Mutt sidled inside with the smug look of the successful hunter.

Kate wasn't sleepy, but she put on a clean T-shirt and a clean pair of underwear and made herself lie down. Her pillow smelled differently. She sniffed and realized it was Jim's aftershave.

Before she knew it the pillow was sailing across the room. When it thudded to the wall and then the floor Mutt's head jerked up. She looked from Kate to the pillow and back again, her ears and eyebrows up.

"Oh shut up," Kate said.

Mutt heaved a sigh and lay back down.

The next thing Kate knew was a knock at the door. She found herself out of her bunk and on her feet, her heart pounding. It was three o'clock in the afternoon by the battered alarm clock on the table, so she must have slept after all.

The knock came again, more firmly this time. She went to the door and opened it.

It was Stephanie.

Kate made her cocoa. It was a family tradition; elders made cocoa for children when they came to call. Emaa had made cocoa for all the kids in Kate's family when they came over after school, kindergarten right up through twelfth grade. Lorna Doones were a poor substitute for fry bread, though.

The red Super Cub sat to one side of Stephanie's feet, Mutt to the other. Stephanie dunked her shortbread into her cocoa with grave precision.

The silence became burdensome. "How are you?" Kate said, and immediately wished she'd kept her mouth shut.

"I miss my mother," Stephanie said.

"Yes. Of course you do."

Stephanie reached for another cookie. "She left something for you."

"What?"

"My mother. She left something for you." Stephanie dunked with one hand and with the other produced a fat, dirty envelope with Kate's name on it.

Kate accepted it with a sinking heart. "Where was it?"

"In her purse. They found it outside the bank. They think she dropped it there." Stephanie spoke with little emphasis, concentrating her entire being on just the right amount of cocoa soaking into her cookie.

Kate opened the envelope and her worst fears were confirmed. Inside was a printout of the deposits and withdrawals made to Alaska First Bank of Bering by all the processors who had delivered to Bering so far this season.

There was a note clipped to the top sheet in Alice's large, round handwriting, which hadn't changed much in thirteen years. She no longer dotted her I's with little hearts, but the big looping tails and extravagantly crossed T's took up a lot of room.

Kate, the note read, *sorry I took so long to get this to you. I got you the other ones, too, like you asked, so you can compare. Funny thing, it looks like Mike has been making some of the entries himself. I knew we were busy but not so busy that the bank manager has to do data entry (giggle). I'll drop this off at Baird's on the way home from work, so you'll get it when you come on shift. Where are you staying? You never said. Don't leave without saying good-bye. Thanks for letting me play Nancy Drew (giggle squared). Am I George or Bess? I'm not Ned! Love, Alice*

Kate closed her eyes, unable for the moment to read further.

Alice had come through for her. Alice had located the information Kate had wanted, had printed it out, and had tucked it safely into an envelope addressed to her friend.

But was what Kate was holding in her hand the reason Alice had been killed?

The only way to find out was to keep reading, to see just how hot was the information Alice had uncovered.

In the normal course of events, a processor came into the fishing grounds flush, prepared to take advantage of the early high market prices by topping other processors' bids in price per pound of salmon. That way high bidders got the best fish first, and most of it, for resale to potential buyers, gourmet restaurants as far away as New York, gourmet grocery stores, caviar makers, smokers, canners and packers.

Because the business was so cash intensive and because Alaskan salmon were considered gourmet, as opposed to farmed European or Canadian salmon which seemed to get more pale and more bland and more disease-ridden by the year, and because the freezer life of even a wild salmon was not long, a quick turnaround was necessary. A quick turnaround was only possible with large quantities of cash on hand, and cash in good old American dollars.

Since the Kuskokwim River was known the world over for the quality of its reds, business had always been brisk in Bering, especially after the Bristol Bay runs had crashed the year before. This accounted for the processors lined up down at the dock.

Alice had printed out a page for every one of them. The *Kyoto Kozushima*, the *Chongju*, the *Northern Harvester*, the *Arctic Princess*, along with others who had docked at Bering that season. All had healthy accounts amounting on average to

223

between one and two hundred thousand dollars, ready to be drawn upon. These looked as if the minimum amount were maintained over the winter, to keep the account open and current, and then were increased by a large deposit at the beginning of the fishing season. Payments went to Chevron for fuel and AC and Eagle for groceries, to the chandlers for parts and supplies and to Alaska Airlines and Baird Air for freight, but the bulk went to individual fishermen in many smaller payments ranging from two hundred dollars to ten thousand. Deposits of much larger amounts came from buyers. At the end of the year, Kate figured, they would clean out the account to the bare minimum and head south for the winter.

She came to the last page and halted. She had to read the numbers twice before she believed them, and that was after she counted the zeroes and the commas.

The *Kosygin*'s cash on hand amounted to one million five and change.

"What?" Stephanie said. She was halfway through the Lorna Doones, Kate was glad to see, while Kate's cocoa had gone cold in her mug.

"I'm sorry, did I make a noise?" Kate said. "I didn't mean to."

Deposits to the *Kosygin*'s account came from someone or something called High Seas Investments, Inc. The deposits were not large by comparison with the beginning deposits of the other processors, one to three hundred thousand dollars each, but there were so many of them, nearly—Kate ran her eyes down the dates—one every two or three days.

It looked like the *Kosygin* intended to buy one hell of a lot of fish.

Kate spread the accounts out on the table and compared numbers. The *Kosygin* was buying less fish from fewer fisherman than all of the other processors combined. At the same time, they seemed to be selling five or six times the amount of fish to their one buyer, a Northern Consolidated Seafood Distributors, Inc.

She sat back and thought of her visit to the *Kosygin*. The small crew. The dearth of fish, and near absence of fish smell. The willingness of the crew to party instead of readying the ship for sea again, to get out there and buy fish and fill up their hold.

Her eyes dropped to the pages spread out before her. She used a magazine as a straightedge and began to compare names with numbers.

The same fishermen were delivering to the *Kosygin* over and over again. This wasn't unusual; with this much money to throw around the *Kosygin* could afford to pay top dollar, but receiving a full load from the same fishermen three and four times a period was testing the bounds of fishing reality for anyone who'd ever wet a net in Alaskan waters. The twelve- and twenty-four-hour periods weren't long enough to accumulate that many loads, not to mention which the *Kosygin* would suffer a great deal of difficulty getting them on board that fast. Besides, the Kuskokwim salmon runs were dropping the same way the Bristol Bay runs were, although not as drastically, and for the same reason—the trollers with their one- and two-mile-long nets dredging up every living thing on the ocean bottom without regard for size, sex or species. There just weren't that many fish to catch, and if that was the case, there weren't that many fish to deliver, either.

A Russian processor. An Alaskan bank. A lot of money coming in. A lot of money going out.

She looked at the dates. The money was going out fast, usually one to two days after it had come in. The amount left was the bare minimum to keep the account open and to cover docking fees and crew expenses.

The pages didn't list the bank's fees, but they would be listed somewhere, and in large figures with lots of their own zeroes and commas, as banks were not in the business of providing their services for free.

The Alaska First Bank of Bering was providing the *Kosygin* quite a service.

She thought about Mike Sullivan. Alice had carelessly dropped a few facts about him. Too carelessly. Mike was divorced, and attractive, and about Alice's age, and Bering wasn't that big a town.

What had Alice said about Mike Sullivan? His father had been an Irish trapper who followed the beaver to Bering and married his mother, Martha Ashepak. His father had left soon after the birth of his second child, Mike's sister Brigid, and Martha had raised them up on her own, if any Yupik could be said to be ever truly alone. The Yupik were strong believers in having family around.

Kind of like Emaa, Kate thought, only more familial and less tribal. Or maybe it was just that to Emaa, everyone was family.

The Yupik were the unspoken envy of many Alaskan Natives, particularly the Yupik who lived along the Kuskokwim. It had helped the culture immensely that there was nothing of value by white, Western standards along the lower half of the Kuskokwim River. It was too shallow for whales to swim up, so the Yankee whalers passed it by, and it was faster to take the Yukon River to the Klondike from Nome, so the Gold Rush passed it by, too, except for the diseases the miners brought with them. Its broad, sandy banks and crumbling bluffs, its lack of trees for fuel and lumber, its sparse and scattered settlements, all these unattractive qualities had combined to allow the Yupik to retain their culture and even their language, which was presently taught half-days in the local school district, with English the other half of the day. "Family first" would have been their motto, if they'd had one. Families lived together, one and two and three and sometimes four generations together. They trapped together, they fished together, they hunted together, and when one family brought home meat the whole village shared.

As Alice had shared with her, she thought. She looked across the table at Stephanie, who had finished her cocoa and most of the cookies and who seemed content to wait in silence.

She didn't ask what had been in the envelope. She hadn't even looked at the papers. Kate didn't offer an explanation. It might be information that had gotten Stephanie's mother killed, and Stephanie was not going to fall heir to that same information if Kate had anything to say about it. She gathered up the papers and put them back in the envelope. "Thank you for bringing me these, Stephanie," she said.

The girl nodded, as was her usual habit keeping her eyes down. Mutt had her chin on the girl's left knee, her eyes closed in bliss as Stephanie scratched between the flattened ears.

"Did the police bring your mother's purse back?"

Stephanie shook her head.

"Somebody, a friend, a relative, went by the bank and picked it up? Maybe someone saw it there on the way into work today? And then brought it straight to your house?"

Stephanie's head bobbed in the slightest of nods. Pick one, Kate thought. Well, that explained why Trooper Mary Zarr hadn't trampled down her door, wanting to know why the deceased had had a letter addressed to Kate in her purse the night she died.

"I mean what I said yesterday," Kate said. "If you ever need anything, anything at all—"

"I want to go to school."

"I'm sorry, what?"

"I want to go to school." The voice was barely discernible but firm enough for all that.

"Okay," Kate said. She rallied. "Your mother said she hoped you would go. How can I help?"

"I don't know."

"Well, you should finish up here, first," Kate said, feeling her way. "Do you agree? You don't want to leave your great-grandfather, or your grandmother, not yet, do you?"

There was a brief silence. By then Kate's face was nearly at table level, trying to see into Stephanie's eyes. "I guess not," the girl said at last.

"Especially now," Kate said gently. "They'll need you, for now. Later, when you're older, when they have other grandchildren, then you can go. When you graduate from high school, maybe?"

"No."

"Oh. When then?"

"I want to go to Mt. Edgecumbe. They have a good sciences program." For the first time the girl raised her eyes, and Kate straightened hastily. "I'm good at science. I'm the best."

Only dimly did Kate perceive how difficult it was for Stephanie to say those words. If one were Yupik, according to Alice, and especially if one were female and Yupik, one did not speak up, or draw attention to oneself, and one never, ever claimed to be the best at anything. It had been hard for Alice to go to school, too. Kate was impressed by the girl's tenacity. "Oh. I see. How old are you, again?"

"Ten."

"Which puts you in which grade?"

"Fourth last year. Fifth next year."

"So you'll have three more years at home, before going off to school. Is that enough, Stephanie?"

"Yes."

"Don't answer so quickly. Think about it. Are three years more long enough?" Something in her voice caught and held the girl's attention. "I lost my parents very young, younger even than you. I refused to live with my grandmother because I wanted to stay on the homestead with my parents' memories. It wasn't the best or the smartest thing I've ever done, Stephanie. And it hurt my grandmother deeply."

Until she'd said the words out loud, she hadn't realized how true they were. Oh Emaa, I am so sorry.

"You have the rest of your life, Stephanie. Many, many years. Your grandmother has not so many, your great-grandfather even less."

Silence.

"Just think about it, all right? But remember, whatever you decide, whatever you wind up wanting to do, I will help. All you have to do is write, or call. Okay?"

"I guess so."

Kate reached across the table and put a hand beneath Stephanie's chin. "You know so."

They stared at each other, considering, evaluating, testing. Kate tried not to blink.

"Is that envelope why my mother died?"

Kate tried not to jump, tried to keep her eyes and her voice steady. She withdrew her hand and sat up. "I don't know. I hope not."

Stephanie regarded her steadily without expression for what seemed like a very long time. After which she rose to her feet, gave Mutt a final scratch, tucked her Cub beneath her arm and left.

"I thought Kipnuk was a dry town," Jim said.

"It is," Baird said, grunting as he shifted another case to a pallet.

"Then what are we doing shipping this beer to them?"

"I just ship it. What they do with it once it gets there is their problem."

Jim was beginning to miss his uniform. He opened his mouth to say more and caught sight of Stephanie standing in the doorway to the hangar, bright red Super Cub clutched beneath one arm.

"You can get that, can't you?" he said to Baird, and walked toward the girl, leaving Baird standing next to a truckload of Michelob and a half-empty pallet. Jim ignored the string of curses that followed along behind him.

"Hi, Stephanie." He knelt down, and didn't make the mistake of reaching for her. "It's nice to see you."

She wouldn't look up, as usual.

He hesitated, and then said gently, "I was really sorry to hear about your mother."

A brief, almost indiscernible nod.

She touched her finger to his wound, so lightly he could barely feel it. He looked like he'd started to get a decorator shave of his scalp and had changed his mind halfway through. "You got hurt."

"Yeah," Jim said, and gave her his best smile. "But you should see the other guy."

She did smile then, although without looking up, and about then the Herc landed with a hold full of reds from Quinhagak. He led the girl to a fifty-five-gallon drum of engine oil and perched her on it, her and her Super Cub. "You stay here until I tell you, okay? You can come look at the plane, but only when I say so, all right?" He grinned. "I don't want you getting in the way of those props. God knows what damage your hard head would do to them."

She did smile then, revealing dimples and straight white teeth. It didn't last long, but at least now he knew she had teeth.

Baird emerged from behind the beer truck and skidded to a halt when he saw Stephanie. He inspected her closely from a distance of thirty feet. "Is that yours?" he said to Jim.

"Yes," Jim said. "I mean no. I mean, she's a friend. She won't get in the way."

"She better not," Baird said, a scowl darkening his face.

"She loves planes," Jim said.

Baird snorted. "Everybody loves planes."

"She builds model ones. She built the one she's holding. You should take a look—it's a Super Cub that's the twin of any one I ever flew in, except for size."

Baird snorted again, although it was less contemptuous this time. "Everybody builds model airplanes."

Jim helped fuel the Herc for its trip into Anchorage and when he returned, Stephanie was no longer on her barrel. He panicked until he saw Baird sitting in the Cessna's left seat, talking to someone in the right seat Jim couldn't see. On a hunch he approached from behind, and heard Baird say, "Okay, we'll have to leave the rudders for when your legs are longer."

"Blocks," Stephanie's voice said.

"Blocks? This ain't no time to play ABC's, kid, we're—oh. Wooden blocks, big ones, we could duct-tape them to the rudder pedals. Then your feet could reach. Good idea, kid, we'll do that next time. Okay, remember what I told you about landing without flaps? We call it landing clean, but you need a lot of runway. Say you're going into a Bush strip in your Cub, maybe all you got is three hundred feet before the alders take over, then you gotta use flaps to—"

Jim tiptoed away.

CHAPTER 12

sounds to sunrise
one clear voice in tongues

—*The Ripples*

KATE WALKED INTO TOWN. The day after the Fourth, the road was littered with the wrappings of fireworks. It would seem Bering had no local ordinance against them. In another town, in a wet town, the feeling would have been subdued, the morning after the night before, but in Bering it was business as usual, traffic nonstop between the docks and the airport, stores bustling with customers, lines at restaurant doors. The joint was jumping.

"Stay," she said to Mutt, who flopped beneath a rose bush with a martyred sigh. Kate trod the steps to the Bering Public Library, a small, square prefab building with coppery brown siding and windows neatly outlined in white paint. Each window had its own flower box, overflowing with pansies and nasturtiums. Twelve-by-twelves cut into four-foot lengths marked a line of parking spaces, only one of which was in use.

Inside rows of metal shelves crowded with books filled the center of the room. To the left was the children's corner, with low round tables and tiny chairs. To the right was the reference section. A few grownup chairs were grouped around a rectangular work table, upon which a dark, burly man had his feet propped. His nose was buried in a copy of

The Carpetbaggers that looked as if it had already seen much use. He didn't bother to look up at Kate's entrance. There was something familiar about the shape of his head, but she couldn't place him and she was intent on her mission so she didn't try very hard. A mistake, as it later turned out, but then Kate wasn't perfect, as she herself would be first to admit.

"May I help you?"

This from a pleasant young woman with a nice smile and a mop of straight black hair that fell into her eyes. She wore a flowered blouse with short sleeves tucked into a loose blue skirt, and flat heels. She looked like somebody's mother.

She looked a little like Alice, in fact.

"I'm hoping you've got the state newspapers on microfilm," Kate said, trying not to sound grim.

"Yes, we do—?" Her eyes flickered to Kate's scar and back again.

"Kate," Kate said. "Kate Shugak." There wasn't much point in trying to keep her identity a secret any longer if Ray Chevak was going to introduce her around.

"Hi, Kate, I'm Heidi. Right over here."

She led Kate to a row of cabinets holding long, small drawers filled with rolls of microfilm in boxes.

"If there is anything else I can do to help, please let me know." She hesitated. "I knew your grandmother."

As who didn't?

"She visited here quite often, Bering, I mean, although she stopped by the library every now and then, too. Of course, she spent most of her time out at the Chevaks'."

Not only had Emaa had a prolonged romantic relationship, the entire city of Bering knew every detail.

While her outstanding dullard of a granddaughter remained totally in the dark.

"Thanks," Kate said with determined civility. "I'll yell if I need help." Her smile of thanks was more of a grimace.

Heidi looked a little startled. "Well, take your time. There's only one other person in here, and he's reading, so I can help whenever you want." She retreated to her desk.

Bering was hooked up to a computer service, so Kate could do a search on the name of Michael Sullivan and another on the name of Christopher Overmore and make a list of dates of articles. Overmore's name got far more hits than Sullivan's, which was not surprising. She concentrated on the articles written within the past twenty years, in the *Juneau Empire*, the *Anchorage Daily News*, and the *Bering Sea Times*.

She hit paydirt almost from the first frame.

Overmore had been a banker before he had been a senator, one of the founders of Great Land Savings and Loan, which in turn was one of the original repositories of funds dispersed under the Alaska Native Claims Settlement Act of 1972. The savings and loan had gone under during the financial bust in the mid-eighties, involving the loss of twenty-three million dollars. Most of that twenty-three million had originally belonged to five Native associations around the state.

Kate was delighted to read that in 1992 there had been an indictment, followed by a trial and, further, that the *Anchorage Daily News* had sicced Sheila Toomey onto it. Toomey wrote smart, always a plus. Kate kept her savings on her kitchen table in a one-pound Darigold butter can. She would need someone who wrote smart to explain major-league banking to her.

Toomey wrote funny, too, although it would be a stretch, even for her, to write funny about mortgage rates.

It took the state six years to hand down forty-two counts of conspiracy and bank fraud, and another two years to bring the accused to trial. The prosecutor claimed that Overmore et al had made a number of unsecured loans in the amount of five hundred thousand dollars each to members of the bank's board, so that the board members could buy stock in an attempt to take over another bank, this one in Fairbanks. Witnesses testified that they thought the loans so problematical that lower management refused to sign off on them. The defense attorney protested that this was simply taking advantage of a good business opportunity, as the bank in question was undervalued and badly run.

The prosecution claimed that the officials of Great Land Savings and Loan had falsified minutes and forged documents to get federal approval of the takeover plan and to prove its adherence to the regulatory process. Witnesses from the Federal Reserve Bank said they'd never seen said documents and certainly had never signed off on them. The defense attorney protested that the allegedly falsified documents were last-minute corrections made sloppily by a legal secretary who wanted to get home to her kids. He attached no blame to the secretary, instead drawing a moving picture of her three children, one of whom had cerebral palsy. He maintained that the paperwork to the Federal Reserve Bank had been lost in the mail.

The prosecution claimed that bank funds had been misappropriated to open a branch of Great Land Savings and Loan in Palm Springs, California, and further, that bank funds had been used to finance a lifestyle that would make Frank Sinatra weep with envy, including a townhouse on a golf course for each board member, a Mercedes-Benz 450 SL coupe in each garage, and ten memberships in Club Palm Springs. The recreation director of Club Palm Springs testified that various board members had, in fact, played golf, tennis or racquetball at the Club three out of every four weeks from November to March, and had the daybooks to prove it. The defense attorney protested that by 1987 there was no banking business left in Alaska. Wasn't it sensible and businesslike for responsible officers of the institution to seek out new investors where the money was? Palm Springs would be such a place. And certainly in seeking out new investors in Palm Springs one wouldn't go down to the local Y.

The trial lasted three and a half months. A great many documents were introduced into the record concerning the laws governing money in America, most of them by the defense. The judge had to wake up on average one juror per week. In the end, the jury was unable to decide if Great Land Savings and Loan's failure was due to embezzlement of funds or just plain incompetence, and Overmore and his partners had walked.

Of course, that was Fairbanks, Kate thought. It was a byword in Alaska that if you were guilty, petitioning for a change of venue to Fairbanks was your best bet for being found not guilty.

The next article, some two years later, announced Overmore's intention of running for office from District S.

"Excuse me?" she said to Heidi.

"Yes?" Heidi hurried over.

"Do you have a *Legislative Review*, going back about five years?"

"Certainly. What do you need?"

"I want to look up Christopher Overmore's voting record."

There was the sound of a book dropping to the floor.

"Excuse, please," a male voice called.

"No problem, sir," Heidi said cheerfully, flapping a dismissive hand.

She consulted the stacks and produced the light green paperbound books for the years required, hovered in case Kate needed help finding her way around them, and returned sadly to her desk when Kate didn't.

Overmore had run unopposed, because you couldn't count the city councilman from Dillingham who advocated Alaska's secession from the Union, the purchase of Siberia from Russia and the formation of their own country, or the mayor of Nome, who wanted to give away condoms in the schools. Overmore was a moderate Republican who had backed rural preference for subsistence and limited sovereignty for Alaska Native tribal governments. Of course, these were safe positions to take, as the Republican Party had a lock on the legislature and there was no way either initiative would pass. Kate suspected the Republican Party allowed Overmore these radical opinions, the outward manifestation of which would keep his seat, so long as he toed the party line in other matters.

This he appeared to do, and with enthusiasm. During the past five years in office Overmore had sponsored a bill that outlawed abortion, and when that failed, cut funding to any agency that offered either advice or monetary help to get one. He sponsored another bill to return prayer to the schools. He cosponsored a bill advocating private school vouchers, and joined with the majority in undermining the public ballot which had legalized marijuana for medicinal purposes. Every year, he sponsored an amendment to the Alaska constitution to return the death penalty for perpetrators of capital crimes. He sat as chairman of the joint banking committee, where further research indicated he favored doing away with banking controls completely.

At least, Kate thought, replacing the copies of the *Legislative Review* on their proper shelf, thus earning an approving smile from Heidi, Overmore hadn't had a vision from God telling him what to do about subsistence, as another honorable—and still in office—representative of the Republican persuasion had had.

She sat down again to review her scribbled notes. Mike Sullivan had not been one of the board members of Great Land Savings and Loan. His name had not been mentioned at trial. The only court case related to him she had found in the judicial listings was the announcement of his divorce from Judith A. Sullivan, nee Calhoun, no children, in 1995. He started Alaska First Bank of Bering in 1992.

His backers were not listed anywhere, but Kate bet she knew one of their names.

She looked up and caught Heidi's eye. The librarian left off arranging by date a year's worth of issues of the *Smithsonian Magazine* and bustled over. It was a slow day at the Bering Public Library.

"If I wanted to know who the names of the board of directors of a corporation were, how would I find out?"

Heidi gnawed her lip. "That depends. I'm guessing you don't have a copy of their latest annual report."

Kate was smiling back before she realized it. "You're guessing right."

"Are they publicly or privately owned?"

"I don't know." Kate reflected. "But if I had to guess, I'd say privately." A privately held company was probably less subject to public disclosure laws. Christopher Overmore et al had been prosecuted over the failure of Great Land Savings and Loan because it was publicly owned, and had to answer to shareholders. Picky people, shareholders. Nosy, too.

Heidi made a face. "That makes it tougher. We've got the *Directory of Corporate Affiliations* and *Standard & Poor's Register of Corporations*, but they are both for public corporations."

"Well, if the corporation isn't in them, at least I'll know they aren't public."

Heidi brought out the volumes, and Kate looked up High Seas Investments, Ltd., Northern Consolidated Seafood Distributors, Inc., and just for the hell of it, Alaska First Bank of Bering.

The bank was the only one listed, in *Standard & Poor*, and the only officer listed was the chairman and chief executive officer, one Michael Sullivan. It very helpfully included his address, which amounted to a post office box and a zip code.

"Hey," Carroll said. She was looking out the window of Zarr's office.

"What?" Casanare said, coming to stand behind her.

They watched Kate come down the steps and turn right toward the airport, Mutt trotting ahead of her, nose to the ground.

"What's she doing in the library?"

"Maybe she's checking out a book," Casanare suggested.

"Which book?"

"Max—"

She glared at him. "Al, I don't care if First Sergeant Jim Chopin thinks Kate Shugak sits at the right hand of God. She's been consorting on a regular basis over a period of at least two months with a known member of a group of foreign criminals we are currently investigating for the smuggling of weapons into this country. I want to know what she's up to."

240

"She went into a library, for crissake, she's not robbing a bank."

"Al, she fits the profile. She's a loner, she has a problem with authority, she's got enough cause to hold one hell of a grudge against the system. She has to be reminded of it every time she looks in the mirror."

"She's a woman."

"So because all domestic terrorists so far have been men, that means there will never be a woman who likes to blow people up?" Casanare was silent, reluctant to endorse Carroll's theory of sexual equality in serial bombers, and Carroll pushed her advantage. "She's got a hundred and sixty acres out in the middle of nowhere to do whatever the hell she wants to on. You've seen the pictures, you've read the reports. She could hide a factory out there if she wanted to. She could hide an army out there if she wanted to."

"You just said she was a loner."

"Quit playing devil's advocate and look at the facts. We've got an incoming shipment of material crucial to the manufacture of an explosive nuclear device, ten of them, for all we know a hundred. It's sitting on a boat on board which Kate Shugak was cordially invited two days ago, from which she was escorted by none other than the man we believe is Ivanov, a point man for the Russian Mafia and a known smuggler of illegal weapons. And she fits the profile."

"What's she using for money? Who's backing her? She can't be going into this alone, not financially, anyway."

Carroll smiled, knowing she had him. "We've got any number of extremist groups with a toehold in Alaska. Could be one of them, or a consortium, maybe with groups in Montana or Idaho or both. Crazy loves company." She looked over his shoulder and purred, "Well, well, well. Look who I see."

Casanare turned and saw the former General Armin Glukhov, late of the sovereign nation of Russia, trot down the steps of the library and head in the direction of the docks.

Carroll looked at Casanare, eyebrow raised. "Any more objections?"

"Not hardly," he said.

She went to the door and said over her shoulder, "Leave Zarr a note to come find us when she checks in."

Heidi looked up as the two agents entered the library, which was empty by then of everyone except her. "Hello. May I help you find something?"

Casanare spoke first. "I'm Al Gonzalez, Miss—" He smiled.

Heidi blushed. "Call me Heidi."

"Hi, Heidi. This is my friend, Maxine Casey."

"Hi, Maxine."

"Hello." Carroll's eyes warned Al to get on with it.

"You're not from Bering, are you?"

"No," Casanare said regretfully. "We sure aren't. Nice little town, though. Different than anything I've ever seen."

"Really? Where are you from?"

Casanare grinned and said in an exaggerated southern accent, "Takes-us."

"Really?" Heidi said again. "I've never been there." She sighed. "Never been much of anywhere Outside, except Seattle."

"Now there's a great town."

"Any town that puts a troll under a bridge can't be all bad," Heidi agreed, and they laughed together.

By this time Carroll had sidled into the reference area. To her acute disappointment, everything was neat and tidy. She prowled over to the fiction area. A copy of a novel was lying on the table. Carroll picked it up. Harold Robbins. She seemed to remember that this particular book was supposed to be a

242

broad fictionalization of the life of Howard Hughes. Who cared? She put the book back down.

"Tell you the truth, Heidi, we were supposed to meet a friend here." Casanare made a show of looking around.

"Oh? Who?"

He smiled at her again. "Her name's Kate. Kate Shugak. You seen her?"

"Yeah, you just missed her, she was working in the reference section."

"Alone?"

Heidi raised her eyebrows, and Casanare said hastily, "We were going to meet another friend. All of us were going to meet here. To work on our project together."

"Well, he must have forgotten, because she was here alone."

"Really. Darn, I thought I saw him coming down the steps. Too far away to catch him."

"No, Ms. Shugak was here alone. Oh."

"What?" Casanare said hopefully.

"You must have seen the Russian gentleman."

"Yes?"

"He was reading in the fiction section, at the same time she was in the research section."

"Oh. They weren't together."

Her brows knit. She was getting suspicious. "No. They never spoke."

"Really. Darn." Casanare scratched his cheek thoughtfully. "We have kind of a project going on—"

"Oh, you were working on that, too?" Heidi said, too affably.

"Yeah, that report on—" He paused hopefully.

Instead, she gave him a considering look. "Which project did you mean? Ms. Shugak was working on two."

"I'm not sure." Again, he paused.

"Take a guess." She waited. He filled in no blanks for her. "You know, you're too old to be a college student."

"So is Kate," he pointed out.

"Yeah, but I know her, or at least I know of her. I don't know you. What, specifically, can I help you with?"

Casanare looked at Carroll and shrugged. Busted.

The Super Cub had broken a seal on the way back from Atmaukluak, much to Baird's loud and profane annoyance, and when Kate got back to the airport they were just loading the engine onto the Herc. Also on board were a Kwethluk cop, his wife and three children who were moving back to Nebraska, the mosquitoes and the muktuk too much for them, and two thousand pounds of smoked king salmon, produced by a local Native cooperative sponsored by the Native association and destined for Anchorage, where it would be packaged and resold at quadruple the price. It was the real stuff, too; long, dark red strips of hard, smelly fillet. Kate's mouth watered. The sharp end of one piece had broken through the plastic wrap—

Baird's bellow made her jump. "Oh yeah, fine, now you show up, after all the goddamn work is done! Where the hell have you been?"

"Out," Kate said. "What are you bellyaching about? My shift doesn't start until midnight."

"But you've always been here before!" Baird sounded aggrieved.

It was true. Since her arrival in March, she had always been there, ready to be rousted out to turn a hand to anything that needed doing. She had been wounded when she arrived, almost mortally. The only way to subdue her own pain had been to work, morning, noon and night. She'd objected to the hiring of another roustabout, for fear it would leave her more time to feel.

What had changed?

She met Jim Chopin's eyes over Baird's shoulder, and repeated, "My shift doesn't start until midnight. I'm going to grab a few hours sleep before then. 'Night, all."

At midnight she loitered deliberately in the bunkhouse, waiting for Jim. The hands crept round on the clock, five after, ten after, and for a while she thought he wasn't coming. He'd probably apologized to Zarr, who certainly deserved one, and had been rewarded for his pains. Chopper Jim, reverting to form.

I should feel relieved, she thought. Everything's back to normal.

The door opened and normal eluded her once again.

"You're late for work," he said.

"I've got something to show you," she replied, and held out the envelope Stephanie had brought.

"What?" He opened the envelope. "What are these?" He walked to his bunk and turned on the light.

To his back, she said, "They are printouts of processor accounts from the records of Alaska First Bank of Bering. You'll see their names at the top of each sheet."

She could tell the exact moment when he came to the account of the *Kosygin*.

The room went very still.

"If you look at those for a while, you start to see some interesting differences in the numbers."

He turned and with one sweep of his arm shoved everything on the table up against the wall. Kate caught the jar of peanut butter just in time. He flicked on the overhead light and spread out the sheets of paper. "Show me."

She showed him. "What it boils down to is that large sums of money are coming in from High Seas Investments, Inc., and being run through the *Kosygin*'s account in the Alaska First Bank of Bering on their way to Northern Consolidated Seafood Distributors, Inc. I don't think I have to point out, but I will anyway just for the hell of it, that the sums of money involved represent larger amounts than can be accounted for by the purchase and resale of Kuskokwim reds. Especially this season. And especially if you see how few fishermen have delivered how often and how repeatedly."

"They're laundering money," he said.

"Give the man a cigar."

He leaned forward again to scrutinize the *Kosygin*'s account. "The fishermen have to be in on it."

She confined her response to a mild, "Why?"

"The *Kosygin* writes them checks for fish not delivered."

"I don't think so."

"What do you mean?"

She held up the Y-K Delta phone book filched from the hangar office. "I looked for the names of the fishermen listed as receiving checks. None of them are in this."

"They could be fishermen from Outside. Plenty are."

"Not one, Jim."

He considered. "So it's all the bank."

"I think so."

"They're in it up to their ears if they're phonying up a record of nonexistent checks."

"Yes."

He looked at her directly for the first time. "Where did you get these printouts, Kate?"

She set her teeth and said, "Alice Chevak. She was the head teller at Alaska First Bank of Bering. We went to school together in Fairbanks. I asked her for a favor."

He nodded, eyes on her face. "I see."

A brief silence. "You want to tell me why you're here, now?"

He thought about it. "I've told you all I can."

She examined her fingernails, clipped short, filed smooth and scrupulously clean for all that she'd spent the last four months messing around with and in airplanes. "You show up in Bering under an assumed name, you're shot within twenty-four hours of your arrival, the first and last thing you say when I visit you at the hospital are two Russian words, *dasvidanya* and *spasibo*, good-bye and thank you."

She stood up and began to pace. He folded his arms and watched her walk back and forth. It wasn't a long walk, three paces one way, turn, three paces the other.

"I, being a naturally observant person, notice that there are two visitors ahead of me. They're trying awfully hard to look like day laborers, but they've got that stink, you know, how to describe it—" She paused and sniffed the air. "—that whiff of Ruby Ridge in the morning, that evening stench of Leonard Peltier." She looked at him. "In short, if I had one, I'd bet my left nut they're FBI."

When he didn't clutch his heart with shocked surprise, she resumed pacing. "So I wander on down to the docks, and I see a lot of processors, and lo and behold, one of them is Russian. I go on board, where I don't see a hell of a lot of fish, but I do see a young crew dressed for success and not wanting for much in the way of liquor, cigarettes or food. They're a little lonely," she allowed, "which led them to invite me to a party, but they weren't worrying about getting back to work anytime soon."

"You sure are a nosy bitch," he said without heat.

"Thank you," she said sweetly.

"You know something else?"

"What?"

"This is the first time since I got here that I've seen the real Kate looking back at me."

"What?"

He stood up and began unbuttoning his shirt. "You're late for work, and I'm late for my shower." Deliberately he summoned up the shark's grin, all teeth and appetite and no discernible trace of sincerity. "Unless you'd care to stick around and wash my back?"

The door was still vibrating resentfully on its hinges a full minute later when he grabbed his ditty bag and headed up to the public showers at the terminal, trying not to wish she'd accepted his invitation to join him.

But it had stopped her from asking any more damn questions, hadn't it?

CHAPTER 13

Dangling time like the poise
Of a dancer's heel

—*Petition for Nuclear Freeze*

THE CHESS BOARD WAS oak, the chessmen ivory. Oak and ivory both were stained and dark. The pieces left were divided up about equally, white in front of Kamyanka, black in front of Glukhov. The air was thick with smoke.

They were sitting in the wardroom of the *Kosygin*. "When do we meet?"

"At eleven o'clock."

"Where?"

"He will come here."

Glukhov moved a pawn. "I am nervous about this, I admit it."

"Don't be. It's all about money, and we have enough."

"It is a great deal of risk," Glukhov said.

"We have a great deal of money."

Glukhov grinned. "And we will have more. Especially when we sell off the rest of the plutonium." He had been angry when Kamyanka had told him the true contents of the truck as they were driving away from the base, but his first sip of a Starbucks cup of the day, with cream and sugar, bought on the free and entrepreneur-friendly soil of the United States of America in the form of Sea-Tac International Airport, had soothed his conscience to an indistinguishable murmur.

Kamyanka moved his bishop to take Glukhov's queen.

Glukhov's grin faded. He studied the board. "An odd thing this afternoon," he said, trying to figure out a way through the impenetrable white defense to move his pawn to the last square.

"Really?" Kamyanka was bored. He'd masterminded the theft of the rubles to pay for the plutonium to resell it for enough money to finance his entry into the fields of commerce and trade in the United States, that acknowledged pacesetter of free markets. Planning fascinated him; operations did not.

He was even more bored with Glukhov, who was insisting they speak English all the time, so as to prepare him for his imminent retirement to a townhouse condominium on a golf course in Scottsdale, Arizona.

Unfortunately, he could not be rid of the general just yet, because the general was the one who had met Senator Christopher Overmore when the general had been stationed in Vladivostok in 1997. There had been a great deal of to-ing and fro-ing between Alaska and Siberia since the Wall came down, something Kamyanka had noticed himself when it began as a possibly lucrative opportunity. Glukhov and Overmore shared an interest in vodka, girls and money, and had kept in touch ever since. Overmore and his brother-in-law's bank were the last part of the plan to fall into place.

No, he couldn't do without Glukhov.

Yet.

"I go to the library this afternoon, as you know."

"No, I didn't know."

"Oh, I am a great reader," Glukhov assured him. "I mention before my interest in the great American authors, like Judith Krantz. Everyone read these. They teach much about life in

America. I will be ready!" He beamed.

"Uh-huh." Kamyanka had never heard of any of them but then he'd never read a book in his life, either.

"There was a woman in the library."

Kamyanka stifled a yawn, and moved a knight in front of Glukhov's advancing pawn.

"She was asking for Senator Overmore."

Kamyanka paused with his hand on his knight. "What?"

"She was in—" Glukhov searched for the right word, failed to find it, and had to lapse into Russian. "She was in the reference section. The librarian was helping her find out about Senator Overmore." He regained his English. "I hear them talk." He corrected himself. "Talking. I hear them talking."

Kamyanka released the knight. "What did she want to know?"

"She doesn't say, but she is in that place for two hours. She takes many notes." Glukhov took the knight with his pawn, and tried unsuccessfully to hide his triumph.

Kamyanka took the pawn with his bishop. "Checkmate."

Glukhov's face fell. He studied the board with dismay, trying to see where he'd gone wrong.

"What did she look like?" Kamyanka said.

"What? Who?"

"The woman in the library. What did she look like?"

"Oh." Glukhov sat back with a sigh. "I don't know. Like all the women here. Small, dark."

"Short hair or long?"

Glukhov thought. "Short."

Kamyanka took a careful breath. "Did she look anything like the woman on board the other day?" Glukhov looked blank, and Kamyanka elaborated. "The woman at the crew's party? The woman Yuri said was asking questions about

Burianovich? The only woman who has been on board this vessel since we docked? That woman?"

Glukhov blinked. "I suppose it could be. I hadn't thought. Yes, I guess it was," he said, marveling.

Footsteps sounded in the passageway, and Kamyanka rose to his feet, Glukhov a beat behind him.

"Senator!" Glukhov surged forward, hand outstretched. "Is delight to see you again!"

"Armin! Your English is wonderful! You must have worked very hard." Overmore pushed back the enveloping hood of his dark blue sweatshirt and smacked his hands together. "Where's the vodka?"

The Herc came in late, delayed by an emergency caused by a Reeve Aleutian 727 limping into Anchorage from Dutch Harbor on one engine. All traffic had been suspended as the 727 dumped fuel over the upper Inlet. They'd landed safely, and when they rolled to a stop the pilot turned to the crew and said, "Let's show a little class, boys and girls, put on your jackets and caps and straighten your ties."

All this Larry Maciarello related to Kate with relish. Pilots loved stories about near disasters. Actual crashes were okay so long as they knew no one on board and could second-guess the pilot, but near disasters, where everyone walked away, were best. Larry would be reflying the Reeve flight for years, and so would every other pilot who heard about it. Before too long, they'd have been on board, and before much longer, in the left seat.

He helped move the load of groceries out of the Herc and onto the back of the AC flatbed. "I hear you're really Kate Shugak," the driver of the flatbed said to Kate.

She looked at him.

His smile faded. "Yeah, well, I guess it doesn't matter much," he mumbled, backing up to the cab. He climbed in and the flatbed would have kicked dirt if the apron of the airport hadn't been paved.

"Kate Shugak?" Larry said behind her. "What, you're here incognito?"

She turned to see him smiling.

"Kind of like Mata Hari."

Kate looked at him. "Uh-huh," she said.

"Kind of sexy, having an alias. Like your scar."

The next thing she knew he had grabbed her and was trying to kiss her. It wasn't necessarily disgusting, but it was irritating. "Larry, knock it off." She squirmed. He countersquirmed. "Larry, damn it, I mean it, knock it off!" She stiff-armed his shoulders and he retaliated by grabbing her waist and pulling her in tight.

"Okay," she said through her teeth, "that's—mmmph—it."

She raised both feet off the ground, and suddenly he was holding her entire weight with two hands. It threw him off balance and he staggered back a step. He couldn't hold her and she slid down. She got her feet planted just in time and stood straight up fast without bothering to move away first.

The top of her head connected with his jaw. His teeth snapped together with enough force to chip two of them. His head flew back and they both heard the distinctive *Snick!* as his back went out.

He shrieked. There was no other word for it. Kate found herself free. One hand went to his head, one to his lower back. "Ouch, oh damn, oh shit, oh damn! Look what you did to me, oh god, my back, my head, my back!"

He looked to be in real and serious pain, and Kate began to feel sorry for him, just a little, not a lot. He wasn't a big bad wolf, after all; in the predator hierarchy he barely ranked at rabbit. "Look, Larry—"

"Don't touch me!" he shrieked again. "Don't help me, don't come near me!"

He hobbled away, moaning.

Kate turned to see Mutt standing in the doorway of the hangar. "You were a big help."

One eyebrow quirked. Like you needed it, the amused yellow gaze said.

Kate retired to the office to make some coffee. All the planes were in the barn or at the dock for the night, save the DC-3, which was on the ground in Iliamna while the Native association board whooped it up with the Iliamna association board. Kate wondered who Cal Kemper had found to seduce. There was always someone.

Unfortunately, with nothing coming in or going out, that left only paperwork. She brought the various logs up to date, aircraft, engine and business, and entered future trips on the four calendars on the wall of the hangar, one for each plane. It was going to be a busy July. She toted up checks amounting to seven thousand dollars—a slow day—made out a deposit slip and tucked them into an envelope for Baird to take to the bank the next day, if he didn't forget.

The Alaska First Bank of Bering, that was. Kate wondered if she should hint Baird into banking elsewhere. She wondered if the bank were FDIC insured. The FBI had no jurisdiction over banks that weren't.

For all she knew, Baird and Sullivan were drinking buddies. Best to leave it alone for now, watch what happened, but she might have to take steps at some point. Baird was often obnoxious in both his personal and his professional habits and he showered far too rarely to suit Kate, but he worked hard to make his business a success, and he didn't deserve to lose it all to a crooked banker.

She was going to have to tell Jim about Sullivan, though, and Overmore, and soon. She would have earlier if he hadn't reverted to his usual pain-in-the-ass persona. It was only a hunch, backed by some interesting coincidences and some even more interesting past history. If she could just hold onto her temper long enough in Jim's presence to get the words out.

It didn't occur to her until much later how long it had been since she'd lost her temper.

It was four in the morning when she yawned and decided it was time to stretch her legs on the way to the outhouse. Mutt, laid out on a rug in the hangar like a sack of potatoes, opened one eye to a slit and promptly closed it again as Kate went past.

It was late enough to do her business with the door open, and she sat for a few moments and contemplated the distant lights of Bering, three miles to the northeast, nearly obscured by the length of the swamp grass and the density of the alders between. A small town, tight knit, as witness the continuous flow of people in and out of the Chevak house the day before. It reminded her of Niniltna. On a larger scale, of course, as Niniltna had less than five hundred people and Bering had over five thousand.

But it had the same kind of village feeling. If everybody knew everybody else's business, then everybody was ready to help in times of trouble. And they were just as ready to help celebrate in times of joy. The four aunties and their quilting bee, who provided every new bride in the Park with a handmade quilt on her wedding day. Dinah's had had the cover of one of her favorite books painstakingly embroidered in every square, twelve squares in all. Bernie, the bar owner who pretended a fidelity to the bottom line that was proved false time and again, when he refused to serve alcohol to women he knew were pregnant, when he cut off known drunks well before closing time, and confiscated their truck keys into the bargain, when he memorized the birth dates of every kid in the local school and threw them steadily and repeatedly out the door of the Roadhouse when they tried to lie their way in. George Perry, who rivaled Jim Chopin for skirt-chasing but who had been known to get up at five A.M. on a February morning to preheat the engine on his Cessna so it would take off in twenty-below weather and the Niniltna High School student council could get to a conference in Anchorage.

Bobby, who pirated radio air to broadcast snippets of Park news, who'd been born, who got married and who died, and notices for the bake sales and car washes the basketball team staged to earn money for away games. Dinah, who edited home videos for Park rats to send to relatives Outside, accepting for payment a quart of blueberries or a promise of one of next year's kings. Mandy and Chick, who brought glory to Niniltna when they raced in the Iditarod.

Old Sam, who had been with her on the hunt, who'd helped get Demetri down from the ridge in spite of a bullet wound and a broken arm, who had helped bring back Jack's body. Old Sam, that crusty Alaskan old fart, who'd been the only one whose company she'd been able to tolerate on the homestead last winter.

Why, I miss them, she thought, surprised.

The horizon brightened. She remembered a poem, one of Roethke's. In a dark time, the eye begins to see, in broad day the midnight come again, something like that. What was the other line? All natural shapes blazing unnatural light? Some people might call the Arctic's midnight sun unnatural light.

In a dark time, the eye begins to see.

Was she?

Bird calls began to sound, chirps to song to honks, but not the one she was listening for.

Birds know their own place.

She was five steps from the outhouse when somebody threw a blanket over her head.

"Hey!" Her shout was loud and immediate and completely muffled by the blanket.

She fought, kicking, struggling. A rope was thrown, fastened tight. "Mutt!" she tried to yell, and then somebody unloaded a ton of bricks on her and she knew no more.

She woke up in the bed of a pickup truck.

At least that's what she thought it was when it bounced over a rut and tossed her a foot in the air. She came down hard with her head jammed into a corner and her shoulder against something that felt uncomfortably like the fender of a wheel well.

She was glad that her head was jammed into a corner because it felt only tentatively attached to her body and might otherwise have fallen right off her shoulders. There was a dull, insistent pain making its presence known to someone, somewhere, but her most pressing concern was her need to breathe. The blanket over her head was smothering her. Her hands had been bound to her side beneath it, pulling her elbows into the indentation of her waist, a natural curve between breasts and hips that resisted efforts to inch the rope up or down.

She was still fighting it when the driver of the truck slammed on his brakes and she slid forward into the cab, hard. She was still dazed when the tailgate went down, although she could hear that he had left the engine running.

Hands grabbed her feet and she resisted the instinctive urge to kick. It hadn't helped last time, and her only advantage might be in leading her captor to believe that she was still unconscious. So far as she could tell, straining her ears, there was only one person.

She was thrown unceremoniously over a shoulder in a fireman's lift. The breath went out of her in a whoof, the pain that had been happening to somebody else was not so distant anymore and she was unable to restrain a faint groan. She gritted her teeth and counted as the man carrying her walked, one, two, three, four, five, six, seven steps in all. There was a grunt, a shift of weight and she fell backwards, knocking her right shoulder on something round and hard and landing on a surface softer than the truck bed but which knocked the breath out of her just the same.

Which was fortunate, as she couldn't move or exclaim as she felt hands at the rope binding her arms. There was a moment of clarity, of realization. He was untying her. This was it, her chance for escape. Her breath returned and she fought to hide it though her lungs were starving for oxygen.

Throughout her captor remained silent, no word, no sound, and for some reason his silence told her that she was about to die. The realization steadied her, cleared her head, and she didn't move as the rope and the blanket were stripped away. She kept her eyes closed, and let herself utter an artistic little moan when she was hauled upright to sit behind a steering wheel. So that was what had hit her right shoulder when he'd dropped her. She was in the cab of the pickup.

He draped her limp body over the steering wheel, and reached around her for the gearshift.

She beat him to it, sitting upright, throwing in the clutch and slamming the gearshift into reverse. Only there was no clutch, and no reverse; the goddamn thing was an automatic.

Hands grabbed her again. Somebody swore roughly in Russian and she turned to see her friend Yuri, her midnight caller, her Snerts opponent, her genial host on board the *Kosygin*, face creased in an open-mouthed snarl that made him almost unrecognizable.

Still, she couldn't help herself, she paused for one stunned second. "Yuri? Not you!"

He hit the side of her face hard with his fist. Her ears rang. He launched himself into the cab and they grappled, struggling. He was bigger and stronger than she was, but she was more frightened, and more angry. His hands came around her throat. She kept her hands on his wrists, ignoring the steadily tightening pressure as her right foot fought for purchase against the dash. She felt a knob break off beneath her sole, concentrated on finding a surface her foot wouldn't slip on, and then straightened her right leg with an abrupt movement.

It didn't have the force she had hoped for because the steering wheel was in the way, but it was enough to send him off balance and staggering backwards. His hands loosened from her throat but didn't let go, dragging her with him. She didn't let go of his wrists, either, using her body weight to keep him off balance. She sagged to the ground and if he didn't quite fall forward he could not stand straight up, either.

And then Mutt landed on his back, a hundred and forty pounds of rage and fangs. She sank her teeth deep into the back of his neck and he screamed, a hoarse, horrible scream, and let go of Kate to reach back to try ineffectually to push Mutt away. She let go of his throat to bite one of his hands to the bone. He screamed again. Somehow he managed to shake

Mutt off and stumble to his feet. Kate, on her knees and gasping for breath, pulled herself to her feet.

The hour before dawn had come, bringing with it enough light to see everything clearly. There was no trace of the husky in Mutt now; she was all wolf, long, slender legs on tiptoe, ruff extended, long, sharp teeth bared, a steady, rumbling growl emanating from deep in her breast. She looked like the lupine version of Satan incarnate; murderous, deadly, relentless. Judgment had been rendered, sentence passed, and there was no appeal. Next to Mutt, Yuri looked like an amateur, and he knew it.

Terrified, mesmerized, he backed away. Mutt stalked forward, matching him, step for step, crabbing sideways the way wolves do when they're going for the kill. Kate tried to say something, tried to call Mutt off, but Yuri's hands had been too strong and too effective and nothing emerged but a weak croaking sound. She tried again. "Mutt. Mutt!"

Mutt either didn't hear her or didn't want to. She continued to shadow Yuri, who was too terrified to turn his back and run. He continued to back away, one careful, trembling foot feeling behind him at a time.

He stepped back once more and his expression changed to surprise, and then panic. He lost his balance, waved his arms in a futile attempt to get it back, and suddenly, he was no longer there.

With a howl of rage Mutt sprang after him.

Galvanized, Kate scrabbled to her feet and staggered after them.

The road ended abruptly, in a cessation of the gravel pad that was twenty feet thick and so made a steep twenty-foot-slope down which to fall. Clumps of alders and thin-boled birch grew here and there, a few poppies, some Alaska cotton and of course tall stalks of the ubiquitous fireweed.

Yuri was lying at the bottom of the man-made bluff, Mutt standing over him in stiff-legged outrage, growling out her resentment at being balked of prey.

Yuri's head lay at an odd angle from the rest of his body. Sightless eyes stared at the sky. He was quite dead.

CHAPTER 14

elusive
as quiet steps
at midnight

—Drumbeats Somewhere Passing

MUTT SQUATTED OVER YURI'S body, cut loose with a stream of urine, kicked a contemptuous pawful of dirt over him and bounded up the bank. She jumped up to place her paws on Kate's shoulders, anxious eyes staring into Kate's own. A steady, worried whine had replaced the menacing growl.

"It's okay, girl." The words came out in a croaking whisper. "It's okay." She let her forehead rest on Mutt's shoulder, and they stood there, leaning against each other.

The truck was still running.

Kate didn't know when that fact impinged upon her consciousness, but it brought her back to herself with a start. Mutt's paws dropped down to the ground, and she padded after Kate as she walked to the cab.

Standing on the ground next to it was a bottle of Windsor Canadian, the seal unbroken. So that was how she was supposed to go out, just another drunken Native boosting a truck, wrecking it and getting herself killed for her pains. Happened all the time, all over the Bush. What could be easier?

She couldn't have said why the realization made her

literally shake with fury, but shake with fury she did. "Mutt," she said, her voice a little stronger now. "Up."

With one leap Mutt was up and over the side of the bed. Kate picked up the blanket and the rope and tossed them in after her, along with the bottle of whiskey, and closed the tailgate.

She was physically unequal at present to the task of bringing Yuri's body up the bank, and besides, the idea of a few carnivores nibbling on him as he waited to be retrieved was attractive in the extreme.

The truck was registered to someone named Paul B. Malloy, presumably the man Yuri had boosted it from. The tank was half empty, but roads leading from Bering never led far, and she turned it around and started back. She drove very slowly and very carefully, negotiating every bump in the road as if it were Denali. The journey seemed to take hours, when in reality it was only twenty minutes. She'd been gone from the hangar for less than an hour.

She parked the truck very painstakingly indeed in front of the office door, descended from the cab with exaggerated care and walked slowly and precisely back to the bunkhouse. She even knocked on the door. She had to knock twice before he answered it.

"Kate!" she heard somebody say, and suddenly what little strength she had left in her knees gave out.

Arms caught her, and she was vaguely grateful. "Thank you," she said politely. "You know, I think I need to sit down now."

Jim had lain awake for some time, puzzling over the accounts Kate had given him. He had debated whether he should go down to the docks in search of Carroll and Casanare to pass

263

this information on, and had decided almost immediately against it. Carroll and Casanare were fixated on the idea that the Russian Mafia was preparing to turn western Alaska into a funnel for the importation of illegal arms and parts thereof to domestic terrorist groups within the United States. He would need more evidence if he was going to change their minds.

When he showed them the processors' bank accounts, he would have to tell them where he had gotten them, and they were already more than willing to lock Kate up as an accomplice to the Russians.

He wondered about Yuri again. Old, young? And just how friendly had he and Kate been?

He wondered then if he should seek out Mary Zarr and offer her the apology she so richly deserved.

In his life he had never treated a woman so shabbily.

Yes, he thought of himself as a cocksman; yes, he'd had a weather eye out for the girl most likely since he was fourteen and had been deflowered lustily and most enjoyably by the girls' softball coach at the Y. He loved women, all women, short, tall, fat, thin, old, young; he did not discriminate. He loved everything about them, the shapes of their bodies as well as the convoluted workings of their minds. He loved the chase as much as he loved the culmination of the chase.

His problem was that he had a short attention span, as the first women in his life had pointed out to him, with emphasis. He made up for it with a combination of truth and good manners; telling the first and displaying the second.

Telling the truth entailed never making promises he knew he wouldn't keep.

Good manners included waking up next to the same woman you'd gone to bed with the night before, remembering her name, and thanking her in word and deed for the privilege.

He'd failed Mary on all three counts.

He was pretty certain she would throw any apology right back in his face. He was also convinced that she ought to be allowed the opportunity. It was only fair.

He must have fallen asleep worrying about it, because the next thing he knew was the knock on the door. He answered it and barely caught Kate before she fell on her face. He carried her to her bunk and laid her down. "No," she said, trying to sit up. "That makes the world go around."

He propped pillows between her and the wall. "What the hell happened to you?" he said, more shaken than he wanted to admit.

And then he had to stop, because the memories slammed into him like a blow. They were separate, and then there were so many of them all at once that they jumbled against each other, jostling for attention. They were continuous, repetitious, vivid and immediate. Kate, bleeding and oblivious, Jack's body cradled in her arms. A rusting trim line too far above the water. Dark, cavernous, echoingly empty rooms, one after the other. A mutter of some foreign tongue. Carroll and Casanare and, yes, and Gamble in his office in Tok. In his hospital room in Bering. No, not Gamble in Bering, Mary Zarr. The missing smell of fish. The smell of missing fish? Incongruously, his mother and father, side by side in their matching La-Z-Boys in front of the thirty-two-inch television set.

He looked at Kate. There was dried blood on her neck behind her ear, and bruises on her throat. "What happened?"

"Somebody tried to kill me." Her voice was hoarse, more so than it usually was.

"Who?"

"Yuri."

265

"Yuri? Yuri the deckhand off the *Kosygin* Yuri? The one who's been visiting you nights?"

She nodded.

"What did you do, beat him at Snerts?"

"Very funny," she croaked.

"Why'd he try to kill you?"

"I don't know. He didn't say, and I was too busy fending him off to ask him," she said, with a returning spark of her old spirit. "Could I have some water?"

"Oh. Yeah. Sure. Sorry." He poured her a glass and watched her sip it painfully. "You want to go to the hospital?"

"No."

He gave her an appraising glance. The sun was up, and he could see color returning to her cheeks. "All right, then. You want to go talk to the FBI?"

"I don't think there's any zirconium on that tub," Jim said flatly. They were gathered in Zarr's office, Zarr behind her desk, Kate sitting with Carroll and Casanare arrayed before her in full interrogatory mode, Jim standing in the middle of the floor with his arms crossed and a frown on his face.

"Let's ask her," Carroll said, pointing at Kate. "She was wandering around the *Kosygin* like she owned it three days ago. She ought to have a pretty good idea what's on it. Or maybe she can't say, because of her financial interest in its cargo."

Kate blinked at her, still not quite back in her body. She was also at a disadvantage because her throat hurt too much to talk. Mutt wasn't. Mutt didn't like her tone and said so.

"Quiet, Mutt," Jim said. "I was all over the boat the day before she was, and I didn't see a goddamn thing."

Both agents turned to stare. "Do you mean you can remember going on board now?"

"Yes." He looked at Kate, at the bruising beginning to bloom on her neck, and looked away again. "It just hit me like a baseball bat, all of a sudden, like the doc said it might. I wandered around on my own for, hell, it must have been forty-five, fifty minutes before they caught me."

"Who caught you?"

Ignoring the question, Jim said, "I was in and out of every compartment in that hold, and I'm telling you there was nothing in it. Nothing, no fish, no zirconium—what does it come in, anyway?"

"Canisters with big warning labels that say, 'Caution, Toxic Substance, Do Not Lift, Filch, Pilfer, Purloin or Otherwise Steal,'" Carroll said.

Jim looked at her, and wondered what there was in the tone of her voice that was making his bullshit detector kick in. "Yeah, well, I never saw anything even remotely like that on board the *Kosygin*. Plus, the trim line is three feet above the water. I'm assuming this stuff is bulky and it weighs a lot, or why did they need a boat that size to bring it in?"

"It has to be there," Casanare said stubbornly. "We got a list of potential buyers out of the Anchorage data base, all of them involved in some way with white supremacist groups in Alaska, Idaho, Montana and Texas. The Aryan Nation, for crissake, is probably waiting delivery on this stuff as we speak. You think they're going to stop with the Oke bomb?"

"Will you shut up and listen to me for just one minute!"

First Sergeant Jim Chopin in full voice was enough to splinter wood. Casanare mastered his anger and said to Carroll, "What the hell, we can listen. Doesn't mean we can't grab her up after."

Kate heard him and sat up straight in her chair.

"Thank you," Jim said with awful politeness. "Kate's found

some information that I think you'll be interested in. It concerns—"

"Oh I'm sure we'll be interested in anything Ms. Shugak has to say," Casanare said silkily, "but if you don't mind, first I'd like to read her her rights."

He smiled at Kate. It was a very attractive smile, and she decided that if she had a choice, he got to put on the cuffs. She took comfort in the weight of Mutt's shoulder, pressed against her knee. Mutt had taken it as a matter of course that she had been invited to this interservice conference, and no one had thought to gainsay her.

The best—maybe the only—way to deal with Feds on a roll was to ignore them.

Jim didn't have that luxury. "It's a money-laundering operation."

"What?"

"They're not smuggling anything into the country except money. They're running a con through the fishing industry, money in from an overseas business run through the *Kosygin*'s account in a local bank to a stateside outfit."

There was dead silence. Jim looked at Carroll, looked at Casanare. "It's true. I'm betting that goddamn zirconium never came within five thousand miles of the Alaskan coastline. Stealing it was probably part of the operation; hell, selling it was probably how they bankrolled it. But this part—what they're doing here in Bering right now—is about money. It is not about weapons smuggling, and it's not about terrorism. It is about money."

"That's not all," Kate said.

"Oh, she speaks," Carroll said.

Zarr was sitting behind her desk and so far had had little to say. At this, she stirred. "Agent Carroll, let's tone it down a little, shall we? You seem to have some suspicions about Ms. Shugak's doings in this matter. You should know that she has a reputation with the law enforcement community in this state, a good one." Whereas I met you two yo-yos only last week, her tone implied.

It was a warning, however gently voiced, and Carroll wasn't so angry that she didn't hear it. She subsided, reluctantly.

Zarr said, "Ms. Shugak? You had something to say?"

"Thank you," Kate said.

She was being excruciatingly polite. Jim wondered just how hard she'd been hit.

"I went to the library yesterday." She closed her eyes for a moment. "Or was it the day before?" She sighed and opened her eyes again. "I can't remember."

"How unusual," Carroll said, shooting Jim a vicious glance.

Zarr cleared her throat. "You went to the library."

"Yes," Kate said, "and I looked some things up. Some background information."

"What about?"

"Who, not what. Christopher Overmore and Michael Sullivan."

Zarr's eyebrows disappeared into her hair.

"Who's Sullivan?" Jim said.

"The owner of the local bank. Overmore you know."

"Yeah, yeah, the senator from this district, running for U.S. senator. What's he got to do with anything?"

"I can't prove it, yet, but I think he's Sullivan's partner in the bank, or one of them."

"So what?"

"So Overmore used to be a banker, a bad one. He came this close to going to jail for fraud seven years ago."

Jim was furious. "Why the hell didn't you tell me this before?"

She looked away, an uncommon thing for Kate Shugak to do. "I must have forgotten."

I ran you off, he remembered just in time, and shut his mouth.

Zarr said slowly, "You'd better know what you're talking about here. Overmore's a big name in these parts."

Kate thought about shrugging but didn't have the strength. "Look it up for yourself. It was in all the papers. How long have you been posted here?"

"Three years."

"Has no one ever talked about it? Twenty-three million dollars went missing, mostly from Native associations. You'd think people would never stop talking about something like that. How the hell did he get elected senator?"

"Before my time," Zarr said, adding, "He's brought a lot of bacon home. State and federal funding for sewer systems for villages in the district, funding from the FHA for low-cost housing funneled through the regional corporation, federal funding for the local hospital, things like that."

"Yes, well, this concern for local affairs is all very well," Casanare said briskly, "but in the meantime, we've got some highly toxic, very dangerous contraband to track down, and—"

"Sure you do," Jim said, "just not here. Get a warrant, get six of them, deputize every citizen of this town and storm on board the *Kosygin*. You won't find anything. And there is no point in waiting for a buyer to show up when there is no buyer."

"So you say."

"So I say." Jim pointed a finger at Kate. "You poked your

nose into Overmore's business. Somebody saw you in the library, didn't they? Who?"

"I don't know."

"Well, we did," Casanare offered. "Or we saw her come out of it. Followed by one of her Russian buddies."

"What?" Kate said fuzzily, but they were all looking at Casanare now.

He reddened, and went on a little belligerently, "We went in afterward and tried to find out what you were up to, but we couldn't flash our badges and the librarian wouldn't play. She started reciting the First Amendment, so we left before she started singing "*My Country 'Tis of Thee*" and citing the United States versus Kramer Books."

"Good for Heidi," Kate said with a sloppy smile.

"She was looking up Overmore and Sullivan," Jim said. "Someone must have overheard her asking for help, naming the names, and got scared." He looked at Casanare.

"Glukhov," Casanare said slowly, and looked at Kate sitting slumped down in the chair. She looked dazed and maybe even a little drunk.

"You're not buying into this, are you, Al?" Carroll demanded.

"Looking up Overmore is what nearly got her killed," Jim insisted.

This earned Kate a long, skeptical stare from Carroll. "So she says."

Jim rose and strode over to yank open Kate's collar. "I don't think she tried to strangle herself. Do you?"

The bruises were going purple at a fine rate, a nice setting for the roped scar bisecting them. Zarr was the only one who stared openly; Carroll and Casanare looked briefly and then away. "Could be a falling out between thieves," Carroll said.

271

"It's happened before. Right here in town, four, five days ago now, wasn't it?"

"There's something else," Jim said, adding in an undertone, "I'm sorry, Kate." He turned to face the FBI agents. "A woman was killed day before yesterday, a local woman named Alice Chevak."

Zarr sat up. "What do you know about that?"

"She was the head teller at Alaska First Bank of Bering. She and Kate went to school together in Fairbanks. Kate asked her to look up those accounts." Jim nodded at the papers spread haphazardly across Zarr's desk, where Casanare had tossed them contemptuously. "She died twenty-four hours later."

"Coincidence," Carroll said, but she was sounding less sure of herself.

Jim held up one finger. "Alexei Burianovich." He held up another. "Me." He held up a third. "Alice Chevak." He held up a fourth. "Kate Shugak. Four murders or attempted murders—yeah, yeah, you think Kate's lying, fine. There's an easy way to prove her story—we'll drive out that damn road and find the body." He looked at Zarr. "You got somebody who can cover the post while you're gone?"

Zarr shook her head. "The sergeant's on a murder case up in Owl Village. The two other troopers are in St. Paul on a drug bust."

"That's it? You're understaffed."

"Tell me about it." She cast Casanare and Carroll an unfriendly glance. "I've got two cases hanging fire myself. And Chevak."

He followed her glance. "They are laundering money," he said.

"They're helping fanatics build bombs," Carroll snapped.

Jim went very still. "Sorry? I thought this zirconium stuff—wait a minute. What else was stolen out of the military base in Russia?"

Casanare tried bluster as a way out of Carroll's blunder. "Zirconium is an essential rare metal in the production of—"

"You miserable sons of bitches," Jim said. Carroll and Casanare didn't precisely cower before his immense wrath, although Casanare did stealthily feel for the butt of his sidearm. "What are you really looking for, U-235? Plutonium? Did you know about this?" he shot at Zarr.

Pale-faced, she shook her head.

"You know what? I'm tired of trying to tell you people anything. You know your own business best. Fine. Meantime, I've got a friend who's hurt. I'm taking her home and putting her to bed."

"I hear that's what you do best," Carroll flashed.

Zarr stared stolidly at the opposite wall and said nothing, although a faint color crept up her neck.

Kate looked fuzzily at Jim and said with what sounded like genuine surprise, "We're friends?"

"Shugak, just stand up and start walking, okay?"

"Okay," she said obediently, and they left, single file, Jim, Kate and Mutt, who bared her teeth at Casanare, just for practice.

The door closed behind them. Carroll and Casanare stared at each other. "I don't know what the hell is going on here," Casanare said, "but whatever it is, it's starting to fall apart."

"It's the plutonium, Al, it has to be. We know Ivanov took it, and he's right here in Bering Goddamn Alaska. The plutonium hasn't surfaced anywhere else, and we would have heard by now if it had. Ivanov, Kamyanka, whatever the hell he's calling himself nowadays, he's into weapons and parts for

273

making weapons. He's not into money, he's never been into money." She was almost pleading.

"He's had a pretty long run," Casanare said slowly. "Maybe now he's into retirement. This would be a way."

They sat in silence for a few tense moments. "All right then," Carroll said, "let's get a warrant and search the *Kosygin*."

"What for?"

"Whatever we can find."

"Okay," Casanare said, "and we're getting the warrant on—what grounds, exactly?"

Carroll looked at Zarr. "Is there a friendly judge in town?"

The trooper shook her head. "A friendly magistrate," she offered.

"Works for me."

The magistrate proved to be an early riser. The three of them, backed up by six city policemen armed with shotguns, went on board the *Kosygin* at six A.M.

Nobody was home.

The staterooms were empty, save for a few scattered articles of clothing and the pinups on the walls. The coffee pot in the galley was warm, half-filled mugs left sitting on the table. The hold and all its individual compartments were empty, and the device Casanare directed in every direction remained silent, the needle on its gauge motionless.

Two of the lifeboats were missing.

274

CHAPTER 15

the seventh sense develops
that we may vibrate to a height

—The Seventh Sense

JIM AND KATE GOT back to the hangar at five-thirty. The sun shone directly into their eyes, which was why they didn't see Baird's body until Kate tripped over it going into the office.

She stared down at him stupidly. He was unconscious but alive if the blood trickling from his mouth was any indication. His right arm looked oddly bent at the elbow, and the knuckles of both hands were cut, bruised and beginning to swell. Otherwise there wasn't a mark on him. "Baird?" she said. She knelt down next to him. "Baird? Jacob?"

About that time the deep, distinctive *wah-wah-wah* of the Herc's engine sounded from the apron in front of the hangar door.

She heard footsteps and looked up to see that Jim had retraced his steps from the bunkhouse, roll of gauze and alcohol in hand. He saw Baird on the floor and Kate kneeling next to him. He blinked and said, "I thought you were my only patient. What happened here?"

"Go get your gun," she said in a low, urgent voice.

"No," a voice drawled from the door into the hangar. "Don't."

The slender blond man Kate had last seen on board the

275

Kosygin, just before she was booted ashore, stood looking at them with the smile on his face that made him look like an archangel. Maybe an archangel named Lucifer, Kate decided now. He held a pistol, dangling negligently at his side, but it came up smartly enough when Jim dropped the alcohol and the gauze and took a step forward.

Kate shot to her feet. "What do you want?"

A warning rumbled out of Mutt's throat.

The pistol swung toward Mutt.

"Mutt! Stay!" To the man in the doorway she said quickly, "What do you want?"

The pistol gestured toward the hangar. "The loan of your plane."

"Go ahead," Kate said. "It's yours. Take it." Mutt heard the tension in Kate's voice and her growl increased in menace if not in volume. Kate's hand dropped to Mutt's ruff and knotted there.

Kamyanka smiled again. He looked less beautiful this time. "And thirty seconds after we take off, you will be on the phone to your police. I don't think so."

"They're already after you, Kamyanka," Jim said. "Or Ivanov, or whatever you're calling yourself lately."

Kamyanka's smile vanished. "And you would be—"

"First Sergeant James Chopin, of the Alaska State Troopers."

On the floor Baird stirred. "They're here in Bering," Kate said loudly. "The FBI, the CIA, the National Security Agency, the Department of Justice, the state police, the local police, they're here in force and they're all looking for you. You haven't got a chance. Give it up now, and they might offer you the opportunity to turn states' evidence."

"Right," Jim said, picking up on her cue, "they've been

looking for someone to tell them what's going on with the Russian Mafia ever since it became a power. You could talk about it from the inside. You don't want to do anything that—"

Baird reached up an arm, caught the near edge of the coffee table and shoved it forward into Kamyanka's shins with all the force at his command.

It wasn't much, but it was enough to throw the Russian off balance. He flung out his arms to catch himself on the door frame, and Jim went past Kate in a scrambling dive that tumbled them both through the door and into the hangar. There was the sound of a shot, another, sounds Kate had not heard since the year before, sounds she was not sure she was prepared to hear ever again.

Mutt crouched, preparing to leap after Jim. "No!" Kate said, terrified. "No, Mutt, stay!"

Mutt barked back, long white canines snapping together with a sound eerily like the gunshots from the next room.

Kate jumped back, startled and then angry. "I said *stay*, goddamn it!" she roared, her bruised throat forgotten, and raced into the hangar.

Jim and Kamyanka were struggling for possession of the pistol. The ramp on the Herc was down and there were people standing in the great maw of the plane, most of whom seemed vaguely familiar to her.

Her eyes went to the window next to the left seat. It was open, and through it she could see Ziven, the Russian who had dismissed her as of no consequence upon discovering she was not a pilot. He hadn't bothered with headphones, as he probably had no intention of calling the tower for permission to taxi and take off, so Kate had an excellent view of the top of his head coming off when the pistol clutched between Jim and Kamyanka went off for the third time.

One of the men on the ramp shouted and ran back into the plane, followed by several others. Everybody else ran toward the fight on the floor. Kate scrambled to Jim's aid but there were too many of them and not enough of her and she found herself caught and held, helpless, as the rest of them swarmed over Jim.

Kamyanka got to his feet shakily, looked down at Jim, prone on the floor between four other men. He said something uncomplimentary in Russian and kicked Jim in the ribs, hard.

"He's a pilot!" Kate shouted. "Shut *up*, Mutt!" she yelled over her shoulder.

The pistol, shaking slightly, raising slowly until it was trained on Jim's head.

"He's a *pilot*!" Kate shouted again, and cursed the scar that made her voice so rough and so low.

Kamyanka looked up at her, the pistol held where it was. "What?"

She nodded at Jim. "He is a pilot. Yours is dead."

Kamyanka swiveled to look. The rest of Ziven's head was leaning out of the window of the Herc.

"You need him to fly you out of here," Kate said. "You need him."

"That's right," Jim said, picking up on her cue. "I'll fly you out of here. Let's get on board and go."

Mutt, snarling, snapping, whining, sidled toward them in her best wolf imitation. "No, Mutt!" Kate said desperately.

Kamyanka looked from her, to the enraged dog, to the prone man. For a moment nothing was heard but the sound of the Herc's engines, *wah-wah-wah*, a buzzing bass voice that at this proximity jarred the marrow in their bones.

The pistol moved, one quick gesture. Kamyanka said

something and Jim was jerked to his feet. His eyes met Kate's for a brief moment before he was jerked toward the plane. Behind them two men were freeing the dead pilot from his seat belt and pulling him out of the left seat.

Kamyanka strolled forward and used the muzzle of the pistol to raise Kate's chin. "And what do we do with you, hmmm?"

Mutt snarled.

Kamyanka looked at her.

"She won't go for you unless I tell her to."

"She won't go for anyone if I shoot her."

"Leave me," Kate said. "You don't need the excess baggage."

"A good point," Kamyanka admitted. "Where's Yuri?"

"Isn't he with you?" she said, but there was a flicker at the back of her eyes and, quick as a snake, he caught it.

"Let's take her with us," Glukhov said, licking his lips. "We can toss her out once we're in the air. That way, no witnesses."

Kamyanka considered. "A good thought, my general. Alaska is a very big place. They will never find her body. Quick, clean, no mess." He smiled, but it was not the type of smile to encourage an answering smile from anyone else, and added lightly, "We will do Yuri's job for him."

They hustled her into the plane, and as the ramp came up Kate saw Mutt shake off her invisible leash and bound forward. She raced next to them as they taxied, jumping and snapping at the fuselage, all the way down the apron, onto the taxiway, and all the way down the runway. They could hear her howling her rage even over the roar of all four engines.

Carroll was in equally full cry in Zarr's office. "Come on, let's get a move on, we need a boat! They're probably meeting someone at the mouth of the river—a bigger boat, or an amphibious plane! We don't have any time to mess around, let's hop to it!"

Zarr was on her desk phone, Casanare was on his cell, the chief of police was removing the live round from the chamber of his shotgun and Carroll was so loud that when the knock at the door came they almost missed it. When the knock came the second time, Casanare opened it and discovered a small girl standing there, one arm clutching a large red model airplane and the other clasping a videotape. "Hi," Casanare said. "Can I help you?"

Carroll, catching sight of the girl over Casanare's shoulder, said, "We don't have time for this, Al!"

The little girl, maybe ten, maybe younger, looked as determined as she did frightened and did not budge from the doorstep.

"I've got to go," Zarr said into the phone. She got to her feet and said, "This is the little Chevak girl. Stephanie, isn't it? Honey, we're kind of busy right now—"She caught herself when she realized that one of the things she could be busy on was finding out who killed Stephanie's mother. "I'm sorry, Stephanie. What can I do for you?" She came forward and crouched down.

Stephanie held out the videotape. "I made this."

Zarr took it. "I—thank you, Stephanie."

The girl whispered something at the floor.

"What?"

The girl made what seemed like a tremendous effort. She even raised her eyes, meeting Zarr's bravely. "You have to watch it."

"Oh for Christ's sake," Casanare said, disgusted. "We really don't have time for this, Zarr."

Zarr examined the tape. It was unlabeled, and was run about halfway through. Depending on the tape speed, that could mean anywhere from one to three hours. "Stephanie," Zarr said, "I promise you, we're going to find the person who hurt your mom, but we've got something really important to do first, and—"

Stephanie took the tape away from Zarr and walked around her, heading for the cart that stood in one corner with a television and a VCR on it.

"Great," Carroll said, throwing up her hands, "let's all settle in for an episode of *Mr. Rogers' Neighborhood*."

Zarr followed and removed the tape from Stephanie's hand. "Look, honey, I—"

Stephanie said something in a small voice.

"What?"

"What did she say?" Casanare said quickly.

Even Carroll paused to listen.

"The big man," Stephanie said, more strongly. "And my mom's friend." She pointed at the tape. "They're on it."

"Oh goody," Carroll said, "not Mr. Rogers, Mr. Robinson."

Awkwardly, as she hadn't put down the model airplane, Stephanie jumped up to grab the tape from Zarr's hand. "This happened this morning," she said strongly. "You have to watch."

She put the tape in the VCR and switched on the television, and such was her dogged determination, no one tried to stop her.

Jim sat in the left seat, the blood from its last occupant seeping through his jeans.

He was petrified with fear. Most comfortable on the stick of his Bell Jet Ranger, the largest fixed-wing aircraft he'd ever

281

flown was a Cessna 180, a bird with a wingspan of thirty-five feet and a payload of twelve hundred pounds. The Lockheed C-130 aircraft had a wingspan of one hundred thirty-two feet and laughed at loads of twenty tons. The Cessna had one engine with a standard two hundred thirty horsepower; the Herc had four, Allison turboprops at four thousand horsepower each.

You could fit six people into a 180, with one ditty bag per person in the tiny cargo area behind the third row of seats, or you could take out the seats and transport six bodies, as Jim had had occasion to discover in the course of his professional life.

You could fit sixty-four fully equipped paratroopers into a Herc, shoulder-held rocket launchers, backpack bombs and all.

He felt like he was riding a dragon, a large, loud dragon with attitude and no tolerance for harness or bit.

There were too many dials and gauges and they were all in the wrong places, and he didn't know what any of the switches or knobs did. He'd only found the flaps by trial and error. The throttles, thank god, were clearly marked. Also there were four of them, which kind of made them stand out. His takeoff had left him with no confidence that he was going to be able to set the plane down in one piece; he was still in shock that he'd managed to get them up into the air in the first place, and he'd fumbled around enough that he'd needed all the runway there was in Bering to generate enough speed for lift. A pilot watching from the ground would have wondered how any owner in their right mind would have allowed him up the ramp.

In the air, he felt marginally safer, with control of the ailerons by the yoke in his hands and of the rudder by the pedals beneath his feet. He grabbed for altitude, as much as he could get as fast as he could get it, and tried to remember every lie he'd ever heard about a Herc in bull sessions around the bar.

One thing he knew for sure: The Cessna flew with one pilot. The Herc had seats for a crew of five. Baird had adapted this Herc for a single pilot on short hops, but Maciarello had flown Hercs in the service. This flight, Jim was it, which did not contribute to his peace of mind.

It didn't help that he had a very intense Russian sitting in the right seat with a gun aimed at him. "Could you put that thing down?" he said, as politely as he could under the circumstances. "It's not exactly helping my powers of concentration."

"Shut up, fucking American cop," the man said. He'd already said it twice in response to Jim's other attempts at conversation. It seemed to be the only English he knew.

They climbed through five thousand feet and Jim still had no idea where they were going. After concentrated effort he located the airspeed indicator. Jesus god. Three hundred and sixty miles per hour. A 180's top speed was a hundred and forty. If they stayed on their present course, they'd be in Anchorage in an hour. If no one in Bering alerted the authorities at the other end, they could land without occasioning remark at Merrill or International. Unless they had the tower controller in the bag, he didn't think they could land at Elmendorf Air Force Base, but at this point he wasn't ruling anything out.

What had that Herc pilot said at Bernie's that night? That a Herc with a full load could make Seattle from Anchorage without stopping to refuel, and that one could make it to Las Vegas if it didn't have a payload? It was twenty-three hundred miles from Anchorage to Seattle and, what, four, maybe five thousand Anchorage to Las Vegas. If that was true, they could be going anywhere. No one had come forward to make him alter course for Russia, the one bright spot in this morning so far.

He tried to think ahead, but there were so many airstrips along the way. They were all gravel strips, but then the Herc was designed to land on rough strips, the rougher the better, combat zones being best of all. He had no idea of the minimum amount of runway a Herc needed to land, or how much weight they had on board even if he did know how to make some kind of guess. He estimated maybe twenty, twenty-five men in back from the quick glimpse he'd had as they hustled him forward. Overestimate, say they weighed two hundred each, that was still only five thousand pounds. A Herc could fly forever with all four tanks full of fuel and a piddly little five-thousand-pound payload. Planet Earth was only twenty-five thousand miles around. They could be going to Greenland. No, too cold, Russians wouldn't want to go to Greenland. They could be going to Mexico—sun, sand, girls, what could be better? Hell, maybe he'd ride along.

The plane shifted in flight, an odd motion not anything like turbulence or dropping the flaps or hitting an aileron or a rudder. "What the hell?"

"Shut up, fucking American cop," the Russian in the left seat said.

He looked down at the panel for inspiration, heart thudding in his throat. A light blinked up at him. A door was open, or opening. Not the ramp, but a door, a door in the back. He looked over his shoulder, but the flight station was separate from the cargo bay. He couldn't see what was going on back there.

The general's words came back to him. *We can toss her out once we're in the air.*

The portside hatch was open, air screaming past. Glukhov had Kate by one arm, her erstwhile drinking buddy Danya had her by the other, and they were slowly forcing her, one step at a time, toward the opening. They were in no hurry. Glukhov was laughing, and none of the other men volunteered to come to her aid. She never had been that much fun at a party.

She fought. She used her fingernails, her teeth, her feet, kicking, struggling, fighting with every part and fiber of her being.

She wasn't fighting because of the betrayal of her erstwhile party mates. She wasn't fighting to contradict the expression in Kamyanka's eyes, the one that said she, Kate Shugak, had ceased to exist. She wasn't even fighting because of Glukhov's laughter.

She was fighting because she wanted to live.

She wanted to go home. She wanted to swim in the little pool in the creek out back of her cabin. She wanted to read late into the night by the mellow light of a kerosene lamp. She wanted to sit at the bar of the Roadhouse and watch the belly dancers shimmy out of the back room. She wanted to go to Bobby and Dinah's and see how much her namesake had grown. She wanted to sit once more at the feet of the Quilaks, on the banks of the Kanuyaq, on the swells of Prince William Sound.

She wanted to live. She fought for it, with every ounce of strength she had.

It was not enough. She was losing the battle, but she would not give up, she would not surrender. She made them work for it.

Work they did. Slowly, inexorably, they forced her to the hatch. She kicked up her feet and planted the soles on either side of the hatch.

Glukhov, still laughing, reached for her knee.

Jim's first thought was to jump the guy with the gun. In a Cessna 180 he might have gotten away with it, but in a Herc the cockpit was too wide, it would take too much time to launch himself the necessary distance, the guy would get off at least one shot, maybe two.

The Russian sitting sideways in the seat next to him had not wavered, the pistol still pointed straight at his chest.

Wait. Sitting sideways. Not wearing his seat belt.

No one in back was, either, as he recalled from the quick hustle on board. And why bother, this wasn't exactly your FAA approved flight.

He was wearing his seat belt. Like any good pilot, strapping it on was the first thing he'd done when he sat down in the left seat.

A steep dive? A power climb? A snap roll? Yeah, put everybody in back on the goddamn ceiling, that sounded like a plan.

But he didn't know enough about the Herc's tolerances. A snap roll at this velocity with this kind of surface area and he'd probably rip the wings off the aircraft.

Something else then.

Suddenly, he knew what else, and with the knowledge came calm. His heart rate slowed, his breath came back. A flat spin. Centripetal force would slam everyone up against the opposite wall. Always assuming he could bring the plane out of the spin again. He had no idea how a multiengine plane would handle a flat spin. Come to that, he had no idea how a single-engine airplane would handle a flat spin, it wasn't a maneuver he practiced on a regular basis. Or ever.

He felt for the pedals. Better pick the correct rudder to push. Don't want to hurl Kate headfirst out of the open hatch.

The indicator said the open door was on the left side of the plane. The altimeter said they were at nine thousand feet. He had no way to know how much altitude he would lose during the maneuver but he didn't have a choice. Nine thousand feet would have to do. He stretched out his legs, testing the temper of the rudders. He eased the throttles back a little. Nobody said anything; why should they, they weren't pilots. He eased them back a little more.

He grabbed the yoke tightly in both hands. "I'm sorry, baby," he said to the plane, and kicked the right rudder as hard as he could.

Air going three hundred ninety miles an hour struck the right surface of the rudder. The Herc's nose jerked around to the right, its tail around to the left and centripetal force slammed the man with the gun hard against the right seat's window. His head connected with the glass with a nice, solid smack, and better yet, he dropped the gun.

There were yells and screams and thuds from the back as everyone piled up against the right bulkhead, one after the other. The Herc lost forward motion, lost lift, spun clockwise, tail going around like the big hand, nose going around like the little hand, the engines screaming a protest almost as loud as the wind. They were losing altitude fast, too fast, falling from the sky like a big black brick. His body strained at the belt that was all that was holding him in his seat. His spine felt like it was going to shake into separate vertebrae. The vibration was worse than what you got at the epicenter of a seven-point earthquake, and he had cause to compare. The engines protested. Loudly, vociferously, angrily.

He tried not to watch the altimeter, and with grim determination kept the Herc in its flat spin until all thumping and screaming and yelling from the cargo bay ceased.

He began pushing the left rudder then, as he eased off on power to the portside engines and increased power to the starboard engines, praying that all the cables would hold, praying the electronics wouldn't fail, praying the hydraulics would continue to function, praying the rudder wouldn't tear off, praying most fervently that they wouldn't run out of altitude. The muscles in his arms and in the leg holding left rudder quivered with the strain. The spin seemed to have taken on a life of its own, the Herc helpless in its grasp.

Come on, baby, he thought. "Come on, baby," he said. "Come on, girl, you can do it, you know you can, come on!"

She responded as only a craft that was as well-maintained and as well-loved as any of the airplanes owned and operated by Jacob Baird could. She came out of it. Slowly, shuddering a protest, she came out of it. The prop began to bite into the air, to pull the craft forward, the wings slowly ceased to be dead weight and began again to manufacture lift.

The tail began slowly to swing left and Jim hastily straightened out the rudder. With a last groaning protest, she leveled out. Once again they were flying straight and forward and, by a miracle, on a course only slightly off for back to Bering.

He looked at the altimeter, which read a little less than two hundred feet. He looked out. The belly of the Herc seemed to skim the vegetation of the Delta. He pulled back on the yoke to put some space between them and the ground, and tried not to think of how close they'd come to augering in. For the first time since he'd arrived in Bering, he could appreciate the lack of mountains, the flat, featureless topography of the Delta. If he'd tried a flat spin at home, he and the Herc and everybody on board would have found a cloud full of rocks almost immediately.

They bounced three times on landing, the third time so hard he thought the nose gear was coming up through the fuselage. But she held together. She was one sweet craft, powerful and forgiving, and he decided he was in love for life. If he ever met Mr. Lockheed in person, he would kiss him on the mouth.

They had barely rolled to a stop when he was up and out of his seat and moving back, pulling at the pile of bodies lying crumpled against the right bulkhead of the cavernous cargo bay.

Kate was the fourth one he came to. "Kate," he said. "Kate? Come on, baby, come on, come out of it, you know you can do it, you know you can. Get your ass back here, Shugak!"

Her eyelids fluttered.

"Kate," he said, unable to keep from shaking her. He didn't care what was broken, he wanted her conscious, he wanted her alive and awake and yelling at him, he wanted the world back the way it was, the way it never would be again.

She blinked up at him. "Jim?"

An immense wave of relief swept over him. He had to check himself from scooping her up into his arms. "Yeah. Yeah, it's Jim."

She raised her head and looked around at the pile of bodies surrounding them, some of them beginning to stir and groan. "What happened?" She looked back at him, and said accusingly, "What the hell did you do?"

He started to laugh, and this time he didn't try to fight it. He hugged her hard, ignoring the protest muffled against his shoulder, the hands trying to shove him away.

There was a thudding against the outside of the plane. Others were beginning to stir, and Jim got to his feet and fumbled around until he found the ramp control. Somewhat to his surprise, it still worked.

The first person he saw was Carroll, who came on board at a quick pace, pistol drawn and held in the government-certified two-hand grip.

She ignored Jim and Kate, heading straight for Kamyanka. "He's not dead is he, damn it?" She nudged Kamyanka ungently with one toe.

Kamyanka groaned and opened his eyes.

Carroll smiled down at him. "Hello, Ivanov. At last we meet. Now, just where the hell is that plutonium?"

He stared up at her. "I don't know what you're talking about. Who is this Ivanov?"

She turned her head. "Al?"

Casanare came up the ramp holding the arm of a man whose hair was just beginning to grow back over a shaved scalp, not enough to hide the scar left behind when they cracked his skull open and got the bullet out. He moved slowly but steadily, his color was good and he looked like he had a long life in front of him.

"Is this the man who held up your armored truck?" Carroll asked him.

"Yes," Kiril Davidovitch said, staring down at Kamyanka with a bright, triumphant expression. "This the man who shoot the girl. This the man who shoot me. This the man."

Kamyanka closed his eyes.

CHAPTER 16

When does your mouth
say goodbye to your heart?
                    —There Is No Word For Goodbye

SHE WALKED INTO THE bunkhouse at noon the next day and found Jim packing. "I'm taking the jet out this afternoon," he said.

"Yeah," she said, sitting on her bunk and watching him stuff balled-up dirty shirts into his duffel.

"You know where that goddamn plutonium is that Boris and Natasha were chasing? Pakistan, is where. Or some of it, anyway. Turns out Kamyanka shipped it out the day after he bought it from Glukhov."

"How much did he make?"

"Enough to start this operation, evidently," he said with a nod of his head in the direction of the docks. "Looks like things were getting a little too hot for him in Russia. He'd been operating pretty free, wide and handsome there for years, but lately he'd been crossing some lines, pulling some shit even the Russians couldn't tolerate."

"Like what?"

"Like buying elections. So the word came down—hell, who knows—maybe from Yeltsin himself, Kamyanka, or Ivanov, had to go. So he pulled one last job, bought the plutonium with it, sold the plutonium and started laundering it through the Alaska First Bank of Bering."

"Why the Alaska First Bank of Bering?"

"Seems Glukhov had met Overmore in Magadan when Overmore was over there glad-handing. God knows why, nobody in Magadan could vote for him. They became bosom buddies."

"So Glukhov put Kamyanka in touch with Overmore."

"Who is the major stockholder in Northern Consolidated Seafood Distributors, Inc. And Overmore roped in his brother-in-law, who is even more stupid than he is greedy. Overmore, by the way, can't talk fast enough. He's stumbling over his own tongue implicating Sullivan and Glukhov, Sullivan is trying to give up Overmore, and Glukhov is telling everything he knows about Kamyanka's operation. Which isn't much, according to Carroll."

"Carroll?"

"Casey's real name."

"Oh. What about Kamyanka?"

"He's not talking."

"Big surprise."

"Yeah, I'd be careful if I was Glukhov. I'm not sure there is a hole so deep that Kamyanka can't dig him out."

"He missed Davidovitch."

"Yeah. He did. For once, the forces for good prevailed."

"He's a cute kid."

"You saying that because he's testifying for our side, or because he was hitting on you before I managed to carry you out of that plane?"

"Still seems strange they'd pick Bering," Kate said. "For that matter, it seems strange they'd pick Alaska. We're not exactly on the cutting edge of the Pacific Rim economy."

"Maybe that's why," Jim said, cramming clean shirts in

after the dirty ones. "Maybe all the usual suspects were busy. Maybe all the usual suspects were under investigation. And Overmore was ripe for the picking. Like you said. Past history of fraud and embezzlement. And he had a nice big expensive campaign coming up."

Kate said somberly, "I can't believe they killed Alice."

He stopped packing to look over his shoulder. "They didn't."

"What?"

"Zarr said they got the guy last night. Alice's ex-boyfriend got liquored up on some imported Thunderbird and sobbed out the story on his sister's shoulder. He picked Alice up outside the bank on Sunday, drove out somewhere, tried to talk her into coming back to him and when she wouldn't, beat her to death. The sister turned him in."

"Alice was killed by an ex-boyfriend?" She remembered the man outside the grocery store. "Was his name Charlie?"

"Yeah, Charlie Hoffman. How did you know?"

"I ran into him with Alice, coming out of the grocery store." Kate sat down on her bunk, dizzy with relief. "I went on board the *Kosygin* because of you, trying to find out what you were up to. But I did the rest of it for Alice. Because I thought I got her killed."

"Yeah. Well, you didn't. Charlie Hoffman killed her. For what it's worth, he seems really broken up about it."

"It's not worth much," Kate said.

"No," Jim said, adding, "They ought to make this town dry and be done with it."

"Yes." She searched for the relief that had to be there, her exoneration, and found only a numb stillness.

"I went to see Stephanie this morning. She's going to be okay, I think. She never liked Charlie, she said."

"Her family will take care of her."

"Yeah." He thought of his own parents, how he wouldn't be telling them of this week of TDY in Bering, how they would never know about any of the close encounters of the homicide kind he had during the course of a working day. He called once a month, he sent a card on Father's Day and flowers on Mother's Day and he tried to get down for an extended weekend every year. They were polite when they were together, but they weren't close. He didn't blame them for it, it was how things were, it was how they'd always been.

Stephanie's family would handle things differently.

"She's not a voyeur," Jim said. "I mean, she doesn't make a habit out of spying on people. She's just lonely. There aren't any other ten-year-olds around here who want to be engineers and astronauts. Even Ray, who helps her a little with her models, doesn't know what she's talking about half the time. She built that Super Cub model almost all by herself, Kate, and she thought up putting the camera in it, and the remote transmitter that could transmit to the rabbit ears of her television antenna so she could record everything on the VCR. She got the idea from communications satellites, she said. She wanted to build her own.

"She went out late at night or early in the morning to test the equipment, less traffic in the air then. Lucky for us that on Wednesday she'd just put the finishing touches to a monitor so she could look at what she was filming from where she was flying the plane, instead of having to wait until she got home to watch it on the television."

"And lucky for us she was in the right place at the right time to see what happened to us."

"Yeah, that tape will come in handy at trial." He shoved

socks into empty nooks. "How about you? What do you do now?"

She made a vague gesture. "Oh, I'll stick around for a while, help the guys figure out a way to keep the business going until Baird gets out of the hospital, train my replacement. They need a good ground crew or they'll go under, and too many small communities up and down the river depend on Baird Air."

He shook his head. "Kate Shugak, Rescue, Inc. Thanks for saving my life, by the way."

"Thanks for saving mine." She rubbed the back of her neck. "Even if you did have to slam me against the wall to do it."

"Still, you kept Kamyanka, or whatever the hell his name really is, from shooting me. So." He repeated it solemnly. "Thanks for saving my life."

I couldn't save Jack's, she thought.

"Here."

She blinked her eyes clear and saw he was holding something out. "What's this?"

He waved it at her. "It's yours, anyway."

It was the picture he had taken from her cabin, the one Bobby had snapped of Jack carrying her off into the woods after Bobby and Dinah's wedding and Katya's unexpected appearance.

"Where'd you get this?"

He made a dismissive gesture. "It was on your kitchen table."

"You've been to the cabin?"

"Yes. When I was looking for you for this job."

She looked back down at the picture. That woman looks happy, she thought.

Without volition, tears slid down her face, long, silent, one after the other. She let them collect and fall, and she made no attempt to hide them.

Those tears shook him to the bone. He took a deep breath, let it out. He wanted to hold her.

He stayed where he was. "Listen, Kate. About what happened between us—"

She said nothing.

"Look, I'm sorry. I should have—"

"No," she said, looking up through her tears. "Don't. I'm sorry. I shouldn't have said what I did. It wasn't true. You didn't take advantage of me. I woke up, and you were there, and I reached for you. I didn't give you a choice."

He patted the air with his hands. "Nice try, but don't fit me for a halo just yet, okay? Maybe I did take advantage of the situation. You were right. I wanted you. I have for a long time. I haven't made any secret of it."

A faint smile. "You want everybody."

He thought of Kathy at Alaska Geographic, with whom he couldn't summon enough energy to strike up even a mild flirtation, of the flight attendant on the plane in, whose phone number he would never have let get away from him in his prior life, of the frank interest in Sophie the waitress's eyes, of Mary Zarr, whom he'd treated so badly. "Yeah. I guess."

She realized she was sitting on the same bunk upon which they had made love, and stood up abruptly. "I was hurting, Jim, and you, well, you comforted me. You held me while I—while I cried," she said, and the strained expression on her face showed him how hard it was for her to say it. "Thank you for that." She took a deep breath. "And then we fell asleep. Understandable, we were both tired out, emotionally at least. Plus you were still recovering." She nodded at the wound, a neat furrow above his left temple. And then when we woke up—" She spread her hands. "It was a once in a lifetime situation, a fluke of circumstance. It'll never happen again."

"No."

"I mean, you're a rounder. No offense, but—"

"It's the truth," he said glumly, and wondered why his heart felt like a stone in his chest.

"And I'm a one-man woman. I don't stand in line."

He smiled then. "No. You don't."

She blew out a relieved breath. "So we'll put it behind us. Move on."

"Okay."

She looked back at the picture. "I loved him," she said softly.

"Yeah, I know," he said. He hesitated. What the hell. "But you don't have to be guilty because you're alive and he's dead. He saved your life, that's what you said."

"Yes."

"Then live it. It was his gift to you."

She opened her mouth as if to speak, and closed it again.

He looked down at the duffel. His voice so soft as to be almost inaudible, he said, "Where did you get the tooth marks?"

"What?"

He gestured. "On your arm. I saw the scar when—well. George saw them, too, when he flew you out, and he was worried. Where'd they come from?"

She looked down at the scar, touched it wonderingly with her fingers as if she'd never seen it before.

"Where'd they come from, Kate? Mutt?"

She nodded, seemingly fascinated by the marks on her arm.

Still that soft, inescapable tone. "What were you trying to do?"

"I had the rifle down." She spoke as one mesmerized. "I was—I don't know what I was going to do."

He closed his eyes, opened them again and spoke very carefully. "Mutt stopped you."

"Yes."

"And you left the Park."

"That day." She looked up, and her eyes were haunted with the memory of those last days, the Quilaks closing in, the silence getting louder and louder. "I've always run home to the Park. This was the first time I ever had to run away from it."

They stood in silence, until Mutt nudged Jim with her head. He knelt down and put an arm around her neck. "Good girl," he said, looking into her wise eyes, her loyal face. "Good girl, Mutt."

She let him have it with the tongue again, all over his face and all of his ears and neck she could reach. Mutt didn't hold back. When she liked, she liked.

He let her go and rose to his feet again. He picked up his duffel. "Jack is dead, Kate," he said. "You aren't. Come home. You've got people there who need you."

At the door he stopped to look back at her, dark head bent beneath the sunshine streaming in through the window.

He went back then, and put his arms around her. She didn't resist, merely rested against him.

He kissed her brow.

He kissed her cheek.

He kissed her mouth, a sweet, tender kiss that went on a little too long for his comfort.

He raised his head, traced the line of her neat cap of hair. "Good-bye, Kate."

She looked up at him with grave eyes. "Good-bye, Jim."

He brushed her chin with a knuckle, turning it into a caress, and let her go. He patted Mutt on the head, picked up his duffel again and went out the door of the bunkhouse they had shared for the last time.

On the walk to the terminal he thought again of his first sight of her at the gold camp the previous fall; torn, bleeding, the body of her lover in her arms, unwilling, no, unable to let him go. He heard again the sound of that muted wail, a distilled grief drifting up into the air like smoke.

When had anyone ever loved him that much?

"Don't forget," Stephanie said.

Kate looked around the girl's room, at the airplane models hanging from the ceiling, at the textbooks crowding the shelves. "I won't forget."

"Don't forget," the girl repeated.

She sounded more forceful to Kate's ears than she ever had before, and when Kate looked closely she thought she saw tears in the girl's eyes. She went down on one knee next to Stephanie's chair. "Stephanie, listen to me. I try really hard not to make promises I can't keep. I promise, when the time comes, I will help you to do what you want. If you need me, all you have to do is write or call. I'll be here in Bering for a while yet, but I gave you my address and my friend's phone number, didn't I? Good. He can always reach me, and I can be back here in a day." She said it again. "All you have to do is write, or call."

Stephanie kept her eyes lowered. She was not a touchy-feely kind of kid, so Kate made no effort to embrace her. She stood up. "Alice Chevak was my friend. Her daughter, Stephanie Chevak, is my friend."

Stephanie looked up, startled. Kate's voice had rung in the little room like the big bell in a tower.

Kate, grave, inclined her head in a small, formal bow.

Somewhat clumsily, Stephanie rose to her feet and returned it, small face solemn and intent.

They clasped hands and shook, formally.

"You'll be all right?" Kate said.

"I will be all right," Stephanie said, still formal. She sat down again, and bent over her book.

"Good." Kate hesitated. "There is a man, a pilot. His name is Jacob Baird."

A peculiar kind of listening stillness came over Stephanie. Kate waited.

"The fat man," the girl said at last. "With all the planes."

"That's the guy. He's in the hospital. He'll be okay, but he's stuck there for a while. He might like a visitor, someone who can speak his language." She gestured at the model of the Super Cub sitting on the bed. "Another pilot."

The back of Stephanie's head was unresponsive.

Either she would or she wouldn't. Kate thought she would, and turned to go.

"*Arrivederci*," Stephanie said suddenly.

Kate looked at her.

"That's Italian for good-bye."

Kate nodded, not trusting her voice to speak, and left the room.

On the porch, Ray said, "Why did you come here without your name, Katya? Were you ashamed of it?"

"No!" she said.

She was startled by her own vehemence. "No," she said

more calmly. "Not ashamed." She leaned against the railing, staring toward the town and the river beyond. "Sick of it, maybe." She thought, and added in a lower voice, "Soul sick."

She turned to look at him. "What did you do when Emaa died? How did you manage?"

His smile was slow and sweet. "How did you?"

She thought of his words as the Alaska Airlines 737 rose up into the sky over Bering and banked east, the first leg of her journey home. *I can't be sad, Jack,* she'd told him, that cold winter day in the Park, when they'd scattered Emaa's ashes up and down the Kanuyaq River. *She's with me, right here, right now.*

She's in every rock and tree in the Park. She's in the water we drink. She's in the air we breathe.

She'll be in every flake of snow that falls, all the winter long.

She'll come up the river with the first salmon in the spring.

She'll be on board every seiner that puts out to sea in the summer.

She'll be on the foothills with the berrypickers in the fall.

She'll always be here. I can't be sad she's gone, when she never left in the first place.

Even over the sound of the jet engines, a faint, anguished howl could be heard from beneath their feet. The other passengers exchanged irritated and amused expressions, but they might as well settle in for the long haul. The back seat of a Cessna was one thing. The cargo hold of a 737 was quite another. Mutt would make her displeasure known all the way to Anchorage.

Kate smiled as the foothills of the Kuskokwim Mountains rose up beneath them, the beginnings of the Alaska Range. If they followed it as it curved around the southern half of the state, the range would lead them unwaveringly to the Quilak Mountains.

And home.

And memories of Abel, and Emaa, and Alice.

And Jack.

Companion to me in every place.

CHAPTER 17

...weightless I
soaring with it shall be for you
Light bright shining

—*Bright Shining*

IT WAS LATE WHEN they landed at the airstrip in Niniltna, almost evening, almost August. George gave her a ride home and a promise to keep her return to himself, "For tonight, at least," he'd added, giving her a hard look. "There are some people who've been worried about you. Who'll need to know you're back safe."

"I know. Thanks, George."

She shut the door of his van and stepped back so he could make a U-turn. It hadn't rained in a long time; the dust of his passing hung over the old gravel railroad roadbed long after he was gone.

She looked down and saw a railroad spike, rusted a dull orange but still a spike, one of those used to hold together the Kanuyaq and Northwestern Railroad track, some seventy years before. Lucky George hadn't picked it up in one of his tires. People did, still, every now and then.

She'd spent the rest of July in Bering, running Baird Air until Baird was back on his feet. She handed in her notice then, over his vociferous protests. He'd even offered her a share in the business. She'd stayed on long enough to train her

303

replacement, a bright, eager eighteen-year-old boy, fresh out of high school with, after one summer on the Kuskokwim, no wish to take up fishing as a permanent way of earning a living. He was the son of a cousin of Ray's, and Ray had vouched for him. Baird had grudgingly allowed as how the boy wasn't a total idiot and a complete waste of time, which Kate correctly deduced to mean that Baird had found himself an employee with more than just a pulse going for him.

The spike was warm from the sun and heavy in her hand. She stuck it in her pocket and hoisted her pack over one shoulder. She took her time going down the path, stopping to pick a handful of salmonberries here, a raspberry there. Mutt plunged into the brush, scattering ptarmigan in one direction and spruce hens in another before leaping back out on the path to run mad circles around Kate, laughing up at her human with her tongue lolling out.

Birds called in the trees, a bull moose with a full, velvety rack munched his way unconcernedly through a stand of diamond willow, and she could hear the gurgling of the creek in the distance. It sounded pretty tame, but then it was late in the season. The mountains would be reluctant to give up the last of the runoff, snowmelt from the narrowest valleys and the deepest crevices that only the longest days of the highest sun could reach.

"Maybe I'll go for a swim," she said out loud.

A single, joyous three-note call sounded from the branches of the spruce tree on her right. There was a quick flutter of wings as she turned quickly to look up, but all she saw was the tip of a branch bouncing gently up and down.

She smiled. "I'm home, Emaa. I'm home."

Mutt shot out from the brush again and shouldered deliberately into her, knocking her on her butt before disappearing again down the path at a mad gallop.

Kate lay on her back for a moment, staring up at the blue sky, stunned.

Mutt came charging back, skidded to a halt three feet from Kate, leaned down on her forepaws and stuck her butt up in the air, tail wagging furiously back and forth. Big yellow eyes pleaded for fun.

"Hey," Kate said, getting to her feet.

Mutt barked, a short, sharp, happy sound.

A surge of well-being swept through her, and she didn't even feel guilty about it. She was alive, the sun was shining and her dog wanted to play. "Hey, you!"

Kate dumped her pack and gave chase. It was tag-you're-it all the way down the path, until Kate tackled Mutt with a low dive and they rolled into the clearing in a tangle of arms and legs and ferocious mock snarling.

Mutt sensed it first, of course. She shook off Kate like she was brushing away a mosquito and stood on tiptoe on all four paws, looking toward the cabin, ears up, nose testing the air.

"What?" The questioning growl had Kate on her feet, hands loose and ready. "What is it, girl?"

She turned to the cabin and saw him.

A boy stood in the open door, a thin boy, maybe twelve, maybe thirteen, already taller than Kate, with the promise of future bulk in the width of his shoulders and the length of his limbs. He had his mother's tow-colored hair.

He had his father's deep blue eyes.

Kate tried to speak, and failed. She licked her lips, and tried again.

"Johnny?"

DANA STABENOW

'UNIQUE IN THE CROWDED FIELD OF CRIME FICTION' MICHAEL CONNELLY

THE SINGING OF THE DEAD

When a candidate for State Senator receives death threats, Kate Shugak is hired to protect her. But what connects the Senator with an unsolved cold case?

A KATE SHUGAK INVESTIGATION

11

She walked out on stage wrapped in fifty yards of sheer white chiffon, a pair of high-heeled shoes with jeweled buckles, and nothing else.

There was a second of stunned silence in the packed, smoky saloon, before deafening and prolonged approval threatened to raise the roof

She waited, a faint smile on her face, for the first roar to moderate and pitched her voice to be heard. "Good evening, gentlemen, and welcome to the Double Eagle's Christmas Eve auction." Her voice was husky, with the slight hint of an accent she tried to control. She let her smile broaden, giving it her special up-from-under and through-the-lashes look, part Madonna, part whore, all woman, and added, "I'm the best present you'll ever find under any Christmas tree you ever saw."

This time the stage literally trembled beneath her feet, and she gave a fleeting thought to all the gold dust spilled on the floor this night, now being shaken through the cracks in the floorboards. It wouldn't go to waste. Japanese Jack and Big Ben Bentson would crawl beneath the building the next morning to sweep it up and add it to the night's till. Likely she wouldn't see her percentage, but at the moment she couldn't allow herself to be distracted by that realization.

Big Ben was the owner and Japanese Jack the bartender of the Double Eagle Saloon, doors open around the clock at the corner of Front and York Streets in downtown, boomtown,

1

gold town Dawson City. The Double Eagle was the biggest building in Dawson, the first to add on a second story. It had a long mahogany bar that matched the mahogany wainscoting, eight mahogany gaming tables, a polished brass footrail that matched the brass spittoons, large, elaborate paintings of reclining nudes lit by tiered crystal chandeliers, windows made of stained and beveled glass, and a dozen rooms upstairs with thick carpets, many more mirrors, and furnished with suites in the very latest style. A cleaning staff of a dozen kept the place spotless, although they kept leaving to stake claims in the search for their very own Eldorado.

They were all men, the cleaning staff. Women could do so much better, selling dances for a dollar, a pint of champagne for eighteen dollars, an hour in one of the rooms upstairs for considerably more. Big Ben got fifty cents on the dance dollar, three-quarters of the price of the pint of champagne, and she never told anyone what the split was on the third.

She had been headlining there for the past year, specializing on stage in the Flame Dance that kept two hundred yards of chiffon in the air at one time, and specializing in what one reporter called "the long, juicy waltz" in the clubrooms upstairs. At the end of fourteen months, she had twenty-seven thousand dollars in the bank. She was twenty-two years old, although she admitted to nineteen, and it was her great good fortune that she looked even younger than that. Most laboring men Outside, of any age, were lucky to earn a dollar a day.

She could have kept working for years, especially here, where men outnumbered women six and seven to one, but she had plans, big ones. One more winter, one last contribution to her savings, and she would be ready to move on.

She looked around the room, at the sea of faces upturned to her, and felt that thrill of power she always felt at being the

2

center of so much concentrated male attention. The chiffon began in a spiral of fabric at her ankles and finished up in a graceful swath around her shoulders, the loose end draped over her bare arm. So closely bound together were her feet that she could take only tiny, mincing steps, which was just as well given the height of the heels on her shoes. Big Ben had wanted her to go barefoot, but she knew what the heels did to the line of her legs, displaying their graceful and well-turned length to best advantage, making a man imagine them wrapped around his waist.

One miner had fought his way forward to the edge of the stage. He was ragged, bearded, and smelled as if he hadn't bathed since the river froze over. He looked hungry, and so very hopeless. She gave him a special smile all his own, inviting everything, promising nothing. She was a whore, but she was an honest whore. She gave value for money received, so long as the money was received. That didn't mean she couldn't be kind.

"It's going to be a long, cold, lonely winter, boys," she said, and there was a shout of agreement. She walked down to center stage and out onto the catwalk thrusting into the room, the little mincing steps causing her breasts to shimmy. The tuft of hair at the vee of her legs was a shadowy patch beneath the chiffon; she put a little extra into the roll of her hips to underline just what was on the auction block that evening.

"For me, too," she added, pouting, and they howled like wolves on the scent.

Again she felt the thrill, a flush of power that began somewhere low in her belly and spread up her torso and down her limbs. A faint film of perspiration broke out over her skin, and a commensurate low, prowling growl rose from the crowd. She performed a three-quarter turn and paused to cast

3

a roguish glance over her right shoulder. "We have a saying here in the north country, boys. I know you've heard it. The odds are good, but the goods are odd." *She winked a violet eye at one man standing in the back, watching her over a glass of Big Ben's watered-down whiskey. He was a regular of hers, a banker who was as conservative with his own money as he was acquisitive of others'. He hadn't liked the idea of his favorite dance partner taking herself out of circulation for the entire winter, but then he wouldn't be bidding this evening, either. She had no doubt that he was ready to take her evening's earnings in deposit, however, just as soon as it had been paid over and Big Ben's commission deducted. She let one hand skim suggestively down her cocked hip, reminding him of what he 'd be missing. His eyes narrowed against the smoke of the cigar clenched in his teeth, and she laughed her husky laugh.* "I'm sure you '11 agree, these goods aren't the least bit odd."

Big Ben and Japanese Jack had been priming the bidders for the last week with announcements of the auction, including tantalizing hints as to exactly what skills and services the highest bid would bring. The flyers were papered all over town and every claim from Log Cabin to Circle City. The always needy miners of the Klondike had been quivering for days at the prospect of the Dawson Darling dancing the slow, juicy waltz just for them for six exquisite months. No one would notice the dark or the cold with the Dawson Darling waiting in his bed.

"Here I am, gentlemen," she said. "It is generally held that my looks are pleasing and that my figure is good." *She waited for the chorus of agreement and was not disappointed.* "What are my terms?"

She tossed the end of chiffon over her shoulder, where it

4

trailed behind her like the train of a wedding dress as she walked downstage again. She came to the end of the catwalk and met the fierce blue eyes of a tall blond man standing near the double doors. In a room full of men who wanted her without reservation, the biting intensity of his look gave her pause, but she rallied and held his gaze, a definite challenge in her own. "Terms? Well, I'm willing to sell myself tonight to the highest bidder, to act as his wife in word—"she paused delicately "—and in deed—" there was another roar "—for the next six months, from this night, December 25th, until June 25th."

"Start the bidding!" yelled one man who had yet to look above her chin.

"Yeah, stop talking and start bidding!"

"But," she said, raising one white, well-tended hand without breaking away from the stare of the blue-eyed stranger, "I reserve the right to accept the next lowest bidder if I do not like the highest." Her eyes lingered on the Greek, who looked at her out of cold, acquisitive eyes that held no lust for her personally, only for the money she could make him when he put her to work in one of his cribs.

"You'll like me all right!" someone yelled.

"The man who buys me must provide a decent cabin and a good stock of food. I'll cook for him, and I'll clean for him, and I'll—"she paused "—dance for him," and again, she was forced to wait for the noise to subside.

"But understand this," she said, smile vanishing, and there was something in her expression that caused all comment to pause. "The man who buys me, and lifts a hand to me . . . "

"I'd like to see him try!"

"We'd fix him for you, Darling, never you worry!"

She waited, and then repeated, "The man who buys me, and lifts a hand to me, will have attended his last auction on *this earth. Am I understood?"*

She looked at the Greek, whose calculating expression didn't change. She waited long enough for her words to sink in, and smiled again to take the sting out of them. "You'll want to know," she said, dropping her voice, "I'm not exactly an iceberg." She turned, contriving so that the top fold of chiffon covering her breasts slipped down to be caught and held, barely, by her nipples.

No one looking at her doubted that she was telling anything but the absolute truth.

Into the dead silence that had fallen, she said softly, "So here I am, boys. Ready and willing." She smiled, making a slow, graceful pirouette, caressing the faces in the crowd with a warm, welcoming gaze. "What are you waiting for?"

Big Ben had a hard time getting them quieted down after that. The bidding opened at one thousand. It was at five thousand thirty seconds later, offered by a squat, dark man with a matted bush of greasy hair and a mouthful of rotted teeth. She repressed a shudder and paraded down the catwalk again. "Now, boys," she said, laughing, "that last bid was only five thousand. Aren't you going any higher than that?" She paused at the edge of the catwalk and put up a hand to the thick auburn hair tucked into a graceful swirl. When the hand came down, it traced an invisible line from throat to breast to waist, to settle again on her hip.

"Sure, girlie," called out an Irishman with a handlebar mustache and a white, wide-brimmed hat, "I was only waiting for the pikers to drop out. Ten thousand, and that's only two days' cleanup on my claim!"

"Twelve!" the squat man growled.

"Thirteen!" yelled a man in spectacles and bib overalls with a watch chain made from gold nuggets hanging from the

6

front pocket.

"Fifteen," the Greek said, his voice as flat as his eyes. There was neither lust nor longing in his tone, only a look that calculated how much she could earn for him when he turned her out. She repressed a shiver, and reminded herself that she had right of first refusal.

"Sixteen," the banker snapped. She met his eyes, startled. He shrugged. She couldn't help it. She laughed. "Sixteen," he repeated, looking faintly irritated at the sound of the word forced out of his own mouth.

"Seventeen," a new voice boomed, and she looked up to lock eyes again with the tall blond man at the door. "Seventeen thousand dollars," he said again. His voice was deep with no trace of an accent. Second-generation Swede, perhaps? He was strong-featured rather than handsome. His face was impassive, but she sensed that he was angry. She didn't know why, but it made her chin come up.

"Seventeen-five!" the squat man snapped. His eyes were little and cruel and calculating.

"Eighteen," the tall man said imperturbably.

The squat man swore in a foreign tongue—Italian?—and said in a rising voice, "Nineteen!"

"Twenty," the Greek said.

Everyone else seemed to have dropped out and were now swiveling their heads among the three bidders. There would be a fight before the evening was over, and they all knew it. Lust and blood lust, thwart one and the other stepped in.

She wasn't going home with the squat man, but she had a good idea of what six months of her exclusive attention was worth, and it was more than twenty thousand dollars. "The last bid stands at twenty thousand, boys," she called out into the silence, and when they turned to look at her, she shook her head once. The single pin, artfully placed, loosened itself, and her hair tumbled down in a thick, gleaming fall to her waist. "I know you can do better than that."

One auburn strand fell forward to curl around her breast. The crowd watched it, mesmerized. Someone gave a little moan. Someone else swore not quite beneath his breath.

"Twenty-five," the man at the door said.

The room fell silent. He drained his mug and said into it, "Oh hell, what's the use of wasting time." He looked up to run a possessive look over the Dawson Darling and said, "Thirty thousand dollars." He smiled, showing strong white teeth. He didn't seem angry anymore.

She couldn't help herself. She had always had a weakness for good teeth. She smiled back.

The Greek said nothing. The banker looked as if he were performing a complicated mental calculation. The squat man saw her smile and screamed, "You crooked, dirty whore!"

He struggled to reach her and was thwarted by the crowd, as protective of her now as they had been avaricious before. With a sudden change of direction, he rushed the man at the door, and this time the crowd parted eagerly before him so that his opponent was grabbed up in a crushing grip immediately. The tall blond man struggled and got one arm free to fend off the hands reaching for his throat.

"I break him! I smash him!" the squat man shouted. His arms quivered, muscles bulging. He lifted the tall man so that his feet dangled a foot above the floor. The tall man went limp. Everyone watching expected to hear the snap of the tall man's spine.

Instead, when the tall man went limp, the squat man's grip slipped, and the tall man smashed him instead, one large-knuckled fist to the squat man's jaw with a force that laid the

8

squat man flat on his back on the floor, out cold. The tall man almost went down with him, then caught his balance and remained on his feet.

There was a roar of approval and a surge toward the tall man, who held up one hand, and such was his presence that they halted. "My name's Sam Halvorsen," he said, looking across the room to where she stood on the catwalk, skin gleaming through white chiffon and auburn curls. "You going to exercise your right to the next lowest bidder, ma'am?"

She could barely speak around the lump in her throat. "No, Sam," she managed to say. "I am not."

The crowd, silent again, parted before him as he walked to the edge of the stage. She didn't have to look down that far and realized he was even taller than she had thought. He held up one hand, and she placed hers into it, only to give a startled shriek when he yanked on it, jerking her off balance. She fell forward, and he caught her neatly in his arms.

He grinned at her. "We've only got until June 24th," he said. "Time's a-wasting."

And, carrying her easily, he shouldered his way out of the bar.

CHAPTER 1

I'M WATCHING YOU.

That's all?" Jim Chopin said.

Darlene Shelikof handed over a manila file folder, and Jim leafed through half a dozen similar missives, all on eight-and-a-half-by-eleven-inch sheets of plain white paper folded in thirds.

He held one up to the light and read the watermark out loud. "Esleeck Emco Bond, twenty-five percent cotton content." He lowered his arm. "Available by the ream from Costco at six-seventy-nine a pop, the last time I looked."

"Can't you tell something from the writing?"

He shuffled through the sheets again. "Looks like he—or she—used a black Marksalot."

I KNOW WHERE YOU LIVE.

"The big block printing is an obvious attempt to disguise the handwriting."

ABORTION IS MUDRER.

"I take it Anne's pro-choice?"

"She started the family-planning clinic in Ahtna."

"That does tend to make the nuts fall from the tree." He held the letter closer. "Probably printed with the left hand, or whatever hand is not their hand of choice in writing poison-pen letters. Also, he can't spell."

10

YOUR HUSBANDS CUTE.

Jim's eyebrows went up. "Is he?"

Darlene smiled. "Not as cute as you are, Jim."

His smile was swift and predatory in return. "Why, Darlene, I didn't know you cared." Even to himself the words sounded formulaic, and tired as well, and he looked back down at the file. Well, hell, he was tired. It had been a long week, what with a rape in Slana, a death by arson in Copper Center, and a suicide by cop in Valdez that he would have missed if he hadn't had to overfly Cordova due to weather and overnight on the Valdez chief of police's couch. He focused on the papers in his hand.

YOUR DAUGHTER WEARS HER SKIRTS TOO

The writer had written in letters so large he or she had run out of room before finishing his or her thought, and had had to add "SHORT" in smaller letters in the lower right-hand corner of the paper.

STAY HOME AND TAKE CARE OF YOUR KIDS.

"Ah, a traditionalist," Jim said.

The seventh letter was more direct, RUN FOR SENATOR AND ILL KILL YOU.

He held it up so she could read it. "This the one that made you bring them all in?"

She nodded. "They've been coming in one at a time ever since she announced. Then last week, we got two."

"All date-stamped except the first one, and you kept the envelope for that one, too. Smart," Jim said. "We appreciate smart in law enforcement."

She smiled again.

He examined the envelopes, all of them stapled to the backs of the letters. "All postmarked Ahtna. Well, I'll give the post office there a call. You never know, somebody might have

11

noticed something."

"You don't sound very optimistic."

"I'm not. The Ahtna post office handles all the mail that goes into and comes out of the Park. That's, what, three thousand people, a little less? And these are pretty anonymous letters, Darlene."

"What about the handwriting? Isn't there an expert you can send them to, figure out who wrote them?"

"Sure, and I will," he said, stuffing them into an evidence bag. "Today. But unless and until the state crime lab already has a sample of the perp's writing to compare them to, we're SOL as far as identifying the writer."

"What about fingerprints?"

He looked at her. What he wanted to say was, "You've been watching too much television," but what he said instead, patiently, was, "Who opened these?"

"The candidate, the first one." She thought. "The rest were opened by volunteers, I think. Oh."

"Right. And then they got passed up or down the food chain to you, and then your assistant had to file them. There are probably ten sets of fingerprints on every letter, and we can't even be sure that every letter has the same set of ten." He sealed the bag. "Have you fingerprinted your staff?"

An expression of revulsion crossed her face. It was a very nice face otherwise, black eyes set in a broad, flat face with a tiny pug nose and a merry mouth, hair in a permed black frizz standing out around it. She was thick through the body and short, although her erect posture made her seem taller. She carried weight, did Darlene Shelikof, and not necessarily just body weight. Her jeans were faded but clean, the blazer over it a conservative navy blue, the shirt beneath a paler blue and open at the throat. Ivory dangled from her ears and adorned her lapel and both wrists.

She had been leaning forward, just a little, and now she leaned back, just a little, not enough to give the impression she was in any way relaxed. "What about protection?"

"What about it?"

For the first time she allowed herself to look angry. He admired her control. "How much can you give us?"

"Darlene, you worked for the AG. You know exactly how much protection we can give you."

Her mouth thinned. "The threats are escalating, in delivery and in degree."

"Yes."

"Chances are he—or she—will try to make contact."

"Chances are he—or she—already has."

"What do you mean?"

He shrugged. "How long has Anne been on the campaign trail? She announced in June, didn't she?"

"Yes."

"What day in June?"

"The sixteenth."

"The first of those envelopes is dated June twenty-seventh."

She thought about it. "So he's been following her since the beginning?"

"That'd be my guess. She's been doing the usual things politicians do, going to church in Chitina, walking the bars in Cordova, shaking hands and kissing babies and promising to throw the bums out, like they all do." Darlene looked indignant. He waved away whatever comment she had been about to make about her candidate being all new and improved and completely different. He'd been an Alaska state trooper for going on twenty years; he'd seen a lot of political campaigns whistle-stop through; he had seen every single

13

candidate of every political party (and in Alaska there were about seventeen separate and distinct political parties with more springing up every year), and he had seen every successful candidate as a first order of Juneau business cuddle up with the lobbyist with the most money to spend. Call him a cynic, but he didn't see anything changing just because this candidate was a woman and a Native and homegrown.

Juneau seemed to have that inevitable and invariable effect on elected officials, he reflected. Or maybe it was just political office everywhere, because the nation as a whole seemed to be in about the same shape. Substitute Washington, D.C, for Juneau and what did you get? Bill Clinton for president. Jesus. It wasn't that Clinton was a rounder that bothered him so much, it was that he'd been so awful goddamn inept at it. If you're going to philander, he thought now, for crissake do it with some style.

"So we have to wait until he takes a shot at her before you'll do anything?" Darlene said.

"It's a big step from writing a nasty letter to someone popping off with a thirty-ought-six." He held up a hand to forestall further commentary. "What I will do is put the word out to all the local law enforcement agencies that your candidate's getting hate mail, that it's personal, and, yes, that it is increasing in amount and degree."

She gave an impatient snort. "What's that get us?"

He was starting to get a little annoyed. "Nothing, if you don't call ahead to let the local agencies know when you'll be there."

She glared, and he sighed to himself. No point in getting the person who was very probably going to sit at the right hand of the next senator from District 41 mad at him. "I'll e-mail all the troopers in the area, and all the police chiefs. I'll

14

give you a list of names and numbers, and I'll tell them you'll call when you know your candidate will be speaking in their jurisdiction. You need to call every time, Darlene," he said with quiet force. "They can't plan to look out for you if they don't know you're coming. They've got jobs, full-time ones, already." He thought about the suicide by cop in Valdez. "Full-time jobs," he repeated. "You releasing this information to the press?" She hesitated, and he groaned. "Don't tell me you think that this is going to get her the sympathy vote?"

She had the grace to flush.

"All you'll do is get him off," he warned. "That's what he wants, attention, film at eleven."

"Or she," she reminded him.

He looked at her in sudden suspicion. She read his thought before he could speak it out loud. "Fuck you, Chopin," she said, her voice rising.

"Okay," he said, patting the air. "Okay. Sorry. Just a thought, a dumb one, I admit, but—"

"As if I would—as if Anne would—just fuck you, Chopin!" She shot to her feet and marched to the door. Hand on the knob, she turned and said, spitting the words like knives, "Thanks for nothing. If—*when* Anne gets into office, if this asshole doesn't kill her first, we'll remember this when it comes time to look at the budget for the Department of Public Safety. I'd say trooper salaries and step rates for Bush posts are way overdue for review."

"Darlene!"

His voice, cracking like a whip, stopped her halfway out the door. She looked back, very ready to escalate hostilities.

"If you're that worried, if you really think Anne's in danger . . ."

She didn't move. "What?"

15

"What about hiring security for the campaign?"

"You mean like guards?"

"I mean like one guard." The one he was thinking of wouldn't need any help.

She let go of the handle, and the door hissed closed on its hydraulic hinge. "You suggesting someone in particular?"

He just looked at her and, being a well-trained law enforcement professional of intensive and lengthy experience, was able to pinpoint the exact moment when realization dawned.

Also because she said, "Oh fuck, no."

"She knows the Park," Jim said. "Who she isn't related to she's drinking buddies with." He thought of Amanda and Chick, Bobby and Dinah, Bernie. Old Sam, the quintessential Alaskan old fart, Auntie Vi, the quintessential Alaskan old fartette. Dan O'Brien, the only national-park ranger in Alaska to survive the change of federal administrations and gain the affection if not the actual respect of Park rats. George Perry the air taxi pilot, next to whom Jim had stood on that airstrip south of Denali last September. He banished that memory the next instant, or told himself he had. "If she was a drinking kind of woman, that is."

"Not her."

"She's probably related to Anne, come to that."

Darlene's voice rose. "Not her, Jim."

He was surprised at her vehemence. "Who else?" he said. "She's a teetotaler. She's a local. She's a Native. She has a reputation—"

"Oh yeah, she's got a reputation, all right, a well-deserved one."

"Took the words right out of my mouth." Curious, the curse of any good cop, he went fishing. "You sound like you know her."

She opened her mouth, met his eyes, and closed it again. "I knew her," she said at last.

He waited hopefully. No weapon in the cop's arsenal worked better than the expectant silence.

"We went to school together."

He raised his eyebrows. "I didn't know you were from Niniltna."

"In Fairbanks. UAF."

He gave a neutral kind of grunt, and waited again. In the ensuing stony silence, he wondered why the feud. If one person hating a second person who, so far as Jim knew, was indifferent to the first person's existence, could be called a feud. Did Kate crib from Darlene's test? Wear Darlene's favorite sweater without permission? Steal Darlene's boyfriend? It irritated him that he would like to know, to add to his fund of Kate Shugak lore. Said irritation moved him to say, "Just a suggestion."

"A bad one," she snapped.

"No," he said, suddenly weary. "Just a suggestion."